SHERLOCK HOLMES AND THE LEY LINE MURDERS

Strange events and fearful discoveries along Britain's ancient ley lines have brought the folk memories of a distant ceremonial past into the modernity of the nineteenth century and to the attention of the latter period's greatest analytical mind.

Allan Mitchell

Copyright

First edition published in 2017
© Copyright 2017
Allan Mitchell

Paperback ISBN 978-1-78705-130-0
ePub ISBN 978-1-78705-131-7
PDF ISBN 978-1-78705-132-4

Published in the UK by MX Publishing
335 Princess Park Manor, Royal Drive,
London, N11 3GX
www.mxpublishing.co.uk

Cover design by Brian Belanger

INTRODUCTION

Sherlock Holmes, first and foremost, was a chemist and, as such, might better have appreciated the role of Stamford, the unassuming human catalyst who initiated the unlikely reaction between himself and Watson but who fell from view immediately after introducing the Sleuth and the Doctor and took no further part in any of their adventures. Such is the fate of catalysts but little would happen were it not for the existence of agents able to cause two otherwise incompatible entities to meet on mutually compatible terms to allow interaction between them to result in a desirable product. The product of Stamford's catalysis was a partnership destined to long outlast its creator and enter the language and psyche of generations, a partnership which continues in the present day and, undoubtedly, will continue for generations to come.

Spent catalyst is often regenerated – not so Stamford. Once he bade Watson farewell and advised him to study the phenomenon of Sherlock Holmes, he disappears, though other less-influential Stamfords do make later appearances.

A debt of gratitude, at the very least, is owed by the Holmesian universe to this enigmatic personality – someone of subordinate status as a surgical dresser for student and instructor and yet possessed of sufficient seniority to be able to approach both senior student and experienced graduate surgeon on terms approaching equivalence, if not equality.

Was it Stamford's fate to live in obscurity or did he move on to help others come together in productive partnerships? We don't know, nor do we know if Arthur Conan Doyle ever gave him a second thought after his pen was lifted from those few pages of Stamford's literary existence. Stamford was just one of a great many significant and sundry characters to enrich the world of Sherlock Holmes and John Watson but, for readers of their exploits, be those readers young or old, past or future, it was, is and always will be Stamford who deserves the credit for bringing together two such ill-matched characters from two completely different worlds and setting the scene for the greatest of all detective duos.

Despite the brevity of his literary interaction, however, Stamford will never completely disappear as long as new generations of readers keep discovering Sherlock Holmes and experiencing the thrill of his first meeting with Watson, a meeting from which Watson and every new reader came to understand that there existed a brain so superior in logical and intuitive thought that it was very little short of miraculous in its workings.

Did Stamford know what he was starting? We can only guess at the answer but we can readily imagine him walking away from Watson grinning with the knowledge that something new and special was about to be created, something of great worth and great endurance, all because he recognised Watson who, in his despair, had gravitated into London's Criterion Bar. Lunch at the Holborn following the meeting set things in motion as it was here that Watson learned of the possibility of sharing diggings in 221B Baker Street, though Stamford did warn Watson of possible domestic disharmony due to Holmes' eccentricities. Stamford led Watson to a hospital laboratory, introduced the pair and, regretfully, was never heard from again.

The reader would like to imagine Stamford going back to his duties and, from time to time, meeting up with his two acquaintances to go over old times and catch up on any news. Alas, even Sherlock Holmes seems to have forgotten the man who helped make it all happen, a man who simply merged into the background of those metropolitan millions and sadly disappeared from the literary record maintained by John Watson, the very man whose life he was instrumental in saving.

Still, life is breathed into this man ever so briefly every time a new reader is introduced to the world of Sherlock Holmes. Without Stamford, there would have been no meeting and without that meeting John Watson may have stayed at the Criterion Bar to drink away his troubles on the way to an oblivion fuelled by alcohol and depression. Without Stamford and that meeting, Sherlock Holmes would never have met John Watson and may have gone on occasionally solving the seemingly unsolvable, experimenting with reagents on himself and dabbling deeper and deeper into the deadly narcotic charms of the cocaine bottle until life could offer no more.

Thankfully, there was someone such as Stamford, otherwise the light of Arthur Conan Doyle's two most famous characters would never have been lit and the concept of a flawed but inspired Victorian consulting detective and a recovering military doctor with a steadfast sense of loyalty and a gift for narrative may have graced the bottom of a waste paper basket. Indeed, what a waste that would have been and how less colourful would have been the literary world but for that one man who formed a human bridge between the highly incompatible natures, though ever complimentary characters, of Mr Sherlock Holmes and Dr John Watson.

We who relive the exploits of those two characters over and over, and even those whose experience is merely fleeting and incidental, must admit to the occasional subconscious utterance of *'Thank you, Stamford! We are forever in your debt.'*. This debt, however, was never so much apparent as when the deductive talents and intuitive insight of Sherlock

Holmes were combined with and augmented by the medical aptitude and military experience of John Watson when both were confronted with the mystery of the Ley Line Murders.

CONTENTS

SHERLOCK HOLMES
AND THE LEY LINE MURDERS

'to the memory of a great and dear friend'

SAVAGE RITUALS

The Crimes

First one, then another, then two more bodies, all killed in an apparent orgy of human sacrifice - their heads missing, their bodies dismembered, their hearts removed, their identities unknown, the gruesome remnants placed at intervals along the ley lines on Salisbury Plain, paths used by the Britons of old, paths as straight as a line of sight could permit, paths harking back to a prehistoric ceremonial past long forgotten but still found as faint echoes in folklore, place names and seemingly innocent nursery rhymes. The Press had made much of the Ley Line Murders, unashamedly suggesting that mystic forces might lie behind the acts, the resulting sensation driving up sales but hampering investigations as over-curious sightseers trampled any evidence into pulp and took souvenirs by the sack load.

The official detectives attached to the Wiltshire Constabulary had been baffled by the senseless barbarity of the acts and could find no trace of the victim's identities, save for a single tattoo suggestive of French military service. John Watson, ever the man of civilisation but no stranger to war's savage turmoil and hideous leavings, had been reading a late account of the murders and commented to his colleague, Sherlock Holmes, who had recently returned from a case involving the Swedish Royal Family, trivial as it turned out but with some interesting and intriguing features, *"Sherlock, you know, it says here in The Times that the four Ley Line Murders may have been Pagan religious observances and that members of the general public need have no fear of the events ever affecting them."*

Sherlock Holmes, taking a puff on his favourite pipe and shaking his head in mock disbelief, replied, *"Well, if that isn't just typical of the incompetent tripe we get served by those who see everything but are blind to the vital clue which a felon always leaves in his wake. And now we get the same dish served up by the Press."*

"But, The Times, Holmes!" broke in Watson, *"Surely we can trust it for its content and its complete objectivity in what and how it reports the news."*

"Yes, yes." replied Holmes, *"I grant you that The Times is in a definite class well above so many of those other publications which dare to call themselves newspapers, but even the Times occasionally lowers itself to a level to which we could scarcely believe it capable."*

Sherlock Holmes had risen from the comfort of his chair and walked over to see what John Watson had been reading while finishing off his breakfast. The latest edition of The Times had been spread out across the table, covering an assortment of breakfast dishes and coffee cups, and Watson had drawn the article towards him, crumpling the page messily into a miniature landscape of high mountains and deep valleys. Looking over his friend's shoulder, Holmes was directed to an uncharacteristic tabloid-style heading of *'Pagan Worshipers Revive Ancient Death Ritual'*, the article then continuing with *'Regional Police spokesman, Inspector Rupert Fleming has refused to comment on claims that the Ley Line Murders had all the hallmarks of a revival of ancient religious practices which involved human sacrifice and the dismemberment of the victim's body prior to distribution of the body parts to places of Pagan spiritual significance. Inspector Fleming's refusal to comment has only served to fuel the already rampant rumours that persons of high status have been involved in the Pagan observances and that Police resources have been diverted elsewhere until the furore subsides.'.*

"Typical, well .. no .. this is untypical and also very unworthy of The Times." ranted Holmes, *"This is not news; this is not the reporting of fact; this is sensationalism, pure and simple, and Inspector Fleming has had words put into his mouth by some incompetent hack who cares little for the truth and less for the unfortunate victims of the despicable acts."*

"These are crimes, Watson," exploded Holmes as his ire rose and the veins in his neck and forehead grew thick and blue. Ire was one of the few emotions Holmes allowed himself, and only then on the occasion when complete incompetence or indifference to the truth was exhibited by those with an obligation to uphold its inviolability. *"These are crimes, no more and no less, My Good Friend. But I do believe they are such as might serve to restore my faith in the creativity of the criminal mind, in as much as they might provide a challenge to my own."*

"Now, steady on, Holmes, surely that is going too far, even for you." retorted Watson in stark disbelief at what had come from his friend's lips, *"You surely can't be equating the criminal mind with your own. That some are fiendishly devious, I am fully prepared to accept, but the mind of the criminal possesses a definite flaw and it is that which puts those warped minds into a class subordinate to your own. If any would even approach your intellectual capacity, I would want them under lock and key and not roaming the streets and going about their*

devious and damnable mischief. Yes, prison is the place for them, some forever and some until they have learned a well-deserved lesson."

"Quite so, Watson, but my whole being needs stimulation ... for my mind to think, for my heart to beat and for my lungs to breathe." declared Holmes going slightly on the defensive after witnessing his friend's distress. *"It is true that I am blessed, if I may be forgiven for using such a self-aggrandising term, with an intellect and insightfulness well beyond the norm and it is these attributes, gifts if you will, which allow me to see beyond the commonplace and into that zone of existence rarely sensed by the average person. I admit that, given the wrong sort of inducement and should my conscience fail me, I could be the arch-fiend, the greatest criminal agent ever known, but it is my Providence-given place in the order of things to see that, for victims from all stations of life, high and low, justice is delivered and done, regardless of what some barely legible statute written in legal gobbledegook might say."*

"So much for The Times." said Watson as he cut out the article and roughly refolded the remaining pages. *"This Inspector Rupert ... er ... Fleming. Do you think he might be appreciative of a little help from that brain of yours? Perhaps we could take a trip into the countryside and check out the lay of these lines for ourselves."*

"Watson, a definite touch, that little pun of yours. I believe you are developing some subtlety in that sense of humour you keep hidden away." declared Holmes with a restrained laugh, *"I admit that I could do with a change of air and the countryside is at its best at this time of year. Perhaps we could spare a few days to enquire how things stand for the good Inspector – he may well appreciate some support in his*

inquiries, both moral and physical. Let us begin, however, by gathering what facts we can from accounts reported so far in the newspapers, as distorted as these may prove to be. Now, it's getting on for nine o'clock so, if you can get going with those scissors of yours, we might catch the afternoon train from Waterloo and be in Salisbury by five. A telegram to a local inn should get us accommodation, at least for tonight. We should then have a few good hours to locate our man and see how we may assist. Could your needy patients go without benefit of your healing hands for a short time?"

Watson replied in the affirmative and then proceeded to dispose of the latest issue of The Times before moving on to the pile of stacked newspapers endlessly building up in a corner of their sitting room ready to be mined of valuable tit-bits should the need arise. The need had definitely arisen for Watson and he went back though issue after issue, cutting out article after article on the gruesome events while Holmes checked his own records for any mention of ley lines. Holmes' records were of little help, however, as any reference he noted was merely incidental, though a brief mention of a little-accessed book on the 'Ancient Ways' was spotted pinned to a file on an old case, one of little consequence at the time and of low memorability in the present.

"Perhaps," said Holmes to a Watson busily involved in digging up informative snippets from the recent journalistic past, *"we might postpone our country excursion until tomorrow and spend the afternoon at the British Museum's grand Library – there is a book I wish to consult which may prove to be of supreme importance in understanding the motivation of the perpetrators and the significance of the locations of the aftermath of the crimes. We can take the early train to Salisbury tomorrow and arrive far better prepared than we might otherwise have been."*

Both men, Sleuth and Doctor, made preparations for an early departure on the following morning and then proceeded to the British Museum to continue their preliminary investigations. Exactly what manner of information was to be gleaned from the Museum's Library sources had not yet fully affirmed itself in the two men's minds but they knew from past experience that the smallest and seemingly most trivial fact might have enormous significance and point to a clue of momentous importance.

The British Museum on London's Great Russell Street held wonder upon wonder from around the Empire and the greater world but its Library held facts, facts by the millions, by the tens of millions, and if Sherlock Holmes valued anything, it was a fact – cold, hard and irrefutable – one which he could set firmly in his mind and on which he could begin to coherently stack others and build his way to the absolute truth, much as a construction engineer might lay down a solid foundation stone on which to start building something enduring and immoveable. The Library had begun its existence more than a hundred years before as numerous even-older private libraries had been bequeathed to the formative concept of a great British receptacle of knowledge. When George II assented to the Parliamentary Act of 1753, his signature had effectively converted the concept into a reality. Since then, its contents had been available for public access and few had frequented the ever-extending shelves of its Library with as much eagerness as had Sherlock Holmes. Upon entry, Holmes made his way to the great catalogue while Watson sought out recent news publications as yet unbound.

Watson discovered a treasure trove of information but found that, as with all buried treasure, much digging had to take place before he could gaze upon the prize within. Still, he did have all day, at least the greater part of it, and so took the opportunity to search the recent contents of regional newspapers available in this great British edifice of information for any further data which may prove useful to the duo, while Holmes found he had to ask for assistance in locating the volume he desired, 'Ancient Ways' - available but only on specific request. He had expected that he could locate it in just a few minutes but it had been placed on a restricted access list, not because of its content but due to its physical condition.

'Ancient Ways' was small, far smaller than Holmes had anticipated, and was not in good condition. It had been printed in 1815 and its disintegration was well advanced. Holmes looked at the small offering and thought, "*This work will soon go the way of so many others from the past and the information painstakingly collected and arranged will be lost forever. Perhaps, in the future, some means will exist to record the information held in these ancient books before it disappears forever, some photographic process perhaps.*"

In the centre of the flyleaf, Holmes could just make out an inscription, unfortunately written with a soft leaded pencil and read only with some difficulty. Looking through his convex lens and positioning the book so that light struck its surface at an oblique angle, the Sleuth was just able to make out the words: '*To my niece, Margaret, to whose interest in the ancient ways this book is dedicated. James Fletcher (Uncle Jim). 1815.*'. Holmes wrote down the name '*James Fletcher*' in his notebook right next to the heading 'Ancient Ways' and, beneath it, recorded '*Margaret – niece – alive or deceased?*' then opened the book at the first page.

The Book

The Introduction to 'Ancient Ways' was brief but did contain a few snippets of biographical information concerning the author. James Fletcher had been a provincial school teacher in Avebury and had become interested in the local legends concerning the works of the region's ancient peoples. He had witnessed the dawn break flawlessly and spectacularly through lines of standing stones on a winter solstice and illuminate a deliberately positioned altar stone and he stood in awe of a people who could go to such lengths to mark and celebrate what to them was obviously an event of prime religious significance. As the hours of daylight diminished and the land produced less and less, the priests would observe the progress of the position of sunrise on the distant horizon. Long experience had taught them that, after the dawn sun's rays had struck the altar stone, the progression of the position of sunrise would start to reverse and the darkness of the day would begin to diminish after that special day on which the sun stood still, the solstice. Thereafter, the sun's light would not continue to fade away for that year but would begin to shine stronger and longer until the summer solstice was reached once more, half a year hence. The cycle was never ending but it was deemed prudent to placate the gods in case they decided to continue the sun's decline and bring eternal darkness to the land.

A teacher's life could be rewarding but few, if any, of Fletcher's students would go on to make a mark in higher education circles – theirs was a rural community and most students had learned enough by the age of twelve to satisfy the basic requirements and join their parents in cottage, field or distant factory in a never-ending cycle of labour and making ends meet. Not educated to a standard which would give him entry to the greater learned institutions of the nation, James

Fletcher none-the-less possessed an enquiring mind and would fill it with all manner of detail on the lives of the ancient peoples as evidenced by their lasting effects of the landscape. He visited the ancient monuments and gradually became aware of lines of connection, perhaps communication, between them and, with his knowledge of the classics, saw them as existing within a greater network of 'ways' by which ancient peoples maintained contact across great distances. Some monuments, he observed, were still intact, others were less distinct on the landscape and still others seemed to have been re-used over the millennia as stone forts and churches usurped their locations of prime significance. Too many, he would find, had been stripped of their usable stone blocks for use in construction of later people's houses, farm buildings and fencing; others had disappeared back into the landscape which they once overlooked.

"If only such a man could have achieved his potential." thought Holmes, *"What knowledge and insight might have been disseminated to scholars about our distant past and how might today's people be able to see themselves as the heirs to a greatness stretching back into antiquity. Instead, a lifetime of private intellectual achievement has ended up in a single book crumbling its way to a dusty and mildewed oblivion. Waste, sheer incomprehensible waste!"*

Enough! The mind of Sherlock Holmes, so alert to its own capabilities, was able to close off thoughts it was not ready to shut down. It could compartmentalise itself to an enormous degree and concentrate on one fact at a time while holding dozens more in a mental limbo, all readily accessible to construct a coherent theme of events. One thought did need to be placed on his ready-access list and this concerned Margaret, the author's niece. Did she go on and expand her interest in the Ancient Ways? At the time, access to higher education was an opportunity denied to the majority of males while the female could only dream of the time she would be able to raise her eyes to the higher things. Still, many had done so in a private capacity and, hopefully, this Margaret had taken her uncle's encouragement and filled her mind with the wonder of the objects and peoples of his own life's interest and made it her own. Finding her would be a major quest in itself but might well provide insight should a critical line of inquiry bog down for lack of hard fact.

The text of 'Ancient Ways' began with a rambling discourse about Saxons and Romans and Celts and how any obvious evidence of thousands of years of movement of ancient peoples across the landscape of Britain had been largely obliterated by those successive latecomers who discounted the prior legends and began constructing new ones of their own. Some was, and could only ever be, supposition based on informed observation but many features seemed to repeat themselves in the same manner and at similar geographical locations. Druids were mentioned, and Caesar, and the peoples of ancient Gaul and Iberia and the way in which the Romans were able to find their way around a vast landscape with apparent ease. Sherlock Holmes had no doubt that there had been movement around ancient Britain but was largely ignorant of the mystical associations those people had with specific locations. James Fletcher's book was to open his eyes to a different way of seeing reality, one which placed influential spirits and gods upon the Earth and kept them foremost in the minds and everyday activities of the 'old folk'.

Mass movement across Britain had significantly stagnated for some two thousand years, ever since the playing off of one tribe of Britons against another by the Romans had interrupted a long-lived equilibrium of local power, occasional battles and strained but generally peaceful accommodation of religious practice. This interruption was further intensified by Saxon and Norse invasions and land grabs, but it was the Normans, in particular, who constructed inflexible power barriers across the countryside and kept the people under control and immobile – new feudal constrictions had finally destroyed and replaced what remained of the old tribal freedoms. Since the coming of the railways, however, some of those freedoms were being reclaimed but 'Ancient Ways' was penned in the days before those 'new ways' of steel rail would snake across the landscape and smoke belching machines with their demonic screeching steam whistles would drag the people along in relative comfort.

Holmes read on, trying hard to envisage the ancient landscape through the eyes of a pre-railway era scholarly investigator who could barely have foreseen the scale of the coming onslaught of industrialisation any more than Holmes could foresee the revolutions which would begin in his own time.

Fletcher, now joined by Holmes, had looked back to a time when the habitat of humanity was defined by that thin region between the surface of the land and the base of the low misty clouds and when the Earth stretched outward to the salty seas beyond which there were other lands, sometimes with people very familiar, sometimes very strange, and where monsters and all types of abominations might be encountered. Above and below this thin region existed other beings, most of whom had no business on the surface of the Earth but who, at times, insisted on visiting, often intent on mischief or even great evil. The sun was a blessing, the moon was a timekeeper, the stars were fires fixed in a heavenly canopy belonging to the gods, gods who could actually be seen as planets wandering about the night sky, perhaps tending to those fires, perhaps warming themselves by the heat given off. Nothing existed which did not have some spiritual attachment and the secrets of that attachment was known to the astrologer and the priest, the ones with 'the knowledge'.

Holmes was taken back to a past in which metal was scarce and the next hardest object was stone which, of course, was plentiful. Also plentiful was wood – trees abounded but would yield increasingly to the stone, then bronze, axe for fuel, building material and space, space to graze animals, space to grow crops, space to deny cover to approaching enemies, and space for extensive religious observances. Stone also would yield to those of the Bronze Age, not just course handy-sized rocks to build a crude wall, nor just large boulders positioned with great effort into alignment with celestial features and events, but huge squared stone blocks cut to size and dragged incredible distances across the countryside to erect huge structures for astrological rituals and celebrations. Not only were they built, they seemed to line up with great accuracy with other distant structures well out of sight across broad expanses of land and even across wide bodies of water. The people of the time not only knew and used the Earth, they also knew and used the Sky.

Copper and Tin were to be found within the Earth or, if fortune was kind, ejected onto the surface out of some devilish underground smelter - it took courage to be a miner and it took special knowledge to take the leavings of the Earth and refine them into shiny materials worthy of the gods. It also took organisation and it needed a transportation network to distribute the materials to those who would use it.

Alignment was important, even critical, if people were to set off on foot and follow the signs, such as they were, to the next way point and then on to a distant destination. Line of sight was the way forward, from one mark stone to another, through a naturally occurring notch in a row of hills or through one painstakingly cut by those who came first; sometimes a tall tree atop a knoll in the distance; sometimes a stone cairn erected long before; sometimes a small pond reflecting the light from a torch at a distant way point. So many paths and marks for the initiated to look for and follow – straight lines and angled deviations to alternative destinations – keep to the straight and narrow and the traveller, merchant or pilgrim, could set out confident of a safe arrival. A group could await the coming of another at a way point, an intersection, what the Romans would come to call the 'trivium', the 'three ways', perhaps, as Fletcher suggested, the source of all the trivia spoken to divert minds from the boredom of the wait.

Modern roads, modern for the late 1700's and early 1800's, would follow the old ways but would often deviate to take the traveller with horse or oxen-drawn cart across a bridge, thus avoiding a river crossing at an ancient causeway, natural or constructed long before and maintained through thousands of years by people completely ignorant of those who came first, save for the legends.

Such places were special; they were places where people congregated and waited for others to come for mutual assistance and made offerings to the spirits associated with a particular location. The spirits would choose locations for themselves and bring down disaster on those whose offerings were not acceptable – these were spirits of the water, of the forest, of the underworld, of the soil, of the rocks – all were looked down upon by the omnipotent gods of the sky, all demanded the unreasonable, even animal and human sacrifice, to let people pass across in peace. Everything the bronze-age person did had spiritual associations.

Sherlock read how the lines often began in ancient Gaul and continued across the water to Britain, the alignment being practically perfect as mark-stars guided the eye of the ancient surveyor as the Earth rotated at religiously special times of the year. The Sleuth had need for further guidance but was unsure of how and to whom to pose the required question and uncertain that he would understand the answer. He knew, however, that the legends were just that, tales told to explain the inexplicable, at least to the ancients. Those legends still held strong in many remote places, however, and some modern-day individuals might even believe in them and observe the old savage rites with religious fervour.

"Wasn't there some mention of a tattoo, one suggestive of French military service?" thought Holmes *"This is rather curious and very intriguing. I wonder if the French Army is missing one of its surveyors?"*.

Holmes did not need to know everything but he needed to make himself aware of the misguided beliefs of the newly converted faithful and the lengths to which they might go to appease the spirits or convince themselves that they were doing so. The little book, the 'Ancient Ways', was in many ways a guidebook, not just across the landscape, but also into the mind of those ancient superstitious and energetic peoples.

Having acquainted himself as best he could with what James Fletcher could make of the thinking of those who had long ago looked to the 'lines' and the 'places' for significance in their lives, Holmes returned 'Ancient Ways' to the attendant saying that the volume needed and deserved to be preserved as an important historical resource, even to the point of being republished and recommended to students of Britain's prehistory. It may not have been excessively rigorous in its presentation of evidence but it contained a wealth of observational detail which could be built upon, expanded and refined with a view to presenting future students, scholars and the general public with a partial view of their collective long distant past. Holmes came away with several notions worthy of further consideration, some suggestive of human sacrifice, though he knew the facts in the book were not set on particularly solid foundations – much was surmise based on observation, on a studious grounding in early British history and on one remarkable man's personal logic and intuition. He had much on which to ponder; many new ideas had to gel in his mind overnight. Holmes put the ideas to one side in his brain-attic and began to wonder how Watson had made out with his newspapers.

Watson had found many articles reporting the 'Ley Line Murders' but was loathe to produce scissors in the great library. A small pen knife to sharpen a rapidly blunting pencil lead would not invite the same sort of threateningly malign look from the attendants and so Watson was obliged to record everything of interest manually in his own notebook. He found little of any novelty, however, as so many of the articles were copied, often inaccurately, from the major publications. The Doctor made notes of a small number of regional journalists, correspondents and editors who might have further facts they may wish to share, especially with the Great Sleuth, the ever-noteworthy Sherlock Holmes.

Before heading off home to Baker Street, Holmes suggested calling in on Lestrade to see if he could shed any light on the crimes, or on the state of the on-going investigation. Lestrade did, indeed, have some knowledge of both, though it was only to the extent of providing potentially pertinent files and offering personnel to assist. The official detective from Scotland Yard had met his rural colleague and counterpart but was unable to offer Holmes and Watson anything beyond a letter of introduction to the man, hopefully making offers of assistance from Holmes and Watson more acceptable. If he could manage it, Lestrade added that he would like to join them but this would depend upon the progress of cases currently ongoing in the metropolis.

The Sleuth and the Doctor then proceeded back to Baker Street via Hansom, both excitedly anticipating what the following day would bring and mindful of what dangers might have to be faced in the days beyond.

The Ancients

Europe, as with most of the Earth's larger land masses, is old, unbelievably old, but the story of its human associations is, to the land itself, relatively new. Over the eons, the landscape has been reshaped as have, naturally, the forms and behaviours of its inhabitants – plant, animal and, increasingly, human. The glaciers generated by the giant freeze of the last ice-age pushed practically all life off so much of the northern land area and crushed and ground the surface rocks until nothing but ice could be seen. Slowly, ever so gradually, the great thaw began as temperatures mellowed and life began to reclaim a newly exposed landscape rich in remnant silt, firstly the plants and, slowly, the animals and then, warily, bands of humans whose distant ancestors had retreated as the greatest of winters came and seemingly, to them, never left. The reclaiming of northern Europe had begun, perhaps, thirteen thousand years before Caesar pondered on Britannia and its potential for the Empire, and himself; and the Romans were only one of many peoples who would desire the prime, rich real estate. Some of the humans who ventured forth as the ice retreated would become the ancestors of the 'ancients' of Fletcher's book, the term 'ancient' referring only to, perhaps, the last six or seven thousand years but, in the human experience, such a length of time seems an eternity into which living memory and numerous levels of legend have disappeared leaving only incidental clues to the lives of those who went before.

Life was harsh and short, winters were bitter and long, predators were many, competition was rife but, for such an inquisitive and inventive species as the humans, these attributes were soon put into a perspective to explain the wilfulness of nature - legends arose and those who lived long enough could tell the stories of the 'old ones' and how they knew to watch for the signals which the Earth, and the Heavens, provided if they were to survive. In time, such knowledge would become the property of the 'wise ones', the forerunners of the priestly castes.

The British Museum, conceived and newly erected in the time of Fletcher and filled with curiosities of all manner by that of Holmes, heralded a new caste of 'wise ones' who would dispassionately examine the clues to those past eras. Much had been learned but the techniques were still being refined and so much had happened since those ancient days that separating the old from the truly ancient could be difficult in the extreme. Regardless of what the new 'experts' said, however, there were and would always be people who looked beyond the obvious limits of reason and saw only what they believed, or what they wanted to believe. The need to see the otherworldly and spiritual in all things was something inherent to the human psyche and some would never overcome the appeal of the mysterious, the fear and awe which accompanied it but also the comforting presence of our all-pervading ghosts.

Britain and, indeed, much of mainland Europe and the Eurasian landmass, has been left marked by the remnants of the many stories of its ancient peoples, the peoples who came first and those which came along later and joined with, or displaced, or destroyed those who were there before. The landscape is itself a book, of a sort, sometimes hard to read, sometimes with pages scraped clean and used again, sometimes missing many pages or even full chapters, often never read but overlooked and forgotten until some need arose to call upon the knowledge it held. The new reader would have little to go on and would have to be self-educated anew in the language of the land, the physical cues which provided the words and told a very incomplete story. Occasionally, however, someone wise enough and with sufficient foresight, would leave a guide to that language and something of the story which that particular someone was able to read. Such a person was James Fletcher, and Sherlock Holmes could not have wished for a better teller of tales.

Fletcher's little disintegrating book told Holmes of the early Britons, a name latterly applied to all inhabitants of what became known as the British Isles but coming from a people who find their earliest recorded mention in the form of the Pretani, an appellation of disputed meaning but written down by the Greek mariner/explorer Pythias who spoke of the Pretanike folk he encountered on his epic voyage around the extremities of the European landmass. A few centuries later and Julius Caesar would speak of the Britannic people of Britannia although the term actually referred to a specific tribal grouping. The author of 'Ancient Ways' asserted that the Pretani were a Celtic people who had arrived from mainland Europe well after the ancient stone monuments were constructed and the long straight ways had been paced out but who found and utilised both. Perhaps they had merged with the original bronze-age people and took on many of the trappings of that much older civilisation, perhaps they had conquered them, perhaps the structures and lands had been long abandoned and were gradually assimilated into the customs and beliefs of the newcomers - all was conjecture, little more than a series of educated guesses which might never be confirmed or refuted due to a desperate lack of evidence.

Who those people were, where they came from, what type of language they spoke, what they actually believed in – all were unknown, but their skeletal remains and the alignments of their monuments pointed to a general European type and a desire to fit in with the comings and goings of the sun, moon

24

and stars. Their priests and astrologers left nothing in written form but there was another later cadre of priests which had found the Europe of the Caesars a little too unsettling as their influence on the Celtic tribes clashed with the ambitions of the rulers of the Land of the Legions. An aggressive Empire was expanding and the uncooperative and antagonistic Druids were prime targets for the armoured juggernaut of Rome.

The Druids may have known nothing of the truly ancient peoples and the Romans would learn little from the Druids but would push them ever westward until they found their last refuge and their ultimate demise in the far reaches of the 'western isles'. The last Druids went into the haze of history on the sacred island of Mona and their religion fell silent as their oral traditions died with the last priest to fall. They left nothing in the way of scriptures to truly tell us who they were and are known only because of numerous derogatory mentions in the annals of the unstoppable victorious conquerors, highly embellished accounts of battles against uncivilised barbarians who were overcome and rendered subject to the Emperor or eliminated completely.

It wasn't that the Romans were not accommodating of local gods and religious practices, many co-existed with the observances made on behalf of the Roman pantheon, it was more that the Druids had too much power over the local tribes. There's was a unifying presence at a time when Rome's all too successful foreign policy was based on the principle of 'divide and conquer'.

With no actual record of the beliefs and practices of the far older bronze-age peoples, Holmes considered that neither he, nor the perpetrator of the ley line crimes, would be able to go back beyond the time of the Druids. Everything he had known previously seemed to mix everything prior to the coming of the Romans in one big pot, a single history of a single people. Now he was reading that this was not the case but, beyond that statement, he could not progress.

The ways, the ancient ley lines were described as features added to and merged into a landscape undergoing rapid transformation from forest to field. The scope of the early inhabitants was expanding and the world-view was altering from the domain of the leafy forest gods to that of the gods of the heavens and the broad expanses of land. People were no longer looking inward to local influences but outward and upward to a greater order of the natural and the supernatural. Fletcher even noted how people of his time, ever so recently, had spoken of the lines in semi-reverent terms, as if one might follow one and disappear into the mists of time and commune with the "old ones', the "ancient folk", who knew the ways of the spirits of the sky and the land. Sherlock found many of the inferences difficult and could not always tell if Fletcher actually believed in the legends or merely rejoiced in their retelling.

The little book of 'Ancient Ways', though actually addressing the system of path-ways and road-ways used by the ancients, was an eye-opener to any reader wanting to glean just a little knowledge of their ways of life. Ancient History was not high on the list of Sherlock Holmes' curriculum as too many unnecessary facts, he would often insist, would fill up the brain-attic and deny any new and potentially important fact a place to settle. He did, he felt, need to get a feel for those long gone days, not for the historical record but because someone may well be trying to recreate them or make it seem as though they had returned.

The time of the 'ancients', Holmes learned, was a time in which those who wished to go somewhere generally had to do so on foot. The Celtic tribes had their war chariots and, no doubt, used horse-drawn carts to move materials around, but the ancient ways were not broad roads, merely tracks along which people predominantly walked. Iron for horseshoes was scarce and, over rough terrain and along ways worn down to a rocky base, a horse's hooves would soon suffer wear sufficient to render the animal lame. In time, all this would change but, until the coming of the Romans, the countryside was predominantly filled with pedestrians, sometimes leading horses pulling carts, sometimes leading horses laden with merchandise, but very few mounted – though powerful, a horse's endurance could be quite short.

James Fletcher had brought snippets of the ancient world back to life, bits and pieces gleaned as best he could from the widely scattered remnants of stone and mounded earth, and given the reader a glimpse of what life may have been like thousands of years and hundreds of generations before. His efforts were remarkable but subject to substantial qualification due to the many assumptions he had to make. Sherlock Holmes found the narrative intriguing in parts but was mostly interested in the motives of those remarkable builders in stone. He needed to know the significance of their human sacrifices, the reasons why a body might be dismembered and placed at junctions of the ancient ley lines. The perpetrator of such acts in his own time, repulsive as they were to those of the latter nineteenth century, may not have actually followed some ancient religious rite out of spiritual conviction but may have been trying to divert attention away from a greater crime by laying down a false scent by way of a highly elaborate and very distracting red herring.

But did these acts follow the ancient practices? If records were absent, from writings, from pictorial descriptions, or even from directly related folklore, then how would anyone actually know what those ancient practices were? There were certainly body parts deliberately placed but did these gruesome items represent offerings made to some spirit? Could the blood, perhaps, have been spilled in such a way as to symbolically nurture the soil and facilitate a bountiful harvest? Could such action have been some form of punishment? Could the dismemberment have been some sort of warning to others, to would-be traitors, to enemies? There was just no way to know and Fletcher's little book could provide little in the way of further assistance. Holmes knew he had much to learn, so many facts to gather before he could get the merest feel for the case, that is if Inspector Fleming did not send both him and Watson packing as unwelcome amateur interferers in a baffling case requiring professional expertise.

The Inspector

Rupert Fleming was not a man of great cultural awareness or involvement but he was a competent and motivated investigator who saw crime as something to be battled relentlessly. He had, however, little to go on for the case at hand, apart from four dismembered and scattered, though deliberately positioned, bodies - all victims being male, all having been in prime condition and all having been of moderate age, all certainly at least thirty and some perhaps as old as fifty. It had been a journalist, Robert Parker, who made the connection with the ancient ley lines as it was he who had noted, or been made aware, that the body parts had been placed at their various intervals where, according to local lore, the spirits of the long departed folk often made their presences known. Any journalist worth his salt would have taken this information as a gift from on-high and Robert Parker, ever eager to earn as much salt as he could and sprinkle it far and wide, was not slow in crafting a coherent story out of loose fact. His was the world of the independent freelance journalist – a story was only as good as the number of people who would buy a newspaper for an entertaining read, and strict factuality often got well and truly in the way of an exciting exposé or juicy scandal.

The Inspector, however, could not present a report to his rather stern and very conservative superiors and place the blame on the spirits of those who had walked the Earth several thousand years before. Nor could the man be seen to place much credence in evidence containing references to the power of a subterranean, living, breathing Earth Spirit which could, if it saw fit, come to the surface and display its displeasure at the antics of the humans which disturbed its peaceful repose below ground. No, Inspector Rupert Fleming could only report facts, facts supported by other facts and by solid, tangible evidence collected by himself or his trusted assistants – the trouble was, however, there were few facts beyond four dead bodies to report. As a result, the Inspector, harried from all quarters, was almost ready to search for the proverbial and ever-elusive straws at which he might clutch in sheer desperation. Little did he know that such a straw was on a fast train headed his way, its name being Sherlock Holmes.

As straws went, however, Sherlock Holmes, many times and to the great consternation and distress of Inspector Lestrade, could also be the one which broke the camel's back, so infuriatingly persistent could the man be when badgering officialdom to act before it felt it was ready to proceed with a successful prosecution. Sherlock Holmes was impatient, to say the least, and the prudent reluctance of the forces of Law presented an impediment to an agent whose life's blood flowed hot and fast through his veins to feed the excitement of the chase but whose involvement ceased when a felon was apprehended. Sherlock Holmes was the frantic hound running fast on the heels of its quarry and eagerly anticipating the kill and the frenzied feast, while Lestrade was the patient hunter carefully stalking his prey but ever mindful of conserving his strength for the long walk home lugging his heavy prize over his shoulders for later consumption in the proper manner and with all the proprieties of civilised dining observed. The Great Sleuth and the Official Detective were worlds apart in motivation and procedure but of one mind when seeking out the wrong-doer and putting an end to criminal disorder. If Holmes could be restrained to hold off just a little longer and if the Police could be pushed into action just that little bit faster, then each man could often provide what the other lacked – it was a system which worked because of the mutual dynamic support given by two agents moving in the same direction to the same end, albeit at different speeds and with different motivations. It was yet to be seen if and how well such an arrangement might work with Inspector Rupert Fleming.

Waterloo Station was, as usual, busy with passengers rushing about while trying to locate appropriate carriages and booked compartments, while porters did their best to keep up with the barrage of conflicting instructions. Late arrivals were also doing their best to purchase tickets before the whistle announced departure, though Holmes and Watson, having arrived in good time, had procured their first-class tickets and were lucky enough to secure a compartment free of fellow passengers - they were unsure, however, if they would have a continued exclusive occupancy as the train's substantial human cargo rearranged itself.

A shrill steam whistle prompted the latecomers into a race against time, the carriage and each other as the entire train of carriages shuddered into a series of staggered movements before the locomotive finally took the strain and pulled evenly on its trailing load. Steam and smoke and high-pitched whistles finally outpaced a group of disappointed runners who now sensed the reality of their situation – a long wait on a platform and a delayed completion for each one's journey. Holmes and Watson, ensconced in their compartment, now apparently one which they would have to themselves, settled in for the first part of a journey which would take them into a landscape and mindset moulded by millennia of human activity, and possibly into significant danger.

Watson busied himself going over the notes from the previous day's investigations, reading over and over the articles held by his newspaper clippings, all the while hoping to discover some as-yet elusive clue. This was never going to yield more than some basic facts heavily laden with conjecture and journalistic hype. Holmes was also pondering on the previous day's investigations but had spent much of a sleep-deprived night putting his newly-won knowledge into order – his brain-attic was now charged with facts, important facts but facts of unknown significance. The Great Sleuth still had many questions but had exhausted his options and would now rest as the train took him closer and closer to the answers he sought. His first question, and its corresponding answer, would reveal the character of Inspector Rupert Fleming; subsequent enquiries, should the Inspector prove amenable, would start with a small list compiled by Watson and could lead them into places and situations unknown. The mind of Sherlock Holmes had been cleared of all unrelated matters and was prepared and eager for the challenge ahead.

Three hours, numerous stops and several cat-naps after departure, Holmes and Watson were stirred into waking by a rapping on the glass of their compartment's door and the pre-arranged call of *"Salisbury, next stop. Gentlemen!"*. The two Gentlemen looked up and acknowledged the call, then stood and stretched, collected their belongings from the luggage racks and retook their seats to await arrival.

"Not a bad little trip – just the thing for catching up on some lost sleep." Holmes declared to his friend who replied, *"Well, I slept like a log last night and enjoyed being awake as our glorious countryside went gliding by our window. You missed a sight well worth seeing, My Friend."*

Holmes smiled a little and admitted, *"Well, I did keep one eye open much of the time but I suspect we will soon be seeing enough of our countryside up close and without recourse to soft seats such as we have just enjoyed. When you find your bed tonight, I expect that it will feel like soft down even if it turned out to be a blanket spread upon the bare ground."*

"*Holmes, sometimes you can be a complete cad.*" said Watson, "*I shall leave the bare ground to those who see nobility in discomfort, types such as yourself who could sleep soundly on a jumbled pile of bricks and not know the difference. We shall seek out a comfortable inn with soft downy mattresses and sleep like kings – there is nothing noble about an aching back first thing in the morning.*"

Sherlock Holmes looked at his friend and grinned, knowingly.

The pair stood once more as the train slowed its way into Salisbury Station then, as they felt their conveyance come to a complete stop, opened the compartment's outer door and stepped onto the platform.

Holmes and Watson both travelled light, their needs being generally simple, but each had brought along a thick coat – summer could be hot but nights out on the open countryside could prove chilly for those who might have to stand sentry exposed to the open sky and the elements. Watson went off seeking transport to the police headquarters while Holmes rechecked his letter of introduction to Fletcher from Lestrade and hoped it would prove to be the key to unlock the often impenetrable gates of local officialdom – his reputation for unreasoning interference would undoubtedly had gone before him and his reception could prove hostile.

The trip to police headquarters in the famous cathedral city took twenty minutes by Hansom and both travellers took delight in sights neither had encountered before. Remnant fortifications stood side by side with new shops, and old, while fine business premises, grand municipal buildings and neat domestic dwellings lined the streets – all was novel, and interesting, and pointed out to the newcomers by the cabbie who eventually called a halt to the sightseeing with the call of, "*Police Headquarters, Gentlemen, if you please.*"

Hopping down from the cab after Watson, Holmes tossed a generous half-sovereign to the cabbie with a smart, *"Thank you, My Man. We may need you later."*

"Just keep a keen eye out for Fred Jenkins, Guv'nor." replied the cabbie, *"I'm bound to be out and about somewheres and I knows this place like the back of me hand, and the land hereabouts."*

"Good Man." replied Holmes, *"We may have need of some good local knowledge, apart from that which the official agencies can provide. We shall, of course, pay well for whatever portion of your time we may take up."*

"Well, I'm your man." came the cabbie's reply as he whipped his horse up into a slow trot.

Holmes and Watson, travelling bags in hand, turned about and stepped smartly into the police building and addressed the Sergeant at the desk.

"Good morning, Sergeant." said the Sleuth, presenting his card, *"I am Sherlock Holmes and this is my friend and colleague Dr Watson and we would appreciate an audience with your Inspector Fleming. We have a letter of introduction from Scotland Yard - from Inspector Lestrade who believes we may be able to provide some valuable assistance with the current unpleasantness and who may be joining us at a later time."*

"Mr Holmes, Dr Watson – yes, I've heard of you and read some of the accounts penned by the good Doctor here." replied the Sergeant, *"I am Sergeant Baxter, gentlemen; I'd not been told to expect such famous visitors but I will inform Inspector Fleming of your arrival. He is conducting interviews at present, I'm afraid, and you may have to wait a*

short while till they are completed. I can offer you a cup of hot tea if you wish, though there are tea rooms across the road should you wish to take refreshments of a more solid character. I shall send word when the Inspector is free to see you. You may leave your bags here with me if you would like."

"Thank you, Sergeant." said Holmes and Watson in unison, obviously grateful for the opportunity, "We shall do as you say." then handed over their bags, retraced their steps outward, located the tea rooms and briskly stepped across the road and through a door whose attached bell announced the arrival of two hungry customers.

Mrs Dalhousie, the aproned proprietress, came out from behind a counter piled high with pastries and indicated to the pair to take their seats at a table close to the main front window. "I see you are new to town, Gentlemen, otherwise my little shop would be well known to you both – you have the look of men who appreciate good cooking, wholesome and tasty. I think I may lay claim to the provision of both qualities better than any you may come across in our county, or even perhaps beyond."

"Well, if the aroma is a faithful herald of the taste to come, you may well be stating the absolute truth, Madam." declared Watson salivating at the thought of treats in store.

Holmes and Watson took their seats, placed their orders and looked outward to Police Headquarters while awaiting delivery of their treats. Hot tea and good food were definitely appreciated by the hungry pair but both were anxious for an audience with the Inspector and quietly confident of his acceptance of their offer of help.

Thirty minutes went by and Holmes was becoming impatient. Watson had called for refills and second helpings while

Holmes had barely finished his first. A constable was then seen coming swiftly in their direction and Holmes nudged his friend, indicating that the Doctor should finish his meal while he paid the bill at the counter. The sound of the door's bell announced the entry of the constable who stepped quickly toward the waiting pair and said, *"Mr Holmes, Dr Watson, Inspector Fleming is free and will see you now, if you are finished your meal."*

"Thank you, indeed, Constable." was the reply as both men showed their eagerness to follow him. Across the road in Police Headquarters was Inspector Rupert Fleming, a man almost at the end of his tether and keen to accept any and all help he could get. As the now-refreshed pair entered his office, he stood and said, *"Thank you for taking the time to offer your services, Gentlemen. Mr Holmes, Dr Watson, your reputations precede you both. I am Inspector Fleming in charge of this Ley Line Murder case and Inspector Lestrade has sent a communication telling me to expect you and suggesting that I offer you every consideration."*

The Case

The morning had started off badly for Inspector Fleming, especially so as he had received a verbal reprimand from his superiors who had taken a lack of results to mean a lack of initiative and competence on the part of their subordinates, specifically him. The Inspector, however, was swamped with work of a most tedious nature and had very little in the way of uniformed personnel to help with the interminable questioning of possible witnesses spread out over a vast area and always suspicious of the Police. He had two 'persons of interest' to interview that morning, the interviews being in-progress when Holmes and Watson had arrived, though Fleming held little hope of receiving any reliable information from either. The two men had been active in the region but were petty criminals who were mostly guilty of little more than being 'drunk and disorderly', occasionally getting into heated arguments but never actually resorting to violence of any great concern. Still, they were both on the list of 'usual suspects' and would have to be interviewed as a matter of course.

Over the course of four weeks, more than one hundred 'persons of interest' had been interviewed and several hundred people across the region had been visited in their homes by police officers gathering information on who the victims may have been and who might be likely suspects in their murders. Nothing of any great worth had been discerned from these activities, however, and the medical examiner had been unable to shed much light on the victims' identities, nor even of their precise manner of death, save for the fact that all had been decapitated and had arms and legs detached and deposited at various locations then regathered for matching up to the four torsos. 'Severe loss of blood' was the recorded cause of death in each case and 'consistent with massive traumatic injury' was the rider, somewhat unnecessary as all victims' heads were missing. Hoping that it might help identify one of the victims, the Police had released the fact that one arm featured a tattoo with a French military theme. They had deliberately omitted the details of the tattoo featuring two crossed sabres set across the background of the French Tricolour under which was the word 'Revanche', French for 'revenge', suggestive of the man being a disgruntled veteran of the recent but ill-fated, for the French, Franco-Prussian War of 1870. The Inspector had, however, received a telegram the previous evening from his London colleague, Inspector Lestrade, which carried a message of hope, or at the least the potential for it – *"Sherlock Holmes and John Watson arriving tomorrow with official letter of introduction. Suggest you seriously consider their offer of help. Lestrade."*

Fleming's greeting of Holmes and Watson was effusive, perhaps a little too much, but the pair could tell that the Salisbury man was significantly stressed and grateful for any and all assistance they might provide.

"Inspector Fleming, we will be glad to offer you whatever help we can." said Holmes as he watched the Inspector rearrange chairs about his desk and place a number of folders in a tray for filing. *"I was unaware that Lestrade had sent word ahead about our pending arrival – he presumably felt it proper and courteous to send word in advance, by telegram, I expect."*

Holmes handed over Lestrade's letter of introduction which Fleming accepted, glanced quickly at its content and placed it in one of his desk drawers.

"Yes. That is the case." replied Fleming, *"And I'm glad he did. I freely admit that this case has me flummoxed and hearing that you and your colleague, Dr Watson, were coming settled*

my nerves somewhat and I was able to get a few hours of decent sleep last night, something which had evaded me for some weeks. This is a horrible crime - four murders made all the worse by the defilement of the bodies after death – well, I presume it was after death."

"Is there any suggestion that that may not have been the case?" asked Watson, aghast at the notion that such a thing might happen in his country in the latter half of the nineteenth century.

"No, indeed, Dr Watson," replied Fleming, "but the medical examiner has not been able to definitely rule out the possibility. Salisbury Plain holds many ancient secrets and many locals and quite a few newcomers are led to believe, or want to believe, in the ancient tales with all of their savagery and human sacrifice."

"Please take a seat, both of you," he continued, "and we may peruse the case files together, though there is little of substance to go on, even at this late stage of the investigation."

The two Londoners sat as Fleming collected numerous folders from his shelves and placed them on his desk. The files contained photographs of the unfortunate victims' remains and detailed sketches of particular features of their injuries, and the tattoo on the upper arm of one of the victims. Each victim had its own folder, each of which also contained photographs, maps and sketches of the locations of the remains, while a fifth folder held maps of the area over which those remains had been scattered, though each remnant seemed to have been deliberately placed with some underlying pattern to the actions.

"The medical examiner is confident that he has put each of the limbs with the proper torso." insisted Fleming, keen to show that, whatever the paucity of clues to the perpetrators or their motives, proper and detailed examinations had taken place and all findings had been documented according to the Police service's guiding rules of evidence. *"We have no idea of what happened to the heads, beyond the obvious fact that they had been removed. Perhaps this action was to prevent their identification but that goes against the deliberate placement of the limbs. I am loathe to say it, but there does seem to be a sense of ritual about the killings."*

"Or perhaps that's what you're meant to believe." responded Holmes, *"There could be pure conniving human criminality behind it all, a case of someone sending you and your men off along false trails and chasing false scents."*

"A distinct possibility," was Fleming's reply, *"but what would anyone want to keep us away from which would require such drastic action? This part of the country is rather quiet as regards criminal activity – mostly nuisance pilfering and the odd big robbery which is generally easy to clean up."*

"What, indeed?" pondered Holmes, *"But, apart from deceiving the Police and keeping you busy, there is the distinct possibility that someone actually places stock in the old beliefs and is keen to revive them. This, in matter of fact, gives us two definite lines of enquiry, one seeking someone who is downright crooked and another seeking someone who is suffering from self-deception, or has gone totally mad."*

"There is much to investigate," Holmes continued, *"but little, as yet, to go on. We do, however, need to think beyond the depraved killer supposition and look for something altogether more devious. Watson and I need to find our digs. We are booked into Cooper's Inn on the Amesbury Road – it promises comfortable lodgings and good sustenance, if we can believe the reports. Then I would like to ask a few questions of some*

of the locals but do want to get out to the sites where the bodies were found in the early morning. I trust you would have no objections. People may open up to us where the Police might find them tight-lipped."

"None whatsoever." was the Inspector's reply, "Can we be of any assistance in regards of transport?"

"No." came the reply, "I believe we will be able to count on the services of a local man, Fred Jenkins, who has indicated that he would be willing to help us in that regard. I will need to locate several maps of the district. The one's I have are limited in their detail but, on our way here, we did pass an excellent-looking shop which should satisfy our needs."

The Inspector nodded approval and added, "I know of Jenkins – a good man and quite trustworthy, also very knowledgeable in the goings-on about town and country. He's very hard to shut up once he gets talking, though, so beware of telling him anything you don't wish spread around. He can keep his mouth shut but it does tend to cost. He operates a Hansom locally but also runs a carriage and wagon for his out of town jaunts."

"Well, a little bit of legal bribery can go a long way," answered Holmes, "especially if there is a definite prospect of more to come. We shall look him up and engage his services and see what comes of it. Rest assured, though, that we shall remain tight-lipped on the possibilities we have discussed in this room. I'm certain you won't want any more rumours circulating around the countryside. Watson here has made up a list of people to talk to who may have information unsuspected by even themselves."

"Indeed." commented Fleming, "Anyone we can help you with."

"No, not really, not at this point." replied Holmes, *"But I don't suppose that you may have heard of an old school teacher, long dead by now I expect, one by the name of James Fletcher who wrote about the ancient paths and people early in the century, one who had a niece called Margaret, though she'd likely be of a fair age by now?"*

"No, I can't help you there." said Fleming, *"But Jenkins may know, or may be able to tell you where to find out. You might try school records, such as they are, if this Fletcher's school is still standing."*

Holmes and Watson collected their bags from the Duty Sergeant and made their way to purchase the necessary maps which would help them prepare a preliminary plan. They would need an ordinance map of the region and maps of the archaeological features of the countryside as well as any general information on local legends as might be held. Much of the latter was of limited use in itself but did point the pair to a number of local characters active and knowledgeable in the ancient lore. These would have to be visited and questioned about any revived religious practices in the region, and who might be involved. Holmes was not exactly starting from scratch, he had read James Fletcher's little book, but he did have a lot of facts to gather, to absorb and to sort, before he could decide on an appropriate course of action. Still, it would be necessary to visit the sites where the various body parts had been deposited even if he did not, as yet, fully appreciate the significance of those particular sites to the ancients.

Having gathered what information was available, the pair made way to the Amesbury Road digs, to Cooper's Inn, where they could spread out their maps and decide just who should be visited first. Before they could do that, however, they would need to make contact with Fred Jenkins and engage his services for the next few days. There was still a considerable portion of the day remaining and neither man was prepared to waste a single minute of daylight. The innkeeper may also have information he could offer – the reports of the Ley Line Murders had been good for business in one sense as ghoulish sightseers flocked to the region, but many regulars had either just not arrived or had sent word that they had made other arrangements due to the terrible events.

A lad the innkeeper referred to as Billy, his son, it was assumed, was sent off to seek out Jenkins and his cab and the pair then took the innkeeper into their confidence and was told, with as few details as possible, of the involvement of the famous detective Sherlock Holmes and his colleague Dr John Watson as ancillary investigators in the official investigations. The innkeeper was sworn to silence for the duration of the investigations and was ever so keen to cooperate, especially as he would be able, after the case's completion, to boast that the Great Sleuth had slept on the premises and had conducted his investigative activities beneath his roof. He also asked if they would object, in due course, to his naming of the pair's accommodations in their respective honours – "*It would be very good for business.*" he asserted – Holmes and Watson agreed with a just modicum of embarrassment but paid the matter little attention.

SALISBURY SECRETS

The Cabbie

After their exertions of the previous day and that morning, and despite the long hours of daylight providing the opportunity for immediate immersion into their investigations, the two sleuths were sorely tempted to take to their comfortable beds to rest up but knew that Fred Jenkins, the cabbie, would be coming sooner or later to hear of their proposal. They did not know the man beyond one trip from station to station, railway to police, but did detect a good degree of competence and knowledgeability complimented by a direct way of talking. Inspector Fleming had indeed warned them of the man's talkative nature but also added that he did not know this from first-hand experience, only from the comments of others. Prudence in what may be said in his presence and what might be entrusted to him would be an obvious ploy, at least until they knew him better, but they also knew that any astute person keenly attuned to the region's comings and goings as this cabbie seemed would already have deduced the reason for presence of Holmes and Watson and made plans of his own which would work to his personal advantage. One troubling notion, however, was that the man had both intimate knowledge of the region and various means of transport and might, however unlikely it might seem, have been involved in the atrocities himself. Caution and preparedness would have to be added to prudence in their dealings with the man.

Young Billy, the innkeeper's lad, had searched the usual haunts of an unencumbered cabbie and finally found the man outside of Salisbury Railway Station resting his eyes and his horse in the generally quiet part of the day. One train had left and another wasn't due for some ninety minutes and the city of Salisbury was midway through the long afternoon of a working day - Fred Jenkins' morning rush and midday outings were over and he had, as had usual, taken a late lunch, fed and watered his horse, and positioned his cab under a tree to doze away the time till his next fare. Billy's yells were not altogether welcome as Fred had just drifted off into a dreamy slumber in the warmth of a summer's mid-afternoon but a fare was a fare and accommodating those who would pay for transport was his business; after all, the horse did most of the work.

On hearing of who was summoning him, however, the cabbie called young Billy to hop into the cab so they could both be off to Cooper's Inn. Fred Jenkins had hoped that the famous pair from London would engage him – he was keen to know more about what had been going on and saw the arrival of Holmes and Watson as a golden opportunity for gathering gossip material, something his two new fares would explicitly forbid as a condition of their arrangements.

Holmes and Watson had deposited their belongings in their respective rooms in the inn and then descended to the commercial room adjoining the bar and dining areas, a facility often used by commercial travellers and others requiring quiet, good lighting and ample desk and table space for preparing their upcoming ventures. Holmes had his maps and Watson his lists and could spread out to their hearts' content, there being no other occupants of the room at that moment. What they did not know was the time it would take and the difficulty involved in reaching their desired locations and contacts, some of which were spread far across a considerable area; they would need a reliable guide, perhaps Fred Jenkins should he prove agreeable, for this information.

The pair looked up from their tasks upon hearing the clip-clop of Fred Jenkins' horse on the cobbles outside the inn and proceeded to cover any reference to mystical causes of the murders. Holmes had spread out the district maps and marked on them the sites where the body remnants had been deposited. These he would definitely wish to see but to do so might require an early start for a long day's excursion – they would have to see to procuring sufficient supplies, possibly for an overnight stay out on the plains.

Fred Jenkins walked into the inn behind a very excited Billy who ran up the stairs shouting out *"Mister Holmes, Doctor Watson, Fred Jenkins is here with his cab."* but to no avail; the pair had exited the ground floor room and had addressed the cabbie by the time Billy returned.

"Oh, sorry Gents, I thought you'd be upstairs in your rooms." said Billy, puffing a little after his unnecessary exertions.

Sherlock Holmes smiled at the lad and reached into his pocket, *"You did well, Young Billy. Now here's a thruppence for your troubles. We may well need your services again."*

"Thank you, Mr Holmes. Just yell out when you need me." came back an enthusiastic reply. *"I won't be far away."*

"Now, Mr Jenkins. Your services." started Holmes, *"We shall be in need of transport within the city itself and around the countryside about over the next few days. We would like to engage your services for a period and you won't find us ungenerous for the inconvenience. How are you placed for time and for transport?"*

Fred Jenkins gave an exaggerated *"Hmmm"* while screwing up his face and pinching his chin between thumb tip and forefinger knuckle. *"I do believe I could forego my usual fares for a good cause, especially if that cause didn't see me out of pocket. I would need to charge for waiting time and special exertions, for the horses, you know, depending on the mode of transport gents such as you might require. I have my cab, of course, and a carriage but for going out into the countryside we'd need the wagon – well, it's fitted out with seats and I often take groups out on excursions to see the old stones and the like – the wagon, two horses and feed and my time will cost more than a cab around town, you would appreciate."*

"*Yes, indeed, Mr Jenkins,*" replied Holmes, "*Here are two pounds on account and we'll pay appropriate extra amounts as we use your services. Would that be satisfactory?*"

"*Yes, indeed.*" was the reply, "*Quite satisfactory.*"

"*By the way,*" cautioned Holmes, "*Our work must, of necessity, be kept secret in as much as we cannot have our movements and activities discussed with anybody. All lips must be sealed on those matters. I expect that you know we are here to investigate some recent unpleasant occurrences – it is crucial that you come on as part of our team and agree, on your honour, not to divulge anything unless we give our express permission to do so. If all this is agreeable, and I suspect that it is, then you are our man, Mr Jenkins.*"

Holmes extended a hand to the eager cabbie who responded in kind and stated, "*Well, I admit I do like a bit of gossip, being a cabbie and all, but you have my word on the matter, Mr Holmes. Not a word on your doings will anyone hear from Fred Jenkins.*"

"*Good man.*" declared Watson who had also extended a hand to the cabbie, "*Now, we have places on the map to discuss.*"

Sherlock Holmes had spread out his ordinance map of the region on the room's central table and marked the locations of interest. He had made note of these locations from the file map held in Inspector Fleming's office but there seemed to be neither rhyme nor reason to the placements of the body parts – the Sleuth would need help though he was expecting that some pattern might emerge once he had been able to pencil in any ley lines passing through the area covered by his map. The modern roads were well marked out and the variations in topography were apparent; town and city areas were detailed and boundaries clearly indicated.

"*These ordinance maps are a godsend, Gentlemen,*" declared Holmes, "*they are so reliable and professionally prepared that without them I would be roaming blind over an unfamiliar landscape, though I expect that Mr Jenkins here might find his way around with ease.*"

"*Yes, the area is quite familiar to me, though it is easy to get lost once night falls or a heavy storm comes in.*" responded an eager Jenkins, "*But a map isn't everything; a map is a guide to an outsider and made for a purpose, not to tell the holder everything about the land he walks over.*"

"*Well said,*" agreed Holmes, "*and very true, and it is for that reason precisely that we have engaged your good self. The information held on these folded pages reflects only what the surveyors chose or were restricted to committing to the engravers and printers. It is the tracks, the ancient ways, those ley lines, and all manner of ancient man-made features which we need to trace out so that we can start to make sense of the landscape from a bronze-age inhabitants point of view.*"

"*You're not saying that someone from the bronze-age killed all those people, Mr Holmes,*" said Jenkins with some little alarm evident in his voice, "*that's beyond even my gossiping mind.*"

"*No.*" said Holmes, "*It's just that someone is acting as though he's some reincarnation of those ancient folk, or is a deluded religious devotee to those bygone rituals, or is someone trying hard to cover up a completely modern crime and leading the Police astray with false trails. My money would be on the last of those three options but it would be imprudent to ignore the possibility of the first two.*"

"*Anyway,*" Holmes continued, "*someone knows a lot about the ley lines and it is those lines which will, in time, lead us to the murderer, or murderers.*"

"*Those ley lines, Mr Holmes, are not all as apparent on the ground as you might wish. A lot has happened since they were first put down, or dug out, or whatever those old folk did to mark out those ancient ways.*" warned Jenkins, "*But a good place to start could be the old stones – some of them are in circles, some mark out lines as straight as a die but disappear into someone's field or heavy forest, some seem to deliberately point toward distant features or other old monuments, and some mark out a well-used straight road together with churches and fortifications only a few hundred years old. Whatever they are, they are not there by accident.*"

"*Yes, yes.*" came from Holmes, "*but Watson here is an ex-military man, a Doctor certainly, but when he wasn't digging out bullets or sewing up a gaping wound, he took in the lay of the land about him with a map and prismatic compass. He has that compass with him, and an excellent pair of field glasses, and we might begin to amend our map with information our talented Doctor may glean from such observations on the Salisbury Plain.*"

"*Oh, good,*" Watson said, somewhat sarcastically, "*I was hoping I'd have more to do than just carry the bags.*"

Watson then produced a number of small publications featuring walking maps of the district, nothing too detailed but indicating the major points of archaeological interest and the best ways of getting there, on foot. Some locations were distant and some of these were accessible using railway stations along the main London to Salisbury line, and some from branch lines, as bases. There were substantial distances to cover in many cases and the walking tourist was advised to leave an expected time of return and an anticipated route with the Police or with representatives of local amateur archaeological groups. Activities advised against were walking alone and without adequate provisions and clothing – high summer and deep winter had claimed many a life over the years and, as Cooper and Jenkins could well attest, such events were definitely bad for business. Of course, there would always be the stalwarts but many more would seek out the likes of Jenkins for an interesting day trip, safe, moderately comfortable and finishing up at one of the many local inns for a hot supper, relaxing beverages and comfortable beds. Just how many of the local legends Jenkins held in his cranium could only be guessed at, but how many of those were actually factual would be extremely difficult to discern – Jenkins, himself, had probably long forgotten which ones were based on fact and which ones were not. His business on the plains was one of transport mixed with a fair amount of entertaining commentary, far more than any desire to improve people's archaeological and prehistoric education, but still he seemed far more knowledgeable that first appearances would have suggested.

The Maps

Jenkins left the two sleuths musing over their scant information and went out to check on his horse and to collect his own map of the area. Holmes took the opportunity of the cabbie's absence to make a few comments to Watson.

"We shall need to make contact with that sensationalist hack who wrote all that rubbish for The Times. He's bound to be hanging around Salisbury making up news when none can be found." Holmes said in a less than enthusiastic tone. *"He may be a great exaggerator but he does seem possessed of great energy – if he applied his mind productively, he might make a superior detective."*

"Oh, you mean Parker, Robert is his first name." responded Watson, *"Yes, he does have a flair for the sensational, I grant you, but he also knows what the Public craves. We should ask about; he no doubt would be staying in one of the local hotels, something fairly cheap as his income would be intermittent. Perhaps we should ask Jenkins if he knows of him."*

"We must tell Jenkins only as much as we need to at this point. There is no reason to let him in on all of our plans." declared Holmes, *"We shall have a few hours before we must be off to Stonehenge and it would be remiss of us not to grasp the opportunity to gather facts. Facts, Watson, not myth or legend or fanciful stories to entertain the Public. We might also query Parker for his opinion of Jenkins, and of Fleming – he may have much to tell us if he can see a story with our names attached to it."*

"You mean your name, don't you Holmes?" demanded Watson, *"Don't let him go bandying the name of Sherlock Holmes around willy-nilly. Remember his way with facts – he'll have you down on your knees with your magnifying lens*

checking out every blade of grass on Salisbury Plain, and a picture of you doing it."

"Yes, yes." agreed Holmes, *"We shall have to offer him something, though, something better than a juicy half column in The Times or even a blaring headline in one of those rubbishy tabloids which will print anything. He will want the story of the year, of the decade, I'd expect, so we shall have to cooperate with him, just a little."*

Jenkins was seen coming back with his map in hand and Holmes gave Watson a nudge and a knowing wink.

"Here we are, Gents." expressed Jenkins, *"My own map, a little the worse for wear but it shows all of the locations of interest for a seeker after prehistoric knowledge. I base my little tours on it but seldom have to refer to it these days, such is my intimate knowledge of the region in that regard."*

Homes and Watson looked at the bedraggled document, the long splits along its folds, the underlined text, the circled features, the pathways marked out in heavy ink lines and the many notations added by its owner over its many years of usage. *"A valuable resource, I perceive,"* said Holmes, *"a tool of your trade, not some fancy chart in pristine and unused condition. I like a man who knows what he's about."*

Watson gave his friend a quick sardonic look as if to say, *"Holmes, don't butter him up too thickly."* and then looked away until he was able to bring his involuntary grin under control.

"Now," said Holmes, *"I notice on some of these leaflets of Watson's that there is a Salisbury Historical Society led by a Professor Tilbury, retired I would assume, going by the scope of his local activities."*

"*Retired from Oxford, yes,*" replied Jenkins, "*but those activities aren't his, but hers. She was one of the earliest women admitted to that august institution but her Professorship, though well deserved, is honorary. I'm not even sure she was able to take a degree in her time but everyone about calls her 'Prof' and many's the visitor she's had seeking knowledge of the ancient times over the years, visitors both academic and private.*"

"*Remarkable.*" declared Watson with undisguised admiration, "*I'm sure that Holmes here wouldn't see the significance but there will come a time when such things will be commonplace and Britain can put all of her mental capacity to productive endeavours.*"

"*Indeed, Watson,*" replied the sleuth, "*but for now we are on a quest and must focus on the matters at hand. We shall call upon Professor Tilbury and prevail upon her to give us some guidance into the minds of those who crave for immersion in those ancient ways. I crave facts or the means to attain those facts from this Professor. Be he or she male or female, it matters not one iota and I judge that she will prove a very useful contact.*"

"*Well,*" came in Jenkins, "*the lady is well into her eighties and, though quite robust for someone of that venerable age, she does tend to tire quickly and a visitor ought not just show up and expect a lengthy interview. Perhaps you, Mr Holmes, and Dr Watson ought to send her a note to expect you, say early in the afternoon of tomorrow, or perhaps mid-morning, after returning from the stones; we should be back in good time.*"

"*That is precisely what we'll do, Watson.*" agreed Holmes, "*Thank you, Jenkins, for the information and for the suggestion. Would you be on hand to take us there at that time*

– we shall of course continue to retain your time over the period? Late-morning would be best, I think – we shall advise her that we'll call at eleven and trust that this would suit her arrangements."

"My pleasure," was the reply, *"I'm your man while you're here. Now, we should get down and have a good look at these maps, yours and especially mine."*

Holmes had cleared the main central table and made room for Jenkins' tattered map of Salisbury Plain and the sites of the stones and the other works attributed to those exceptional builders of so long ago. Jenkins placed his map at the table's centre and oriented it so that it received maximum daylight from the room's large window.

"Salisbury, Gentlemen." the cabbie said, somewhat dramatically as though he was giving one of his commercially enhanced entertaining spiels to a group of amazed tourists, as he pointed to a cluster of blocky images at bottom left of his map. *"And up here is Avebury and the rows of stones, all having stood sentinel over the district and over the centuries, indeed over the millennia."*

"Stonehenge," he continued, *"is but a relatively small way northward and is but one of many structures close by, albeit the most spectacular and memorable, and it is to here we shall proceed this evening by way of the Amesbury Road. It would be illogical to take in the entirety of the sites in just one day, so I would suggest we plan a series of sojourns and prioritise them in some way."*

"Well, our cab driver's a showman. Or is it a cab driving professor we're listening to?" Watson remarked to himself while trying to catch Holmes' eye.

Holmes, though, was concentrating less on what Jenkins was saying than on the map itself. He did agree that it might take some little while to see everything but that was not his intention. Holmes wished to feel what his adversary felt, at least to some degree, so that he could better appreciate that adversary's motives should they be based on ancient belief or on that adversary's logic should that stem from an intention to deceive any investigation.

"*I would certainly like to see Stonehenge,*" said Holmes, "*and I would like us to visit the sites where the body parts were deposited. On my map, the locations seem unconnected, but on yours, if I have those locations correctly transposed, there is a dotted pathway connecting three sites and another connecting four while the eighth site seems isolated. They were, indeed, laid out in straight lines over a broad area, presumably along ley lines, but access is apparently possible via modern trails, some meandering about wildly. How passable are those dotted pathways, Jenkins?*"

"*Quite passable, Mr Holmes,*" replied Jenkins, "*especially in the drier times. They can be a bit boggy in places in the wet but even then the walker just gets muddy boots. They are of little use for my cart but a horse would quite easily manage, though because of the fences we never see any but the hiker on those trails, quite often in groups of four or five, rarely more. You might note that much of the area is in private ownership and there the lines indicate rights of way – it is necessary to observe the proprieties in those cases, you'd understand.*"

"*Of course,*" agreed Holmes, "*but still I must see those sites, though any evidence is sure to have been trampled underfoot by all those sightseers.*"

The cabbie shook his head and said that there had been trouble on the private lands, *"People just went stupid and pushed down fences to get access to some sites, ignoring the paths and the signs and even the directions of the constables standing guard. It was madness, Mr Holmes, and the constables had no chance of controlling the fools, so many were there. I can't see how it could have been but the whole thing seemed almost deliberate, even organised."*

"Indeed!" mused a fascinated Holmes, *"We shall talk more on that point later."*

"So, I see here on your map," Holmes continued, resuming his focus on the actual geographical arrangements indicated so much better on Jenkins' document, *"that Stonehenge is no more than two miles from the furthest of the sites of interest."*

Jenkins nodded in agreement, saying, *"It is no distance at all for an able-bodied person. We can't get to them by wagon so we should leave it at Stonehenge and then walk, though we do have to make a longish diversion before we get to those dotted trails lest we fall foul of a landowner or two. Best to keep on the right side of some of these fellows; they have been known to shoot at trespassers, or set the dogs on them."*

Holmes knew that there would be little chance of detecting useful clues around the sites themselves but needed to stand on the ancient ley lines, as it was reported, and get a sense of location and outlook. *"Perhaps,"* Holmes began pondering audibly, mostly directed at Jenkins, *"Watson might take sightings with that compass of his and we might scan the horizon for any distant feature which might have been of significance to those ancient people, and perhaps to the murderer, or murderers. The old soldier always carries his field glasses along with his medical kit."*

There was little more that the trio could do beyond looking at the maps and examining, in broad detail, the geographical arrangements which defined the area of interest. Jenkins' map was a godsend in that much more pertinent detail had been added but, beyond allowing for a plan of action, could tell them nothing of the sites themselves. There were no ley lines indicated on either map but, at least, the two sleuths would be able to see for themselves what the murder saw when depositing his ghastly remnants.

Jenkins could see the frustration on Holmes' face and read the determination in Watson's. He knew from experience that all who saw the stones and the other monuments were somehow changed in their outlooks – he knew that, for all of their experience and pragmatism with criminal investigations, Holmes and Watson would be no different. He folded his map and returned it to its oilskin folder and decided it was time for the tour master to take charge.

"There is much for the curious tourist to marvel at on the Salisbury Plain," declared Jenkins, *"but for such men as you who seek the significance of and the truth beyond the ancient artefact, there could be no better place to begin your surveys than Stonehenge."*

The Spirits

Circles and lines, of stone, of long-decayed wood, of raised earth, dot and crease the countryside of Britain and, indeed, of Europe, all structures pointing to the energy and enterprise of the ancient peoples who felt compelled to honour the gods of the natural world and the heavens by bringing the landscape into line with celestial events. In the stone and bronze ages, they may have lived, but their minds were as keen and alert and creative, perhaps even more so, as those of people one might encounter in the nineteenth century. There's was not a subsistence level existence – that had long passed and agriculture, supplemented by organised hunting, had seen them move from hunter-gatherer societies into tribal civilisations raising crops and keeping livestock. The working year was divided up and regulated, far more than ever before, according to the seasons and the dictates of the gods, gods who had provided signs for the people to observe and obey. Those signs were recorded in monumental stone and bequeathed to the generations to come. When the old beliefs faded, though, the stones remained to fascinate all who gazed upon them.

The age of stone had given way to the age of bronze and that to the age of iron as described by, and for the literary convenience of, much later scholars, but two educated men in the more enlightened modern age of steam and steel were now immersing themselves in the mixed remnants of all that had occurred over the six thousand years which had passed since the stone monuments began appearing.

Salisbury is rich in the magic of ancient legend – its very name records a succession of occupations, though for only the last third of the age of the standing stones. The Old English scribes of a thousand years past had written Seorobyrig for what the Celtic peoples had called Sorviodunum and the Welsh chroniclers recorded as Caer Caradog, all names indicating a fortification, and a fortification meant one thing: that enemies abounded seeking dominance over a vast and valuable tract of real estate held by someone else.

The magnificent Salisbury Cathedral, the crowning glory of the region, it too aligned on the landscape according to belief, was begun 750 years before Holmes' and Watson's investigations commenced but is a relative newcomer to the landscape, being a monument raised to the glory and beliefs of the last group of invaders, also great builders of enduring monumental structures, these being the Normans. An ancient hill fort, perhaps built by the Celtic peoples more than 1500 years before that, or perhaps by the far earlier stone or bronze age folk, was located on a site of prime strategic significance which was not lost on the Romans who were desirous of controlling the region and the Celtic tribes within. The Romans were apparently happy to let one local tribe dominate and therefore occupy the fort but the Saxons, some 500 years later, took control and later fortified the structure considerably to counter the threat of the rampaging Vikings.

Old Sarum, a name bequeathed to the hilltop fort and its cathedral, was in a state of ruin by the time Holmes and Watson would get to see it but its demise and demolition had materially aided in the birth and development of New Sarum, some two miles distant, the Norman cathedral around which the city of Salisbury would grow and prosper.

A sight, strangest and most intriguing by far, however, is to be found in the ancient rings of massive stones, all deliberately shaped and squared, dragged into position and stood upright, some then to hold their fellows aloft after these had been raised upward and made horizontal. What its makers called the structure and what ceremonies were conducted within its precincts can never be known with any great accuracy, those people and their knowledge are separated by the long silence of the millennia between their demise or dispersal and the coming of the Celts, but all know it today as Stonehenge.

"Stonehenge, Gentlemen." repeated Jenkins, *"You will no doubt have heard of the structure and read of its antiquity and of the many and varied and outrageous stories told about its origins and use. I must admit to going along with many of those tales when standing on the Plain, particularly at sun-up, with a group of enchanted tourists, just to give them their money's worth, you know. The fact is, as far as I can tell, no one actually knows who built it or why, though it apparently has something to do with the rising sun on the winter solstice."*

"Indeed." replied Watson, looking quizzically at Holmes, both having noted how the subservient cabbie's expression had changed when speaking of the stones, how his accent and intonation had altered from that of a rustic dialect to the expression of someone imbued with an educated and confident enthusiasm for the wonders of his region. His was not the overused and misplaced showman's hyperbole, it was the articulation of someone immersed in and part of the region's rediscovered ancient culture.

"Just how far away is Stonehenge?" asked Holmes, noting from the guide map that it seemed to offer a readily achievable easy day's outing for the seasoned hiker, *"Could we go there in the morning?"*

"We could, Mr Holmes," replied Jenkins, *"but the best time to see it is at dawn as the sun's first rays of the day burst through the stones. We're a long time to the winter solstice but the effect is still spectacular and, once seen, it leaves the pilgrim changed in some way as it merges the present and past in the*

mind, if you take my meaning.   Anyway, you will fully understand only when you have sat within the circles and watched as Old Sol starts to fill the world with light and the land is reborn once again."

Watson again looked at Holmes with both eyebrows raised to express the intrigue he felt for the cabbie's expression.

The cabbie, noting the unvoiced communication between Holmes and Watson, added, "*It's an eight mile drive in the wagon, two hours with a good team in front. If we prepared ourselves this afternoon, we could camp out on the plain overnight and experience what those old ones did all those years ago. Dr Watson can take his fancy compass and draw lines on that map to his heart's content.*"

Holmes, noting well how the cabbie's speech had regressed into its rustic subservient style, said, "*Well, Watson. Are you up for a bit of camping and early morning surveying. Stonehenge does seem a good place to start our investigations of the lines.*"

"*Agreed,*" replied Watson, "*Cooper's soft beds will just have to wait, I suppose. It looks like we'll be sleeping on rocks after all.*"

"*Nonsense.*" Jenkins retorted, "*I'm fully stocked with camp stretchers and tents. They'll keep you high and dry off the ground and protected from the elements. And I'm a fair cook – nothing fancy but you won't go hungry.*"

He continued with a broad grin, "*Let's hope the spirits of old stay put this night. Can't have them upsetting our guests.*"

Watson laughed, as did Holmes, but the Sleuth also noted the cabbie's use of 'our' in his last statement.   Was Jenkins referring to Salisbury and its people as a whole or was there something the cabbie was hiding, something devious, perhaps diabolical?

The cabbie continued, cheerfully, *"Good. So I'll pick you up at seven this evening and we'll have an easy ride out to the stones. We can have a look around, a hot supper and then turn in after sunset, all ready for an early start before dawn. In the morning, I'll have the porridge heated and tea brewed so we can breakfast before the apparition. I'll leave you both to sort out your maps and such and return later with all that we'll need for an overnight camp."*

Holmes and Watson were both keen to see the stones at daybreak but would first arrange a solid hot meal before embarking on their outward trek.

Jenkins having taken his leave, the pair returned to their maps and leaflets, studying all for anything which might suggest a clue to the perpetrators of the crimes or to the motives they may have had in committing them. Nothing, however, could be gleaned but the two men were at least familiarising themselves with the district and its major features and made notes on visitations they would have to make, geographical and personal. Holmes was still a little uneasy about Jenkins' use of 'our' when speaking of them as guests. Was this a local mannerism, a figure of speech peculiar to the region or was the term an accidental reference to others with whom Jenkins was in league?

Holmes was never very forthcoming with unresolved mental dilemmas but he felt that he owed it to Watson to discuss the matter. He did not want to make too much of something which might turn out to be a trivial matter but they were both in territory new and largely unknown to them both and did not know of in whom trust might be placed implicitly. Perhaps

Inspector Fleming, as unlikely as it would seem, may turn out to be involved or at least knowingly compromised in some way.

"*Watson,*" said Holmes, "*this Jenkins seems an amenable fellow but we both noted the change which came over him when talking about Stonehenge. It was as though the simple cabbie had left and the eminent professor had taken his place, such was the fervour and apparent depth of knowledge he showed. This may have been something practiced or there might be great depths to the personality of the man perched on top of that cab.*"

"*I did notice that, Holmes,*" replied Watson, "*and I must admit to being a little unnerved at the change. The original Jenkins was likeable and pleasant but his altered manner of speaking was a little too intense and cultivated for a simple rustic type. I agree that there is much of the performer in the man but perhaps he knows and says too much.*"

"*Indeed,*" Holmes responded, "*but we have committed ourselves and must now trust our instincts. We shall go with him to Stonehenge but not unarmed, nor unprepared in other ways. These are still dark times, Watson, and a murderer is still at large, or murderers, and no one knows the who or the what or the why or the when of those involved. Are we to face a lone deviant with a little local knowledge or are we up against a well organised group of conspirators intent on sending a drastic message to others? We just don't know and we are just starting to gather our facts. Caution should be our watchword and we must keep our thoughts and findings close to our chests.*"

Both men had gone upstairs to collect any necessities for the overnight camp and returned on hearing Cooper's call to dine. The men would eat well and muse on the unresolved matters in a mood mixed with great anticipation and some little disquiet. Both men, however, and despite the uncertainties of their positions, were determined and keen to run their quarry to ground after it had been flushed from hiding. What fangs and claws that quarry might wield at that time was unknown but four dismembered bodies could attest to the fact that the hunters were almost certainly in for a fight.

All that could be done for that day had been done and the next stage of their adventure was about to start. When dealing with the suggestion of otherworldly beings, most people would find it difficult to keep their primeval fears in check, despite the knowledge that they were up against mortal humans, and both Holmes and Watson were susceptible to flights of panic should they let those fears take hold. Watson was determined to keep his mind focussed on reality while Holmes was able to compartmentalise his mind and lock up all unnecessary wandering thoughts.

Yong Billy Cooper was sent for and given a hastily written note to deliver to Robert Parker. They had assumed that the journalist was staying in one of the lesser hotels of the city and Billy would go from one to the other asking if he was registered. On finding the hotel, or the actual man, Billy was to hand over a sealed envelope which also contained the card of Sherlock Holmes – the note requested a discrete meeting with the journalist and asked that a written reply be given directly to Billy or sent in another sealed envelope to Cooper's Inn. This done, all that remained to do was to wait for their ride.

Just on seven, the pair heard Jenkins' wagon draw up to the inn. They picked up their small bundles of necessaries and proceeded out and climbed aboard. *"Ready, Gents?"* came from Jenkins as he cracked his whip in the air and the horses responded with slow steady steps, *"We'll be off for something which will challenge the knowledge you hold of your own native land – we are going deep into the Britain of the ancients."*

"Never readier." came the reply, *"Take us to those stones so we can truly begin our quest."*

Off the group was carried at a steady trot through the town and out onto the plain. Watson would keep his loaded revolver handy, Holmes would have his single stick at his side and his knuckleduster in his pocket – they may well have a visitation of some sort but both knew that, if such did come to be, it would be in a devilish human form which would pay dearly for interrupting their exertions.

The Stones

Just when the small roaming bands of humans coalesced into crude political units in the distant past is difficult if not impossible to determine but there must have come a point in time when an individual looked about and felt part of something bigger and more extensive than its close family unit. And how many would have been the generations which would then have to pass before a caste of individuals with special retained knowledge would emerge to guide the rest and tell them of the gods and lesser spirits which abounded on the earth and how they, the mortal humans, must act and show deference before they, too, passed into that ethereal spirit world? But such was and is the power of belief that people can be urged to perform magnificent and seemingly impossible feats, and the ancient Britons, well before that name would come to fit much later inhabitants, were driven by that faith to move mountains, literally, across the landscape and create structures which would outlast those builders and all who would come after them.

Stonehenge, a simple name, misapplied as it turns out by those latecomers who saw the long horizontal stones, each held high by two of its fellows mounted vertically and reminiscent of a gallows, a henge or hanging structure in the dialect of the later invaders. Though latterly named for a place of death, Stonehenge had marked and celebrated life, the reviving life of the land itself as the sun regathered its strength and began to reconquer the day – its original name is unknown and unknowable but the massed believers of old would gather to shed fear and gather hope as the sun's dawning rays passed through a strategically placed aperture and illuminated the altar stone. The modern visitor could barely imagine the feeling of euphoria this generated in the minds of those ancients but, if that visitor closed both eyes in the dawn's silence and slowly opened them to receive the sun's first reborn light, it was just possible to link momentarily with the minds of those who so long ago gathered at that very point on the ancient landscape.

Holmes and Watson were not pilgrims, they were detectives seeking facts, facts whose significance could only be fully discerned after the pair had experienced just a little of the ancient atmosphere. To win the fight, it is necessary to know one's enemy, and the duo now approaching Stonehenge had much to learn, much to take in, before they could arm themselves against a mysterious foe.

The sketches Holmes had taken from Fletcher's book of the 'Ancient Ways' were neither to scale nor oriented precisely but showed an obvious and intriguing ley line bearing directly from beyond Old Sarum, through New Sarum, the Cathedral, and then on to and through Stonehenge. This was not, Fletcher had argued, by coincidence but by design, though the two Sarum cathedrals, Old and New, had been constructed at way points important to the ancient peoples and recognised as significant by all subsequent newcomers.

Once Holmes had been able to transfer various layers of information onto his own map he was able to see the pattern – none of the human relics of the recent atrocities had been placed along the Sarum-Stonehenge bearing but along three lines radiating outwards from Stonehenge through three lines of mounds, possibly tombs or possibly navigation markers but too precisely placed not to have connections with the great stone monument. He had not discussed this information with Watson as an opportunity free of the ears and eyes of Jenkins had not yet presented itself. The inclusion of the mounds made the pattern far more obvious but, "*Why,*" Holmes asked himself, "*had the official agencies not commented on this?*

Why was this detail not in the Police report? Why had the newspapers not built up and reported an exaggerated story which would have intrigued the Public and driven up sales even more? And who first had reported that the relics had been placed on ley lines?"

This latter point was intriguing, more so than the others, and Holmes would ponder on its implications as Jenkins' wagon rattled its way toward Stonehenge on a decidedly erratic bearing while managing, Watson complained, to find every rock and hole on their outward journey. That journey, short though it would be and reaching almost to Amesbury before turning west toward Stonehenge, seemed to take both Holmes and Watson back to a meeting with the Britons of old, such was the effect of the landscape on the human mind. If magic could ever be said to inhabit a region, it was experienced that evening on Salisbury Plain as the two sleuths momentarily left the nineteenth century behind and touched the stone age as the distant form of Stonehenge came into view and grew larger. Watson was transfixed by the apparition; Holmes felt emotions he had never known nor suspected possible – he was a detective trying his hardest to remain detached and pragmatic but finding himself being more immersed in the atmosphere of the stones than he ever imagined possible.

Both men had been prepared in part for the experience having seen the ruins of a reported Roman camp at Amesbury, this having been named for Vespasian by Elizabethan era visitors but never actually visited by the Roman general. It was one of the many hill forts constructed well after Stonehenge had fallen into disuse but 'ancient' was 'ancient' to the local population and myths and legends merged as the storytellers took every opportunity to embellish an already confused history. Jenkins was to be no different and he rambled on about Roman campaigns against the British tribes in the region paying little attention to factual accounts compiled by scholars who had painstakingly examined the physical evidence and the historical records and refuted many of the legends long assumed to be true.

To have argued truth versus legend at this point would have put the investigators at odds with their goal, that of finding a motive for murder and then finding the murderer, and led them into conflict with many who might hold information pertinent to the case.

Watson had fancied Stonehenge to have been larger but was dumbfounded upon entering the site and touching the stones, stones so large that it seemed a race of giants had placed them there unfinished and yet unbelievably impressive. The sun had yet to set and Jenkins was eager for his charges to view the sunset from Stonehenge despite there being little chance of any significant alignment for many weeks to come. Holmes stood upon one stone and looked outward toward a mound some half mile distant and wondered at the industry of those ancient hands which toiled so laboriously to construct such monuments, such practically eternal expressions of devotion to their gods.

As Holmes and Watson hopped about and clambered onto one stone after another, a practice frowned upon by archaeologists and half-heartedly discouraged by tour guides, Jenkins had taken his wagon off some three hundred yards to a site suited to overnight camping. Here he had begun erecting tents and selecting a site for a campfire from several previously-used locations marked out by previous campers who had made their own small circles of stones in more recent years. Hot stew, porridge, bread, coffee and rum were Jenkins' staples when on the Plain though he did keep supplies of biscuit, tea and whiskey for those who tastes differed from his – he considered each trip, though short and in close proximity to several sizeable habitations, a small adventure, and adventurers had no need of civilised niceties. Unusually for that time of year but not surprising given that there was a mass murderer running loose in the region, the three men had Stonehenge to themselves.

Sunset was not to prove disappointing but Jenkins was keen for the spectacle of morning and eager to show Holmes and Watson the majesty of Stonehenge in its element, a circle of ancient stones illuminated by the golden light of the dawning sun. Salisbury Plain took on a ghostly appearance as the sky grew darker and pin points of light began to manifest themselves as stars, suns at incredible distances to the modern eye but fires lighting up in the heavens to the ancients. Now Holmes and Watson could feel the exertions of the day catching up with them, their eyelids drooping as the pair gazed into the flickering campfire while disposing of their meals and, opting for the alternative spirit, finished off with two whiskeys apiece and retired to their tents. Jenkins rinsed off a few items, checked on his horses, doused the campfire and followed the lead of his two charges and took to his tent.

Holmes and Watson found sleep very quickly that night, sleep which for Watson was all too soon interrupted by Jenkins' rattling of metal pots and the crackling of his pre-dawn fire. Despite the season being warm, the mercury had dropped precipitately overnight on the broad extent of the Salisbury Plain and a good serving of hot porridge washed down by strong tea was just the thing to keep the body from seizing up in the morning's chill.

"One hour to dawn, Doctor." he said outside Watson's tent, *"Time for breakfast."*

A series of slumber interrupted grunts signalled Watson's sleepy response and Jenkins moved on to Holmes' tent which he found empty. Holmes, never one to sleep much more than four hours at any one time, had been up and about for some considerable time.

"*Mr Holmes.*" cried Jenkins, a little alarmed at the possibility of losing one of his charges, "*Mr Holmes. Where are you?*"

"*Out here, Jenkins.*" came a distant reply from the darkness, "*I've been out absorbing the atmosphere of Salisbury Plain and pondering imponderables – I'm half way through a second pipe and shall be with you directly.*"

Watson emerged, sleepy but ready for the coming of dawn, and breakfast, having heard the call and response of the guide and his errant charge. Joining the cabbie-turned-guide at the campfire, he stated despairingly, "*He does that, Jenkins .. goes off by himself to who knows where with nary a word to those who need to know his whereabouts. It's a wonder he didn't fall down a hole or into a bog of some sort, or get carried off and dismantled bit by bit by some axe-wielding fiend dressed in long flowing robes. We could well have found the fellow headless with his arms and legs and whatever deposited along one of the ley lines we've come to examine. With a brain such as his, one would expect him to show a little more care for himself, let alone consideration for others.*"

"*He's a type, alright – one of a kind - and I dare say you'd not have a snowflake's chance in Hades of making him change his ways.*" chuckled Jenkins, "*I didn't hear him rise and I'm a light sleeper – that comes from dozing on top of my cab whenever I get the chance. Perhaps he's part ghost himself, part ancient wizard and part modern man, and has been here before in one of his past lives.*"

"That makes more sense than you realise," retorted Watson, *"but I think he's actually part cat and moves about in stealth while risking those nine lives every feline possesses."*

Jenkins was scooping out hot porridge into Watson's bowl when Holmes appeared. *"Yours is next."* said the grinning guide, *"Then we'll make way to the stones – the reddening horizon tells us Old Sol is up and about and ready to start a new day. Can't be late, so eat up, down that tea, and then we'll be off."*

Holmes and Watson did as directed and the three men made their way to Stonehenge to await the spectacle. There would be no special alignments that morning but the effect was to prove both spectacular and humbling as the sun's first golden rays burst across the horizon and through the tall uprights of Stonehenge. Jenkins had seen it all before but always felt a thrill at the sight; the two sleuths were mesmerised and felt a momentary communion with those long-ago folk – one had to see Stonehenge in its dawn glory to appreciate just how significant a structure and location it was to those ancient ones. There's was a baptism of light, in a manner of speaking, and they could now converse with others in knowing terms.

The group spent the next two hours locating the ley line bearings and following these to the sites of the gruesome discoveries. Alas for Holmes, there was little left to observe, such had been the effect of disruption and trampling by hundreds of pairs of meddlesome booted feet. Still, Holmes was able to see the locations in relation to each other and the general landscape and its major features. He had taken in all he saw, the mounds, the stones, but there was one feature, indistinct on Fletcher's map but continuing outward on a side opposite that of one of the 'victim lines' and which did need investigating. The long indistinct feature seemed to start within the outer stone circle and follow a line formed by two low stones, an outer one called the Friar's Heel by the locals and the other, the inner, intriguingly referred to in Fletcher's 'Ancient Ways' as the Slaughter Stone.

Locating the Slaughter Stone, the group observed an altar-like arrangement in direct alignment with the opposite ley line and further on to what fitted the description of the Friar's Heel.

"*Is that dried blood?*" asked Watson, pointing to a dull brownish stain which seemed to have flowed across the stone's top and down one side, "*If it is, it is certainly not fresh; but could it be human?*"

"*You ought to know blood when you see it, Army surgeon and all.*" interjected Jenkins who received a quick defensive reply from Watson:

"*A surgeon knows blood, alright, but that blood would be fresh and red, perhaps a little congealed after an operation. We tended not to observe the stuff's condition after weeks of its standing in the hot sun on some rock. This could be the site where those victims were despatched and dismembered, though the amount produced would have been prodigious, far more than may be indicated here. Perhaps they were killed here and butchered elsewhere.*"

"*Quite likely.*" agreed Holmes, "*And we need to find out where. But, for now, what of that Friar's Heel?*"

That stone feature was a short distance away and, when approached, could be seen to have supported a fire of some sort, the charred woody remnants of a fire still being apparent.

"*Illumination, perhaps? Or a beacon to signal to others?*" Holmes mused, "*Is this ceremony or ruse? We must find out but, now we must be getting back and cleaned up. We have an appointment with an eminent Professor.*"

The Professor

A long summer's day had started off well and promised more. Holmes and Watson had gotten a basic feel for the stones and the associated 'ways', and clambered aboard Jenkins' wagon for their return trip. Jenkins knew a shorter way back than that of the outward journey as the banks at several required river crossings were more easily traversed at their lower angles of approach for those travelling southward. Back at Cooper's Inn, the pair found a note from Parker waiting for them and suggesting a meeting that evening at a his hotel. The two Londoners, despite their unfamiliarity with Salisbury, would go on foot without Jenkins – it was considered prudent to keep journalist and tour guide apart for the present.

There was an hour and a half before their meeting with the 'Prof' and Jenkins left his two charges at their lodgings to clean up and prepare. He proceeded back to his yard to exchange his wagon for his cab and returned just as Holmes and Watson were walking out of the inn. Onto the cab the two hopped and they were once again on the road, this time to visit a very remarkable woman.

'Prof' Tilbury could have been sixty, such was the vitality of her constitution, the result of a life spent in vigorous outdoor activity and protracted interest in the matters of truly ancient Britain, but her knowledge betrayed the great number of years she had spent in pursuit of those lives passed so many eons ago and the significance which the landscape held for them.

Holmes and Watson had arrived a few minutes before time and had been ushered into the waiting room by the Professor's maid. *"Please take a seat, Gentlemen, the Professor shall be with you directly and will likely invite you into her study. She likes to be surrounded by her books and artefacts, you know. They are her children, in a manner of speaking, though she does have a human family as well, despite their visits being all too infrequent – two sons and four grandchildren she will tell you, as well as their names, their ages and what they have all been up to lately. She is an absolute marvel but is no spring chicken so be wary of tiring the great lady with lots of questions – just start her off and then let her do the talking. I shall be serving refreshments before too long."*

Holmes and Watson sat in silence awaiting the Professor who, when she did appear, made them feel they were in the presence of someone of great significance – her demeanour was such that the two men immediately stood regardless of what the rules good manners would dictate, and then she spoke.

"Good morning, Gentlemen. Welcome to Netherfields, my home. I have been looking forward to meeting with Mr Sherlock Holmes and his good colleague Dr Watson. Your names are well known to me; you see, I have been following your exploits which have appeared in the Strand. You have a gift for narrative, Dr Watson, and your investigative colleague must truly be remarkable should your accounts mirror the truth to even a small degree."

"Good morning, Professor Tilbury." came from the two men in unison, after which Watson continued with, *"Thank you for that compliment, and I can assure you that the powers of Sherlock Holmes, my good colleague here, have not in any way been exaggerated."*

Sherlock Holmes, ever the pragmatist, broke in on Watson's praises with, *"Professor Tilbury, it is a great honour to meet you and we both thank you for allowing us some of your valuable time. I'm afraid, however, that Watson here is a great embellisher of fact in that I believe he wastes his considerable talents pandering to the dictates of an editor bent on making sales. I am hopeful of one day producing a text on deductive theory and practice which would instruct the investigator on how to observe and understand what the eye merely sees."*

"*Well,*" laughed the Professor, "*I see turmoil in the camp – not such a bad thing, either – too much agreement in a team leads too often to acceptance of lower grade information whereas a bit of vigorous and determined questioning of respective positions forces each party to fully consider its stance and rule out nonsensical notions and arrive at the truth. This is true for archaeology and, I am certain, it would be true for detective work.*"

"*But enough of this prattle in this drab room,*" she continued, "*Let us continue in my study, my own little world, where we will be more comfortable. Your note, Mr Holmes, said precious little but if you would allow me some licence to do a bit of deducing of my own I would say that you've come about these ley line murders.*"

"*Are we that obvious?*" asked Holmes, "*This is a direct result of Watson's scribbling. There are few places I can now go without being recognised and I have to resort to disguises to avoid being questioned myself.*"

The Professor led the way along to her study into which they entered, the two visitors gazing at the books and unbound manuscripts lining the walls and piled up on tables. Taking her seat behind an impressive old desk, Professor Tilbury gestured to her guests, saying, "*Now, Gentlemen. Please make yourselves comfortable in those chairs – I'm used to having visitors and enjoy discussions on all manner of subjects concerning the ancient lives whose efforts we see about us in these regions. I'm not actually entitled to call myself Professor but many do afford me that honour, none the less;*

those who know me, and many who don't, simply refer to me as 'Prof'. Now, just what can I do for you two detectives on this fine morning?"

"Well, Professor Tilbury, Prof," began Holmes, *"I believe I would be correct in presuming you do not see mystical forces at work here, rather the work of a despicable criminal making use of people's fascination and fear of the supernatural to cloud a yet to be discovered plan which involves real live human beings anticipating great ill-gotten rewards of some kind. Those human relics were left where they would be found and the only reason I can be satisfied with is that of drawing attention away from something else, though I'm unable to say what that might be at this juncture."*

"I have visited the sites," Holmes continued, *"and felt the atmosphere of the location and admit that there is something otherworldly about it but put this down to the scale of the landscape overwhelming our human senses used to the much smaller scale of our cities and towns. Mix this sensation with talk about ancient peoples and the actual encounter of those ancient structures and those who want to find ghosts will certainly do so, though those spectres will be of their minds' own making."*

Prof Tilbury thought about the question for a moment before responding, then said, *"Well, Gentlemen, I do share that general view and have been troubled by the sensational statements made by ill-informed and irresponsible types or by straight-out devious exploiters of other people's foolishness. I am truly glad that you have come for I fear that the Police have been overwhelmed with information, much of which is utter rubbish, and that a murderer is living among us, perhaps several. I tire far too easily now but, could I shed twenty or thirty years, I'd be out after this fiend myself."*

Watson kept quiet throughout the dialogue between Sleuth and Prof but could not help thinking, "*May Providence protect me, now I have two Holmes to contend with. Holmes and Professor Tilbury think along similar lines and express a disdain for the official agencies charged to look after our wellbeing. Lestrade and Gregson would suffer apoplexy were either one of them foolish enough to get between these two. Elderly this lady may be but she possesses the mind and spirit of a Sherlock Holmes, in an academic sort of way, but despite her age, has energy and spirit such as might do justice to a hundred Scotland Yard detectives.*"

Holmes chuckled a little at the fighting words expressed by his very learned host and then posed a series of questions. "*Extending from Stonehenge is a longish feature which seems to stretch out directly opposite one of the ley lines on which several human body parts had been found. Does this feature have any great significance and, if so, could you also enlighten us as to the significance of the Slaughter Stone and the Friar's Heel?*"

"*Now, those who believe or want to believe in the spirits,*" replied the Professor, "*may be forgiven for calling a particular feature the Slaughter Stone in that pools of reddish liquid accumulate in several small hollows on its upper surface. From a distance, it takes on the appearance of a blood-splattered rock upon which something or someone had been ritually sacrificed but up close, so many knowing locals and a few scientific types with tell, it turns out that a common type of red algae grows in those depressions after the rains and this dries off to a ruddy brown, just like dried blood.*"

"*Who first called it the Slaughter Stone,*" she continued, "*is impossible to say. It's just one amongst so many local tales and misapplied names of features which the local people have* repeated generation after generation, the details varying a little over the years."

"We did notice a dried blood-like stain on the stone," said Holmes, "and could not say if it truly was blood or not. Perhaps a chemical analysis of the residue might confirm the situation, one way or another. It did occur to us that anyone determined to conjure up the spirits of old in people's minds might just despatch their victims on such a stone. I have taken a small sample of the material for later testing. But there is that other stone, that described as the Friar's Heel; what can you tell us of it?"

Prof Tilbury smiled and replied, "The Friar's Heel is a common rendering of what folks in the not so distant past called the 'Friar's Heol', the latter term being what the Britons called a fire, a beacon in fact, something which could be used to line up Stonehenge along the opposite ley to another beacon sited on the distant horizon where another such stone is to be found."

"A beacon, you say?" interrupted Holmes, "We did see definite signs of a recent fire on that stone. It seems as though someone is re-enacting some ancient rite – we must check out that Slaughter Stone residue without delay. If I could get access to a chemical laboratory I would be able to sort this out in a few hours."

"I have a laboratory of sorts - well, all serious archaeologists do – and you're welcome to use it." volunteered the Prof. "It's fairly basic but it could possibly help distinguish dried blood from a decomposed algal residue. Dr Watson has you described as a very competent chemist to whom such a procedure would be child's play."

"*There's that scribbling Watson at work again,*" declared Holmes, rolling his eyes in the direction of the Professor, "*though it is true that I can claim significant prowess with the test tube. I have developed a reagent which will produce, when added to a dilute watery suspension of dried blood, together with a catalyst of my own making, a mahogany coloured solution which develops into a fine brown precipitate over the course of a few minutes. I carry both reagent and catalyst with me when in the field and require only the means to put them to work.*"

"*I do believe,*" he added, "*that we have the beginnings of a line of enquiry, something tangible which will begin to shed some faint light on a very dark crime.*"

Watson had said little in the meeting, listening to the discussion and letting his eyes wander about the room to see and admire the many pieces of fine, though somewhat dated, furniture. As the meeting came to its end, he could not help himself, and stated, "*I would say, Professor Tilbury, that much has passed across this old desk of yours, much in the way of observational records and new ways of viewing our past history, that dealing with the old stones and the societies which took it upon themselves to make such exertions. I dare say it could tell a few tales were it given the chance.*"

"*You would be right, Dr Watson,*" replied Professor Tilbury, "*but this old desk is not particularly valuable as a collectable piece of furniture though it does have great significance for me. I would never give it up for it was at this very desk, as a very young girl, that I was introduced to the study of the ancient monuments. It was my late uncle's, he being something of a true pioneer in the scientific study of such matters. He was a school teacher in these parts early in the century and became completely absorbed by the atmosphere*" *about us. You would likely not have heard of him but his name was James Fletcher."*

ANCIENT ECHOES

The Blood

Holmes, on hearing a name newly encountered but wholly unexpected in this instance, gave out a surprised *"James Fletcher!"*, then continued with a restrained chuckle to his voice, *"Yes of course I know that name, though I must admit that my knowledge is only days old. I had reason to visit the grand library at the British Museum seeking out a book entitled 'Ancient Ways' written by that very gentleman. The book was not in the best of conditions and I felt moved to recommend its renovation or copying to preserve its contents which must surely be lost if left to the unremitting devices of mildew."*

"Your Uncle, you say?" he continued in a quizzical manner, *"I noted a handwritten dedication to Margaret, a niece, one with a budding interest in the subject and one whom I had hoped to seek out."*

"Well, seek and ye shall find, goes the saying," replied the amused Professor, *"and found what you sought, you most certainly have. I was a very young girl when that dedication was made and I've often wondered what had become of that particular book, though I do have several other copies – perhaps the library might be interested in exchanging that copy for one in much better condition. Uncle James was a man of great energy and insight but with few resources beyond his teacher's salary and what he could raise by giving lectures on the old stones at odd times. He had to pay for the publication of his one and only book himself and could afford to have only a small number printed. He remained a bachelor but my mother, his sister, had married well and, fortunately for me, found that her husband, my father, valued vigorous outdoor activity and broad education for all of his children.*

Alas, I am the sole survivor of that latter generation and the last link with that previous, that of Uncle James, but I do have my work and my children and grandchildren, though all those stones put in place so many thousands of years ago will outlast us all as surely as those ancient builders intended."

"You have seen many changes in this century of ours, Professor," said an admiring Watson, *"and I daresay there will be many more to come. However, I'm not entirely sure they will bring us what we human beings seek, whatever that is."*

"We are an enquiring species put on this Earth to discover our ultimate destiny and then to achieve it." declared Prof Tilbury in an unabashed and forthright tone, surprising for one who looked so deeply into the past, *"Though what that might be and how many generations it might take to get even close to that point, I am unable to say. Mr Darwin tells us we have come up step by step from the primates, leaving our distant ape cousins behind and perfecting our brains and intellects along the way. Perhaps we will one day think our way beyond the Earth and see wonders untold. I believe, though, that we should continually remind ourselves of our humble beginnings and record and remember the beliefs and exertions of our ancestors. To know what we'll become, we must first know what we are and what we have been."*

"Quite a philosophic point, Professor." stated Watson, *"I see that you look well beyond the stones of Salisbury to all of the people who have seen and touched them over the eons."*

"Indeed." remarked the Professor, *"all buildings have been built for a purpose, even if some seem to be monuments to someone's over-inflated ego – humbug! Architecture reflects the world of the architect and is meaningless unless it says something of the people inhabiting it."*

"Agreed." interrupted Holmes, *"But there are people alive right now who may be planning the demise of yet more of our fellow human beings and I feel we should be about stopping them. Perhaps you might direct me to your laboratory while I have Jenkins return to Cooper's Inn for my valise and the reagents within. I have a sample of the Slaughter Stone residue in my pocket in a paper envelope."*

"Excellent, Mr Holmes. It's time we were about solving these murders." declared the Professor, *"Now, I'll have Julia, my maid, show you the way to those test tubes but I usually have a nap about this time each day. I just don't seem to last as long without rest these days but you two gentlemen do what you must – my library is open to you, and the laboratory. We shall have a light meal at one o'clock and we can discuss things further when you have discovered the nature of those reddish brown stains from the Slaughter Stone; if you find algae, so be it; but if you find blood, then the plot thickens and we are up against someone with a better than average knowledge of ancient rituals."*

Holmes rushed out to get Jenkins to return for the valise without revealing that it held the key reagents for a definitive test for dried blood, one of his own devising. The cabbie had been dozing while Holmes and Watson were inside; he too needed to catch up on sleep whenever the opportunity presented itself. Jenkins asked no questions but immediately rushed off – he was being well paid for his time, whether that involved taking his wagon across the plains or waiting half asleep while his charges went about their business. It would be about ninety minutes at a good gallop, he judged, before he'd be back.

On returning inside, Holmes found that Julia, Professor Tilbury's maid, had arrived and was escorting the grand lady to her bedroom for her regular late-morning nap. Watson had begun to take more than a casual interest in her health and began to lecture Holmes on the need for a gentle approach when speaking of the recent deadly events as, although she was extremely keen to be involved and was of a strong constitution for her age, the Professor might well suffer if excited too much. Holmes agreed and, when the maid Julia returned, proceeded with her to the Professor's laboratory to prepare a sample of the residue for testing, a simple procedure involving a little grinding, vigorous shaking in water containing a commonly-found salt to keep the sample suspended and another specific salt added after some ten minutes to cause impurities to flocculate and fall from suspension, leaving a clear sample solution ready for the application of Sherlock Holmes' specially devised reagent and catalyst. It had been used before to determine if brownish stains on a suspect's clothing were blood or not, and it had sent several men to the gallows, though some did avoid such an undeserved fate when such stains were proven completely innocuous.

Fred Jenkins had been spot-on with his estimation and returned exactly ninety minutes after setting out. He had with him the valise which Holmes had required and also a note which Inspector Fleming had left and which had been waiting for him at the inn. Holmes came out and took possession of both items while Jenkins stated his intent to return to his slumbers; the note from Fleming was a request for Holmes and Watson to call in to the Police Station at their earliest convenience, preferably that afternoon; the valise contained the reagents needed by Holmes.

Holmes hurried back down into the laboratory where he was able to continue with his analysis of the Slaughter Stone's scrapings. He had prepared three samples of the scrapings, each with a slightly different appearance; he then mixed his special reagent with a small quantity of water and added a few drops of this to each sample held in its own test tube, then added similar quantities of catalyst and shook all three vigorously and returned them to the test tube rack to await the results. After a very long ten minutes, Holmes fancied he could see a slight reddening in one of the tubes and took the rack over to the window to better observe the developments. Yes, there was a definite reddish colour forming in one, and then another began to show similar signs. Finally, Holmes could see the desired mahogany colour in all three test tubes and had only to wait several more minutes until the definitive red-brown precipitate began to accumulate at the bottom of each tube. *"Blood -"* he said to himself, *"and all over the Slaughter Stone. The game is now definitely afoot."*

Watson had been busying himself in the Professor's library while Jenkins had been away and Holmes was ensconced in the Professor's laboratory; the Doctor had found much to interest the experienced military man given the region's long and tumultuous history. He had begun to read about the history of New Sarum cathedral when Professor Tilbury returned from her late morning nap.

"Lunch," she announced, *"will be served on the terrace in ten minutes' time. We shall continue our discussions and perhaps Mr Holmes may have something extra to tell us."*

Watson rose, closed and returned the book to is correct place on its shelf, then walked over and offered his arm to the great lady who graciously accepted the gesture and took some pleasure in being escorted to lunch by such an obvious and somewhat famous gentleman as Watson. On their reaching the table on the terrace, he drew out a chair and the Professor sat, rather pleased with herself, and began reminiscing about the days of her childhood and youth and of modern times and how so many things had changed in the intervening period. Watson could scarcely get a word in except to give a supportive *"Goodness me"* and *"Amazing"* when he felt that he should add something to the conversation.

She spoke emotionally of her late Uncle and of how he had tried to decipher the clues to the multiple histories of Salisbury Plain with his limited resources and how he took her on so many short excursions to the stones and the numerous incredible features hard-worked by the ancient peoples. Together, they had made studious pilgrimages to the site of Old Sarum and then returned to New Sarum and the magnificent cathedral and its many links with the history of the modern English state. They had walked along the lines of stones at Avebury and marvelled at the effort required to erect such an extensive and enduring monument. They had ambled over the remains of the old fort at Amesbury and pondered on the way its ancient inhabitants thought about the land about them. They had stood in the centre of Stonehenge and watched as the dawn broke over the horizon and flooded the stones with light. Her Uncle had taught her about the ley lines and the alignment of the monuments with the stars and the rising and setting sun at times of the year significant to people entirely reliant on the reliability of the seasons to provide for their bodily needs.

Watson, finding his opportunity, asked the Professor if she had ever lived away from her Wiltshire home.

"Well," she responded, *"there were those stints away at the university and the times I had found it necessary to visit London and its great collections of books and artefacts, but I really did not relish being away, especially in London – such a jumble of people and maddening rush. I could never stand*

to be too far away from my ancient landscape for too long – it's where I belong and where I shall be buried when I'm finished with this life. Perhaps I, too, shall become a mystery to people in the far distant future – someone may well try to discover if I had been of the age of bronze or iron or even of steam, if that is what our current time shall be called in centuries to come."

Watson laughed and added, "*I wonder what those future archaeologists would make of Holmes and that brain of his. Someone may hold up his skull and ponder on the mind it once held and have no understanding of the difficulties it once faced and overcame with its almost miraculous workings. Would they appreciate Holmes and the greatness of the London he knew or would they just see the remnants of something so old and very mysterious, such as we might do when gazing on Stonehenge?*"

As Watson and the Prof sat chatting about times ancient, modern and future, city versus country, London versus Salisbury and a host of subjects unconnected with the murders, Sherlock Holmes rushed out and interrupted both with an excited declaration: "*Professor Tilbury, Watson - mahogany solution, then ruddy-brown precipitate – we have blood splattered on the Slaughter Stone.*"

The Reports

"Then the victims were killed there, or someone was." retorted Watson, *"But the blood, Holmes, there did not seem to be enough if someone was indeed slaughtered there."*

"Perhaps the stone was the site of a ritual stabbing or blood was put there to suggest as much." countered Holmes, *"These are things we don't know but the blank sheet we started with is beginning to fill out with facts, some of which will prove useful, some not. However, we must return to Salisbury and meet with Inspector Fleming – he seems to have something to share with us, and we with him."*

"Not before you've sat down and eaten something, Young Man." said an insistent Professor Tilbury, *"You'll need something inside you to keep up your strength for whatever lies ahead. There may well be danger – I'd be surprised if there were not. Just know that this house is always open to you and you will find a meal and a bed here anytime you may have need of either, or both. Now, eat up and then you can be about your business – I admit that I'm finding this whole business a little exciting, having Sherlock Holmes and Dr Watson here and going about all that sleuthing they get up to. There is evil about but that evil is to be found in men's minds, and possibly women's as the gentle sex is not always so gentle; so be on your guard and be ever so careful with those to whom you speak your mind and in whom you place your trust."*

"I have had a plate of food taken out to Mr Jenkins." she continued, *"He's a likeable fellow, and knowledgeable, but he's also a bit of a busybody and likes nothing more than the opportunity to show himself as important by repeating gossip he's overheard in that cab of his. So, be warned – if you don't want everyone to know your business, don't talk about it in*

front of him. Still, on the other hand, he may be a useful source of information – other people's."

Holmes nodded his assent and then did as directed – he sat and ate his fill, far more than Watson could ever get him to do. Perhaps there was something of the maternal about the great lady whose table they were sharing and Holmes had reverted to the obedient child of old for just a while. Whatever the cause, the sleuth admired her spirit and proceeded to eat enough to keep him going for several days, if need be, and then rose and announced that he would like to speak further on matters of ancient ritual, or ritual revived by those who sought to relive the ancient practices.

"Thank you, indeed, Professor Tilbury." he remarked, *"You have provided us with food, not only for thought but also for sustenance, and our understanding of the ancient beliefs is improved. I still have no clear picture on exactly how or why the murders were committed but I do see a conspiracy of deception in progress. The mists which had been hugging the ground are beginning to rise and soon, I believe, we shall start to make out many details currently hidden from us."*

"Watson," he continued, *"we have work to do and must bid this grand lady a fond adieu for the present. Jenkins is outside and we must be off to Salisbury to meet with the Inspector. I hope that his news will prove to be as promising as ours."*

Watson, rose, turned to Professor Tilbury and thanked her for her assistance and hospitality. Both men then approached and shook her hand, a hand raised in determined friendship though her eyes betrayed a subdued desire to be out there with them.

"Ah, yes," the Professor declared, *"you two must be about your important work, so be off and be careful for, as the good*

Doctor here might have written in those stories of his, a deadly game is most definitely afoot."

Waking up a snoozing Jenkins, the pair clambered on board a cab somewhat unsuited for country roads but fast when commanded by one such as their determined cabbie. Off went the pair toward Salisbury where Holmes and Watson would dispense with the cabbie's services for the day and proceed on foot after their meeting with Inspector Fleming.

The steady trot back to Salisbury took a good deal longer than Jenkins' rush to retrieve Holmes' valise but there was ample time to meet with the Inspector and then to meet up with Robert Parker and receive a journalistic slant on the happenings and the state of the investigations into them. Parker would, no doubt, have sound commercial reasons to hold back various details until he felt the Public was growing weary of repetitive reports – he had to play both his Editor and his Public and release a carefully considered combination of information and innuendo, much like an angler playing with a feisty pike caught on an understrength fishing line.

Before meeting Parker, however, they had to face Inspector Fleming who would be busy dodging the jibes of not only that same Public and Press but those from the senior echelons of the Police Service. The man, his resources already stretched far beyond their operational limits, would be keen for any snippet of new information and appreciative of anything which would relieve the weight of mounting pressure impinging upon him. He would likely have heard Jenkins' cab pull up outside the Police Station and silently rejoiced on hearing a familiar voice.

"We shall send young Billy for you in the morning." he heard Holmes yell, *"We do not yet know how things will stand until*

we speak with the Inspector. Perhaps there'll be another trek onto the Plain or we may be visiting people around the city."

"*Here is a little more on account,*" Holmes added as he handed up a crisp new banknote, making the cabbie's eye's gleam.

Accepting the note and touching the side of his forehead with it in an appreciative salute, the cabbie simply replied, "*My horse and I thank you, Mr Holmes. Just yell out when you need us next. We're never far away, unless it's with you and the good Doctor.*"

Holmes and Watson watched as the cab trotted off down the street and then saw it turn out of sight. The two men then mounted the steps of the Police Station's entrance, pushed open the two doors and went inside where they were greeted by the same burly Sergeant who had been so agreeable and helpful on their visit the previous day.

"*A very good afternoon to you, Sergeant,*" burst forth from the lips of Sherlock Holmes, "*I believe your good Inspector Fleming is keen to speak with us. We did receive his note and have hurried here from Netherfields.*"

"*Ah, yes, Mr Holmes.*" came the Sergeant's reply, "*Your good self and Dr Watson are expected. If you will be so good as to wait for a few moments, I'll see if the Inspector is free.*"

The Sergeant hurried off to the Inspector's office and the two sleuths heard a few short muffled words exchanged, after which the Sergeant returned saying, "*Yes Gentlemen, the Inspector is quite free – he awaits you in his office. I believe you know the way.*"

"Thank you. Sergeant." was the reply and Holmes and Watson made their way down the corridor and knocked on the Inspector's door.

"Come in, please." was the enthusiastic response, and Holmes turned the handled and pushed open the door. Both men then entered to be greeted by Inspector Fleming standing in front of his desk and positioning two chairs for his guests.

"Ah, Gentlemen." said the Inspector, *"You've been out to the stones, I believe – with Jenkins, no doubt. Impressive, aren't they? And just a bit spooky, especially at dawn. See them by moonlight on a cloud-free night, though, and you'll find out what true spookiness is and you'd be glad of some company about you. I've been meaning to take a greater interest in the ancient objects in our region, though one does not have to go far in Britain to make contact with the distant past."*

"That is certainly the case," replied Watson, *"but those stones are incredible. We did experience dawn amid those stones but' alas, the moon had not risen when we took to our tents the previous night. It was cloudy, somewhat, and the moon was just a little beyond new, so we would not have seen much anyway."*

"Watson tells no lies, Inspector," demanded Holmes, *"but I was up before dawn and caught a glimpse of Stonehenge by starlight – the clouds had cleared away in the very early morning and I would agree with you that 'spooky' is the correct term for the atmosphere generated by the apparition. Professor Tilbury had much to say about the ancient monument – and very knowledgeable she was, that grand lady; full of spirit, too, despite her age."*

"So, you caught up with one of Wiltshire's greatest assets, I see." said the Inspector, with more than a little note of pride

detectable in his voice, "*She is absolutely remarkable ... for her energy, her spirit, not to mention her knowledge. She is a magnet for all those who seek knowledge of the ancient folk and the artefacts, large and small, which they left behind. You could not have done better than to have sought her out for insight into the mysteries of our ancient landscape.*"

"*Indeed.*" remarked Holmes, more than a little surprised at Fleming's tone, now exhibiting a somewhat more optimistic quality, "*We met with the lady this morning and have come directly here after taking lunch on her terrace. Jenkins had gone back in to Cooper's Inn for a few items and returned bearing your note, so we have made haste to see what you had in mind. We hope to return and obtain her views on a few matters which are swirling around in my mind and just waiting to settle down in some semblance of order. We shall wait for a day or so as the lady seems to tire and we do not want to tax her.*"

"*Well, Inspector,*" Holmes continued, "*you have summoned us here for some purpose, so how can we be of assistance?*"

The Inspector pushed back in his chair, pleased to have something to report to his two distinguished visitors, and gave a brief report, "*I have had a communication from Inspector Lestrade and it seems that, Mr Holmes, your brother Mycroft has been seeking you out with little success. Your landlady had been able to tell him very little beyond the fact that you weren't there in your lodgings so he then sought out Inspector Lestrade who took it upon himself to relay your brother's message to me. It seems the French government is missing one of its officials who, together with three rather excitable ex-military types, is loose somewhere in Britain. The matter would not normally have caused even the smallest ripple in government circles either side of the English Channel but*" someone in the French Embassy in London noted the mention of a tattoo reflective of French military service on the arm of one of the victims. Mr Mycroft Holmes, it seems, is very keen to involve you in some unofficial capacity to investigate matters."

"Well," exclaimed Holmes, "Isn't that just like my brother. I don't hear from him for months and then he comes running for help. I suppose I will have to see him at some point – he is sure to have much more information than he is first ready to disclose. I declare that pulling out a back molar is far easier than getting information from his lips."

"But, Holmes," broke in Watson, "if Mycroft is involved then the matter must be considered to be serious – he is, as you have so often said, The British Government."

"Yes, yes, I do see that there may be a significance beyond the commonplace if both the French and British governments have been communicating, albeit at a presumably low level," agreed Holmes, "but when Mycroft gets involved he is likely to drag others into waters deep and dark and beset by treacherous currents. He just cannot help himself - he was born to conspiracy and intrigue and seems to know no other way. The man is simply compulsive."

"Well, I wonder if that's a family trait?" asked Watson with more than a hint of sarcasm.

Holmes smiled at his friend's remark and continued, "I will, I suppose, attend to Mycroft's request in due course, particularly as it must pertain to this case, but I'll do it in my own good time and not when the man snaps his fingers and barks out a command. Anyway, I haven't told Inspector Fleming about the blood."

"*Blood. What blood?*" retorted the Inspector, "*Tell me; I'm all ears.*"

"*Well,*" said Holmes, "*I had noted that Stonehenge featured a low horizontal stone which someone has dubbed the Slaughter Stone assuming that it had been used for some sort of human sacrifice. There was a dull reddish-brown residue on its surface, something Professor Tilbury suggested might be the dried reddish residue of the algae which grows in its depressions after the rains. I took some scrapings and, with my special blood-sensitive reagent and using the Professor's laboratory, was able to verify my suspicions that blood had recently been spilled on that stone, though the amount was not suggestive of that resulting from the dismemberment of a single human body, let alone four of them.*"

"*This suggests we are being duped,*" remarked the Inspector, "*and your stated possibility of a red herring seems quite plausible.*"

"*Indeed it does,*" replied Holmes, "*but we ought not to broadcast that fact too early. We should proceed as though looking for overzealous religious types trying to revive the ancient savage ceremonies.*"

The Journalist

Having spoken with Fleming and exchanged information, Holmes and Watson begged their leave of the Inspector and made their way back to Cooper's Inn on foot. They were to meet with the journalist Robert Parker that evening and wanted to rest up and go over the facts collected to date, such as they were.

The pair had not mentioned Parker's name to anyone but young Billy had been sent to search him out. Billy had been sworn to secrecy but Holmes knew that the young lad's lips could not be sealed for long, if at all. Still, they had not made much of the matter and would keep their meeting with him undisclosed but not deny it took place should they be queried about it – they may well be under surveillance, official or criminal or even for the sake of gossip by Jenkins for all they knew - a denial would be futile and counter-productive.

A walk through the streets of Salisbury proved a tonic, especially to Watson who had grown up on the tales of Old and New Sarum but had never previously had the opportunity to pay a visit. He looked about him at the old buildings and occasionally remarked on the difference of the city from the giant bustling metropolis they inhabited. Holmes proved a difficult conversationalist, however, and was generally oblivious to his surroundings while contemplating the development of the case and of what might eventuate should Mycroft's news prove true and significant. He had little data on his brother's information and refrained from coming to any conclusions until they could meet – he knew that Mycroft would never venture beyond Whitehall and its precincts and so he, Sherlock, would have to go to him and possibly waste a good day's investigating.

"If I must go to London and meet with my intractable brother," said Holmes to Watson after both had been silent for at least fifteen minutes, *"could I prevail upon you to remain here. Perhaps you might see the sights, visit the cathedral or do any of those tourist things people do. Should anyone ask, I have returned to London to trim up the loose threads in some unconnected case and will return in a matter of days."*

"Of course. You should confer with Mycroft and see what he has to say, or what the French have to say, that is." agreed Watson, *"The fact that the French Embassy has become interested should be reason enough to spur you along, especially to find out what that official, as they called him, was doing in Britain. I wonder what sort of official he was."*

With Holmes' visit to London decided, the pair walked on, again in silence, until Cooper's Inn was reached. In the pair went and sought the host to arrange for dining; then each took to his room to clean up and ready himself for the evening and their meeting with Parker. Thirty minutes went by with two men dozing on top of the bed covers, each jumping up with some expectation on hearing the gong sound for dinner. Neither man had realised just how famished he was, not even Holmes, but this became clearly evident as they hurried downstairs almost as though neither had eaten for a week.

"I could eat a horse." declared Watson knowing full well how his friend was likely to reply, *"And before you say it, they do not serve horse in Salisbury, not at Cooper's Inn."*

"There is nothing wrong with eating horse, I'll have you know," replied Holmes, *"just as long as it's not something left over from the Charge of the Light Brigade. There are many in this world who would not turn their noses up at the prospect and regularly feast on some superannuated Dobbin or Sunbeam."*

"Not in the England I know, they don't." retorted Watson, feigning outrage with a half-smile on his lips, *"Now, no more talk of equine fare – the only horse a la carte I want to experience belongs to Jenkins, cart and all. Look, here comes our meal – soup for starters and then good British beef with all the lashings – No, Holmes."*

With talk of horses behind them, the sleuths demolished their meals and then accepted second helpings from their host. They had no firm plan of action beyond talking with Parker and trying to determine if he knew as much as his newspaper stories would suggest. On finally finishing their meals, the pair sipped on their coffees until Holmes spoke up. *"Time to get going, Watson. We must see if this Parker is as knowledgeable as he makes out – what he writes and what he tells us may be two entirely different tales and, hopefully, what he tells us will have some basis in fact. I would like to talk to his sources but he may well be guarded in that area. Still, we may be able to glean something from the fellow, especially if he sees a bigger story with us than he has by himself."*

The pair made off to meet this new journalistic colleague, as Holmes was hoping he might be able to call him, at a steady pace as if on an evening's stroll so as not to attract attention for, who might be observing their movements, they could not be sure. The way to Parker's hotel, being near the railway station, was fairly well known to them, Jenkins having taken them on the same route just one day before. They would stop to look in shop windows and at various notable monuments and statues until they finally found themselves outside Parker's diggings. Swiftly entering, they approached the desk attendant and asked to be announced to their quarry. The attendant sent a boy off with a note and Parker had responded within a few minutes and descended the staircase to greet his new acquaintances.

"*Mr Holmes, Dr Watson,*" he exclaimed, stepping forward with his hand extended, "*it is indeed a pleasure to meet you both. Your respective reputations precede you, Mr Holmes for his art of detection and Dr Watson for his journalistic endeavours.*"

Holmes and Watson shook hands with Parker but were taken a little aback with the man's forthright and effusive manner. They had expected some cringing and deceitful character totally devoid of all civility and regard for the niceties of common courtesy. Instead, here was a man of charm and charisma demonstrating a professional outlook toward what he seemed to regard as two colleagues come to discuss matters of mutual concern.

Before either Holmes or Watson could respond, the journalist jumped in with, "*This matter of the Ley Line Murders is truly perplexing and I don't mind admitting that I'm largely at sea and battling worrying undercurrents swirling beneath a turbulent surface.*"

"*Well put.*" said Holmes, noting a sense of honest frustration in Parker's voice, "*Perhaps we can help steady the boat and get her on an even keel. To say it plainly, we had been worried about the sensationalism of the reports in the newspapers.*"

"*Ah, yes.*" Parker replied, "*Well, getting people to buy newspapers to read The Story is my stock-in-trade and if I'm unable to keep the Public enthralled and maintain its interest, I'm afraid that I'll be relegated to describing the Glastonbury Flower Show or doing some exposé on the state of the Fish Markets in Bristol. News which nobody reads is not news at all, just a waste of paper and printers' ink. I'm sure that if Dr Watson here merely reported your escapades as a table of facts he would make no sales at all and the usefulness of your*" *methods would not be appreciated anywhere near as much as it is."*

At this point, Watson gave an amused "*Hurrmff!*" and looked at Holmes as if to say, "*See! How many people would read that manual of deductive reasoning you say you will write in your declining years?*" Instead, he made the comment that, "*Your reports, Mr Parker, have included many gruesome details but fall well short of coming up with a tangible explanation – we have read of ancient rituals and demonic practices but not of who might profit from the deaths of four men.*"

"*The reason I report such things,*" replied Parker, "*is that, in the absence of any plausible explanation, those rituals and practices are all I have. They are reports of what people are fearing and saying – there are other matters which I am investigating but, while I can say what I like about the ghosts of people long gone, I must show great restraint when discussing living characters who may well be acquainted with the laws of libel.*"

"*But enough of this sparring,*" continued the journalist, "*I have engaged a private saloon room where we may speak freely and not be overheard. Salisbury, I declare, seems to have more ears than London when it comes to picking up bits of gossip. It is not only murderers that I fear, but other journalists too lazy to find their own facts.*"

Holmes and Watson followed Parker into the saloon room and took their seats. Parker ordered drinks for his guests and the publican appeared in due course with a tray laden with three glasses, a whiskey decanter and a water jug, saying, "*If there is anything else you gentlemen may need, just give a whistle and I'll be right back.*"

Parker nodded to the publican who then took his leave. The three men sat around a circular table while Parker began to pour drinks which were taken with some relish by the trio. As Parker refilled the glasses, he looked at his two guests and stated, *"Well, Mr Holmes, Dr Watson, you did request an audience with this sensationalist hack writer so I presume you have something to ask of me. Please speak freely – I do understand that you may possess sensitive information and I give you my word that nothing of that nature which we discuss will appear in print unless you give your specific and prior assent. I am interested in the big story, the whole story, not just titbits of journalistic nonsense to keep the Public's interest honed."*

Holmes looked at Watson, smiled and nodded and then looked back to the journalist to respond. Regaining his serious countenance and feigning almost complete ignorance, Holmes began by saying, *"To be honest with you, Parker, Dr Watson and I have little of any great substance to go on at this point. We are here, not at the invitation of the authorities, but because the case intrigued us, well, me that is, and partly in response to the wild conjecture made about rituals and ancient pathways and monuments. I had used our occasional working relationship with Scotland Yard to approach Inspector Fleming who has, I must admit, been keen to have us involved. His resources have been overstretched, as you must appreciate, and two extra pairs of experienced eyes would not go amiss in the situation."*

"Ah, yes," replied Parker, *"the good Inspector Fleming. A fair man, competent to be sure, but not over-endowed with a great imagination, something required when one is trying to sort out the motives behind people's actions. He is a plodder and does not put one foot forward until the other has been set firmly on the ground – he is not given to great leaps of foresight but he*

is thorough and would likely stumble upon the truth in time, though his methods may result in his being too late to catch those responsible. One hopes that he would not take a set against a convenient local villain just to close the book on this case."

"He does not strike me as that sort." interrupted Watson, *"He could have done that already but has taken great pains, with the scant resources at his command, to gather facts which he can take into court when the offenders are eventually caught."*

"That is a reassuring thought." Parker agreed, then he added, *"But you say 'offenders' – do you have knowledge that the murders are the work of more than one man? Is that something Inspector Fleming has confirmed?"*

Watson, as did Holmes, realised that he had said too much to this collector of notions, factual or fanciful, and knew that he must be far more careful with his words in the future. *"No."* he replied, *"One or many, it is unknown at this point, as far as I can discern. My own leanings would be to the multiple for there is much effort required to commit such dastardly acts, though I suppose that one man could do such things on his own."*

"At this point," broke in Holmes, hoping to rescue Watson from the quagmire he had just blundered into, *"that is just one of several points of conjecture. There are too few facts at this stage to make assumptions and it would not be useful to an investigator to close his mind to all possibilities at such an early stage. You seem an intelligent man, one not given to convenient half-truths, despite what we have read in your articles, and we have sought you out to hear your thoughts on the matter. Watson and I have been here in Salisbury for just over one day; we have had a cursory look over the field of action and are just beginning our preparations for the hunt."*

The journalist smiled a little and then gave a hesitating laugh at Holmes' comments. *"Intelligence goes only so far, but I do thank you for the compliment. More important for any investigator is energy and an attitude of dissatisfaction with the knowledge he holds, and that goes for a journalistic snooper like me or a detective such as yourself, and it should hold for a policeman like Fleming. They call him an Inspector but he falls well short of being a detective; though, in many ways, his hands have been bound by legal mumbo-jumbo."*

"It seems, though, that we all have our jobs to do and we all seem to think the efforts of others are misdirected." he continued, *"But we blunder on and things get mixed together and the resultant mess generally finds its own level, that mess being society in general. I enjoy being in a position to know things, things which others don't; I don't know if you sometimes feel the same way but I suspect that you might, at times. If I didn't feel that way, The Times wouldn't accept my stories and pay me to get more, though I don't work exclusively for one newspaper. One day, however, I will earn my way to Editor of a major newspaper somewhere in the world. By the way, did you learn much from Professor Tilbury?"*

"Professor Tilbury." exclaimed Holmes, *"How did you know we had paid her a visit?"*

"Well," replied Parker, *"you'd be surprised at how many people tell me things, just to show me that they know things too. As well, I'd be the one surprised if someone such as you, and Dr Watson here, had not been there. She is the fount of all knowledge and quite a good deal of wisdom about these parts and one should always consult the oracle before embarking on a perilous quest. Anyway, I saw you come back from her general direction and deduced the rest. It would*

make a good headline: 'Sherlock Holmes Consults Grand Lady of Salisbury Plain on Ritual Murders.' – it's a pity I won't be using it."

Holmes looked a little worried but was grateful that Parker was not going to compromise his visit. "*It would certainly be telling the truth but prove rather unhelpful to our efforts.*" he said, "*It may also place Fleming in a difficult position if his superiors block my access to Police resources and files. Those superiors may have to trip over Stonehenge to find it but they can be very jealous of their official positions and authority, not to mention their reputations. What I would ask of you, though, is if you have sensed something else happening, something which might drive people to commit murder and mutilate their victims. The heads are still missing and somebody knows what became of them.*"

Holmes stopped talking at this point as the adjoining room began filling with patrons and hearing became difficult without voices being raised. Parker suggested another meeting at a different venue in a few days when more information might be forthcoming. He did leave Holmes and Watson with a snippet of information by saying, "*Mr Holmes, Dr Watson, there is something but I've not yet got my source nailed down – one of the big landowners is up to something, something about land use, but all attempts to track down the details have come to nought, so far. Keep a keen ear for any mention of such things but don't ask too many direct questions – it could be extremely dangerous to do so. I carry a small pistol with me and I'd suggest you might consider doing likewise.*"

With that, the journalist rose, opened a side door and told the two sleuths they could escape that way and not be seen. He would leave the same way and then re-enter his hotel through the main door, there to mingle with the ever-talkative patrons in the noisy bar-room.

Out in the street, Holmes turned to Watson and expressed the opinion that Parker had given them a major clue, though in a very elementary form, "*He didn't say too much but he did say something. We must take what he said as probably true and we may find that it fits in with Mycroft's revelation, if that's what it ends up being. Things are developing, Watson, and we may find ourselves up against far more than misguided murderous make-believe high-priests – Salisbury Plain is likely to prove the site of something old-fashioned, something born of good honest greed and deceit.*"

Watson nodded, saying, "*Quite likely, Holmes. But you do have to get on that train in the morning.*"

Being quite near Salisbury Railway Station, the pair walked on over and Holmes purchased a return ticket for London for early the next morning. He would not employ the services of his retained cabbie the next day, the ever-talkative Fred Jenkins, he would walk; after all, it was summer and the sun would rise almost as early as him.

The French

Waterloo-bound, Sherlock Holmes set out early, just before the dawn sun made its appearance and once more cast its light through the stone pillars of Stonehenge. He was to catch the first London train of the day and hopefully make good time to his destination. Watson would still be hard at his slumbers and would not rouse for several hours but, by then, Holmes would be on the approaches to his metropolitan terminus and readying himself to make way to Whitehall and his insistent brother.

What Mycroft was to disclose was impossible to predict but Sherlock knew that his brother did not involve outsiders without a very good cause. Murders, mutilations, missing French officials and 'excitable' ex-military types were suggestive, collectively, of something significant. Add to those factors Parker's hint of involvement of big local land owners in some sort of land use problem and the situation gets even more interesting.

Holmes exited Waterloo Station and hailed a waiting cab, giving instructions to head for Whitehall. He carefully looked about to see if anyone obvious was following him but could see nothing overtly untoward. He threw his valise inside and mounted the step and swung himself inside, prepared and yet unprepared for the coming meeting.

France and Britain, he well knew, were not on exceptionally good terms but he was also aware that the balance of power in Europe had shifted abruptly with France's defeat by Prussia in the relatively recent Franco-Prussian War and the emergence of a newly united Germany, a Germany predominant in military prowess on land, expanding and modernising its navy, and jealous of the Empires of both France and Britain, not to mention those of Austria-Hungary,

Russia and Turkey. Germany's Emperor, Kaiser Wilhelm II, was a grandson of Britain's Queen Victoria and cousin to the Crown Prince but, despite the pomp and ceremony purporting strong royal family ties, the lust for power was and always would prove stronger than the bonds of kinship. France and Britain were being pushed closer and closer together – France and things French had always been held in high esteem in Britain when considerations of culture were involved and the enmity born of the early medieval claims on Normandy, the push for sections of Aquitaine, the sea battles for imperial supremacy and the losses on the bloody fields of North America had been getting hazier as time marched on and new enemies emerged.

France and Britain were not allies but might become so, in time. *"What then,"* Holmes asked of himself, *"can Mycroft have to tell me? What, given his position of great trust, could he possibly risk telling me?"*

The Great Sleuth, beset by problems he could not overcome without further data, did what he would always do in such circumstances – he would retreat into his mind and organise his cerebral filing system so that, when required, what he did know would be fully documented and readily at hand. He would remind himself that, *"Ideas without foundation are not facts, facts without context are not data, and data without connection are not knowledge. Stout bricks and strong mortar make a solid wall, not random rumours of building materials."*

Holmes knew that his brother would, at that time, be making his way from his home in Pall Mall to the great edifices of Whitehall – he never varied his route, never failed to arrive exactly on time, and never failed to carry out his duty - he also never took time out to personally confirm his theories, he had others to do that, even his more energetic brother Sherlock could be engaged should special insight be required.

Sherlock Holmes had breakfasted lightly on the train and taken a passable mug of hot tea at one of the longer station stops. His food requirements were moderate, despite his exertions, and tobacco often took his mind to places a full meal could not. Mycroft, however, exerted himself as little as possible and seemed to operate well on a full stomach. Moreover, Sherlock knew all too well that his brother would insist on him sharing in his many snacks and take offence if a refusal was offered. He would arrive before Mycroft and await his brother whose person would open almost any of the many doors in Whitehall – he would not have to suffer the regular delays and checks imposed on unaccompanied visitors. A tap on the roof of the cab and a coin tossed to the cabbie mounted above finalised the inward stage of the urgent trip and Sherlock Holmes found himself standing outside the building housing his brother's office at Whitehall – he was ahead of time, just, but knew that nothing short of a major catastrophe would or could persuade his brother to hurry.

Holmes had to wait only five minutes before seeing the bourgeoning form of his elder brother powering around a corner like some force of nature on two legs, sporting the obligatory top hat and tails and steadied by a rolled umbrella, all the while expecting those in his path to make way or be trampled by this human juggernaut.

"*Sherlock.*" he shouted, "*I knew you would come when summoned. Come, you are just in time for a light refreshment – such a good way to start the working day.*"

"*My working day,*" the younger Holmes replied, "*started hours ago; well before dawn, in fact, as did the working days of most of our countrymen. But I would be grateful for a cup of tea."*

"Tea without cakes or buns is uncivilised, Little Brother." came the reply, *"We owe it to the Empire to keep up our standards. Think of all those bakers and pastry cooks who have worked so hard since before first light – it would be unpatriotic not to partake of the fruits of their labours."*

Mycroft's walk to work each morning was the only time he could be observed exerting himself physically. Once he had reached his office, the hub of a vast network of information-gathering gnomes and secretive operatives charged with carrying out his demands, he would sit and read, receive visitors and give instructions, and take tea and nibble at the supply of fresh pastries delivered daily. Interviews with the man were generally short and sharp and even government ministers grew nervous about him. He knew things, things some thought he couldn't possibly know but somehow did, and a visitor was well advised not to omit parts of any message, let alone falsify its text or alter its meaning. Mycroft was a power because of what he knew but, luckily for the civilisation he served, he was a patriot and deferred in all things to high principle.

All discussion, even with his younger brother, was made without stopping or even slowing down and Sherlock had to keep up or be left behind as Mycroft passed through the impressive doorways and halls of power. As he reached his own office, he barked out a sharp, *"Tea for two and cakes for both."* at one of his attendants who were, as ever, well prepared for the master's all-pervading voice. Two minutes passed and Mycroft had settled into his seat, directed Sherlock to another, and then a trolley arrived laden with tea pot, saucered cups, milk jug, sugar bowl, lemon slices and an assortment of rich pastries. The attendant poured and asked for Sherlock's preferences as regards to milk and sugar and lemon, poured his master's standard cup, bowed at the guest and left without a further word.

The senior Holmes looked at his brother and told him, *"Drink up and help yourself to the treats, Sherlock - I shall be with you in just a few minutes. There are a few communications on my desk which will not wait – you know, stuff of State and all that – boring mostly but sent from on-high."*

The junior Holmes leaned back and sipped slowly on his tea, a vast improvement on the railway fare and very refreshing. He forced the smallest pastry he could locate and managed to swallow it and watched as his brother's eyes flicked back and forth as they scanned the official letters, taking in each detail and judging how much of his time and effort it merited. Mycroft picked up his pen, dipped its nib into the ornate inkwell and started to scribble out brief messages to his attendants – matters of the highest significance would pass his desk as well as base trivia but each received its due attention from this human automaton.

At last his first task of the day had been done and he could address his brother, *"Now, Sherlock, uhm ... oh yes, bits of bodies and missing Frenchmen – now I remember. The French Embassy is in a tizz and can't find one of its minor officials, thinks he's gone off with some old soldiers and might have met a sticky end on the blade of an English axe, or some such nonsense. Anyway, I said I'd check it out but I can't go through the official channels for the moment as some delicate negotiations are underway between Whitehall and Versailles – tight lips and all that, for me and for you but I'll tell you what I can."*

"Have you read the Police report on the Ley Line bodies?" asked Sherlock, *"There could be something of interest to the French as the tattoo mentioned has a definite message, a call to arms, in fact."*

"It does?" queried Mycroft, *"But, no, to answer your question on the Police reports, I've just had a sketchy outline of the doings at Salisbury. What does my man on the spot, my younger brother, know? Has he seen the tattoos? Details, Sherlock, give me details."*

"Details are what I was collecting before being summoned to Whitehall." replied Sherlock, *"But I have seen the Police report and the photographs of the tattoo. They are not in colour but an accompanying coloured sketch shows the French Tricolour, a couple of crossed sabres and the word 'Revanche' in bold blood red, not some picture of a Parisian dancing girl as one might find on a soldier's arm after a night out in the Capital."*

"Revenge, hey? Now that is something - well it may be." commented Mycroft, *"I presume you've not fallen for all of that prehistoric mystical rubbish flying about, Little Brother. That would be all we need: Sherlock Holmes dressed up like some resurrected Druid chanting at the morning sun and chopping up Frenchmen. Our negotiations would end in outright warfare."*

"Certainly not," came the curt reply, *"but someone possibly wants us to think along those lines. I have made contact with a journalist, one who wrote such rubbish. He is an intelligent sort and extremely interested in getting the complete story but keeps the shillings flowing in with his lurid and fanciful reports. He seems able to approach people at all levels and is investigating, so he informs me, some business concerning land owners and land ownership around Salisbury Plain."*

"*It has just occurred to me,*" Sherlock continued, "*that this man, this journalist called Robert Parker, should be working for you – he's sneaky enough but uses his brain.*"

"*If I didn't know better,*" responded Mycroft, "*I'd say you were paying the man a compliment. You know we don't make jokes about such things around here so I'll assume your comment was a serious one. I'll have the man checked out – we can always use a useful contact, especially one with good Press connections. Anyway, how is the good Doctor? How is Watson?*"

Sherlock thought on his good friend before replying, "*Watson is on-station, as it were, being my eyes and ears while I'm away. He will play the tourist as in so many ways he will be, but will record any developments, even suggestions thereof, and communicate these to me on my return.*"

Putting down his tea cup and moving in closer to his brother, the Great Sleuth took on a quite serious appearance and demanded, "*Now, I've told you what I know, which isn't much at this point; now you must tell me why I'm here. You know I'm like a fish out of water in this place – people just aren't normal in Whitehall and I can get more sense and straight-talking out of a house breaker caught red-handed and headed for prison. So, don't be coy, just tell me what's going on.*"

Mycroft swallowed the second of his pastries, washed it down with a large sip of his excellent brew and looked squarely at his brother. "*France,*" he said, "*finds herself between a powerful Britain and an aggressive Germany and dislikes us somewhat less than her militant neighbour to the east. Our own frontiers are largely settled but France has lost a sizeable province or two, German speaking to be sure but no less a part of France for that, at least to the French. She also feels a sense of humiliation and that Revanche tattoo expresses a*" common sentiment – some wish to recommence hostilities, with anyone it seems, just to get back in the fight."

"*And this missing official?*" broke in Sherlock.

"*Not so much an official as a Colonel, one forced, as a brevet officer, to surrender at Sedan, at the breakthrough.*" was the reply, "*A loose cannon, no less, and one who would stir up trouble between Germany, Britain and France and scuttle the current negotiations or even start a major war.*"

"*And the current negotiations are?*" probed Sherlock.

"*Sensitive.*" was the reply.

"*Mycroft!*" shouted Sherlock.

A laugh, then a sustained grin and the elder Holmes continued, "*And could lead to an accord between France and Britain, perhaps even a treaty in response to Germany's new status and enhanced power and reach. But it's early days yet and there are many perils to overcome, allies to avoid upsetting, adversaries to avoid provoking, not to mention our domestic aversions. But, you know nothing of this, of course, nor can anyone else, not even Watson, as much as I trust the man and hold him in high regard.*"

"*But if these four men were French and were bent on causing trouble, why would they be on Salisbury Plain?*" pondered Sherlock, "*Surely there would be ample opportunity to upset things in London, or Paris or even Berlin or has something else been going on, something you won't or can't tell me?*"

"*I have told you too much as it is.*" replied his brother, "*But, having done that, I suppose I can tell you that the Army has its sights on sections of Salisbury Plain to test out its new toys. Our Army is quite proficient as it stands but is hardly the most extensive in Europe, not by a great stretch, and needs room to manoeuvre, literally. There are good security, cultural and commercial reasons that this information is not known outside of certain offices in Whitehall and we don't want to read this Parker's exposé of it in The Times or anywhere else.*"

"*He'll hear nothing from me on the subject.*" declared Sherlock, "*But someone knows something – remember I mentioned some rumours of land owners and land usage. This came from Parker but, who told him and what he was told, I'm not in a position to know or say as yet. Would the matter be worth the lives of four men, though? And what would it profit the French to know of such plans?*"

Mycroft replied softly but firmly, "*Those are questions which you will answer for me, Sherlock. I can't command you but I do implore you, both as brother and countryman, to use all of those special skills you possess to find your way through this maze without starting off a major war.*"

"*I will do my utmost.*" was the reply, "*After all, starting off major wars is your department.*"

The Return

The two brothers sat quietly, each unsure if the other had more to add. Finally, Mycroft reached for the tea pot and poured another cup for them both. He also reached out for another sweet treat – he felt he deserved and needed the extra boost.

"*So there it is,*" came forth from his pastry-laden mouth as he pushed the pastry dish toward his brother, "*Now, eat up, drink your tea and be off back to Salisbury and get to the bottom of these doings. You have only to send for any funds you require and they will be made available to you. Remember that no one can learn of what we have discussed and, as far as anyone else is concerned, you are there to solve a murder, nothing more.*"

Sherlock Holmes drank his tea, refused the extra pastry and stood, ready to leave. "*I will call into Baker Street for a few supplies.*" he said, "*Just a few extras for my defence.*"

Mycroft nodded and opened a drawer, reached in and drew out a small revolver and a packet of bullets. "*Don't hesitate to use this,*" he said, "*I don't want my brother turning up in bits.*"

Sherlock thought about it for a few seconds and then pocketed the weapon and box of bullets. "*I suppose,*" he said, "*that it might be of use should things get out of hand. Hopefully, I'll return it unused.*"

"*Just make sure you return yourself.*" was his brother's earnest reply.

Sherlock bade his brother farewell and made his way to the street, hailed a cab and started for Baker Street, then had the cabbie wait while he attended to a few items and re-mounted the cab to set off for Waterloo. He was aware that, unlike with his inward journey, he had been followed by a second cab, a Hansom, and that the same cab was now stationary farther down in Baker Street. While most cabs of that sort appeared almost identical, the garb of the cabbie and the lightness of the horse's colour made it stand out to the observant eye.

Sherlock had made no great secret of his destinations, though only Watson, Lestrade and Inspector Fleming knew he would be visiting his brother in Whitehall by special request, but here he was being followed. Who was in that cab, and why?

The ride to Waterloo was trouble-free and Holmes stepped from the cab and paid, taking his replenished valise and seeking out the platform for his return to Salisbury. The cab following stopped right behind but Holmes made no attempt to confront its fare, he would just walk at a moderate pace, not hurrying, not dawdling, until the mystery man made his move, if such was his intention. All of a sudden there were sounds of running feet and Holmes swiftly turned about and raised his stout walking stick above his head.

"Holmes, you wouldn't strike an Officer of the Law, would you?" was the response from the owner of those running feet.

"Lestrade," shouted Holmes as he lowered his weapon, *"you almost got yourself brained. You've been following me since I left Whitehall. What's going on? Oh, and by the way, you're an inept sort of spy for I spotted that horse and driver in seconds - they stood out like the flag of Spain in our London streets."*

"Needs must, My Friend." replied Lestrade, *"They were all that was to hand at the time. Anyway, I wasn't hiding from you, only from others who had no business knowing our plans."*

"*Our plans. What plans? I don't even know our plans.*"
complained Holmes.

"*The plans that we're about to make on our way to Salisbury.*"
was the Policeman's reply, "*I've been given leave to help out
Fleming and put all those Frenchmen back together, with or
without heads. I knew you'd be going to London to see your
brother and thought I'd join you on your way back. Fleming
sent word to me and I thought I would intercept you without
your brother knowing; I mean, he might suspect you of
sharing his secrets with me.*"

"*Well ... yes,*" stuttered Holmes, "*there are things which I
cannot share for reasons which I cannot divulge, but if you
think Mycroft would not have seen you then you would be
wrong; he sees everything, or those gnomes of his do and then
report it all back to him. At this very moment, I'd say that
your name is on several bits of paper being sorted for filing.*"

"*No doubt.*" laughed Lestrade, "*My name's always being filed
by someone, but if I can help Fleming with a bit of the drudge
work, he may be able to see over all those piles of paper to the
actual truth, at least who was killed and who did it, regardless
of any 'why' that Mycroft doesn't want us or anyone else to
know about, though that may prove difficult to keep secret for
long. Whatever it is, the Yard doesn't want to send a trainload
of blue to trample the region with big plodding boots; perhaps
it's been warned not to alert the world to the secret goings-on
around Salisbury.*"

"*Some of those secret goings-on may well become generally
apparent in due course,*" commented Holmes, "*but I can't be
the one to tell you. My lips have been sealed for very good
reasons. Now, I believe we should be boarding our train; we
can speak further out of public view.*"

Holmes walked to the carriage and opened the door through which Lestrade then stepped. Taking one last look around in case anyone else was following, Holmes joined his official colleague in an empty compartment. Preparations for tobacco consumption were then made by both men, Holmes taking out his tobacco pouch and pipe and filling its bowl and Lestrade producing a fine cigar, one saved for a special occasion such as discussions with Holmes. Holmes lit a match and offered it to Lestrade who leaned forward to draw air and flame to the tip of his cigar and then puffed vigorously as ignition took hold. Next, Holmes raised the match above the bowl of his pipe and repeated Lestrade's actions. Smoke started to fill the compartment and both men sat back in their seats and began to withdraw from their troubles with relaxation telling, particularly on Lestrade.

Whistle blowing, carriage shuffling and the pair was off and watching the platform going by until the train had cleared the station. Then the speed picked up and the rocking of the carriage relaxed the two detectives even more until they entered that state of semi-stupor which led to their occasional dozing off and experiencing hazy daydreams. There was no chance of either man speaking or even listening to whatever either one might have to say – it was the best of states for men deprived of sleep, especially for Lestrade who could rarely justify or countenance snoozing on Scotland Yard's time.

The journey to Salisbury was not a long one but the two men dozed for some time before waking from their sleepy states to see their countryside in its glory. It was not yet high summer but the patchwork of greens and golds and the passing parade of picturesque villages and darkened woodlands made for a very pleasant ride, despite the knowledge that somewhere out there was a murderer and a very enigmatic mystery lurking among the old stone monuments.

"*What are these ley lines, Holmes?*" asked a curious Lestrade, so suddenly that Holmes was a little startled, "*Do they really exist or are they just some sheep trails fancied to be ancient pathways by locals with too much imagination?*"

"*They are real enough, My Friend, and seem to predate any written record, on paper or in stone.*" was the serious reply from one now somewhat fascinated with the ancient network devised by people he had once thought of as somewhat brutish but now saw as people working to the limits of their capabilities and in tune with the land, the seasons, the sun and the stars. "*Those lines run as straight as a die for miles and join up points on the landscape, some natural, some man-made, and some of our straightest streets seem to owe their origins to them.*"

Lestrade, still mystified as to the significance of the lines but first and foremost a policeman, went on, "*And why would anyone want to chop up a body and place bits of it along one? Is this what those old timers did all those years ago?*"

"*I believe,*" stated Holmes, "*that someone is trying his best to make us think they are still doing it. But no one knows what those old timers, as you call them, got up to – everything is conjecture mixed in with a lot of wishful thinking, also a bit of loose logic mixed in with some reasonably reliable common sense. But something real is going on: I don't know exactly what that is or who, for that matter, is doing it. Parker, the journalist, seems to have a nose for such things and we ought to listen to what he has to say, if we can get him to say it. There is more to that man than I first thought and he's as much a detective as anyone bearing the title.*"

"*Praise from Sherlock Holmes is high praise indeed.*" replied Lestrade, "*Those fellows are generally fast and loose with the truth so what makes this one so special?*"

"Well, he does seem to appreciate the need for some restraint, although he's certainly paid to keep the Public's interest." said Holmes, *"But one gets a feeling about someone; you'd see that in your own work. He thinks he's on to something quite significant, and more than a bit dangerous I'd say. Something is brewing and it has something to do with someone who owns some of the land thereabouts – he feels it and I am inclined to think that he's correct. He wants to write the bigger story when the quarry is cornered and seems willing to cooperate to stay close to the hunters."*

"Did your Brother Mycroft happen to tell you of the Army's desire to acquire large swathes of Salisbury Plain?" enquired Lestrade, unsure if Holmes had been aware of the secret plans, *"It's not generally known but such things are hard to contain as time goes on – too many people become involved and someone is sure to let something slip. If the Army sent a survey team out it would be spotted in no time and then everyone in the district would know about it before sundown - it's how things work in the country."*

Holmes was quite unsure of how to respond to Lestrade's question. The official detective had obviously learned something of the Army's plan but, though he did trust the man implicitly, Sherlock had given his word to his brother to stay mute on the matter.

"What do you know of such things?" asked Holmes, hoping to avoid the need for a direct answer, *"And how would you come to know them?"*

"A detective gets to know a good many things, as you would well appreciate, Holmes." was Lestrade's reply, *"A policeman picks up a crumb here and a morsel there and, before you know it, there's a whole meal of a story before his eyes. Somebody always knows something and someone will always*

talk; it's the way of things and if a plan is too complicated there are too many things to go wrong."

"*Well,*" said Holmes, a little sheepishly, "*can we agree that this is a subject we should not discuss unless we really have to? Neither of us wants to fall foul of Whitehall or the Army.*"

"*Agreed. But the time will surely come when we must discuss it with someone.*" Lestrade conceded, "*Then, I'm afraid, unless I have direct orders from The Yard to the contrary, I must proceed using every fact at my disposal – like a lot of people, I too have a duty to uphold and few options for discretion.*"

Holmes smiled and nodded his assent, then leaned back into his seat and checked his pipe which seemed to have extinguished itself while the two men were in discussion. The pipe's bowl found itself refilled and relit and Lestrade decided that a second cigar was in order. They still had thirty minutes of travel time to fill but had run out of things to safely discuss. "*Too many tempting and tenuous notions and too few hard and fast facts.*" went through the mind of the Great Sleuth as he sought the sanctuary of his brain attic.

Eventually, though far too soon, the two men felt the train slow as Salisbury was approached. Lestrade stood, stretched and said to his colleague, "*Time to get back to work, My Friend. Let's see what Fleming and the rest of the cast in this comedy of horrors has to say.*"

GALLIC INTEREST

The Priests

Almost two thousand years had passed since Caesar drove the Druids from their Gallic homeland to the doubtful sanctuary of Britannia, there to repeat the exodus onto the Isle of Mona and extinction at the hands and swords of the Roman legions whose Generals were keen to be rid of a disruptive and uncooperative priesthood. Since that time, empires had fallen, particularly Rome's, and other empires had risen while the face of Europe altered immeasurably as tribal peoples invaded and settled and coalesced into quarrelling kingdoms and eventually matured into formative squabbling nation states.

The great stones, the ancient sentinels set in place during a time too remote for anyone to remember why or by whom, looked out and saw all these changes but stayed impassive and mute as the sunlight's annual oscillations came and went with no one to observe them. The Druids had paid homage to the deities in their sacred groves of trees, the groves and the spirits they nurtured being destroyed by the Romans who then sought to render any resurgence by the priests impossible by killing every last one. The Romans, however, as thorough and as ruthless as they could be, were unable to find every last priest and pockets survived, isolated and vulnerable, in the dark forests of both Gallia and Britannia.

The only way for such besieged remnants of the old religion to survive was to change, to adapt to new circumstances and try to retain as many of the old observances as possible through the centuries. How many of the Druids survived and for how long they maintained their devastated religious practices cannot be known but a resurgence of old ideas and a longing for some mythical lost golden age brought many in modern times to see the standing stones of Europe as part of that lost heritage, something to be regained without ever truly knowing just what those people of old actually believed.

Old Gallia and Britannia began to fade as the Roman Legions withdrew and, as the Germanic tribesmen crossed the North Sea and the Danube, each former Roman province started to become something else, the land of the Franks and the land of the Anglo-Saxons, each to become powerfully Christian but never completely expunged of their ancient mysteries, secrets kept in trust and memory as the ancient Gauls and Britons were pushed to the limits of the land. Peoples beliefs shifted from the spirits of the land about them to a kingdom in the sky and, one by one, the links with the old ways broke and fell away to oblivion until those ancient ways once again beckoned and small isolated groups of people began to yearn for the certainty they were sure that a return to the old observances would bring.

The Druids were reborn after so many centuries had passed that no one could possibly have known what they truly had been, beyond the vague descriptions of ancient chroniclers and the fanciful imageries of the modern romance writers. Still, there was a need, a void which needed filling in the lives of the new adherents and anything ancient was to be revered and honoured, and possessed. Where the Druids of old clung to their sacred groves, the new observers looked to the rings and lines of great stones, structures erected thousands of years before the original Druids came but now part of that ancient world the newcomers wanted to reclaim.

Across nineteenth-century Britain, France and parts of Spain, groups of two, three and four people gathered to discuss their views, often divergent but maintaining the central unswerving theme that contact with the spirit of the Earth should be re-established. Over time, groups coalesced into small local movements whose activities were seen as eccentric by some, threatening by others, while most paid little attention at all. Contact between the groups began as local meetings which traded views and generated links before forming regional movements with national and international followings. Nothing like a formal religion was in view but the fervour of the participants in the newly introduced, some would say resurrected, rituals was becoming apparent.

The new Druids were not quite an underground movement but did tend to gather furtively at night, some to perform their rituals around a sacred fire and some to await the glory of the dawning sun and its gift of spiritual light. Some of the adherents liked the spectacle and the trappings of the ritual much more so than the meaning behind it; some, however, drew strength from their leanings and became true believers in something they saw as eternal and linked with both past and future events. The Druids were now the totality of followers, not just the high priests and educated elite, but when those priests appeared, the followers listened and believed and some, in moments of great religious fervour, acted to render any opposition powerless by any means necessary.

Salisbury Plain was a place sacred to the new Druids, perhaps as much as it had been two thousand years before but now the high temple of Stonehenge was the centre of their religious observances. Other lesser monuments were visited as the new observers set out across the landscape along the ancient ways, the ley lines, though the land was not as open as it had once been. Much of the land was now in private hands and fenced off to the general public, though numerous rights of way still existed – a battle of wits had been waging between those who saw private property as sacrosanct and others who saw it as theft. Mostly, though, if there were no great diversions off the old tracks, the landowner was happy enough to let the generally harmless practitioners come and go; some even joined in and a few turned a profit from the novelty it presented to the ever-present tourist.

Pilgrims began attending from across Britain, and even from France and Spain where the old religion had been harried to virtual extinction and the new observers were generally not appreciated, not by the established church, nor by that church's adherents. Britain, especially Salisbury Plain, proved a magnet to believers otherwise assailed in their homelands for quasi-heretical behaviour and they came, generally small in their numbers but always great in fervour. There were, however, differences between British and Continental observances and serious disputes often arose as to whose rite should take precedence and, as seen on so many occasions, petty religious differences often led to horrendous repercussions.

The lands of France, Italy and Spain, now modern states drawing together often disparate territories, had been integral parts of the Roman Empire while Britain was a distant and difficult province of doubtful worth to the Caesars. In those countries, the Druids had been ruthlessly eliminated except in a few remote areas in which they could continue their practices, often disguised as Christian monks. Those false monks had maintained a continuity through the centuries but eventually lost their links with the Earth while preserving their lives. Their chanting became meaningless repetitive verses recalling the faint and garbled echoes of the dying gasps and protests of their ancient slaughtered brethren. They served an ever-retreating distant memory, not the living spirit which those ancestral communities felt in those groves of sacred trees. Even to them, though, the new Druids would have been seen as pretenders with profane beliefs and meaningless rites, their observances neither legitimate nor acceptable but offensive and often laughable.

Ancient Gaul, now modern France, had been the heartland of the Druids and it was here that resurgent communities saw the opportunity to emerge from obscurity and not be hunted down and despatched as heretics and devil worshippers. No one could recall a time when the Gauls and Britons had not been separated by a strait too wide to swim and too deep to ford. On a clear day, those standing on high cliffs in either land could see a hazy distant landform come in and out of the mist and knew that there were people looking back, often people of peaceful intent, sometimes not, but always people of like belief.

The France and Britain of Sherlock Holmes' day could claim much the same, though their peoples were separated by the politics of empire and commerce and their common religious observances had diverged considerably. When the new Druids of France met the new Druids of Britain, the groups had come from several centuries of quite different political and religious conventions and backgrounds and this was to tell in the way the groups interacted with each other, disastrously in some cases. There would be no central authority to arbitrate disputes and no ancient scripts to refer to for guidance; each movement involved a completely new basis of belief and each had usurped the same ancient mystical name. For the majority of adherents, however, those who had been attracted by the trappings of ceremony and costume, there would be little reason for serious dispute, but for some, those who believed in extreme earnest, there were bouts of open hostility and occasional violent clashes.

The weather was perfect around Salisbury and pilgrims were beginning to converge on Old and New Sarum to fulfil some pressing need; some would come to pray at the famous cathedral and ponder the site of the former structure; some would come to fulfil a pledge or submit a plea for divine help; some would come to see the grand structure itself and wonder at the great effort required for its construction; others would come out of pure curiosity – for whatever reason, all would make their own grand tours and some would be branded as tourist, someone and something to be milked of money by the locals.

Telling a visiting Druid from a shuffling pilgrim could be quite difficult – they tended to look much the same as anyone else and most Druids probably had some interest in the modern cathedral as well as the ancient stones. They would never wear the ceremonial robes and headgear in public and would never speak about their own special secret pilgrimages.

James Fletcher's 'Ancient Ways' had paid scant attention to the subject of the Druids. He had little actual information to go on but had made mention of their being magicians to the Celtic peoples, the term 'magician' having had a more mystical meaning than the modern 'sleight of hand conjuror' which most people associated with that word. Sherlock Holmes knew virtually nothing about them, nor of the new movement – they had not been involved in recent crimes nor were they seen as a subversive movement, merely a harmless curiosity with a rather eccentric membership. That they had originally been priests vital to the Celtic tribes was little appreciated and the mention of human sacrifice and other savage rites in ancient writings had placed them into a brutish class. Still, the very word Druid would likely strike a chord somewhere in most people's minds, something old, something mystic, something mysterious, but also something destroyed long ago and swept from the annals of history.

Several ancient writers had recorded accounts of the Druids and their practices though these, for the most part, were second-hand at best and often written down well after the prime sources had long disappeared. The only reliable account, though some definite bias ought to be expected, was from the pen of Julius Caesar in his 'Commentaries of the Gallic Wars' written, of course, by the victor. Roman victors, particularly those aspiring to sit upon the Imperial throne, were not known for their humility, nor were they given to complete honesty when it came to the character of their defeated foes – the worse the enemy, the greater the victory and the greater the victory the bigger the reception the victor would receive in Rome, all necessary for the support of the Roman Senate and People and, especially, the Legions. Druids were never portrayed as push-overs.

So far, though, no one had mentioned the Druids to Holmes and Watson but the two men were about to experience something unexpected, though with hindsight, neither should have been in any way surprised.

The Colonel

Colonel Baudin, patriotic in the extreme and given to being impetuous, was attached to the French Embassy in London and held a position which defied all logical attempts at definition except that he sounded for all the world like a spy. While holding a Captain's commission, he was raised to the equivalent of Brevet Colonel for the duration of hostilities during the Franco-Prussian War and, despite a commendable effort in battle, had found himself and his unit isolated when the Prussian cavalry broke through the French lines at Sedan. The supporting Prussian forces then made short work of the defenders who found that they had few options – some had stubbornly fought on but Prussian short range artillery and mobile Gatling guns wielded by the Prussian infantry silenced the desperate French protests and took many into captivity. Baudin had wanted to fight on but was persuaded, uncharacteristically, to think of his men before his personal glory, his superiors telling him that France would need zeal such as his in the future. That future had yet to come and Baudin, forcibly retired from the army at the cessation of hostilities, had joined the equivalent of the Foreign Office in his country's civil service, though he insisted on still using his brevet title.

To be a private soldier serving under Baudin had not been something to relish; the man was demanding of himself and demanded that his men be prepared to die willingly whenever ordered because 'that was what Frenchmen did'. He was unceasing in his demands, intolerant of any perceived weakness and thought that withdrawing to a more defensible position was sign of base cowardice – he was the sort who would engage superior forces and consider the loss of his men with little more concern than a young boy would when knocking down his rows of toy soldiers, except that his fallen men rarely got the chance to rejoin their ranks. He was not popular with the rank and file; he was not popular with his brother officers; but he was the right man for the job when it came to a small force needing and willing to take chances and push a position – he was, in short, considered quite useful at times but also quite expendable.

Decidedly disinterested in archaeology and history, particularly British despite being posted to Britain to 'make observations and report', Baudin had heard rumours of something stirring military-wise around Salisbury and had decided he should investigate. He was far too much the Frenchman to ever hope to infiltrate military units or political organisations but he did have a good eye for military developments and could suggest where such preparations might be taking place or be about to do so. Apart from being overtly militaristic, the man was also extremely religious and saw the once-Catholic now-Protestant Norman cathedrals of England as bastions of enemy power in hostile territory under temporary truce. Many had expected him to cause trouble and were sure they would be proven correct, though they were also pleased to be rid of him to an overseas posting.

Baudin, however, had not been seen or heard from for some weeks and the French Embassy was worried, particularly as discussions had begun on the possibility for some future military alignment of France and Britain. The Colonel had been off, in his own unique way, watching and listening for developments or rumours thereof on Salisbury Plain. Unlike France's army, Britain's land forces were not large and were also spread across a world-wide empire, so any local increase in their size or effectiveness was of interest to France, less so for any threat it might pose but as general intelligence of matters of military significance. If Baudin could be trusted to observe and report only, there would be no problem; if he entered and probed military installations as he was inclined to do, he risked jeopardising the chance of a military understanding between the countries and could possibly alert Germany whose nervous leadership might well feel the need to launch a massive pre-emptive strike against France and then consider its options in respect of Britain.

The man and his situation presented an enigma; he was both an official charged with gathering information useful to his nation's negotiations with his host country and, at the same time, a frustrated energetic soldier who considered himself to be behind enemy lines. Wiltshire, inclusive of Salisbury and its ancient monuments, had been strategically important in past centuries when Britain had been beset by internecine warfare but was now a showcase of peaceful countryside and stood out as an icon of Britain's idyllic rural shires, one steeped deeply in history. France, too, had regions of similar significance but Baudin could not, to twist an oft-encountered phrase, see the forest for the enemies hidden behind the bushes. Problem was that there was little to see and the man was finding himself pushed well beyond his normal level of frustration and paranoia.

He had noticed one thing, though, this being that small groups of men could at times be seen walking sections of Salisbury Plain and making observations of some type using ordinance maps, compasses and sometimes theodolites – they were making surveys. To Baudin, this was proof that Britain was about to significantly increase the size and military preparedness of its ground forces – to simply observe was out of the question, he had to infiltrate the groups and determine their motives. Moreover, some of the men in the groups were French and this pointed to treason and, to Baudin, one French traitor in British service was worse than twenty-thousand blue-jacketed Prussian infantrymen crashing through the French lines.

Partly because of Baudin's appointment being forced upon them, French Embassy staff had considered his deployment ill-advised as they knew his character, his tendency to see enemies at every turn and his dislike of anything non-French – he was not driven by patriotic fervour, rather by nationalistic rage, and this would prove his undoing. Hopefully, many of his countrymen thought, it would not see France placed between two enemies with powerful military and naval forces and huge industrial resources and might. France had been weakened and recently lost two important provinces and could not afford to lose more – a Britain aligned to France's prosperity and renewal, to many at the Embassy, was a prize worth the sacrifice of a dangerous war-mongering fool. Still, he was a loyal and steadfast Frenchman in the service of his country and could not be disposed of for being an embarrassment.

Mycroft Holmes had been aware of this man, not just for his being missing, but for comments made about him by contacts Mycroft maintained at the French Embassy. Being fluent in French and of French extraction on his mother's side, Mycroft was held in some esteem and trust by his French counterpart who had alerted him to the man's disappearance and character. Mycroft, however, was loathe to divulge all he knew to his younger brother Sherlock lest his relationship with his French contact be compromised. If the elder Holmes knew anything about his younger brother it was that, being put on to a scent, Sherlock would track down the quarry with the nose of a bloodhound and persistence of a bulldog just for the challenge the hunt presented. Too much information at Sherlock's command might alert others as to the nature of the quest and the younger Holmes knew enough to keep quiet when Mycroft insisted on discretion.

Monsieur Baudin, 'Colonel' to those under his command and at his insistence, had convinced his superiors or, more correctly, his superiors' superiors, that he ought to have a small detachment of hand-picked men at his disposal, men who would follow orders, men who would not quibble about the nature of those orders. In short, he wanted his own miniature army, a squad to do his bidding, a squad with which to begin the recovery of France's lost honour, an honour which only he, as he saw it, seemed willing to seek out.

"*Surely,*" came a commonly expressed sentiment from the French Embassy's staff, "*in the wilds of Wiltshire and the vast expanse of Salisbury Plain the man could do no harm. There is nothing there of military significance, just cattle, grain and a few churches.*"

This was a sentiment held by most, including the Ambassador who had not been impressed by having such a character dumped on his doorstep, as he had once put it, though he would have little to do with the man's day to day activities. These were the province of one particular Under-Secretary who had been too junior in rank and status to refuse his superiors' directive. Having no specific instructions as to the Colonel's duties, the Under-Secretary made sure the man was paid on time and requested, with futility, that he report regularly and diligently and file accurate reports of his activities. Baudin, considering that he out-ranked his administrative overseer, ignored the request and became a law unto himself and was lost in a very cumbersome system, one keen for him to stay lost.

Only when queries about the Colonel's requests for additional funds had gone unanswered did anyone realise that the man was missing, or at least unaccounted for. The Under-Secretary, not unduly perturbed but none-the-less being cautious, took both the requests and the newspaper reports of murders on Salisbury Plain, and the fact that a French military man may have been a victim, to his superior but still it took some time before any sort of alarm was raised, and that was a half-hearted one, at least at first.

No one, it seems, was certain of where the missing Colonel should have been, nor any of his three underlings – 'somewhere around Salisbury' was the closest anyone could suggest and this was on the basis of information more than a month old. The Embassy did not want to involve the British agencies in tracking him and his small group down but if it came out that the dead men were indeed Frenchmen in the service of the Embassy, there would be a series of embarrassing and awkward questions to answer, all at a time of sensitive diplomatic manoeuvring by both countries.

Avoiding official channels, Mycroft Holmes' unofficial contact in the French Embassy, one of the Ambassador's permanent secretaries, had put out feelers to his unofficial British counterpart in the hope of avoiding any unnecessary unpleasantness. Mycroft had asked the usual questions and sent out one of his operatives to seek any information on groups of Frenchmen who might have been noticed in the region in recent times. Nothing of any great use was uncovered but Mycroft's luck changed for the better on hearing that Sherlock had decided to offer his assistance to the Wiltshire police based in Salisbury. This, of course, was now additional to the extra help Inspector Lestrade would be able to provide now that he had been released to assist his rural colleague.

Mycroft had told Sherlock precious little about the man being sought but well knew his brother's capabilities. It would be for the Great Sleuth to find out the man's name in the course of his investigations but he was now aware of the military designs on Salisbury Plain and that the French were somehow involved. The French military motif tattoo and the four bodies possibly corresponding to four missing Frenchmen, including a Colonel attached to the French Embassy, suggested some level of French interference in British military matters. Mycroft could see that this could indeed be so but was not totally convinced, after all, the French Embassy had contacted him about the missing men. With the efforts of the local Police now bolstered by the presence his younger brother with his incredible powers of insight and helped along by the sturdy presence of John Watson, Mycroft was certain that a motive for the murders would soon be found. He could only hope that journalists like Parker could be kept in check and not ruin the delicate diplomatic machinations of the two nations, though he could not comprehend the sense of the murders nor of the reason for the victims' horrific mutilations.

The Supporters

The train bearing Holmes and Lestrade from London came slowly to its termination at Salisbury and as the carriages jerked to a halt the two men pushed open the door and burst forth, each seemingly charged with a new and invigorated determination to have the matter of the Ley Line Murders solved once and for all. Mycroft had given precious little away in terms of actual detail, especially the name of a significant potential victim, but had provided numerous very strong hints as to what and who should be looked for. This was always the way of Mycroft, to hold back and not divulge every detail, rather to rely on his trusted operatives to use their initiatives and work through the problem at hand. This had the effect of separating Mycroft from both the operative and the operation but also making sure that each operative would make certain of all facts gathered and not simply rely on delivered information which may have been compromised before being received at Whitehall.

Holmes and Lestrade, in their respective unofficial and official capacities and backed by Watson with his tempering ways upon his friend's impulsive tendencies, would prove a positive boon to the embattled Fleming, especially now that the newcomers had been provided with strong hints as to secret goings-on in the greater Salisbury region. Fleming had made little headway with his investigations but the information he had been able to collect had been helpful in that the man had been meticulous in his reporting of what detail he had managed to collect. His fortunes were about to change, however, as the two detectives walked from the railway to the street and hailed a cab, not that of Jenkins who was uncharacteristically absent from the rank which was just as well in the circumstances, and set off for the Police Station.

Inside the cab the two detectives remained silent lest the cabbie's ears be primed for any bit of stray gossip. Lestrade looked out at the passing buildings trying to get his bearings in a new location while Holmes looked down at his clenched hands trying hard to recall all that his brother had revealed, checking his memory all the while to be sure that he had not missed anything of vital importance.

Holmes looked up and saw the tea rooms he and Watson had visited two days earlier coming into view. *"We're getting close."* he uttered softly to Lestrade, as though the cabbie might be listening and inadvertently be let into some secret, *"Just at the end of this road."*

Lestrade nodded and picked up his bag; Holmes did likewise. The cab swung around and stopped outside their destination and the two men exited, Lestrade tossing a coin into the cabbie's proffered top hat. Then came *"Ta, Guv."* as the cabbie cracked the whip to get quickly on his way looking for another fare.

The Duty Sergeant greeted Holmes very cordially and looked at Lestrade suspiciously, only to come to attention on learning of his rank and status.

"I beg your pardon, Sir." he stated, *"I knew Mr Holmes here, and of course his colleague Dr Watson, but was unaware that we were to have a visit from Scotland Yard in the form of your good self. Let me have your bags, Gentlemen; they'll be here behind my desk when you need them."*

"Thank you Sergeant," replied Lestrade handing over his bag, *"We don't wish everyone to know I'm here, though I suppose it won't be a secret for long."*

"*No indeed.*" came the reply, "*And I'd say that the railway attendants and the cabbie have started spreading the word about some new official-looking arrival at the Police Station. But if folks come asking about you, I'll direct them to Inspector Fleming – they'll get nothing from me you may rest assured.*"

"*I am sure of that, thank you, Sergeant.*" replied the London Inspector, "*Now, if Inspector Fleming is presently available, you might direct us to him.*"

Before the Sergeant could respond, Inspector Fleming appeared, effusively greeting his two visitors. "*Welcome back, Mr Holmes, it seems a week since you left. And I presume that this gentleman at your side is Inspector Lestrade.*"

"*Yes, indeed.*" was Holmes' reply, "*Inspector Fleming, may I introduce a professional colleague of mine and a brother officer of yours, Inspector Lestrade of Scotland Yard.*"

"*It is grand to finally meet you, Inspector,*" said Fleming, firmly gripping Lestrade's hand and shaking it enthusiastically, "*I don't mind admitting that I could do with some help, though I had been hopeful of some extra constables as well.*"

"*There is little chance of constables at present.*" declared Lestrade, "*We seem to be short of men everywhere and no one wants to release what they have. But we do have Mr Holmes and Dr Watson with us and no doubt they'll be worth a dozen constables each, Mr Holmes with that nose of his for detail, and Dr Watson ... well, there's no sturdier man in a difficult situation; why, with my own eyes I've seen him outnumbered by armed felons only to stand and face them down with that revolver of his and win the day. He doesn't seek trouble but he has been known to put an end to it at times.*"

"*By the way,*" he continued, "*where is the good Doctor?*"

"*Jenkins drove him to the Cathedral, I believe.*" said Fleming, "*I think they might be keeping an eye on each other. I must say that Jenkins is a little too sly for my liking, though I can't lay anything specific on him. Just a type, I suppose.*"

"*But a sly type, you say?*" queried Lestrade, "*And you don't trust him?*"

"*Yes to your first question and no to your second.*" was the reply, "*though he is a very good cabbie, very knowledgeable and very accommodating; too much in my opinion. Mr Holmes can tell you about him, he and Watson having driven out onto Salisbury Plain and camped out overnight at Stonehenge with the man.*"

"*Well,*" Lestrade started, "*we do have much to discuss and I'm sure that man's name and whatever he gets up to will come up at some point. Now, the day's getting on and I'd like to know what I'm about, that is what we're about, before sleep catches up with me later tonight.*"

"*Perhaps,*" responded the Salisbury Inspector, "*if you and Mr Holmes find your ways to Cooper's Inn, I might join you later this evening to discuss what needs discussing; say about nine o'clock.*"

"*A capital idea,*" agreed Lestrade, "*Holmes and I will start walking and try to catch a cab on the fly, so to speak. A ride in a Police wagon would certainly start the tongues awagging. So, it's farewell until nine o'clock; we shall see you then.*"

That said, the two visitors stood, shook the hand of the local detective and exited his office. They picked up their bags from the Desk Sergeant and continued through the front door on their way to their accommodations where they would meet up with Watson and partake of an evening meal. There would be much to discuss now that the game was well and truly afoot.

"*Holmes,*" said Lestrade, lugging his bag and trying to keep pace with Holmes, "*we do need to talk in earnest before we meet with Fleming at nine. He has been the man on the spot but seems somewhat out of his depth; I fear that he's not looking for help but for someone to divert his problems to. He seems a good man but also very provincial in outlook and experience and it may well be that I'll have to take charge officially, or perhaps give the orders with him notionally in charge as far as outsiders are concerned.*"

"*I do fear that you are correct in that assumption,*" responded Holmes, "*and we will discuss that and many other matters when we meet up with Watson who, if he has noted the train timetables, should be at Cooper's Inn awaiting our arrival.*"

Cabs were scarce as Holmes and Lestrade made for Cooper's Inn, each looking forward to what the evening would bring. A full thirty minutes would pass before their destination came into view and Lestrade gave out an involuntary "*At last!*" while his companion simply kept walking, faster than before as it seemed to Lestrade.

"*Mr Holmes,*" came from Cooper's husky throat as the two men entered the innkeeper's domain, "*and an official friend desirous of some anonymity according to Dr Watson and who I have listed as Lester in my guests' register, though I doubt that his true identity isn't known throughout the town by now. It's hard to keep such secrets in these parts. By the way, Dr Watson is upstairs in his room just waiting for you to return.*"

142

"*Ah, thank you, Mr Cooper,*" came back from Holmes, "*Mr Lester here might just keep his registered name for the moment; there's no point loosening the local tongues any more than they have been. Our rooms are ready for us, I presume?*"

"*Yes, indeed.*" replied Cooper, "*but young Billy is about his chores at this moment so if you'll give a moment I'll show you both up myself.*"

"*No need,*" countered Holmes, "*I know the way and Mr Lester here is in the room next to me, if I read your register correctly. We should like to make use of your commercial room in a short while; would there be a chance of us being uninterrupted? We also have a colleague arriving at nine o'clock.*"

"*A fair chance, Mr Holmes,*" said Cooper, "*but there are a couple of commercial travellers registered with us; they are out and about their business at present but will return this evening and may require its use as well and, of course, I can't deny them that. You should have it to yourselves for an hour or so, however.*"

"*Excellent.*" replied Holmes, as he took to the stairs, "*We shall be down directly for a conference. Could we trouble you for coffee and some light refreshment – we've been chasing trains and have not eaten for some time.*"

Cooper smiled and nodded while saying, "*Well, certainly, if it won't spoil your suppers. This sleuthing business certainly seems to make a person hungry.*"

The pair continued they ways to their rooms, deposited their bags and the went to wake up Watson. Watson's day had been a full one and he was snoozing away, hazily recalling the details of Salisbury's impressive cathedral and of the many chapters of his country's history held within. In his mind he actually stood on Runnymede watching the proceedings as King John gave in to the Barons and started Britain's division of regal powers more than 700 years before his own time. This perfect daydream was rudely interrupted and put to an end by the bark of his friend, Sherlock Holmes, *"Watson. There's no time to sleep. We have work to do."*

Watson sat bolt upright on his bed, rubbed his eyes and replied, *"Holmes, why do you do that? You have the uncanny knack of spoiling my most perfect dreams at their most critical points. I do believe you can see inside my head and wait till I'm most enjoying my slumbers before shouting my name in my ear. I'd do the same to you if you'd ever sleep for long enough. I'll be down directly; just give me a few minutes."*

Holmes and Lestrade went down to the commercial room only to find it occupied by two men who were busily checking over what seemed to be orders taken that day for merchandise prior to sending off the details to their employers' main offices. The two detectives dallied for a few minutes before Watson joined them and a quick discussion ended with a decision to divert their refreshments to a small but less private room off the main bar area.

"Strange that ... our publican not seeming to know that his own commercial room was occupied." commented Holmes.

"Even stranger that those men were there at this time of day." added Lestrade, *"It is getting on a bit but there's still plenty of selling time left. That both would run out of customers at the same time is a little suspicious. We ought to find out who they are without the publican's knowledge; after all, we don't really know who we can trust around here."*

The three men moved off to their smaller room and sat around a small table to await their host. They had only to wait for a few minutes before their refreshments arrived – a plate supplied with bread slices holding slabs of cold lamb with generous dollops of mustard and pickles on the side. It was simple fare and, with hot coffee, very welcome by a trio eager for both sustenance and information.

Holmes spoke first and told of his meeting with Mycroft and of the French Embassy's fears for its man and several of his subordinates. He revealed some details, but not all, of the Army's plans for sections of Salisbury Plain as Lestrade seemed to think the whole matter was an open secret. He did not, however, make any mention of negotiations between France and Britain toward un understanding which could result in a military alliance between the two formerly belligerent and now somewhat mutually suspicious nations, each now facing a potential threat from a Germany growing more powerful each day.

Watson came in next and said he had little to add to what was already known except that Jenkins, the ever inquisitive cabbie, was more than a little pushy on the reason for Holmes' absence. It seemed to him that such knowledge was unnecessary for someone interested only in hearsay and gossip; he thought the man wanted to know specific and critical details of their investigations.

Lestrade said that he had very little information on any goings-on between France and Britain and was there in Salisbury in his official capacity as a Police detective. He declared, *"We must consider all aspects of what has been discussed as being linked in some manner but should also be mindful of the position of Inspector Fleming. He is the face of lawful authority in these parts and has asked for our assistance; we owe him that courtesy and he is entitled to our respect and our support though, again, none of us really knows the man. We three trust each other and, at this moment, that is as far as our trust can truly stretch. Even this Professor Tilbury, though grand lady of venerable age she may be, is unknown in respect of her allegiances and in her religious beliefs, orthodox or unorthodox. After all, she may be some Grand Master Wizard of the British Druids, for all we know, or a pot-stirring practicing witch."*

The Investigators

Who truly to trust was something difficult to ponder for three London men new to the district and holding information which made everyone seem potentially untrustworthy. Lestrade had checked on Fleming, his Salisbury colleague, and could find no blemish on his record, no suggestion of his being anything but an upright officer of law and order, a Queen's man sworn to protect the people and the peace of the nation. Watson could not visualise Professor Tilbury bent over a large pot full of some potent witch's brew bubbling within, nor could he see her as anything but that which she seemed, an old lady full of life and knowledge and purely academic interest in the myths and legends and revealed history of the district in which she was born, a district she obviously loved as much as she disliked pretenders to its heritage. Holmes placed the balance of probabilities on the side of his two long-trusted colleagues but held information which required him to question all that he, and his friends, knew or even suspected. All that the Great Sleuth could tell them was that he did hold such information but was sworn to secrecy about its nature for reasons which he could not divulge, reasons which were not his to explain and certainly not theirs to know.

Apart from these two apparent bastions of respectability, the three men had to weigh up the balance of probabilities for Jenkins the cabbie, Cooper the innkeeper, Parker the Journalist and now the two unknown commercial travellers of suspect working practices. Lestrade had been able to find nothing against Fleming, nor could he discover the least suggestion of wrong-doing by Jenkins, Cooper or Parker, apart from the latter man's tendency to stretch the truth almost to breaking point when preparing a story where none actually existed.

"I'd trust Parker before I'd trust Cooper and I'd trust him well before I'd consider trusting Jenkins," declared Holmes, *"but facts are sparse and their actions mostly point to them taking action for purely commercial reasons associated with getting paid for a good story on the part of Parker and getting money out of tourists by both Cooper and Jenkins. This is not to say that either man might not be up to his nose in no good, though Parker would be foolish to draw attention to the situation if he, in fact, had some connection with the crimes."*

"So," said Lestrade, summarising what he thought Holmes was declaring, *"Parker joins Fleming and the Professor on the 'probably trustworthy' list while Jenkins and Cooper remain in the 'currently doubtful' column with those two men in the commercial room. We need to get close to those latter two. I suggest we join them straight away on the pretext of preparing our own individual reports and I believe that between the three of us we should be able to spot a fake or we're not entitled to call ourselves detectives."*

This agreed, the three men stood and withdrew from the smaller room and proceeded to the larger, Watson hurrying upstairs to procure pen, ink and paper for their task.

"When we go in, we should say nothing; just sit and begin writing something, anything." insisted Lestrade, *"Just keep one eye on the two men and occasionally stop and look up as if thinking of what to write next. This will give us all an opportunity to see if they are what they're reputed to be or something else entirely."*

In went the trio with the necessities for writing a report. Each sat away from the other with neither directly facing the two suspect commercial travellers. Watson got to work scribbling furiously as if having much to say in an investigation so far devoid of hard facts. Lestrade sat back as if in deep thought about what to write but then inked his pen and began to write in short bursts. Sherlock Holmes started in much the same manner as had Lestrade but took up two sheets of paper and wrote four words only on each. He stood, walked over to each of his two colleagues and place one sheet in front of each of them; on it he had written the words: '*Mycroft's men – keep writing*' and then resumed his seat, somewhat annoyed with his elder brother.

Watson and Lestrade did as Holmes' note suggested, each wondering how their friend and colleague would handle the situation. Holmes continued writing, stopping every few minutes as if stuck on his next word but watching the reactions of the mystery men, reactions which did not vary as much as might be expected in a real situation. Twenty minutes went by and Holmes rose, indicating to his colleagues to finish off and exit with him.

"*Gentlemen. The room is yours!*" he stated politely and softly to the two men remaining, each responding involuntarily with a curt "*Thank you.*" before resuming their activities. Holmes noted what he took to be a Suffolk accent in those two words from one man and a decided French inclination from the other.

"*One man from Whitehall, one of Mycroft's gnomes it is to be assumed – he stands out a mile.*" Holmes admitted to Watson and Lestrade as they went back to their small room near the bar, "*The other I expect would be from the French Embassy, here to identify a particular man of interest to both our countries and to witness our manner of handling his fate if and when he is found, though that particular man may well be one of the headless victims.*"

"*Just what is that brother of yours up to?*" asked a somewhat annoyed Watson, "*Are those men truly here as observers and, if they are, are they here to help out in the investigation or just to check on us?"*

"Either one, or both." was his friend's reply, *"Perhaps even something else. Nothing is ever clear with Mycroft. If he tells you something you can be sure that he has left much unsaid and that there are many things going on quietly in the background, things which most people will never find out about. To answer your question as best I can, I would say that the two men are here primarily to keep an eye on us and report back. They are probably harmless but might well get in the way if their inability to look like commercial travellers is anything to go on. A little observation of the real thing would have told them that these 'knights of the road' will spend only what time they must in an inn's commercial room and then congregate in the bar where much wheeling and dealing takes place amidst all the ragging and bragging with their fellows. No, they were stalling, going over their orders and reports with excessive zeal, obviously waiting for us to return."*

"Should we confront them?" asked a puzzled Watson.

"No. We'll leave them with their delusions for now." replied Holmes, *"They may well be useful in the days ahead but we should keep an eye on them both in case they stir up more trouble than they've come here to stop."*

"Someone we ought to meet with, and soon," broke in Lestrade, *"is that Parker fellow and see what he has to tell us about land deals and land owners. Such seems to be the key to the goings-on in these parts. A murder to keep something quiet I can understand but four done in such a manner as to focus all the country's eyes on Salisbury must refute any such suggestion. It seems more like a dire and very public warning to members of some organisation to behave or be chopped up."*

"*Or a mass murder made to look like a ritual killing.*" added Holmes, "*Possibly one principal murder with three extras and some additional dismemberment to confuse the authorities and get them chasing after ghosts. My thinking is towards them all being French, the missing Colonel and his three soldierly henchmen who had stumbled or intruded into something sinister or just plain illegal but with rewards worth killing for. Remember that tattoo, the French Tricolour, the crossed sabres and the word 'Revanche' – who else but a French veteran would bear such a strong statement on his person?*"

"*This is old ground we're going over.*" stated Watson, expressing some frustration with his two colleagues, "*You're always telling us we need the facts before coming to any conclusion, even a conditional one, and the big facts are held, as far as we can tell at this point, by Robert Parker, somebody actually unrestrained by facts. When we can question him furher, and whether he will tell us anything of actual worth when we do, that will be the time to start making our preliminary hypothesis, not before.*"

"*Yes Watson, you are indeed correct on that point.*" agreed Holmes, "*We have four missing Frenchmen, four dead and dismembered bodies, one of which bears a French military tattoo, land hereabouts being sought by the Army, a gathering of pilgrims and tourists, and suggestions of resurrected Druidic practices at Stonehenge, and don't forget the blood on the Slaughter Stone. We also have a somewhat suspect cabbie who knows the region well and has auxiliary transport in the form of wagons able to transport bodies, an innkeeper of unknown intentions, an aged Professor steeped in the ancient ways of the land, and an Inspector of Police who has found himself a little out of his depth; and now we have Mycroft's gnome and his French friend. Parker seems keen to help out, for a price; that price being, I suspect, exclusive access to the details of the case at its conclusion; that is at least an honest desire for something of value, at least to him, despite his tendency to exaggeration to keep the Public's morbid interest. There are other matters which may have a bearing on recent events but I am sworn to absolute secrecy on them, and I believe our Whitehall gnome and his Continental companion are here partly to see that my lips let nothing slip."*

"Right, then." stated Watson, *"It's decided. We seek out Parker before making any more decisions about who did what and who might have seen whom and where anyone was when all this was going on. I admit that I'm getting ready to chop off someone's head, I'm so confused. He's probably at his digs at this moment, in the bar and listening to all of the stories the locals are distorting. We could be there in twenty minutes if we move along."*

That said, and with approving nods from Holmes and Lestrade, the trio left Cooper's Inn and proceeded at pace and on foot to find Parker and divest him of what he knew.

Parker was indeed ensconced in the bar, acting the innocent to draw out more and more information which anyone might be ready to divulge. Numerous pints of ales and drams of spirit had the tendency to loosen the most reticent Wiltshire tongue and the listener had only to prime his source a little to receive a great bounty, mostly an extended barrage of exaggerated rubbish but sometimes a snippet of revealed, previously obscured truth. Many were the contradictions but someone such as Parker could filter these out to find a glimmer of factual information, something which might support other glimmering items of gossip, something around which to build a story. He was truly, as Holmes had rightly observed, a detective whose skills might well compliment those of himself and his companions. If he could be brought on-side, the tally of detectives would then count five – Holmes, Watson, Lestrade, Fleming and Parker.

Holmes went on in but did not directly approach Parker; rather, he stood off at some distance and tried to catch the journalist's eye. This done, Parker gave the Great Sleuth a knowing nod and started to draw away from the garrulous gathering with the promise to return and continue their argumentative discussions.

"Too noisy in here. Let's be off to somewhere quieter." suggested the journalist, *"There's a small storeroom out back and the innkeeper will be too busy plying drinks to notice us. It has a lamp and if we're quiet we should remain uninterrupted."*

The four men retreated to the storeroom and Holmes introduced Inspector Lestrade to the journalist saying, *"Inspector Lestrade, I'd like you to meet Robert Parker, sometimes special journalist to The Times and to other worthy newspapers; Parker, this is Inspector Lestrade of Scotland Yard and you'll not meet a finer nor a fairer policeman than he."*

The two men greeted each other cordially, Parker saying, *"Your name is well known to all journalists, Inspector; it is good to meet you face to face."* while Lestrade responded with, *"Sherlock Holmes tells me you are as much a detective as any who bear the title; a greater compliment I could not envisage."*

Sitting on an assortment of boxes and barrels, the four men settled in. Inspector Lestrade spoke first, saying, *"Parker, Holmes here has explained to me that you are willing to temper your urge to report all that you see and hear in return for some significant consideration information-wise when the case is solved. I have no problem with such an arrangement but it is possible that I may be over-ruled by higher authorities. You don't seem a fool so you'd know how things work in official circles but you do have my word that I will do all that I am able when the time comes."*

"Inspector Lestrade's word is rock-solid." commented Watson, *"There are things, however, that Holmes is not permitted to disclose, not even to me or Lestrade; matters of the highest significance. Holmes, tell Mr Parker here what you can about those matters we've discussed."*

Holmes laid such information as he might about missing Frenchmen and tattoos on body parts and of a Colonel who may well be one of the victims. He also explained about old Druids and new Druids and their rumoured but wholly unconfirmed practices of human sacrifice and of the blood which he found on the Slaughter Stone. He mentioned nothing about possible pending military ties between France and Britain; it would be breaking his word to do so and it would be tantamount to treason in his brother's eyes.

"And the land requirements for the Army?" queried an expectant Parker.

"An open secret; even Lestrade has picked up on that." the Great Sleuth replied, laughing.

"But it is the matter of land issues that we wish to discuss with you." continued Holmes, *"What are you able to divulge and how much credence can we place in it."*

"My land owners of interest had been down to four when we spoke last; Billings, Barraclough, Fernmount and Franklin."

admitted Parker, "*Since that time I have been able to strike the first and last mentioned from my list. The two remaining names are from families long in the district and belong to two men fervently against canon fire disturbing their fox hunts or sleep. I'm told it's extremely dangerous to stray onto their lands unless one is partial to buckshot in one's rear, or worse.*"

"*No favourite at this time?*" asked Lestrade.

"*Not as yet, but I've yet to question a disgruntled yardman recently sacked by one of the pair.*" was Parker's honest reply, "*Things might gel quickly after that. I will let you know when I know.*"

Watson tapped Holmes on the arm and stated emphatically, "*Holmes, we ought to be off now if we're to be back at Cooper's Inn at nine.*"

"*Ah. Your nine o'clock meeting with the good Inspector Fleming.*" said a grinning Parker to an astounded Sherlock Holmes, "*That cabbie Jenkins has big ears and an even bigger mouth if offered the right incentive. Just be careful what you say in front of him, and especially in earshot of young Billy Cooper, particularly about Mr Lester here.*"

The Contact

Parker rose, eager to get back to the noisy patrons in the main bar. Holmes, Watson and Lestrade made their way outside after thanking the journalist for his information.

"Should we risk a cab or should we walk?" asked Lestrade, *"We do have time if we don't dawdle along."*

"Let's walk." said Holmes, *"I fancy that the only cab about will be that of Jenkins and it seems we've told him too much already. That young Billy Cooper is as bad, or worse. Perhaps we can use their proclivities to good effect, planting an idea and seeing how and where and from whom it turns up."*

"As long as it doesn't come back to bite us." warned Lestrade, *"But a few innocent statements would be safe enough, just to determine who might be talking and who might be listening. Obviously young Billy talks to Parker but, then, it seems that everyone talks to him; he's that sort of fellow. He's obviously hungry for facts – a good detective, as you say Holmes, in his own way, but he doesn't have to prepare a case to face a court of Law with its rules of evidence. Nor do you for that matter."*

The three men walked on at a brisk pace and, with no prying eyes and ears nearby, each felt able to speak his mind.

Lestrade felt the need to reiterate his official position, *"I don't mind admitting that I feel a little less than comfortable speaking of Fleming in terms of suspicion, even at such a low level. He is my colleague and I'm actually here to support him."*

"No need to feel any sense of guilt." said Holmes, *"Up until a few days ago, the man was unknown to us all and, given what I know but can't tell you, the three of us ought to place implicit*

trust in none but ourselves. The pressing matter for now is that of approaching the land-holders mentioned by Parker. Do we dare risk compromising his investigations or do we trust him enough to leave such matters in his hands? After all, he has been sniffing around for clues longer, and more effectively, it seems, than anyone, including Fleming."

"I was a little surprised," continued Lestrade, *"that Fleming suggested I go to Cooper's Inn at our first meeting this afternoon. I had expected to go over the case in as much detail as possible, policeman to policeman in the confines of the Police Station, not within the walls of some inn with, dare I say it, two unofficial persons present, despite the implicit trust which I hold for them. It is not good practice and certainly not the way I would do things, nor should I expect that any of my colleagues would as well. Our meeting should have been a formal affair, not a casual chit chat over drinks."*

"He was not expecting you." Watson broke in defensively, *"Perhaps he had made other arrangements which he did not wish to bring up in front of Holmes and I."*

"Perhaps." agreed Lestrade, *"But the man did know that I'd be arriving, just not the exact time. I'm not trying to make too much of a trifle but, if you'd read all those stories you write about him, you'd know that Holmes thrives on such trifles and he's come specifically, though unofficially as far as the Police Service is concerned, to help out. What Mycroft has him doing, we don't know."*

After Lestrade's response, neither man felt it proper to continue but thought it best to await Fleming's arrival at Cooper's Inn. Nine o'clock was approaching, as was the trio to Cooper's Inn, and Fleming would be able to tell them, optimistically, what they wanted to know and put their minds at rest as to his trustworthiness. There were many questions

Lestrade wanted to put to his official colleague, many gaps in the record of the sequence of events and persons involved which needed filling. Everyone would need to be reinterviewed, reinterrogated if necessary, and the investigation would have to be put on a more professional footing. The feelings of Fleming were of secondary importance as each of the trio knew that something of great national importance was happening, but only one of their number, Sherlock Holmes, knew exactly what that was.

"Here we are at last." declared Holmes as the trio approached the main door of Cooper's Inn, *"I suggest we say nothing of Mycroft's two men to Fleming – it may lead to questions we don't want asked, let alone answered."*

"They may continue to seem what they want to appear, just a couple of commercial travellers going about their business." responded Watson in agreement, *"They are here to watch us, not to solve a murder, so we believe."*

"Quite so!" said Holmes as he pushed open the Inn's main door, *"Now, Gentlemen, after you."*

In went Lestrade and Watson followed by Holmes, all expecting that Fleming might have arrived but, the man being a stickler for punctuality, would wait till the clock struck the appointed hour.

Holmes made his way to the Cooper's Inn main bar where its regulars had collected for their nightly carousing, an occasionally rowdy though mostly quite tame occurrence which acted to help the patrons shake off the cares and stresses of the working day. Catching Cooper's attention, he was able to communicate his need for refreshments in the commercial room, a space now clear of curious eyes and ears and in which four men would soon meet to discuss the official position of the Ley Line Murders case. Apart from holding an assortment of quite vocal patrons, the main bar also held the two characters Holmes had identified as 'Mycroft's men' and who were now sitting in a corner in close conversation with another who looked quite out of place being, Holmes thought, a little overdressed for the collection of casually dressed revellers milling around him.

The curious trio did not appear to have noticed Holmes, their discussions being quite intense at the time, and the sleuth was hopeful of their remaining oblivious to the forthcoming meeting. Holmes would have to enquire, however, of who and what the man might be, a colleague of Mycroft's two or a contact being interviewed or even interrogated. When Cooper brought in their refreshments, he would ask if the innkeeper had any knowledge of the fellow who seemed just a little out of place.

Holmes, Watson and Lestrade made their ways to the commercial room and sat, silently awaiting their official visitor as well as Cooper, the innkeeper, bearing food and beverages for four. On Cooper's arrival, just before nine, Holmes made a seemingly casual enquiry.

"Mr Cooper, there is a well-dressed gentleman sitting with two other guests, commercial travellers as you described them - they were busy at their records in this very room earlier. Their companion, the well-dressed one has a very familiar face to which I cannot put a name or place. Would you know his name, if that would not be too much of an intrusion into the man's privacy?"

"No, Mr Holmes," was the innkeeper's reply, *"He joined the other two men, guests of this inn as you have observed, half an hour ago and I served him and his two companions whiskeys. One of the men is definitely a native but the other*

two were speaking French if I'm not mistaken. At least it sounded like French to me. We have been getting quite a few visitors from across the Channel lately ... you know, to see the stones up at Stonehenge and at Avebury. I'm afraid my attempts at the Parleyvoo are not what you'd call good but the French voice is distinctive."

"Quite so." agreed Holmes, *"But I cannot say that I know the man, being French. I'm sure I would have remembered if the man I had met was a Frenchman. But, thank you, all the same."*

"My pleasure, Mr Holmes." responded Cooper as he turned to move away, *"I'll be looking in on you later to see how you're faring victual-wise."*

Closing the commercial room's door behind him, Cooper quietly returned to the main bar and its thirsty patrons. He could see the three men huddled in intense conversation and, picking up a cleaning cloth and tray, walked in their general direction, picking up empty glasses and wiping down tables until he was beside them.

"May I clear those glasses, Gentlemen, and wipe that table for you?" he asked, *"And can I get you anything more? Whiskey's each, perhaps?"*

The two Frenchmen looked up and the Englishman, looking at his two companions and then he, too, up to the innkeeper, replied, *"Well, yes ... thank you ... and three more whiskeys would be welcome. Thank you."*

Cooper returned to his bar and poured out three measures of whiskey which he promptly served to the huddled trio. Without any delay, he continued attending to other seated customers and, after several minutes, left the main bar-room and entered his office where he took pencil to paper – he had something of interest for Sherlock Holmes. Picking up his ever-present tray and cleaning cloth, he went directly to the commercial room, knocked, heard the response to enter and opened the door. Within were the trio he had left minutes before and one more. Inspector Fleming had joined them on the dot of nine. All four men looked up to see why the innkeeper had disturbed a private conversation between guests.

"*Gentlemen, forgive this intrusion,*" said Cooper, offering Holmes a folded note, "*but I have something for Mr Holmes.*"

Holmes took the note from Cooper's extended hand and nodded knowingly at the innkeeper who turned and exited quietly. Opening the note, he read its contents with interest. "*Mr Holmes,*" it stated, "*Your French 'suspect' was addressed as Barrallier by the Englishman. Couldn't make much sense of anything else, they were all speaking French.*"

"*Well,*" said Holmes to his companions, "*Some news, of sorts. I don't know if this doesn't muddy the waters more than it clears them. At least it's a fact worthy of following up. I must reappraise my thoughts about Cooper somewhat. We should continue our discussion, though, before I confuse the matter further; the contents of Cooper's note can wait till later.*"

Inspector Fleming had come into the room minutes earlier and had just settled into a brief appraisal of the state of official investigations to that point. He had begun going over matters which constituted old ground to Holmes and Watson but of which many were new, in part, to Lestrade. Fleming now continued with the evidential facts of the bodies and with those he had been able to ascertain from his enquiries.

Lestrade interrupted at this point, saying, *"Pardon the interruption, Fleming, but you didn't say just who it was that discovered all those body parts up near Stonehenge."*

"Oh, of course. Did I not say.?" responded the Salisbury Inspector, *"That was remiss of me. It was that cab driver, Jenkins – Holmes and Watson know all about him."*

Holmes glared at Watson who did likewise in return. This fact had been withheld from them in their discussions with Fleming and, though they too were remiss in not asking such an obvious question, the local detective's omission of this fact now served to intensify any simmering suspicion the pair held of the man.

"Indeed we do." was Holmes' response, *"And yet we do not know the full character of the man. He seems to have knowledge beyond what one might expect of a cabbie, even one who takes tourist abroad to the Salisbury Plain monuments for a fee. Perhaps, though, that is merely a consequence of his show-business approach to archaeology and the man is simply making a living as best he may."*

"Undoubtedly." agreed Fleming, who then continued with his report.

The Inspector went on with details of the body parts, where they were found and how they were arranged and how one of the arms displayed a tattoo featuring the French Tricolour, crossed sabres and the word 'Revanche' suggesting its owner had been in the French military. Beyond those basic and early facts, Fleming had little to offer. His investigations had involved questioning every establishment offering accommodation in the district but, beyond a few French archaeological and religious types who had all been accounted for, had little to show. Fleming had not dug very deeply into

162

local political dealings and business concerns which might have had some French involvement, nor had he paid much attention to the congregating Druids, the French visitors mostly staying with their local co-adherents. Considering the reports of ancient Druidic ritual human sacrifice in the more lurid newspaper reports, Holmes, Watson and Lestrade were surprised that this line of inquiry had been left largely ignored.

The meeting wound up in less than forty minutes, the London investigators being left no better informed and less than impressed, and Fleming made his excuses and left.

Lestrade, quite unimpressed, commented, *"Well, it's no wonder nobody has been arrested. The man isn't looking anywhere near hard enough. I'm loathe to criticise a brother officer, but the man is not doing his job. Simply collecting obvious facts is not enough; he ought to be out looking under all of those stones out there for what they may be hiding."*

"By the way," he added, *"what did that note of Cooper's say?"*

"Cooper seems a better detective than Fleming could ever hope to be." Holmes replied, *"He has told us that the third man out in the bar is a Frenchman called Barrallier."*

EMBATTLED FIELDS

The Innkeeper

Holmes, Watson and Lestrade sat around the large table in the Cooper's Inn commercial room hardly able to believe the apparent disinterest shown by Inspector Fleming. He had seemed so enthusiastic about the prospect of help from the famous consulting detective team of Holmes and Watson and the subsequent arrival of Scotland Yard's Inspector Lestrade but now seemed hesitant to proceed further than he already had. After the initial surprise had subsided, the three men were forced to re-evaluate the situation.

"So," Holmes mused, *"Cooper now ascends to the 'probably trustworthy' list while Fleming holds his current classification but only because of his being disinterested and ineffectual, or so it seems."*

"I could barely believe I was listening to the same man." continued Holmes, *"Fleming had seemed completely overwhelmed but, at the same time, expressly determined. If something or someone intervened to cause such a reversal, I would like to know."*

"As would I." added Lestrade, *"He is not the man I expected from reports of that Glastonbury business two years back. He had gathered information none had suspected existed and, though I was set to travel, the case was solved with no help from me. His move to Salisbury was a promotion largely due to his efforts at that time. No, there is something else behind this and the man may have more need of our help than he dares to ask."*

"*Do you mean he may have been threatened?*" asked Watson, "*He may be subject to a threat so horrific that he dare not share the details with us. Perhaps it concerns his family, if he has one.*"

"*It's the only explanation that makes sense.*" commented Lestrade, "*That the man could have become corrupted or is cowering away from danger to himself is something I just cannot countenance.*"

"*We appear to be up to our necks in a soup getting thicker by the minute.*" said Holmes.

"*And deeper.*" added Watson, "*And soon we'll be drowning as we find ourselves out of our depths. Holmes, we promised to help the man with his enquiries so shouldn't we help him out with this matter, whatever this matter happens to be. If he's not to be found at the Police Station, do we know where he lives?*"

"*We will need to seek him out at his place of work,*" suggested Lestrade, "*but if he does have a family and it is being threatened, we shall need a plan to remove its members to safety. But where can we be certain of such safety?*"

"*What about Professor Tilbury?*" suggested Watson, "*The lady did offer us shelter should we need it. Perhaps she might extend that offer to a family in some danger; it would be worth putting such a question to her.*"

"*Indeed it might.*" agreed Holmes, "*Though we will need transport to get there and Jenkins would smell a rat if we engaged someone else.*"

"Can't we just go there as part of our general investigations?" asked Watson, *"That way we can make our visit and keep a close eye on our suspicious cabbie."*

"That does make sense." added Lestrade, *"I can approach Fleming as a brother officer offering help while you go off and see this Professor, though we don't actually know the nature of Fleming's dilemmas."*

"Well, that's settled; that's a plan." continued the Scotland Yard man, *"Now off to our beds; my eyelids are fast succumbing to the force of gravity and the effects of whiskey. We've a big and possibly dangerous day ahead of us and we need to have all our wits about us."*

That said, the three men stood and started for the door, then for the stairs which would take each to his room and his rest. None wanted to say more on the subject at that point but Lestrade was worried that Fleming may have already compromised both himself and the investigation. He knew that there was more to this case than simple murder and mutilation, there were suggestions of conspiracy and espionage if not downright interference in and sabotage of vital matters of national significance of which Holmes was aware but, acting on his brother Mycroft's official directive, could not tell.

Despite his concerns, Lestrade found sleep rather quickly, as did Watson, but Holmes decided that it was worth a pipeful of tobacco to go over what he knew and what he needed to find out. He made his way to the main bar-room, now being emptied of its patrons as the innkeeper called 'time' and those delaying the inevitable reluctantly downed their 'last drinks' and rose slowly to make for the door and the darkening night beyond. There were the usual grizzles and Cooper had, as was usual, to encourage the most reluctant of his customers to their feet and to the door; the intriguing threesome, however, was nowhere to be seen.

"*Have I time for a pipe?*" asked Holmes of his host busily ejecting two grumbling regulars.

"*Yes, indeed.*" replied Cooper, "*You are a guest and the rules are different, though I would ask that you adjourn to the saloon room where I'll join you, if you can stand my company.*"

"*You would be a most welcome companion.*" declared Holmes, hopeful of getting a little more information on the man called Barrallier and with whom Mycroft's two inept spies, if such they were, had been so engrossed. Holmes also wanted to size the innkeeper up, generally. Was he involved in more than providing accommodation and refreshments for the traveller? Was he a general gossip like Jenkins or did he draw a line at discussing his guests' business with others except, as Holmes had experienced that very evening, when matters were of an earnestly important nature. Was he, though it went against all Holmes' instincts, involved in the murders or perhaps just in some sort of cover-up? Was his son Billy primed to gather information for his father or was the boy merely an over-curious imp, a nuisance eager to earn a few pence for bits of other people's business?

Many questions were circulating in the mind of the Great Sleuth but few, if any, answers worthy of application came his way. He had gathered a few facts but these were not accompanied by a clear context for them to be called knowledge, but things were picking up as vague and indistinct pictures were beginning to form. He would speak with Cooper about the mood of the people of the district since the murders became known and how the news had spread and drawn in all manner of people from all over Britain and even a few from beyond her shores.

That there were Frenchmen involved was obvious to Holmes, and no doubt to others, but he could not disclose any of the more politically sensitive reasons for the presence of some, not even to Lestrade and Watson, and certainly not to Cooper just to get him to come forth with what he might know. No, Cooper was a suspect, though not one of great significance in the eyes of Holmes, not since he came forth with the name of Barrallier, though this may well have been by way of a bait laid in a trap set by those involved in the murders, or a diversion to keep Holmes off the main scent.

Holmes had settled into the saloon room, primed and lit his pipe and was busy puffing his way to a relaxed state when Cooper came in to join his celebrated guest in what the ancients might have seen as a communal tobacco consuming ceremony, as indeed it had become and remained in the modern nineteenth century. Such an activity allowed all parties to find that particular harmonious state in which they could speak without the need for the other to directly respond, just to speak generally about whatever subject was on each mind. Minds often found they could meet and exchange, not so much the information each held, but a sense of the importance each placed on that information. Tobacco had become the medium to the soul of the consumer, despite often slowly destroying the consumer in the process. Watson, himself the possessor of a well-utilised pipe, had often warned Holmes about his overindulgent dependencies and their harmful consequences.

Cooper sat opposite Holmes in a comfortable cushioned chair and repeated the actions of his guest, now puffing away and ready to receive whatever his host may have to give. The innkeeper ignited his tobacco, drew its magic into himself and joined the detective in that state of semi-stupor each sought and by which they might communicate.

"*Interesting, those two commercial traveller fellows.*" started Holmes.

"*Commercial travellers, my Aunt Sally!*" retorted Cooper, "*I took them as government men, both of them; I could tell they weren't what they claimed a mile off. One gets to know the type in my line of business, though I couldn't tell just what their game was, one being French and all, just like that third fellow. It might have something to do with the murders – you know, that French tattoo on one of the chopped-off arms. Perhaps that arm belonged to one of their own out spying on something. Who knows? Who can trust the French?*"

"*Who indeed?*" stated Holmes in mock agreement, "*But one Englishman did seem intensely engaged with two of them this very evening.*"

"*Yes. Barrallier they called him.*" replied the innkeeper, "*He waltzed into the main bar this evening and made straight for the others. They called for a whiskey each and got into some sort of intense conversation, mostly in French, at least the bits that I overheard.*"

"*I overhear a lot, you know, in my line of work,*" he continued, "*though I don't normally tell the business of my patrons and guests to others. But, with you being here, and the Doctor and the two Inspectors, and the two dubious commercial travellers with their mysterious French friend, and it all adds up to something sinister; well it does in my book. I don't normally tell tales out of school, Mr Holmes, but it would be an unconscionable fool of a schoolmaster who wouldn't shout 'fire' if he saw smoke billowing forth from his schoolroom.*"

"*Indeed it would, Cooper.*" agreed Holmes enthusiastically, "*And you don't strike me as the foolish type.*"

"*Such don't last long in this business, I can tell you.*" responded the innkeeper, "*There's many an innkeeper who's trusted his patrons and suppliers too far and lived to regret it in the poorhouse. It's money up front from my drinking patrons and money on delivery to the breweries; it can't be done any other way. I extend a facility for those seeking accommodation but it's always at my discretion, and I've never been let down yet.*"

"*Take those two fellows posing as commercial travellers.*" he continued, "*As I said, I spotted them as phoneys the minute they walked through the front door. There's a type as does the rounds of the business houses, you see, and that type wasn't theirs. They had the look of government men but were not here to check out licences and such, they were here on other business. What that might be, I couldn't and can't say, and they didn't say much either, just seemed to know their way about and want rooms for two. The Frenchman said nothing at all – don't even know if he speaks English though the Englishman spoke French, at least enough for him and his friend to get by together, and the other man from this night, that Barrallier.*"

"*Yes.*" broke in Holmes, "*That Barrallier! I admit that he does intrigue me. Two secretive Frenchmen and an enigmatic Englishman; it must add up to something, though perhaps to nothing and we're seeing trouble where none exists.*"

"*Mr Holmes.*" said Cooper through a knowing grin, "*I have a nose for trouble, an innkeeper has to have one, and you are a detective whose reputation says 'bloodhound'. Our two noses smell something and it's not the scent of freshly picked roses,*" it's the smell of death, violent death, and those three men simply reek of it."

"The first two paid for two nights' accommodation each in advance," he continued, "all without being asked and all in crisp new notes, so crisp and new that I had to have a good look at them in case they weren't real. I don't really know if they were government types but that's how they first struck me; now they seem like something else, something I don't want in my inn, something very nasty indeed. The other man; well he must have other accommodation nearby."

"I must admit to holding similar concerns." conceded Holmes, "But can we keep this to ourselves until I am able to check a few things out? My colleagues should not be alerted lest they alter their behaviour in the presence of these men. They, too, suspect something but suspicion is no reason to give ourselves and our suspicions away."

"That's agreed." said Cooper, "If I do hear or see anything more, I'll mention it to you, and you alone."

"Excellent." commented Holmes, taking yet another deep draught of his pipe and relaxing further back into his chair before declaring to the innkeeper that the day had taken more out of him that he had suspected and that it was now time for him to retire to his bed.

The Game

Holmes took to his bed and managed to fall asleep using all of the discipline his great and active mind could muster. After more sleep that he usually allowed himself, he rose early and wrote out a message for his brother Mycroft seeking knowledge of two men, one English and one French, who might be in his service and operating as commercial travellers in Salisbury. He would send a coded telegram to his brother which would inform him of the letter's despatch to a post office box across the Thames from Whitehall and addressed to a Mr Simmons. This name would alert Mycroft to a potentially serious situation which needed his immediate attention and a response without delay. He would also add the name Barrallier in a postscript followed by 'also French' and a question mark. He then walked to the post office and mailed his letter and noted that the nearby telegraph office was not yet open for business.

Watson had woken as well but Lestrade could still be heard snoring away, enjoying his slumber as no one else within earshot of him could. Holmes returned to Cooper's Inn looking forward to his breakfast, something unusual for someone who so often went without, and found Watson up and dressed and reading the newspaper.

"*Holmes,*" said the Doctor, "*I thought you'd gone off sleuthing without saying goodbye. I declare you've the energy of a dozen horses.*"

"*No, I've not abandoned you.*" Holmes replied, "*I've just been sending off a few urgent letters about the pressing matters of which we've been speaking. I will have to be off to the telegraph office directly it opens to despatch more messages. Now, I hear that Lestrade's snoring has ceased and we should soon hear his croaky voice seeking out us both and calling for* breakfast. *I'll send that Billy off after Jenkins and ask if he could pick us up at ten o'clock for a trip out to Netherfields and Professor Tilbury. Lestrade can then be off after Fleming to discover just what's troubling the man.*"

"*Should we not be off earlier?*" asked Watson, keen to be on the hunt.

Holmes looked about for any prying eyes or ears and replied, "*Ordinarily I'd be off at this moment but we do not want to alert anyone that we are about urgent business. Any appearance of urgency might send up a flag and send our quarry off into hiding. No, we'll enjoy a good breakfast and take out time over it; I'm sure that would meet with your oft-quoted dietary approval.*"

"*Yes, indeed.*" was the Doctor's eager reply, "*But I think I hear Lestrade's oversized Police boots galloping down the stairs. Time to eat, Holmes, time to eat.*"

And, eat, the men did, till each was full. Cooper was also about but had many tasks to attend to before he opened for business and did not seek out his special guests. Holmes checked his watch and said it was time he was off to the telegraph office. Watson would await his return by which time Jenkins would have arrived to transport them both to see Professor Tilbury. Lestrade would be off on some pretext and seek out his beleaguered colleague at the Police Station; later the three men, possibly in the company of Fleming, would meet to discuss possibilities and plan the way ahead to alleviate Fleming's concerns.

Sherlock Holmes went straight to the telegraph office and sent his cryptic note to his brother. He knew that the letter he had posted earlier would go to London by the first train and be in the post office by three o'clock at which time one of Mycroft's assistants, alerted by the telegram, would collect it and then place it in Mycroft's hands. He knew that his brother, on seeing both telegram and note, would respond immediately in some way and then follow this up with further suggestions or instructions. It was imperative that Mycroft should do this as his younger brother could not proceed without the risk of alerting parties now oblivious to the detectives' motives or in the process of planning more atrocities.

Holmes arrived back at Cooper's Inn just as Jenkins cab came into view along the Amesbury Road, the sleuth being grateful that the inquisitive and suspicious cabbie had not observed his movements, unremarkable and mundane as these would have seemed to anybody watching such an auspicious visitor maintaining his communications with London. Lestrade had left fifteen minutes earlier on foot and would make way to the Police Station, and his troubled colleague Fleming, after wending his way through the unfamiliar town centre.

Calling out for Watson, Holmes hailed the cabbie as his cab trotted its way into the inn's grounds, indicating to the seated Jenkins that the Doctor would be with them directly. With Watson's appearance, both men climbed on board and informed Jenkins that they should be on their way to Professor Tilbury's at Netherfields but that there was no need to hurry, they would enjoy their journey. Jenkins could make the trip in forty-five minutes but would not suggest going faster – his clients had paid in advance and had paid well and a gentle trot was much better for his horse.

Watson looked out at the countryside he had only recently traversed but saw it in a different light, figuratively and factually. He could now visualise teams of men and probably a great many women and older children straining to drag one of the great stones into place knowing that the gods would be pleased with their actions; he could also observe that storm clouds were gathering to the north, filtering the sun's rays and giving the whole region an attractive but spookily ethereal appearance. Holmes could see all of this but his mind filtered such unnecessary input as it went over the possibilities as currently perceived and how much of a risk placing trust, albeit very low, in the Professor might present.

The two men were arriving unannounced and hoped that the Professor would not object once she had heard of Fleming's situation. If they could obtain even temporary shelter for Fleming's family, if indeed he had one, it would go a long way to getting Fleming back into the fight. After almost an hour's easy trot, the cabbie's horse slowed considerably as one on several rivulet causeway crossings was approached. The roof of Professor Tilbury's house could be seen in the distance but the journey would take as long as it would and Jenkins chose not to press for greater effort and speed as his clients seemed keen to enjoy the ride.

Netherfields was located some two miles beyond a small village and the Professor's house was one of the area's more significant dwellings, though its extended gardens bordering onto broad fields did seem to make it detached from any population centre, small or large. From the house, as the cabbie and his fares made way along its short driveway, the form of Julia, the Professor's maid, could be seen scurrying outward and adjusting her bonnet to greet the unexpected visitors. On seeing the faces of Holmes and Watson, she gave a broad smile and a brief curtsy to two visitors she knew would brighten up her mistress's day.

"*Good morning and welcome, Gentlemen.*" she said enthusiastically, almost giving the visitors a small laugh of appreciation, *"We had not been expecting, you though Professor Tilbury said you might call in at any time."*

"We hope we are not intruding on the good Professor's time," replied Holmes, trying hard not to seem too eager for an interview with the learned lady in front of Jenkins, *"and trust that she is feeling well enough for a brief visit."*

"Well, you know her day," Julia explained, *"a nap before too long and then lunch. But she will be down directly to greet you both and Mr Jenkins' horse will be grateful for the grass and water in the near meadow, I'm sure, and the shade of a broad tree. That storm brewing to the north will come to nothing, you'll see; we call them Wiltshire Bullyboys, always threatening at this time of year but they usually back down at the last minute."*

"Come in, come in." she continued, *"You shall have refreshments with the Professor as you discuss what you will; I shall send a brew out to Mr Jenkins."*

Holmes and Watson entered into the darkened interior of the house and, as their eyes adjusted to the reduced light of the hallway, they saw the Professor stepping toward them. *"A surprise, Gentlemen, and very pleasant it is. I wondered who might be calling when I heard the hooves clip-clopping along the drive but could not quite make out the faces with these old eyes of mine. The voices were a different matter; I knew I was in for good company and conversation when I heard them, though I'm equally certain that your errand is an urgent one."*

"Indeed it is," replied Holmes, *"and a somewhat presumptive one as well, I'm afraid. May we speak freely and in earnest with you about a possibly dangerous matter?"*

"*Ahah!*" was the Professor's eager response, "*As the good Doctor here might say in his stories, 'the game is afoot', and I'm to be in it. Good! I was wondering when things would heat up around here and those murderers would know what it was to be caught and chained up like the dogs they are. Tell me what it is that you wish of me and see if I don't say 'yes'. Now, come along with me to my study; we can speak freely in there.*"

The two men followed the Professor into her study and each took the same chair as in their previous visit. The Professor made her way behind her uncle's old desk and sat just as Julia, the maid, entered with a tray containing teapot, cups, saucers, milk, sugar, lemon slices and sundry biscuits and small cakes. Watson looked on, eagerly approving of the treats presented, while Holmes seemed almost oblivious to all but his mission.

Their teas poured and treats selected, the two men sat back to await the Professor's invitation to speak. A good long sip and she was ready.

"*Well, Gentlemen.*" she started, "*Now you can tell me of your troubles and how I can help alleviate them. The look on Mr Holmes' face tells me he is somewhat hesitant to ask the favour he needs.*"

"*That is one for the books, Professor.*" commented Watson with an involuntary grin and looking toward his friend, "*Someone out-deducing the great Sherlock Holmes. Come, my friend, tell the good Professor all. To ask a favour requires that we trust her confidence.*"

"*Indeed, Watson.*" was his reply, "*Now, Professor Tilbury, we find that Inspector Fleming seems greatly distracted somehow. He has suddenly lost that zeal he exhibited on our first visit and subsequent meetings and we fear that he has been intimidated in some manner. Now, we don't even know*" *if he has a family but, if he does and threats against its members are the source of the change in his enthusiasm, we would like to remove those members to a place of safety, somewhere close but out of Salisbury."*

"You mean somewhere like here." broke in the Professor, *"When can they come? I will have rooms readied for them and we are well supplied with victuals. Do you know how many there would be?"*

"There lies the second part of the problem." admitted Holmes, *"We don't know how many, if any. Nor do we know that the Inspector has such a problem; it's simply the only thing which makes any sense. Lestrade if off at present trying to find out just what is troubling the man and we have come hoping to make arrangements contingent on what he finds."*

"All will be ready for the time such arrangements are needed." said the Professor, *"But don't tell Jenkins if you want your secret kept."*

"Certainly not." agreed Holmes, *"We plan to keep the man close but not too close. It was he who discovered the bodies and he may well have more things to tell us on which he is currently keeping mute. We need him in sight at all times, if possible."*

The two men declined the Professor's invitation to lunch, explaining that it was imperative they get back to confer with Lestrade, and possibly Fleming, as soon as possible. They finished their teas and made their excuses as they rose from their chairs, thanking their host for being so generous and understanding under such potentially pressing circumstances.

"Wait, Gentlemen." she exclaimed, stopping each man's retreat, and taking two small books from her desk drawer, then

making an inscription in each. *"Take these with you and keep the memory of a great man alive."*

Taken by surprise, each accepted a copy of 'Ancient Ways' which they opened, reading what seemed a dedication. Watson's inscription read, *'Dr Watson, please accept this from one enquiring mind to another. Margaret Tilbury.'* while that of Holmes brought a grin to his countenance; it read, *'To Sherlock Holmes. Now the game is truly afoot. Margaret Tilbury.'*

The Threat

The pair thanked the Professor and then made way towards Jenkins' cab. Jenkins was snoozing away, as was his horse, it seems, but both responded quickly as they heard their fares approaching.

"*All finished, Gents?*" asked the cabbie.

"*Yes.*" replied Holmes, "*The Professor has made us each a little dedication of a most welcome gift. Time, now, to go back to the inn but there's no great hurry; Watson is a man who loves scenery and this is a place well-blessed with that commodity.*"

Jenkins laughed in genuine agreement but was clearly interested to know what the two men had received during their short visit.

"*Could be useful, these books.*" commented Watson as the horse started off, pulling its load toward Salisbury, "*There might be something within to show us the minds of those strange Druid types we hear of in these parts.*"

"*There might, indeed.*" agreed Holmes, "*But I did peruse the book quite thoroughly at the British Museum's library just a few days past, though I admit it does seem an age since we were there. There was little actual detail of the Druids in its pages, as I recall, they being relative late-comers to the land, but the ley lines are described in some detail and that could well be of great help.*"

Holmes raised a forefinger to his closed lips and pointed upward toward Jenkins to tell his friend that it was time to keep mute on the book's subject matter, and that of the case at hand. Midday had just gone and there was still a great deal of daylight in which to continue their investigations. Firstly, though, it would be necessary to make contact with Lestrade and see how things stood with Fleming.

While Holmes could lose himself within his mind, given sufficient intriguing facts which needed sorting out, Watson could draw on the inspiration which the vista of his native land provided in generous profusion to relax his mind. Holmes spent the return to Salisbury looking inward while Watson looked out upon the rolling hills about him, never happier than when a new feature came into view. All too soon, however, the pair's contemplation and daydreaming ceased as Jenkins yelled, "*Cooper's Inn, Gents. We've arrived.*"

The two men climbed down from the cab, each clasping James Fletcher's little volume of 'Ancient Ways' and each looking forward to finding out what Lestrade had uncovered about Fleming's problems and if, indeed, there had been some extreme personal pressure put on the man. This would have to wait, however, until Jenkins was well out of earshot and Lestrade had returned; meanwhile Holmes and Watson could only ponder on the possibility of needing to relocate the Inspector's family without the knowledge of the likes of Jenkins.

"*It was good of Professor Tilbury to open her home to people in need,*" remarked Watson on seeing Jenkins' cab disappear, "*people who might possibly draw danger to her doorstep.*"

"*Yes, it was.*" agreed Holmes, ever so anxious to hear what Lestrade had to say, "*But without data we are groping in the dark and can make no progress or plan toward it. I dare say that our Scotland Yard man will soon return with news of serious intervention in local Police investigations, intervention perhaps brought about by our very own presence and involvement. We must clear our minds to receive whatever he has to provide; I am in the process of doing so and perhaps you could read a bit of Fletcher's 'Ancient Ways' to aquaint yourself of some ancient ways of thinking and living."*

The time was approaching for the midday meal and Cooper was advised of the two men's desire to eat theirs at the inn, with the probable inclusion of Lestrade at possibly the last minute. Watson, taking his friend's advice, repaired to a chair in the saloon bar and began to read about the monuments and pathways and people of truly ancient Britain, subjects beginning to grow on a man whose appreciation of Britain had not previously extended back much farther than the Britannia of Roman times.

A gong sounded the commencement of meals and Watson looked up from his book, stood and proceeded without delay to the dining room. The Doctor had been seated for several minutes before Holmes joined him at the table, both hopeful of seeing Lestrade walk through the door. It was standard fare at Cooper's, fairly plain and typical of the region but tasty and nutritious none-the-less, and each man eagerly ate his fill – the pair's adventure in the Wiltshire countryside, particularly on Salisbury Plain with its ancient monuments, seemed to have increased the appetite of both. Lestrade, however, did not appear, not until the meal was well and truly over and Holmes and Watson had settled into the main bar room for an after dinner drink.

Almost an hour had gone by before the heavy-footed gait of Lestrade could be heard on the inn's well-trodden floorboards, the two sleuths recognising the distinctive and often anticipated sound at the same time and rising simultaneously, each hopeful of positive news. Lestrade did carry the expected message to his two colleagues and told them about a man overwhelmed by worry and not knowing what to do next.

"*It is much as expected,*" said the Scotland Yard Inspector, "*the man has a wife and young daughter and has received suggestions that their mutual safety could be in jeopardy if investigations continue along present lines. The Inspector's wife is rather concerned, as you would expect, but the daughter, an eight year old, is oblivious of the threat.*"

Holmes, worried about the existence of the threat but relieved that some response had been generated by their efforts, advised Lestrade of Professor Tilbury's offer of sanctuary. "*Our visit to the good Professor Tilbury has yielded positive results in that she has offered accommodation and victuals for whom-so-ever we should like to send, especially as this puts her in the hunt, as she puts it.*"

"*Well, that is good news.*" declared Lestrade, "*We should get both mother and daughter moved as soon as possible.*"

"*How can we do this without alerting everyone in town, especially Jenkins?*" asked Watson, "*We don't want him knowing more than he needs to with that mouth of his, and we don't really know that he's not involved in some way in these crimes.*"

"*The Salisbury Police Station does have its own wagon,*" replied Lestrade, "*one unmarked and suitable for transporting its personnel as well as the odd felon. It's cage and canopy come off readily and, though it's none too comfortable, I'm certain Mrs Fleming and young Nancy, that's the daughter, won't object too strenuously to a bumpy ride for a bit of a holiday. It should be available; I don't know of any pressing need which would prevent us from using it. I'll sort it out with*

Fleming this very afternoon. Now, not a word to anyone, anyone at all."

"Quite so, Lestrade." agreed Holmes, *"Now, we have both eaten, but what of you?"*

"Me?" queried Lestrade, *"I'm full; there's a fine tea house across the way from the Police Station and I grabbed a bite there. Very nice too. You and Watson should look in when you have time."*

"Yes, we shall do so." said Holmes, not wanting to tell his colleague of his and Watson's prior looking in on their arrival in Salisbury and risk getting involved in frivolous banter about tea and cakes, *"But, for now, we should be about advising Fleming of our plans and getting his family away to safety. Perhaps if you returned to the Police Station there would be less suspicion raised than if Watson or I did so."*

"First, though," continued Holmes, *"tell us of this threat made against Fleming's family."*

"Well," started Lestrade, *"that threat was more strongly implied than given straight out. Fleming's wife was approached in the High Street by a well-dressed gentleman who told her that her husband was very unwise to risk his family in matters of local unpleasantness. Mrs Fleming told the Inspector that the man spoke very good English but had an accent of some sort, possibly French but she couldn't be sure, so taken aback was she with the man's message. The lady was considerably shaken but when the man made explicit mention of their daughter by name she became quite frightened. He then opened his coat and she saw the hilt of what she took to be a concealed pistol and the threat then became very clear and very real to her."*

Lestrade, giving both of his colleagues a long knowing look, continued, "*She immediately communicated this matter to her husband who went directly to his daughter's school and removed her under some pretext or other. So, we now know the reason for Fleming's recent bouts of reticence.*"

"*Indeed, but was Mrs Fleming able to describe the man,*" asked Holmes, "*beyond his being well dressed and possibly French?*"

"*Not really,*" was Lestrade's reply, "*but I was hoping, seeing that Professor Tilbury is keen to take them in, that you and Watson might accompany mother and daughter on what will seem like a trip to London for any busybody eyes lurking about. You could travel to Wylye by a round-about route by rail then alight and go overland in the Police wagon, perhaps, or by some other appropriate means. On the way, you and Watson, here, might question Mrs Fleming yourselves after she's had time to settle her nerves.*"

"*A quite workable plan, Holmes,*" exclaimed Watson, "*don't you think? We can get Fleming's family to safety and learn a bit about these fiends who would threaten a woman and her child. A policeman or soldier signs up for whatever danger may come his way but only a base coward threatens a defenceless woman, let alone a young child.*"

"*We must meet danger in whatever form it appears.*" countered Holmes, "*These men are not cowards, I would presume, but are totally devoid of any human compassion and will do whatever it takes to achieve their despicable ends. Don't be deceived, My Friend, for we may not dealing with misguided religious devotees but with hardened criminal types or types well used to dealing in death in all its guises.*"

Holmes, here, was thinking of the missing French officer and his attendant troopers who would have seen death in abundance in the recent war between France and German forces headed by Prussia and may well have seen other action in the restive French colonies. Such men had possibly been born to the colours and had known no other life; their existences would likely have been ones of service, obedience, harsh discipline and little expectation other than death and pain and an eventual pensioned retirement for those who survived.

"But a religious type can be driven to a maddening state." argued Watson, *"Remember those ancient Druids and their appalling human sacrifices; mass death by fire is not what I would call misguided, I would call it atrocious and evil. Remember, too, that some of our own countrymen resorted to much the same thing on religious grounds just a few centuries back. Many a chest-pounding prayer-chanting Christian has resorted to such abominations in the name of God and religion and I'm not so sure I would write off these modern Druids so easily – a new devotee to a religion is the worst of all bigots."*

"Indeed." agreed Holmes, supported by Lestrade who had witnessed so many despicable crimes committed by the most unlikely people, *"So we should not only keep open our eyes and ears, but also our minds to all possibilities in this confusing case, a case whose perpetrators are beginning to show their true colours at last."*

This said and a general plan of action agreed, Lestrade started back to the Police Station to advise Fleming of the Professor's offer and of Holmes' and Watson's willingness to accompany Mrs Fleming and daughter, firstly on a ruse by rail, and then overland to Netherfields and safety. The two inspectors would see to Fleming's family arrangements while Holmes and Watson would visibly purchase tickets for London; further arrangements would have to be made for transport from Wylye Station to the Professor's house, details of which could not be allowed to get back to the likes of Jenkins.

The Sanctuary

The group thought it might be a useful ploy to have Jenkins transport Fleming's family to Salisbury Railway Station and then proceed with a sealed message to Professor Tilbury rather than employ the Police wagon in the town. To have left the cabbie out of the proceedings would only have served to raise his suspicions. It was agreed that Holmes, Watson, Mrs Fleming and daughter Nancy would purchase tickets for London but alight at Basingstoke in order to reverse the direction of flight and proceed back through Salisbury and on to Wylye where the Police wagon would be waiting.

With the cabbie otherwise occupied, the Police wagon would be able to make way to its rendezvous without Jenkins' knowledge while Professor Tilbury would be advised of the imminent arrival of the woman and child and of Holmes and Watson, and the wagon's driver. The message to the Professor would not specify the details of the plan nor who would be arriving in case Jenkins was able to open the envelope and reseal it after reading its contents, but there would be no misunderstanding of the need which had arisen.

Watson got busy checking train timetables but found the group would have to wait till the next morning if their plan was to work with minimal waiting time on railway platforms. This was not desirable but, given the hour and the amount of organising which was needed, was the only way the plan would work. It would give the Police wagon more time to reach its first destination, that of Wylye station, after arranging for a trusted driver able to make the journey, given the shortage of Police personnel available. Fleming and Lestrade would have to be advised of the delay and their charges would need to be guarded overnight.

Holmes, meanwhile, had penned a short message advising the Professor that guests would be arriving toward the middle of the next day, not specifying any sense of urgency, and sealed it securely inside an envelope. The plan had called for Jenkins to carry the envelope to the Professor after taking the Flemings to the station, but he would now be called on to deliver it that afternoon and pick up his two passengers the next morning. Together with Watson, Holmes then set off after Lestrade toward the Police Station and Inspector Fleming, catching up with the Scotland Yard man to revise their plan and prepare for the next day's escapade.

Convincing Mrs Fleming to leave Salisbury with her daughter was not a difficult task for Rupert Fleming, it was one made all the easier when she heard that Sherlock Holmes and Dr John Watson would be accompanying her all the way to her place of sanctuary. Arranging for the Police wagon was similarly straightforward but finding an appropriate driver was not. This was a great stumbling block for the plan but a solution was found, after much deliberation, when Lestrade was convinced to drive the wagon himself. He raised a few reasonable objections but finally saw that becoming a wagon driver for a day or so was the only way forward; he had, he was reminded, spent worse days in a wet and freezing London waiting in the shadows of a dingy inner-city lane for a gang of bank robbers to appear.

Billy Cooper was sent scurrying off to find Jenkins and summon him to the inn, there to pick up Holmes' message to the Professor and convey it to her without delay. The cabbie was then instructed that he would be required to take both Holmes and Watson to Salisbury Station on the next morning on the pretext of them travelling to London on urgent business and then returning by the early evening train or possibly some time the next day.

Jenkins responded quickly and was soon trotting off in the direction of Netherfields with the sealed envelope. There was little else the detectives could do that day but go over what they knew for certain to be true and what they suspected, though beyond the threat made to Mrs Fleming by some well-dressed foreign thug who spoke rather good English, they had little new information to go on; they were, however, reassured of Fleming's intention to continue the fight.

The evening proved to be a long one but morning eventually arrived at Cooper's Inn with Jenkins following soon after. Holmes and Watson wanted to arrive at Salisbury Station early and have a somewhat less than adequate breakfast at its small kiosk while Mrs Fleming and Nancy would arrive just before the train's departure time. There was no way to be certain that Jenkins would not observe the arrival of the mother and her child but Holmes had Jenkins off on a small errand back to Cooper's Inn to deliver a note which he pretended to have inadvertently forgotten to leave for Cooper. While Jenkins' ignorance of events was not crucial to the plan, it was certainly desirable given the many questions which surrounded his possible involvement in the atrocities on Salisbury Plain; it was assumed, though, that the ever-inquisitive man would eventually learn of the group's departure with tickets for London and hopefully be content to accept things at face value and not nose around further.

Breakfast for Holmes and Watson was better than they had been led to believe that it would be and, having eaten, the two men sat sipping their teas, watchful and impatient for the arrival of both the train and the carriage bringing their two charges. Right on time, the London train's shrill whistle could be heard alerting its human cargo just as the three Flemings arrived in a private carriage driven by a trusted friend of the family. Holmes and Watson rose from their seats, picked up their valises and proceeded to the platform, there to meet both the incoming train and the somewhat emotional family Fleming.

Steam and smoke were two very reliable constants of platform existence and both came in great profusion as the London train slowly screeched its way into Salisbury Station and came to a jerky halt. Passengers of all sorts alighted and porters rushed to pick up heavy items of luggage and sundry items of freight. Holmes and Watson stood stationary as the Flemings approached with numerous satchels carried by mother and daughter and one heavy portmanteau lugged along by the Salisbury Inspector. With little time for drawn-out formal introductions, Holmes relieved Fleming of his load while Watson fussed about getting hold of the smaller items, as well as his luggage and that of Holmes.

"We'll be inside when you're ready," instructed the Sleuth, *"so say your goodbyes, for the train will remain at Salisbury only for a short time."*

The goodbyes were brief, and somewhat emotional for Mrs Fleming, while the Inspector maintained a stoic countenance for the sake of daughter Nancy who was aware only of the prospect of a short holiday in the countryside and was excited and keen to get going, especially as she was to miss a bit of school. She knew nothing of the fears which her parents held for her safety, and their own.

The doors were shut and the train started its faltering movements before the strain from the locomotive evened itself out along the length of carriages. Holmes and Watson made sure that all was secure in the compartment and then went about with their introductions. The Sleuth stood, faced his charges and stated, *"Mrs Fleming and, of course, Miss Fleming, I am Sherlock Holmes and this gentleman with me is*

Dr John Watson. We are to take you to the home of Professor Tilbury, a lady who has studied all of the ancient monuments in the district, and many beyond, and has a wealth of interesting information to share. Getting there will require a change of train at Basingstoke so that we can reverse our direction and travel to Wylye, not too far beyond Salisbury, where we will be met and taken to Netherfields, the home of the learned Professor who has graciously offered her hospitality."

Watson stood and bowed slightly to his fellow passengers while Mrs Fleming gave her thanks that she and her daughter were being given such attention. She did not wish to make any mention of danger and threats though she was obviously apprehensive. *"Thank you Mr Holmes, and you too Dr Watson. Mr Fleming has told me of the assistance which you have been providing and that there were mysterious happenings in the district that needed urgent attention. I hope that we shall not be intruding too much on Professor Tilbury; a woman with a young child can be a great imposition if their host is elderly and set in her ways."*

"Well," laughed Watson, *"a younger octogenarian you're not likely to meet. Her energy is remarkable and her wit is as sharp as that of any twenty year old. I suspect that it will be you and Miss Fleming here who will tire before she does. As for imposing, it was at her invitation that we are to be her guests and spend whatever time it takes for the situation to resolve itself."*

"Now, Mrs Fleming." continued Watson in a somewhat more serious vein, *"Holmes and I need to ask you a few questions about that gentleman who spoke to you yesterday."*

"Yes," replied Mrs Fleming, *"Rupert said you wanted more information, though I don't know what else I can tell you."*

"Well," prompted Holmes, *"you called him a gentleman. Does that infer that his manner was polished and that he at least attempted to sound polite, at least at first?"*

Mrs Fleming thought about this for a moment, trying to recall as much detail as she could, then looked at Holmes, saying, *"His manner was always polite, in a mocking sort of way, if you take my meaning, but his voice did have a polished tone to it, at least it had the harsh edges trimmed from it. And his accent; I studied French at school, and while I'm certainly no expert, his accent was slight but reminiscent somewhat of that of Madam Foucault, my old French teacher. It was his English, though, which most impressed me; it was very good but also very deliberate, as though the speaker was trying to emulate some politician making a speech with all of the rhetoric he could muster. I think the man was trying too hard but, when the threat in his message took hold and I saw what he had concealed inside his coat, I forgot all about his accent and elocution and wanted only to see to Nancy."*

"Yes. A parent's first and best instinct is to see to a child's safety." commented Holmes, *"You have done quite well to remember what you have. But is there anything you might add? Is there something more you might remember about his dress? Any distinctive accessories such as a cane, a watch chain, eyeglasses? Anything at all could provide a vital clue to the man's identity. Relax your mind and think back and, if anything of note comes to you, just let Watson and I know, no matter how trivial it may seem."*

Mrs Fleming closed her eyes and leaned back into her seat, trying to relax but struggling to put the words used by her threatening assailant out of her mind. It did not take very long, however, and the lady was off into a shallow dreamy state, dozing to the gentle rocking of the train carriage.

"She probably didn't sleep a wink last night." commented Watson, *"A short nap will do her a world of good and may well allow a few memories to shake themselves loose. It is often the case, as you well know, Holmes."*

"Indeed it is." replied Holmes, thinking back to his impressions of Barrallier in Cooper's Inn and whose command of English might have been sufficient for him to repress his native accent leaving only a faint trace. He would not disturb Mrs Fleming's well-needed rest and would wait to see if and what the lady could further remember.

Basingstoke Station neared and the four travellers got ready to quickly disembark. Holmes had chosen the rear carriage so that other passengers could not observe their exit; it would not do for others to see them getting off so close to Salisbury as local tongues tended to wag freely about anything unusual. Their exit from the train was uneventful and, as soon as the train had cleared the station, the foursome walked to the waiting room, anticipating the arrival of the west-bound train which would take them back through Salisbury and on to Wylye. If all ran to schedule Watson had calculated they would have to wait little more than twenty minutes before they could reboard and Holmes had only to purchase four tickets westward to Westbury, well beyond their actual destination. Any wastage in ticket costs would be worth the extra degree of safety such deceptions would provide.

Lestrade had started his journey with the Police wagon an hour after the Flemings had started for Salisbury Station. It was judged that he should have more than ample travel time and should arrive a good hour before the train pulled into Wylye. Given the round-about route he was to take to avoid prying Salisbury eyes, the distance he would travel was a little more than ten miles, no distance at all on a good road and no challenge at all for a good team of horses; Lestrade would even have time to rest and water his horses along the way and take a break from the driver's seat to which he was long unaccustomed.

Right on time, the west-bound train stopped at Basingstoke and picked up new passengers including, of course, four who were to choose two separate compartments, one for the two men and another for the mother and daughter. As ruses go, this one was not the most elaborate but would serve to not draw attention by over-observant types. Salisbury was transited without incident and the train then continued on toward Wylye, there to be met by Lestrade who would, it was presumed, be waiting for the four travellers.

The Scotland Yard man had made good time to Wylye, even with a short watering stop for the benefit of the horses, and had taken up his post below a shady tree and began to snooze, revelling in yet another rare opportunity to sleep on the job. A shrill whistle woke the slumbering man, alerting him to the train's imminent arrival as it approached the small rural station. Disembarking, again from the rear carriage, Holmes, Watson, Mrs Fleming and Nancy waited for the train to move off before proceeding to Lestrade and his not-altogether-comfortable wagon. The trip to Netherfields was to take forty minutes at the slow speed commanded by Lestrade but the Professor's impressive house, this time approached from a different direction than Holmes and Watson had previously experienced, eventually came into view as the Professor and her maid Julia emerged to greet them.

Mrs Fleming and Nancy found they had been provided with a large room to share, well appointed but not too visible from the house grounds should unwelcome visitors approach. Holmes, Watson and Lestrade, however, were quite happy to accept bunk beds into which they could settle and find a deep slumber which even Lestrade's snoring couldn't disturb. The plan to remove Mrs Fleming and Nancy to safety had proceeded well, seemingly without mishap; from a nearby hill, however, several figures were observing the goings-on with powerful binoculars and great interest.

The Watchers

Watson was the first to notice the watchers on the hill; he had seen the glint of sunlight reflected off a lens, something he had been told to watch out for during his ill-fated military exploits in Afghanistan when being watched was something to be expected. Knowing that he should make no show of awareness of the fact, he continued with the task at hand, that of assisting Fleming's wife and daughter with their luggage, and signalled to Holmes that he should definitely come to his assistance, immediately.

"*I see them too.*" said the ever-observant Sleuth to his keenly watchful friend, both men being careful not to look in the direction of the mysterious watchers, "*But, whoever they are, they are inept sorts of spies, giving themselves away like that. I doubt that an experienced military man would make such an obvious blunder but I can't make any guess as to their actual identities. The sun is behind us so, if you could get to your own excellent binoculars and take cover behind those shrubs to our left, I dare say you might be able to turn the tables on these peeping Toms and get a glimpse of them without their knowledge.*"

Watson continued with his chore, taking several items of luggage into the house where he collected his own binoculars which had served him well when on active military service. He exited the house through a side door, taking care not to alert anyone to the new complication lest it cause further distress, and took up a comfortable and concealed position behind the clump of shrubbery. From this concealed vantage point, he was able to make out three figures with his naked eye, figures whose identities he hoped to determine as their magnified images were brought into focus.

Watson could see three men who seemed dressed more suitably for the rugged rural pursuits of the district than for a short country jaunt by townsfolk or spies from the metropolis, be that London, Paris or even Berlin. He could make out general features and get impressions of dress but could not, even with the excellence of his field glasses, say whether he recognised any one of the three, the distance being too great. He was, however, reassured a little by being unable to observe any weapons they might be carrying, though neither could he see farming implements or detect surveying instruments; horses or wagons were not apparent either, though these would likely be kept beyond the hill's summit and well out of sight if the watchers did not wish to be seen themselves. If the trio's intentions were benign or malign, Watson was unable to tell and knew that a closer inspection would be required and warranted to determine which; he had given his word to Fleming that he would protect the policemen's family and was honour-bound to do his utmost in that regard.

Lestrade had moved the wagon and unhitched the horses, then taken the animals off to grass and shelter in the near meadow. Holmes had assisted and waited until the Scotland Yard man had completed the task and then joined him to clean up in the lower floor laundry before entering into Netherfields proper. The Flemings had retired to their room to await their promised midday meal but the Professor had not gone off for her usual nap; instead, she was in an upper room and calling out for her three gentlemen visitors.

"*Mr Holmes, Dr Watson, Mr Lestrade. Quickly, up here.*" she yelled at a volume scarcely believable for one of such age and presumed fragility, "*It's that dashed Fernmount, nosey blighter that he is.*"

The three gentlemen visitors, as the Professor liked to describe her male guests, raced up the stairs to find the source of the outburst. Watson reached the room first and entered to find a highly animated Professor Tilbury peering through a powerful telescope at the group on the far hill, the threesome recently, though imperfectly, observed by Watson and Holmes.

"Forgive my coarse outburst, Gentlemen," she exclaimed as she turned from the swivelling instrument, *"but it's that busy-body Fernmount snooping into my business again. He wants to buy me out for a song but I can't stand that Devil's tune that he plays. Netherfields and its grounds are to be gifted to the nation when I'm gone. I've made good provision for life for Julia, she whose been like a daughter to me, but I'll be dashed if that smug boorish farmer will ever place his boots on my soil, not while there's breath in my body and lawyers to keep him away when that breath has departed."*

"We've heard tell of this Fernmount." said Holmes, well remembering Parker's recent comments and concerns, *"What is his story and what is his problem?"*

"His estates used to be far more extensive," replied the Professor, *"but he still tries to play the lord of the manor despite the ruinous state of his financial affairs, and his estates. His recent ancestors had gambled away a good portion of the family fortune and lands and his own stupid vanity has seen what was left heavily mortgaged to maintain an image which fools no one."*

Holmes nodded and said quizzically, *"We had heard rumours of problems of land ownership. That Parker fellow, the journalist writing all that stuff in The Times, had mentioned that he was following several vague leads concerning the lands around and about Salisbury Plain. I believe he did mention this Fernmount's name, or perhaps he was referring to a relative with other holdings."*

"Interesting man, that Parker.", commented the Professor, *"Turns up now and then, but I fear he's more interested in my Julia than in any knowledge which my brain may hold. Each of them could do worse for a companion but I fear that Parker's current lifestyle has little time for such complications."*

"I must admit that I've warmed to the fellow." replied Holmes, *"He is not the irresponsible hack I once thought, though his job does see him concentrating on the sensational more than the substantial in order to sell newspapers."*

"That's the fault of the people who read them," countered the Professor, *"and if the general public could raise its collective eye to the factual more so than the fantastic, we would see far less of the emotional hysterics exhibited than we currently do in this over-informed but under-critical nation of ours."*

"Well said." exclaimed Watson, *"I wish I had said that. Perhaps you'll permit me to use it in one of my unexciting but substantial Sherlock Holmes tales."*

"Enough, Watson." countered Holmes, *"We have serious business to attend to."*

"More than that," interrupted the Professor, *"it is now time for us to attend to our lunches. That Fernmount irritation can wait until we've eaten."*

The midday meal was taken in silence by the Professor, her three gentlemen visitors and her two refugees from, to her, unspecified threats. Though nothing had been said about the danger which the mother and daughter had faced, the

Professor knew that such danger must have been both dire and pressing for the three men to have gone to such lengths to protect them and get them away from its source. With eating finished and dishes cleared away, Professor Tilbury called for Julia, her maid, to take Mrs Fleming and Nancy on a tour of the house and the gardens as there were matters she must discuss with 'her detectives' who, now that their two charges were out of earshot and sight, seemed to have had their status significantly altered and were no longer merely 'her gentlemen visitors'.

"*Fernmount. Yes, now ... where were we?*" started the Professor, "*Parker was asking me about the fellow and the lands immediately to our east. These are, at least for the present and until his creditors close in, the westerly remains of a once-greater estate. That estate was effectively split in two with an easterly portion transferred in some manner to a line of cousins - yet more Fernmounts, though they spelled their name Fernmont and were of lesser impetuousness when it came to managing their affairs. The westerly portion had progressively gotten smaller as sections were sold off to pay off debt and maintain a pretentious lifestyle. This western Fernmount likes to ride around his estate but this does not take him anywhere near as long as it once did for his ancestors.*"

"*And of the eastern Fernmonts?*" queried Holmes, "*I take it they are of lesser concern, being completely separated from Netherfields.*"

"*They concern me not at all, Mr Holmes.*" was the Professor's reply, "*I have met two or three of the younger ones who had questions about ancient monuments. They made no mention of their now-distant and disagreeable cousin and were very pleasant. I believe, though, that the western camp has some deluded notion of reclaiming the easterly portion, the lands around and beyond Stonehenge."*

"Now that does interest me." exclaimed Holmes, surprised at hearing of an unpleasant type who had caught Parker's interest and who had ambitions toward lands near Stonehenge and the murder sites and who was, perhaps, observing the movements of his colleagues and charges.

"His ambitions may well be associated with the Army's interest, as yet officially unexpressed." commented the Professor, *"He'd want to be in on the sale, if that is what is to take place."*

"How does everyone know of the Army's supposed plans?" asked Holmes, *"Can't anyone keep a secret in these parts?"*

"Obviously not." answered Lestrade before the Professor could comment, *"Who needs the telegraph around here when news and rumours get around like they do?"*

"It's something not openly spoken of." explained the Professor, *"But too many official types have loose mouths and talk too much in front of servants and field workers, people they think wouldn't know what was what but who really know far more than those official types think they do. They're not tied down like they used to be and they get together after work, particularly the field workers, and talk about anything and everything. Facts get around and often get altered in the process and so there's really no such thing as a secret in the country."*

"Nor in the city." added Lestrade, *"The corner pub is the place to go to learn what's going on. No point waiting for any Police report to arrive, it's all old news by the time it lands on the Super's desk."*

"*It's the same here.*" he continued, "*I was booked into Cooper's Inn as Mr Lester but all Salisbury knew that it was Inspector Lestrade of Scotland Yard upstairs in his room. If anyone didn't, that nosey little Billy Cooper would soon let them know; I might sign him up as a Police detective one day, if he stays out of gaol.*"

"*Yes, young Billy.*" agreed Watson, "*Though I do feel that he'll end up owning a string of hotels and other enterprises before he's through; he has his father's eye for detail and a great deal of energy, and he'll know everything about the business before he's much older. For all we might say about him, nothing goes missing from any of the rooms, so I'm told, so he's either honest by nature or knows that taking things from guests is bad for business and counterproductive profit-wise.*"

"*I wish there were more like him, then.*" added Lestrade, "*But, of course, Holmes and I would be out of a job if that were the case. A saw-bones like Watson can always find someone to patch up but we two will be out on the street with beggar's bowls. Perhaps Holmes could do his special tricks telling people what they've been doing and I could play the monkey running around with a tin cup collecting pennies.*"

The Professor smiled at the banter between three men who have had to work closely together and depend on each other, then commented, "*Fear not, Inspector, the nature of the beast is such that there will always be work for the policeman and the detective. Anyway, you could always come here and I'd keep you well fed and productively occupied digging up old stone artefacts. You would still be a detective but witnesses to any crimes committed, I fear, would be very hard to find.*"

Watson excused himself saying that he needed to check on something pressing. He picked up his binoculars and proceeded outward to take up his concealed position behind the shrubbery to check the hill, and any watchers who might still be observing the movements at Netherfields. One figure remained, seated and apparently not overly interested as he seemed to be gazing all around, his own binoculars slung uselessly around his neck. Beyond that, Watson could not discern anything, just a figure on the hill making all in Netherfields a little nervous. He returned to the group and reported what he had seen and Professor Tilbury, interested and determined to see for herself, climbed the stairs to get a better view through her telescope.

"It's not Fernmount," she called out, *"just one of his underlings, and a disinterested one at that. He's not looking at anything much. One could sneak up upon and give him a good scare. And he's not on Fernmount's land; he's crossed over to mine to get into the shade of that tree."*

"The Devil he has!" exclaimed Holmes, *"Then he's opened himself up to a little surprise, and an unpleasant one at that. "Gentlemen, are you up for a little sport. There is game on that hill and I'm ripe for the hunt."*

"Mark my words, Gentlemen," he continued, *"we'll take this fellow and find out if this Fernmount intends harm to our charges, or to our host. We are three men, able, fed and rested, and we have more than ample daylight to creep up and beat those watchers at their own game."*

MARKED MEN

The Sentinel

The three men were as one in their desire to catch one of the watchers and Watson, ever the military man despite his medical proclivities, got busy assessing the hillside for the best line of approach which would not alert their quarry. The hill's summit was a good mile from where they stood in Netherfields but they would have to swing wide to avoid being seen and then come in almost right under the man's line of sight but remain unseen due to the hill's somewhat precipitous profile on that aspect. Each man was armed but, whether their adversary was also, they could not tell; they could see neither rifle nor shotgun near or with him but a pistol on the man's person was a distinct possibility. Watson could see that they could approach unseen to within fifty or sixty yards of the man but then they would have to cover open ground; over this last distance, they would have to approach at the run and with pistols drawn and pointed. Hopefully, Watson thought, they could take the man by surprise and he would yield with neither fuss nor fight.

"What about the ladies?" asked Lestrade, *"What if this is a ruse to draw us away from our posts and leave them unprotected? One of us ought to remain here. I would suggest that should be you, Dr Watson; I can offer official authority on that summit and Holmes needs some action to keep his brain busy."*

"No." replied Watson, *"You may be right about the ruse but it is you, Lestrade, who needs to stay. I could be needed to provide urgent medical attention if our pistols need to be used and, to say it plainly, official eyes make me nervous when*

Holmes gets going with that attitude to proper legal procedures he has. We don't want you having to perjure yourself to keep Holmes out of gaol for being a bit overzealous in convincing the fellow to talk."

"Alright, then." agreed Lestrade, somewhat reluctantly, *"Have it your way, but don't shoot unless you truly have to. There have been four bodies too many in these parts and we don't want to add another one to the tally, especially if Sherlock Holmes was the one who pulled the trigger; The Yard would likely have me drawn and quartered while Holmes would end up talking his way out of it all."*

That said, the three men agreed; Holmes and Watson checked their pistols, took two long draughts of water each to counter the heat of the afternoon sun, and proceeded out on their long round-about approach toward Fernmount's unsuspecting sentinel. Mrs Fleming was advised of the situation and reassured that this action was precautionary and the presence of the watchers may have nothing to do with the threats against her and her daughter. Professor Tilbury, however, was excited and couldn't wait to see it all through her telescope. Her life had been one of activity and, despite her age, she was in no way done with the thrill it provided. Still, it was felt prudent for her to stay away from the instrument until Holmes and Watson could get into position lest her actions in some way alerted the man that something was afoot.

Afoot, something was, as Holmes and Watson walked briskly down the pathway and out onto open fields before turning to sneak under the watcher's line of sight. The two men would trace a long snaking figure-S and come up on the hill's oblique side; for a while they would not be visible from Netherfields but would emerge to surprise their quarry, approaching at the run and prepared to shoot, up in the air if the man ran, or at the man if he produced a pistol and made ready to fight. Each hoped, however, that the sight of two armed men suddenly approaching at the run would cause the man to give the game up immediately and surrender without fuss.

Mrs Fleming and Nancy, accompanied by Julia, had moved to a room on the western side of the house so that any sounds of gunfire would be muffled; they had been warned to expect that two shots in quick succession might be heard if Holmes and Watson were required to fire a warning shot each. More than two shots, however, would signal that the man was putting up a fight and that the mother and daughter's safety had likely been compromised, requiring Lestrade to move both charges to a more secure location.

Without the aid of her telescope, Professor Tilbury could just make out two forms making way across the base of the hill before they moved around to make their ascent. Shortly after their ascent began, she lost sight of both forms and could only wait until they re-emerged closer to the summit and the apparently snoozing sentinel. Ten minutes went by and the Professor could stand it no more; she took hold of her telescope and pressed her eye to its eyepiece, swung the instrument to get the sentinel in her field of view and adjusted focus so she did not miss any smidgen of detail of the upcoming assault.

"They must be there soon." she said under her breath, breath which she held for another half-minute before she saw the forms of Holmes and Watson appear, each man down on hands and knees and moving slowly but steadily toward the open ground over which they would have no cover. The Professor could make out the vague shape of a pistol in each man's right hand and watched, breathless, as they both rose in unison and began to walk quickly, pistols poised, toward the

still-unaware sentinel. Thirty yards from their quarry, the sentinel awoke and stood, startled and panic-stricken at the sight of two armed and determined men approaching. Professor Tilbury gave a short gasp as she saw the man turn and begin to run and the gave another as she saw Holmes and Watson raise their pistols and shoot into the air; she saw two puffs of smoke emerge as two small flashes came forth from the pistols, saw the man stop in his tracks and then heard the retorts of the pistol shots, delayed as they were due to the distance the sound had to travel. She watched as Holmes and Watson ran to the now-stationary and soon-to-be captive sentinel who, it seemed, had no weapon and posed no physical threat, despite being on Netherfields land. It was enough; too much, in fact, for the Professor and she found that her heart was beating faster than it ought. She relinquished her telescope to Lestrade and took to the nearest chair, exhilarated well beyond what any of her Doctors would have recommended but also well pleased to have witnessed the forces of good in action and victorious for it.

Lestrade saw that his colleagues were in command of the situation and were bringing their restrained captive down the hill toward Netherfields for questioning. He had been caught trespassing and could be brought before a magistrate; he had also been captured while unarmed by two men wielding and using firearms and a magistrate might just consider the action to have been heavy-handed and this could work against them, despite a Scotland Yard Inspector being involved and the Salisbury Police Inspector's family having been threatened. That family had to be reassured that all was well and that no one had been hurt, just startled by warning shots fired by two of their protectors. Lestrade, satisfied that his colleagues were indeed in charge of the situation, left the telescope and Professor and went to advise the Flemings and Julia that all had gone to plan and that they could now move about the house, though prudence would suggest they remain indoors. The two Flemings were pleased to be able to move about and Julia ran upstairs to see to her mistress who, she insisted, should not be allowed to get over-excited.

Julia insisted on bed rest for her mistress but the ever-insistent Professor said she would go only after seeing the captive sentinel up close. She may well know the man, she argued, and her presence might go a long way in getting the fellow to tell all that he knew. Julia had to agree, particularly as there was no getting the Professor to do anything she had decided not to, but insisted that she retire straight after she had seen and spoken to the man.

The return to Netherfields was a great deal shorter in distance and in time than was the adventurous foray outward and Holmes, Watson and captive soon arrived at the front door, ready to turn proceedings over to the official Scotland Yard Inspector, Lestrade. The captive was nervous, to say the least, and his resolve was further tested when introduced to the scowling countenance of Inspector Lestrade, its less than friendly official expression having been practiced and perfected over more than two decades of dealing with the worst of Britain's most violent criminals, many of whom had found themselves marched off to end their days at the end of a stout hempen rope. To ignore Lestrade in his element was to risk the wrath of one of the most proficient and successful, if not over-imaginative, policemen in the country and the captive cowering between Holmes and Watson was to find that the nightmare he had just woken to was about to get a great deal worse.

"Well, what have you brought me, Gentlemen?" asked Lestrade, with a mocking tone of threatening irony, *"A rabbit for me to cook and eat? And here am I hungry and eager for*

a good meal, though I'm sure that this skinny morsel won't satisfy me and I'll be ready for another in less than an hour. Are there any more like this one out there? I may well have to send you out hunting again."

Holmes grinned broadly and laughed out loud, then answered with, *"No, Inspector. We'll all have to nibble on this one. I'll have a leg but we'll save the tail for Watson, it's for luck, good for Watson, bad for this fellow."*

"Well, I'll have his guts," growled Lestrade, *"and I'll make garters out of them if he doesn't cooperate. He has the look of someone who wants to tell me everything. What do you say, Holmes."*

"I'd say he has that look." replied the Sleuth, *"But I could be wrong. He may prefer to end up in tonight's stew. That would, of course, be up to him."*

"I agree," said the Inspector, *"now bring this rabbit in here to face the Professor. Maybe he can explain to her why he threatened to kill a woman and her child."*

The captive tried to respond but found his voice had abandoned him. The sight of the Professor, however, someone he recognised, someone from his home region, caused him to break down and plead for understanding. He was, he insisted, only doing what his employer, the man he would generally refer to as his master, had told him.

"And did he say why he wanted to keep tabs on the Professor's house?" asked a very emphatic Lestrade, *"Was it so that he could do harm to the Professor's guests, or was it to the Professor herself? You know, this sort of thing can get you led straight to the gallows."*

"The gallows?" asked a very alarmed captive, *"You wouldn't hang me just for watching a house, would you? I was just told to watch and tell what happened."*

"Tell who? And why?" continued Lestrade, *"We can hang people for helping others kill people, that's the Law and I know where they keep the rope."*

"It ... it was the Master, Captain Fernmouth." fumbled the terrified captive, *"He took Frank and me up to the hill to see what was happening at Netherfields, then Frank and him went back. The Master told me to stay and watch what was happening; we was at Wylye and saw you in the wagon and the Master knew you was a copper and wanted to know what was going on. That's all. No one wanted to hurt no one. I only jumped over the fence to get some shade under that tree and sit on that big flat rock and you can't hang someone just for that."*

"Captain Fernmouth?" cried Holmes, *"Captain of what?"*

"His family bought him a commission in his younger days." broke in the Professor, *"They must have had something against the Army. Everyone thought he'd go off to do a bit of fighting but he resigned his commission after only two years; someone probably told him that whoever he was meant to fight actually got to fight back and so he thought better of it. Anyway, he kept his uniform and his rank and now tries to lord it over everyone in the district."*

"Yes," said the captive, *"that's what everyone says. But you can't forget to call him Captain if you work for him; he'd skin you alive if you did ... forget, that is."*

"This is George Perkins." added the Professor, letting the detectives know that the fellow was known to her. She then

continued on, suggesting, *"George, if you have anything to tell these gentlemen, I would suggest you do it quickly. They are here looking for murderers and you don't want to get between them and a suspect, not even accidentally; they're all armed and are quite prepared to shoot if necessary, and you know that for a fact."*

George, the captive, looked around and then straight at Lestrade, saying, *"No, I don't know nothing more than what I've said. I was just there doing what I was told."*

Lestrade then gave an noncommittal *"Hurrmff!"* and, pointing to a nearby chair, indicated that George ought to sit and wait for further instructions.

"So," mused Lestrade, *"this Fernmount character ... we have a former Army officer of relatively low rank and even lower commitment, a fellow who likes playing the squire, a bully who doesn't mind beating his workers and a land owner with designs on other people's estates, estates which may have been the sites of some rather nasty murders. I'd say we may have to pay this pretender a visit."*

"A wholly unpleasant type he may be," said Holmes, *"but that doesn't make him a murderer, nor a threatener of woman and children, though I'd not put it past him from what I've heard."*

"But hearsay isn't necessarily fact," continued Holmes, *"though it could be the smoke from a smouldering fire and it does warrant our attention. I suggest we send Perkins here off with a message for his master. Perkins should tell him that three able-bodied men, one from Scotland Yard, will be paying him a visit and intend to take him to task over his dealings with the Professor and with the Fleming family."*

The Captain

George Perkins was a small straw caught up in a whirlwind and was never so pleased when the whirling stopped and the wind abated. He had been given the quite easy job of observing a house at a distance and relating whatever he saw to his master. To George, sitting under a tree on a warm summer's day was a far better way of spending his time than would have been swilling pigs or cleaning out stables, but this rare idyllic opportunity had been suddenly and frighteningly ruined by being shot at, as it had seemed to him, wrestled to the ground by two armed men and frogmarched to face an extremely menacing police inspector who seemed intent on hanging him from the nearest tree. All of a sudden, carting buckets of stinking swill through the putrescent muck of a malodorous pigsty seemed a far more attractive proposition.

George's ordeal, however, was not over, not fully, as he had to agree to relay a stern message to a master who, to vent his frustration on being caught out, would likely give the servant one or two swipes of a cane he always carried with him. The servant, however, had few options and did agree, fully knowing the consequences, and was sent packing after being given food and drink to sustain him on his long walk back to Fernmount House.

"Poor fellow." commented Watson showing some degree of pity for a dupe caught up in something not of his making, *"I hope Fernmount doesn't vent too much anger on him."*

"If the blighter does, I'll run both of them in and give that Fernmount a good taste of his own foul tasting medicine and the servant a couple of day's good rest." declared Lestrade, *"Captain Fernmount, indeed. If a Captain needs to take the lash to an underling for delivering an unpleasant message, then he's not much of a leader, not in my book nor in my*

experience. *"I've been in the Army, you know, I've stood in the ranks and would have readily followed my Captain's order to attack the gates of Hell without being poked or prodded; he was a real Captain, a true man of substance not just of show."*

"Well, we should give the man a good hour to get back and deliver his message," proposed Holmes, *"then we should arrive on Fernmount's doorstep breathing a little fire and brimstone. He may or may not be involved in these murders but I'd wager he knows something."*

"He can send us packing." said Lestrade, *"We have nothing on him beyond being a bully and a bombastic interferer, but he may actually be no fool, not in matters of Law, so we should only come down hard with the matter of threats made to the Flemings and not bring up the murders, not straight away. And he may have powerful supporters in the region. This is one time when we need Fleming's local knowledge."*

"What about the Professor's local knowledge?" asked Watson, *"Cannot we avail ourselves of that? Surely our friend here at Netherfields could advise us of who we may trust and who we should be cautious of in regards to this Fernmount."*

"Fernmount," said the Professor, *"is definitely a buffoon, but a cunning buffoon, and he does have his supporters. I can't say that he has friends in high places but he does have connections via his being a land-owner of some standing, despite his failings in management. This Army business about Salisbury Plain that no one is supposed to know about, it could be that Fernmount has connections with some of his old officer friends and the man's positioning himself for a huge windfall from the sale of land he thinks he ought to own but doesn't."*

"Well, greed has so often turned out to be at the bottom of so many bizarre and confounding cases which I've investigated," agreed Lestrade, *"and, unless it was crime of straight-out passion, I was generally able to follow a trail of money to the guilty party."*

That said, George Perkins was released and told to go directly to Fernmount House and deliver the message and that he would be done for if he ever trespassed on Netherfields land or in any way disturbed the peace of the Professor or the Flemings. A little uncertain of whether there was more to hear from Lestrade, Perkins jumped up and flew out of the door and up the hill toward his master's estate upon hearing the Scotland Yard Inspector roar, *"Well, be off with you! Now! And don't stop till you see that infernal master of yours; and be sure you tell him everything we told you to say."*

Rarely, if ever, had Netherfields seen such a rapidity of movement than that made by George Perkins on being told to leave. That the fellow had been doing nothing more than half-heartedly watching Netherfields on the instructions of his master was now obvious but Fernmount's motives were less apparent. The man may have been acting from simple though perverse curiosity or he could have been keen to see if Sherlock Holmes had really gone to London with the Flemings, if he had even known that any threats had been made. The detectives would find out, in little more than an hour, in which direction the facts would point.

"Refreshments, everyone." was a call by Julia to tell everyone that tea was being served, together with a few morsels of sweet cake and bun, as she was sure that the excitement had made everyone hungry, and as lunch had been finished well over an hour before. The Professor's maid could tell that there was no hope of sending her mistress to bed and that she might

as well get on with her domestic duties, particularly as there were guests staying at Netherfields.

"We ought to be off to Fernmount House," remarked Lestrade, unsure of exactly how long it would take to get there, especially as it would be him driving the Police wagon, *"but I don't think we ought to leave Netherfields unguarded. One of us should stay and I think I would choose you, Dr Watson, as I don't expect any serious opposition to our visit from this jumped-up Captain, nothing presenting any danger and a doctor to keep an eye on our Professor would be a positive asset."*

"But," he faltered, upon considering the refreshments, *"we could spend a few minutes regathering our strength and accept a little more of Netherfields' hospitality."*

Watson, seeing the sense of Lestrade's words, agreed. Lestrade then gathered Holmes and the two men proceeded to the wagon in the lower meadow where the Scotland Yard man declared, with an undertone of warning, *"It's a bumpy old ride on this wagon, I'm afraid, Holmes, but we'll get there."*

"Wonderful." commented Holmes, *"It's a pity we don't have Watson with us to tell us how uncomfortable the Army's wagons were out in Afghanistan compared with the comfort of this conveyance. He complains a bit but seems able to sleep anywhere he can get his head down – says it's his Army experience but he did get an officer's tent and stretcher."*

The banter continued for forty minutes or so, each man being reluctant to discuss matters without access to further facts, until the unfamiliar road brought them to the entrance to Fernmount's estate, much reduced as it was from its former glories.

A five minute ride took the two men to the main door of Fernmount Hose, a somewhat dilapidated structure in dire need of attention. Lestrade, alighting from the wagon first and being the official detective, went ahead of Holmes and pulled on the bell to announce his arrival. A dishevelled person in the guise of a butler possessed of an ill-fitting coat over what looked like a field hand's clothing answered the bell and asked what business they had with his master.

"*Police business,*" answered Lestrade, "*official and pressing, so if you would summon your master here forthwith, myself, that's Inspector Lestrade, and my colleague here would like a few words with him.*"

"*I don't believe the Master is receiving visitors today.*" was the curt reply, to which Lestrade gave his own counter reply.

"*You and your master may well be receiving visitors at Salisbury Police Station if we are made wait. This is an official visit and we will not be delayed in performing our official duty by someone refusing to help in our investigations.*"

The unusual butler was about to reply when Lestrade and Holmes heard the sound of a voice raised in anger and threatening violence on someone. The two men ran to the corner of the house and, looking down toward one of the out-buildings, saw Fernmount raise a stick and bring it down hard on the back of Perkins who had just delivered the message.

Fernmount saw the men running his way and stood back, lowering his cane and holding it behind his back. "*Just who are you? Get off my land; you are both trespassers and I'll have the Law on both of you.*"

"*I am Inspector Lestrade of Scotland Yard and this is my colleague Mr Sherlock Holmes. We entered your lands via your main gate and proceeded directly to your main door along your main drive, all of which were open and unimpeded.*" insisted Lestrade, "*Now, that's not trespassing, that's paying you a visit in a legal and respectful manner but, if you insist on extra formalities, I'll return with a warrant and numerous heavy-booted Police constables. So, answer our questions and we'll be on our way and you can go about your business. Oh, and another thing; we both witnessed your assault on Perkins and if he would desire to make a complaint I'm sure we can continue our discussions through the bars of a Police cell.*"

"*The Commissioner shall hear of this.*" retorted a cornered and flustered Fernmount.

"*I can deliver the message myself, if you wish.*" countered Lestrade, "*I'll be lunching with him the day after tomorrow. He'll be here, in Salisbury, to check on progress and he doesn't like people who threaten the lives of women and children any more than I do.*"

"*Threatening women and children?*" Fernmount exploded, "*Who said anything about that. I haven't threatened anyone and neither have any of my men here.*"

"*You were seen spying on an official Police operation,*" was Lestrade's response, "*and I have every right to haul you in for questioning if you don't cooperate. As well, you had instructed one of your men to enter Netherfields' property and that makes you complicit in a deliberate act of trespass, if not conspiracy to pervert the course of justice. I have three very reliable witnesses to the act and all three, and myself, would readily stand up in a Court of Law and testify to the same.*"

"Now," Lestrade continued, in a less forceful manner, despite placing his heavy Police boot inside the door frame, *"as the potential charges against you keep mounting, I suggest you invite us in and tell us just what it is that you've been up to."*

The three men went inside, Fernmount now rather worried that he had overstepped the mark by spying on Netherfields just as some Police operation was underway. He was also unsure of his position with his man illegally entering Netherfields' land on his instruction and of the legality of the beating he had been giving Perkins. He was not now the old country squire exercising his feudal rights but a suspect in numerous wrongdoings witnessed by a Police Inspector and several prominent citizens, all seemingly antagonistic to him personally.

Fernmount rushed to a cabinet and poured himself a large whiskey, a point of hospitality which he neglected to offer to his two uninvited guests. Thus fortified, he began demanding to know who the threatened people were and how the Police could possibly believe that someone of his standing in the district would have anything to do with it.

"I'm not interested in what you want to know," countered Lestrade in a calm but determined and authoritative voice while ignoring the man's insistent plea, *"I want to know what you have to do with death threats made against a woman and child in Salisbury yesterday. You were seen spying on the intended victims today and therefore must have some felonious interest in their whereabouts so that you can carry out your intended attack on two innocent and defenceless people ... a woman and a young child, as I have said."*

Fernmount gulped and took another large sip of whiskey but failed to reply and, so, Lestrade continued, *"It would be better for you to cooperate at this point and tell all you know to my colleague and myself. We've both seen that you are a violent man, we saw you savagely attack George Perkins just for delivering our message, an official Police message telling you that we would be visiting Fernmount House this afternoon. A man who would attack another able-bodied man for that would surely not hesitate to kill a defenceless woman and child. All of today's events, and those involved in them, will be the subject of a full report made to the Chief Constable and the Commissioner, both of whom have a keen interest in the murders which have confronted the Police in Salisbury, and Wiltshire in general. The presence of a Scotland Yard Inspector should tell you that these men are in earnest and are desperate to find a culprit."*

The master of Fernmount House sat heavily in a chair and looked up at the two detectives standing before him. His hands held his empty whiskey glass between his knees, and his face spoke of a bully who knew he was up against forces he could neither bluff nor beat.

"I just wanted to know what the Police, that is you, were doing." the man sheepishly confessed, *"I saw you at the station in the Police wagon. I don't know anything about threats to anybody and I don't know anything about these murders. I just want to sell some land to the Army. My reserves are depleted and the mortgage on Fernmount House's estates is about to be called in by my creditors. I stand to lose everything if I can't raise the full amount owing. Everything I own is owed to a bank and to a few old friends, all of whom refuse to grant me any more time or extend any more credit."*

"It sounds like you'll be the one getting whipped in the future." said Lestrade in a voice devoid of any pity. *"Perhaps you*

ought to confess so we can hang you and put you out of your misery."

"That's not the least bit funny." demanded Fernmount.

"It wasn't meant to be." replied Lestrade, *"Just trying to make a point, you know. My friend and I need information and you have information to provide so, if you don't want your day getting a great deal worse, I'd suggest you have another whiskey and relieve yourself of what you know and avoid taking on a burden which I can guarantee you will not be able to bear."*

The man stood, poured another glass, retook his seat and looked down at the floor.

The Admission

Captain Fernmount, as he liked to be known, was defeated, and knew it. His bluster was exhausted and his options, if he indeed had any, were few. Such a man in such a position might fill himself with enough liquid courage and then retire to the woods to blow his brains out. This man, however, was not yet there and might yet provide valuable information, information he might be unaware could pertain to the murders and murderers. Despite their aversion to the fellow, neither Holmes nor Lestrade wanted another senseless death as the man might, in time, redeem his estates and himself, resume his station and live a respectable life within the community. The two men had their doubts, though they were not there to act as deliverers of justice but as accessors of facts and detectors of parties involved in criminal activities. Becoming absorbed in ensuring the man got his due comeuppance was not conducive to their aims and could well distract them from their goal enough that the guilty parties might escape.

The Captain, gathering himself and begging the detectives' indulgence for a few minutes while he composed himself, walked from the room and down a corridor to find water, soap and towel and a change of clothing to replace the threadbare work clothing he wore.

"He's been all bluff and bluster." said Holmes, dismissively, *"He's truly broke. Did you see the stables? There were no horses, no signs of the necessary clean up characteristic of a string of fine mounts which a gentleman of Fernmount's pretended standing would be expected to run. He has a single nag pulling a wagon in need of repair; the weld in its left front wheel tyre is about to give way and I'm surprised it made it here from the station. A wheelwright or even a decent blacksmith could fix that in no time but wheelwrights and*

blacksmiths like to be paid and I believe that Perkins and the other man have done what they can to keep the wheel intact. Very soon that wheel will fail and the nag will have to pass for the master's steed and there will be no way of getting anything of bulk or value in or out of Fernmount's withering estate."

"He'll soon have no men if he treats the ones he has the we saw him treat Perkins." observed Lestrade, *"He can't plant anything, and there'd be no point as he'd have no one to do any reaping. And where are all his stock?"*

Holmes nodded in agreement, adding, *"A few sheep are all he seems to have; I saw them from the hilltop above Netherfields and I'd wager that they belong to someone else paying for the benefit of Fernmount grass. The man is desperate and about to take a fall from which he will not recover. He could be desperate enough to agree to participate in criminal activity, or to look aside while others did so for the promise of a substantial payment, though he does seem to be counting on a sale to the Army."*

"The Army may want his land or it may not but we may well have seen how such men are paid." uttered Lestrade, *"The man may well become the fifth dismembered victim."*

"Well, we're still no closer to an answer to the question of why the four were actually murdered, let alone dismembered." commented Holmes, *"By the way, are you really having lunch with the Commissioner tomorrow? Even I couldn't tell if that inscrutable face of yours was telling the truth or if you were lying through those clenched policeman's teeth of yours."*

Lestrade nudged Holmes to indicate the return of Captain Fernmount, now a little refreshed and dressed in a manner more befitting the country squire which he considered he was.

"Now, please." Fernmount started, *"Where are my manners? Can I offer you two gentlemen a refreshment, a whisky perhaps?"*

The man seemed renewed, not the cowering weakling he seemed a few minutes before. Holmes and Lestrade could barely believe the transformation and wondered on the man's sanity. Or had the man reverted to his outward persona, something practiced and perfected but requiring considerable effort to maintain and being a long way from his true nature? Had the man, once straining at the end of his tether and now suddenly overflowing with regained confidence, been showing two sides of his nature or were both of these manifestations simply those of a man acting out two well-rehearsed roles? Lestrade sensed a trick but Holmes looked deeper and saw that these dual manifestations of despair and defiance were methods by which the real Fernmount managed to retain a smidgin of sanity in a situation in which those around him might respond positively out of sympathy or out of fear. Holmes felt that the real Fernmount, his true persona, had long disappeared.

Deep down, Fernmount knew he was beaten and that personal degradation was looming but the confident Fernmount was once again ascendant and keen to show that he was in charge, a force in the greater community. Holmes thought that the time was right for the man to be drawn into revealing all he knew, just so that he could show that he was someone to be reckoned with. The man was deranged but his knowledge was likely to be deep and probably intact.

"Captain Fernmount," started Holmes, *"perhaps we have overstated things and misunderstood your motives. You are a man of some standing in the district and, as such, would hold knowledge that ordinary people would never be privy to. We*

would be grateful, as would the Commissioner, if you could, with your intimate knowledge of the more important matters, put us in the picture as to new arrangements for and newcomers to the greater Salisbury area."

"*Thank you, indeed, Mr Holmes for that recognition, and the compliment.*" replied Fernmount, maintaining his confident and somewhat pompous bearing, "*There are things about these parts to which few of the common folk are privy, as you so appropriately put it. I am a gentleman fallen on hard times, temporarily I might add as my fortunes are definitely set to change for the better, but I am also a soldier, not currently active but still, as you have acknowledged, bearing rank. I am indeed a holder of knowledge of the type to which you have alluded and, as you are an obvious gentleman and the good Inspector Lestrade is here under the auspices of the Commissioner, a great gentleman himself, I feel that I may share at least some of that which I, in my elevated position in the community, would know.*"

"*Excellent.*" exclaimed Holmes, playing to the man's ego and desire to display superiority, "*I knew that we had misread the situation, new as we were to the district and coming from the metropolis where the natural order of society is not maintained as it is in our rural communities.*"

"*Quite so,*" agreed Fernmount, eagerly taking the bait dangled by Holmes and keenly observed by an amazed Lestrade, "*people do come to these parts without a proper understanding of how things work. Now, a case in point, some two months ago I was approached, being one of appropriate community standing, by a brother officer, senior to me though in French service and desirous of smoothing the way for an understanding between our two nations. He was genuinely respectful but did not wish the news of such possibilities to cause international complications. He had with him three others, all of ordinary rank who insisted on addressing me as 'mon Capitan'; I do admit that it made me chuckle at times. Salisbury Plain, he said, looked just the spot for combined military manoeuvres out of sight of the keen-eyed Prussian and needed my help to assess the possibilities."*

"That my lands," he continued, *"those current and those formerly ancestral to my family, might host such important matters was of course of immense interest to me. As it happens, however, the lands of greatest interest were farther to the east and occupied by a very junior cadet branch of my family, the Fernmonts, different spelling, one of less noble occupation and with no military standing whatsoever. I was able, by virtue of my military standing, to determine that the Army was indeed desirous of procuring land to the north and east of where we sit and was able to put this Colonel Baudin at ease by pledging my support."*

"And this Colonel ... Baudin, was it?" probed Holmes, *"Has he been active in the district since that time?"*

"For a week, we met almost daily," replied Fernmount, *"and then he was suddenly nowhere to be found. I had expected him to leave for France to report but was surprised that he gave me no word on the matter. But the military, you know, sudden orders come and they are to be obeyed without question or delay. I dare say he will contact me when he can. Patience is one of the soldierly virtues, you know."*

"Indeed." said Holmes, with a muffled *"Hrrmff"* from Lestrade.

"And have any other French personnel made contact with you?" asked Holmes, thinking of Berrallier in particular.

"No, nary a one." replied Fernmount, *"Though the circle of trusted people must, of course, be a small one. I've heard nothing but I must keep my eyes and ears open for the time that the Colonel returns. He will need me ready and up to date with all the goings-on about Salisbury Plain."*

"Well, thank you, indeed." said Holmes, standing and indicating to Lestrade that there were things to discuss away from those eyes and ears of Fernmount. *"We shall leave you about your business but would like to call again on other matters which may require your intimate knowledge of local affairs. Oh yes, it would be a great favour to us if Netherfields could remain unmolested; we have people there who require secrecy and we know that we can entrust such matters with someone such as yourself, someone of rank and standing."*

"Of course, and you may return at any time. Come when you will." said the enthusiastic Fernmount, his ego now swollen to bursting point.

Holmes and Lestrade stood and turned and made their ways to the front door and over to their wagon. Fernmount stood at the door and saluted the two detectives, both astounded at the way the man could change his nature, depending on the stimulus he was given.

"The man's as mad as a meat axe." said Lestrade when they had put a small distance between themselves and Fernmount, *"One minute he's thrashing people, the next he's going to have us taken to task by the Commissioner, then he's grovelling on the ground like a whipped dog, and now he tells us he's been in league with some French tearaway and giving away military secrets."*

"Open military secrets." Holmes corrected his colleague, then added, *"The sudden disappearance of Baudin does point to*

him being one of the murder victims and his three men could well make up the macabre set. This is not new information but Baudin's active interest in British military matters is confirmed. I need to advise Mycroft of this; all of it."

Holmes pondered on the matter as Lestrade drove the wagon along the narrow road back to Netherfields. He knew he was somewhat isolated from points of rapid communication with Whitehall but also knew that facts were Mycroft's life blood and that he needed as many pertinent ones as he could obtain to help complete a hazy picture. Lestrade dearly wanted to take Fernmount into custody and wring as much out of the man as possible but Holmes knew that the man's mobility was limited and that arresting such a prominent, if unpopular man, would alert others that he was about to tell all he knew. Army types from all nations and many country residents tended to be good shots and Fernmount might well not make it back to Salisbury and yet another murder would need to be explained and solved. Evening was approaching but sundown was still some time off as the two detectives reached Netherfields. Watson was out like a flash to greet them both and to find out what had been discovered.

"Could be a schizophrenic." said the Doctor, *"It's a new line of medicine but the study of the split mind is of intense interest to some of my colleagues. Of course, one ought to visit Germany for the best assessment and treatments, there it is treated as a science but cures, as I understand it, are difficult to attain. Provocation can set a sufferer off but reversal is much less abrupt."*

"He's a loony." demanded Lestrade, *"But he could be putting it all on."*

"Perhaps that's what he's been doing, Lestrade," countered Holmes, *"but the fellow finds his loony side, as you so nicely*

put it, the side of him he likes the best. His fortunes are about to collapse and he may be refusing to face that uncomfortable reality."

"*Anyway,*" the sleuth continued, "*I must send a communication to my brother without delay, no matter the condition of Fernmount's mind.*"

"*There's a train to Salisbury stops at Wylye at four in the morning,*" broke in Julia as she brought refreshments to the gathered group, "*but you'll have to be there and wave a lantern to stop it. It'll be full of milk churns and boxes of all sorts but it's better than walking.*"

"*Well,*" said Holmes, looking at Lestrade and smiling, "*it seems I'll need transport to Wylye, or perhaps I'll walk. It couldn't take longer than that wagon with Lestrade driving. Yes, I think I'll walk and perhaps you, Lestrade, could drive the Police wagon back to Salisbury at your convenience. Watson might remain here at Netherfields to provide protection, and to eat more of Miss Julia's delicious cakes.*"

A grinning Watson responded with, "*Well, seeing you put in that way ...!*" and it was agreed.

The Trek

Holmes had never been a heavy sleeper and was often up well before the cock crowed to announce the coming of dawn. This night, however, would see the man get little if any sleep as he dozed in an easy chair and smoked a pipe's worth of tobacco before walking outside to look at the stars. He had been pondering the nature of Fernmount and wondered if any of his more-distant relatives suffered from the same affliction, especially the branched-off Fernmonts which the 'Captain' had relegated to being a cadet branch in less than flattering terms and who lived, he would assume, within the Army's zone of interest for its soon to be acquired land.

As he had more than ample time before setting off to catch the pre-dawn train to Salisbury, Holmes had taken his time over a communication to his brother Mycroft which would inform the senior Holmes of new developments, at least of newly acquired data which might help clarify the situation, now involving murder, espionage, diplomacy and possible corruption within the Army or in one or more Government Departments servicing the military. The sleuth still had too little data to go on but knew that he would be hard-pressed to get anything more out of Whitehall, despite his brother's influential position, but hoped for a few hints none-the-less. Lestrade may have more luck with Scotland Yard, though its information may well have come from a different source than Whitehall's. It was impossible to tell who was speaking to whom and what was being said and how reliable had been the matters discussed. It was time for a second pipe.

Midnight had sounded on the hall clock and the house, apart from Holmes, had been soundly sleeping for some hours. A few cat naps was all the sleuth would need to replenish his vigour and these he had taken earlier, each ending as the clock chimed out the quarter hours. At two o'clock he would set out for Wylye Station, much less than an hour's walk at the brisk pace Holmes was able to maintain. Julia had provided him with sandwiches and a water bottle for the trip and these he was able to slip into side pockets of his jacket; he would also carry a candle, matches, a rough route map, a stout walking stick, a folding knife, his brother's loaded revolver and numerous coins and bank notes as well as pencil, notebook, envelopes and stamps, and a book of blank telegraph forms. Holmes travelled light but always seemed ready for any eventuality. Most of Salisbury would still be asleep when he arrived and he could rest while on the train and, upon his arrival, post his letter to the usual London post box and when the telegraph office opened, send a coded message to Mycroft to alert him to the letter's despatch. Then he could make his way, possibly with the help of Jenkins' cab, to Cooper's Inn for breakfast and a few short hours good bed rest.

The trek to Wylye Station was uneventful for Holmes, the night being clear and with an almost full moon rising to illuminate the way ahead. He enjoyed the invigorating exercise and the cool of the night air, though its rural cleanliness caused him at times to think something was amiss. Here and there, a distant light would filter its way through trees and shrubs along the way, indicating that he was not the only one out on a quest, though the lights were associated with locals attending to rural duties of which Sherlock Holmes had little knowledge and even less experience.

An hour's wait on the station platform gave Holmes time to locate the lantern provided for stopping the train and then wait, somewhat less than patiently, for the signs of the approaching conveyance. There was little to do beyond walking up and down the platform and thinking about the case while puffing away on the third pipe of the evening, but

Holmes, ever in pursuit of something to entertain his mind, had so much to keep him occupied, though he was careful not to come to any premature conclusions. At last he heard the train in the distance and lit the lamp, readying himself to attract the engineer's attention and board for Salisbury. He had no ticket but could purchase one from the guard or possibly pay at Salisbury on arrival; either way, he would enjoy the sensation of actually getting somewhere.

Salisbury was, as expected, just starting to emerge from its slumbers as the train pulled in and Holmes, having paid his fare, stepped out of the station and headed off toward the Post Office to mail his important letter. Nothing was open as yet and no cabs were waiting at the rank so Holmes sat and finished off the last of his sandwiches and washed it down with the water Julia had provided and settled in to await the arrival of the telegraph office staff. He still had two hours to wait and, so, the sleuth made an attempt at a cat nap of considerable length; he dare not entrust his coded message to anyone, especially young Billy Cooper, so his enforced vigil on a bench across the road from the telegraph office was as unavoidable as it was uncomfortable.

Minutes went by, street sweepers went by as did, in ever increasing numbers, those starting their early morning occupations. Bakers had been up since before Holmes arrived and the Great Sleuth, ever the disciplined investigator when on the job but now forced to languish on a municipal bench, was being distracted by aromas he would normally have admonished Watson for mentioning. Holmes tried his best to ignore the fragrant temptations and retreated into his brain-attic to do a bit of disciplined file sorting which, as his cranial files had been well arranged previously, was a futile endeavour.

"It's to no account," he said to himself, *"I'll just have to yield to the insistence of my olfactory senses."* That decided, Holmes stood and walked to the nearest bakery and selected an item he would dare not admit buying to his friend, the good Doctor.

This turned out to be not the best decision he made as, with his mouth full of a most delectable treat, he spotted Jenkins' cab coming around a near corner; worse still, Jenkins spotted his elusive client and sped up to catch him.

"Mr 'Olmes." Jenkins shouted, as if to awaken the entire street, and reverting to his subservient rural jargon style, *"I thought you was off to the Big Smoke with the Doctor."*

Annoyed at being found out, firstly about his feigned trip to London and then for being spotted back in Salisbury by Jenkins, of all people, Holmes swallowed an inadequately chewed mouthful of pastry and replied, with some difficulty, *"Urgent business called me back, I'm afraid, and I'm just waiting for the telegraph office to open to confirm my return. Watson shall return in a day or so. Could you pick me up in about twenty minutes and take me back to Cooper's Inn."*

Holmes was incensed at his bad luck and bad judgement. Jenkins would certainly be one to know that the train from London had not yet arrived, he was actually heading toward the station to pick up fares arriving on that very train. It would be necessary to concoct a simple, though convincing, story about his return; perhaps the cabbie would accept that he had travelled to London only to be recalled, not to Salisbury, but to Westbury, changing at Reading and waiting at Patney en-route. Holmes was unsure of the actual timetabling but gambled that Jenkins, though an expert on Salisbury, would be just as ignorant as he of such matters farther to the north. He had, in fact, picked up the train from Westbury at Wylye.

Finally, signs of activity appeared through the windows of the telegraph office and the sound of a heavy bolt being pushed open announced the unlocking of the front door. Holmes entered without delay with his pre-prepared form containing a coded message for Mycroft which would alert him that a letter for the fictitious Mr Simmons would need collecting. That task attended to, it was now time to confront the ever-enigmatic and always-inquisitive Fred Jenkins.

Holmes had only to wait for three minutes for Jenkins to appear, right on time at twenty minutes precisely after Holmes had engaged him. The cabbie listened to Holmes' feigned indignation at being dragged back from London to interview a potential witness to the murders. He explained that he had to catch the night train from Westbury to arrive in Salisbury at an ungodly hour and that the aroma of freshly baked pastries had proved too much for an overnight traveller deprived of sustenance.

"And a fool's errand, it turned out," declared Holmes, *"and a great waste of my valuable time. My business in London has been compromised and half a dozen people greatly inconvenienced. Such is the life of a detective, though, Jenkins. I'm sure that you have been let down by the occasional prearranged fare which dissolved into nothing as soon as you appeared."*

"Yes indeed, Mr Holmes." replied the cabbie, his interest now diverted to one more of his favourite topics and his rural accent forgotten, *"They're the bane of my life; I don't mind waiting in the rain or carrying heavy bags up flights of stairs but a booking is a booking, a contract for my time and my service, and to send me away without recompense or to be absent when I arrive is just plain ignorance in my book; and*

if I'm late by even one minute, the same people would berate me all the way to the destination and then dispute the fare."

Cooper's Inn approached and the cab began its turn into the courtyard, readying to deposit its passenger at the front entrance. Holmes hopped out and asked Jenkins to call for him at noon and take him to the Police Station. He assumed that Lestrade would have returned sometime during the morning and would likely have returned the Police wagon before moving onto either Cooper's Inn or to meet with his colleague, Inspector Fleming. Holmes rebuked himself for not having made more definite plans as he would need to consult him about the next phase of their investigations but hoped that, if he had not met with Lestrade at the Inn, the Inspector would be with Fleming awaiting his arrival.

Cooper greeted Holmes as the sleuth entered, "*Ah, Mr Holmes, your rooms are ready. Will you be requiring a meal? Breakfast is still on and I can have cook whip something special up for you should you wish.*"

"*No thank you, Cooper.*" was Holmes' reply, "*I've been in town since early morning and picked up a morsel to keep me going. I shan't need any lunch, either, but I will put my head down for an hour or so to rejuvenate both body and mind.*"

"*I could,*" Holmes continued with an afterthought, "*have need of young Billy, if he's about. I have a note for him to deliver.*"

"*I'll fetch him and send him right up.*" replied the innkeeper, busying himself with the myriad tasks involved in running an inn.

Holmes took the stairs two at a time to have the note written and consigned to an envelope before Cooper's lad appeared. The envelope was marked simply with 'R. Parker'; Billy would know where it needed to go to earn his thruppence, hopefully from both sender and receiver.

With the note to Parker despatched, Holmes settled into a sleep beset by images of dead bodies and pompous gentry, all chasing French spies, interrupting local fox hunts and seeing off Prussian cavalrymen, all watched by Lestrade through the Professor's telescope while Watson ate cake. It was nonsense, merely his mind randomly putting the thoughts of the day into some sort of semi-permanent order within his deeper memories while confusing and confounding his sleeping form without his conscious mind alert enough to be able to maintain control. *"The mind,"* he had often expressed to many a puzzled listener, *"is a wondrous thing but should never be allowed to run things it doesn't understand."*

Noon came soon enough but Holmes had anticipated it by fifteen minutes and was up, washed and had changed clothes ready for a meeting with Fleming. Once again Holmes chastised himself for not sending word ahead to Fleming; this was the second error of judgement he had made in less than eighteen hours and Holmes realised that he had been more tired than he realised, and more distracted. Jenkins pulled up outside the inn right on twelve noon and Holmes was ready and eager to get on board to be taken to Fleming and, hopefully, Lestrade. On arrival, Holmes advised Jenkins that he may have need for a further excursion to the Plain, out near Stonehenge but this time to visit the Fernmonts, those the self-important Captain Fernmount had described as belonging to a much-inferior cadet branch of the family. Jenkins said he could be ready with minimal notice as his horse raised a slow trot, pulling the cab after another fare.

Sergeant Baxter greeted Holmes on entering the Police Station but had to advise that, *"The two Inspectors aren't in, I'm afraid; they're off in conference over at Mrs Dalhousie's Tea House opposite. Our Scotland Yard visitor did look a little famished and somewhat the sorer for his ride on our wagon so our Inspector took pity on him and said he'd treat him to a fancy meal. You might join them if you are of a mind to, or you may wait in the Inspector's office."*

Holmes nodded, thanked the Sergeant and turned around to find the tea rooms and his two official colleagues.

The Brothers

The door of Mrs Dalhousie's tea rooms opened with the inevitable peace-disturbing ring of its bell and both Lestrade and Fleming looked up, teacups in hand, to see the tall form of Sherlock Holmes stoop a little to gain entrance.

"Holmes," began Lestrade, *"we knew you'd find us sooner or later. I did what you said and drove the Police wagon back and now Fleming and I have been eating like kings without you. Sit down, will you, and join us. We've been discussing our favourite lord of the manor and that changeable mind of his."*

"A topic which could keep us all occupied for days," responded Holmes, *"but it's his relations, the Fernmonts, that I find more intriguing and have notified Jenkins to be ready to take us there. We could take the Police wagon, though; Inspector Fleming doesn't realise how fond you've grown of that particular conveyance's driver's seat."*

"I won't be going anywhere without a cushion to sit on." insisted Lestrade, giving his colleagues a wry smile, *"But the Army's possible interest in that family's land, land associated with these murders, and all the other things we find going on, does warrant a serious look in that direction. Perhaps you might like to bring Inspector Fleming here up to date on various matters. I have told him that his wife and daughter have settled into Netherfields quite nicely and that Watson is there with them. I've also told the tale about how you and Watson stormed the hill overlooking Netherfields and scared poor George Parker near half to death."*

"Well," replied Holmes, *"If Watson and I sent him half way to that state, you had him terrified and standing on the trapdoor of a gallows to send him the rest of the way."*

"Yes, just a little technique of mine to loosen unwilling tongues." explained Lestrade, *"The image of noose dangling from a cross beam in a suspect's mind tends to put matters clearly into perspective and makes him remember just what the most important thing in life is; you know, being able to continue breathing."*

"Quite." commented Holmes, knowing full well that Lestrade was in deadly earnest and supported in like manner by Fleming, as well as much of the general public as long as the typical citizen didn't have to get involved in the unpleasantness.

Holmes went over the events of the previous days, some of which were well known to Lestrade but new and of considerable interest to Inspector Fleming. The Salisbury Inspector, now that his family had been removed to a place of safety and provided with a very stalwart armed guard in the person of John Watson, had found he was able to focus on the matters under investigation and help plan for their resolution in whatever way was necessary. Holmes had become convinced that the four murder victims were the missing French official, Baudin, and his three cohorts, all of whom had probably blundered into matters of international intrigue at a delicate stage and had fallen foul of corrupt officials and local land owners hoping to make significant commercial gains from land sales. The dismemberment was, he thought, an overdone attempt at pointing blame elsewhere and the disappearance of the heads possibly stemmed from the desire to hide the victims' identities.

But it all seemed too much, too elaborate, too outrageous for those who would be desirous of secrecy. Bodies could be hidden, bodies could be buried elsewhere, bodies could be burnt. Why go to all the trouble and unpleasantness of chopping up corpses and distributing them around sites of archaeological significance and tourist interest? Why draw attention to crimes which would be better left undiscovered and uninvestigated? There was something more, something even more sinister … perhaps.

Holmes found the two official detectives ready to venture out to Salisbury Plain to speak with the Fernmont family; however, he impressed on them that, *"Before we speak with the Fernmont people, I'd like to see what Parker's been able to dig up. I ought to get back to Cooper's Inn to see if he's responded to the message I sent him."*

His colleagues agreed and said they would wait on Holmes to pick them up on the way out to the Plain, hopefully in Jenkins' comfortable carriage and not his wagon; there were official files for the two policemen to complete and set straight and they could use the intervening time productively. Holmes then left Mrs Dalhousie's establishment and headed off, hopeful of finding a cab to speed his return to his lodgings, and Parker's response. Lestrade and Fleming would revel in a few more minutes of leisure sipping the last of the tea before returning to the onerous and never-ending task of attending to the crucial paperwork which, if left incomplete, could see all their efforts come to nothing as the case against the yet to be apprehended murderers failed for lack of fully documented proof.

Holmes, having found a convenient cab after several minutes of brisk walking, found himself deposited back at Cooper's Inn, there to be informed that Parker had responded by sending a note back with young Billy, a note which Holmes found suggesting they might meet at Parker's hotel which was somewhat less troubled by eavesdroppers than elsewhere. Holmes ran to catch his just-relinquished cab and reengaged it, puffing prodigiously despite his good level of physical fitness. Hopefully, Parker would still be at his digs and the pair could compare notes. A telephone would have been a boon in the circumstances but such convenient luxuries were still few and far between in the metropolis and rare novelties in the country and held in some disdain by Holmes who preferred the authority which a telegram possessed and the considered response it commanded.

Parker came down from his room on being summonsed and took Holmes into the same small room in which they had previously conferred. Holmes gave Parker a sketch of what had occurred and ended by saying that he did not regard Fernmount as a serious contender for the murders but had been a willing dupe in some dubious land sale collusion, something complicated by the involvement of a missing French official, someone operating without official sanction. The journalist seemed unsurprised and told Holmes that he had questioned some of Fernmount's former employees, most of whom said that the man was mad but cunning.

"*I was unaware of any firm connection with French officialdom,*" he explained, "*but was able to find out that he had his eyes on the lands of his distant relatives, the Fernmonts, lands squarely in the middle of the Army's zone of interest. He doesn't have much in the way of capital or credit but he does have contacts who might be able to steer things his way, somewhat illegally but also somewhat improbably. I doubt that the man could raise a penny more than he's done to this date.*"

"*Watson and I witnessed extraordinary changes in the man,*" said Holmes, "*changes from an offensive brute to a cringing weakling and then to a confident lord of the manor type who might just convince someone that he is a force to be reckoned* with. *If he could maintain the latter image and keep his cunning, he might well be successful in his aims, though I do doubt that he could retain the appearance of sanity for any significant length of time.*"

"*There's also that Barraclough.*" broke in Parker, "*He lives up near the Fernmonts; his lands abut theirs actually, but he doesn't receive visitors and his workers are tight-lipped about the fellow and that is unusual, to say the least. Most field hands are more than ready to spread a bit of gossip about their masters, often without any inducement but especially when plied with a bit of liquid tongue loosener. I don't know if Fleming had been able to get anything from them, or from the man himself.*"

"*Nothing of any note.*" commented the sleuth, knowing full well that Fleming had recorded nothing about the man but did not wish to make the Inspector in charge to look bad or even a little incompetent.

"*Lestrade, Fleming and I are off to see the Fernmonts this very afternoon,*" continued Holmes, "*and, time permitting, we shall look in on this Barraclough to see if he will refuse to see two Police inspectors, one local and the other a very persuasive one from Scotland Yard.*"

"*Excellent,*" responded the intrigued journalist, "*just make sure the three of you keep those pistols close and loaded; there are killers somewhere out there on Salisbury Plain. I admit it would make a great story, but three dead detectives would be very bad for business, the locals would be sure to tell you.*"

"*Quite.*" said Holmes, rising and thanking Parker for sharing what he had discovered. He then left Parker's hotel and walked to the nearby Salisbury Station, hopeful of finding Jenkins snoozing on top of his cab. He would get the cabbie to take him back to the Police Station and then return with his carriage, if it was available, otherwise his bone-shaking wagon.

Luck was with Holmes and Jenkins did as requested, returning some little time latter with his carriage in which the detectives would ride out to question the intriguing Fernmonts and, possibly, the reluctant Barraclough. Holmes, Lestrade and Fleming would have preferred to discuss matters during the ride outward but the presence of the keen-eared Jenkins made anything more than small talk a risky proposition. On reaching Fernmont land and approaching the main house, Holmes suggested that Fleming open the conversation with questions about their distant relative while Lestrade could jump in with his heavy Scotland Yard boots should anyone prove to be elusive or uncooperative. Holmes wished to say little but observe the response of the Fernmonts to specific questions.

The great house of the Fernmonts contrasted in the extreme with that of their distant cousin, its condition proclaiming the estate to be both productive and profitable and the residents to be energetic and industrious; it was almost too orderly, Holmes considered as he and his two colleagues approached. Their visit had been unannounced but not altogether unexpected and Richard, the eldest of three brothers, came out into the courtyard to greet the three men on recognising Inspector Fleming.

"*Ah, Inspector,*" he exclaimed, walking toward Fleming with his hand outstretched, "*I had wondered when you would be paying us a visit. Your constable had called in to get a few details after those ghastly remnants had been discovered and said you would be following things up.*"

"Yes, it has taken some time for us to contact all those in the area." admitted Fleming, *"But I now have reinforcements. May I introduce Scotland Yard's foremost detective, Inspector Lestrade, and Mr Sherlock Holmes who, as you may know, is often called in to assist with his unique speciality."*

"Good afternoon, Gentlemen." replied Fernmont, *"Both of your reputations precede you. But let us not stand out here under this hot sun, come in where we may find shade and refreshments. You may tell your driver he may wait around back where he will find shade and water for himself and his horses."*

Jenkins did not need telling, he just rolled his eyes and flicked the reins to get his team mobile and moving where directed. Fernmount and the three detectives then walked into a well-ordered and somewhat darkened house to be offered cool drinks by a fawning servant over-keen to be seen to please. Seats were offered to the visitors and Fermont excused himself for a few minutes to give servants directions and to send for his two brothers who were nearby in the surrounding fields. On returning, the senior Fernmont pulled a chair close to the visitors, sat and prepared himself for their questions.

"We have questions concerning your distant cousin, Captain Fernmount as he calls himself," started Fleming, *"his actions have been erratic and somewhat hard to reconcile with his current financial position. Have you had any contact with the man recently, in person or by other means?"*

"No," replied Fernmont, a little cagily Lestrade thought, *"not as I can recall. Perhaps one of my brothers may have seen him in Salisbury but, to my knowledge, he hasn't set foot on this property in years."*

"Any others, people representing him or offering to act as an agent in some negotiation?" broke in Lestrade, trying to get the man off-balance, *"Anyone foreign sounding?"*

"Well, no; that is ... I don't think so." replied Fernmont, *"We do get representatives from time to time asking about acquiring land, generally via our Salisbury solicitors, but it has been known for hopeful individuals to approach us directly."*

"What about these Druids?" continued Fleming, *"Have you experienced much activity by these people, these devotees to ancient beliefs and rituals?"*

Fernmont sat back in his seat and gave a long sigh, saying, *"These Druids ... mostly harmless people playing at dress-up and chanting away with some sort of gibberish at the dawn light on the solstice, though some do get active at other times of the year. They mostly assemble over at Stonehenge, not on our land, though a few do hop the fence and wander across our fields in search of evidence of wandering spirits and forces emerging from the Earth. We put up with it if it doesn't get out of hand and as long as they don't damage anything or interfere with our stock. We get the occasional lunatic demanding that we vacate holy ground, but the threat of buckshot and the sight of our dogs has generally settled the situation."*

"Generally?" asked Lestrade.

"Yes." was the curt reply, *"We did have to manhandle one fool and escort him to the public road. I don't believe we ever saw the man again. He wasn't a local, I believe."*

"Ah. Here are my two brothers." he announced, breaking off his discourse on Druids, *"The one with the hat still on in the*

house is my younger brother James and the other one is John."

"*Brothers,*" he continued, addressing the two newly arrived Fernmonts, "*These gentlemen are detectives; Inspector Fleming you will know, or at least know of and the gentleman to my left is Inspector Lestrade of Scotland Yard and, to my right, is the celebrated Sherlock Holmes of London fame and some celebrity in the popular press. They have come to ask questions about the recent murders and about our estranged cousin over toward Wylye.*"

"*How can we help?*" asked John, the middle brother, "*We don't really see anything of Fernmount and have no desire to do so. He has made all sorts of unsavoury remarks about our branch of the original family, we spell it Fernmont as you would probably know, and somehow thinks he has some sort of claim on our property despite the break having been made three generations past. We may have stepped into help him by extending him some credit but he has friends who have been left wanting for doing the same. We just don't like the man and do not much care what becomes of him; he's just not family.*"

UNWELCOME STRANGERS

The Fernmonts

Family did seem to be of paramount importance to the Fernmonts, no more so than many families isolated but largely self-sufficient and having run things pretty-much as they wished for centuries, but Holmes, Lestrade and Fleming found that they had stumbled upon one of the strangest families in any of their experiences. Fernmount and the three Fernmonts were all bachelors, no wives anywhere apparent and no children running noisily about announcing their existence and demonstrating that the family was set to continue indefinitely into the future. In fact, there were no other family members, senior or junior, to be seen. Even Holmes, the eternal bachelor himself, could see that, unless the Fernmont men began their own personal families sometime soon, there would be no continuity of the intimate culture that binds a family together and that both branches of the Fernmount/Fernmont clan would end in oblivion as the members died away.

Holmes had been pondering such matters while Lestrade and Fleming had been occupied with their questions when the arrival of the two younger Fernmonts broke into his line of thought an immediately provoked a new one. From what he could observe in the short time he had been on the estate, the senior Fernmont ran the farming enterprise and household operations from the main house while the two younger brothers laboured in the fields alongside numerous field hands, possibly day workers living away from the property. They did not act like any gentry he had experienced, not even junior branches given to pretensions, despite the family name in either of its forms being quite an old one. Holmes presumed there must have been servants other than the two elderly males

247

he had seen being given instructions when the three detectives first arrived, someone to cook, someone to wash, with both occupations generally taken up by women; the sleuth, however, was getting the feeling that the female on the Fernmont estate was obvious only by her absence.

"Yes, we have spoken with your estranged relative." said Fleming, responding to the middle Fernmont brother's statements and totally overlooking the fact that he had actually been absent from the Fernmount interview, *"He does seem to have fallen on hard times and is given to occasional bouts of melancholy."*

"Those black humours stem from a black heart." insisted James, the youngest brother, only to be rebuked by Richard, the eldest.

"James," he retorted, *"your feelings toward our distant cousin are well known but we ought not to lower ourselves to his level and resort to personal vilifications. It suffices to say that relations between the two family branches have soured to the point from which there can be no return to civility. If you must take perverse satisfaction from his predicament, you will have ample scope when his finances finally fail, which soon they must do."*

"My apologies, Gentlemen." Richard continued, addressing himself to his three visitors, *"My youngest brother feels very strongly about family and becomes incensed and given to rash statements when the subject of our unfortunate cousin comes up. Please forgive the unfortunate outburst and put it down to a youthful lack of restraint."*

"All families fall out." observed Lestrade, *"Christmas with my relatives always turns into a battleground and the casualties*

go back to their homes to lick their wounds only to do it all over again next time. But family is still family."

"*Indeed.*" agreed Richard, "*But I perceive that you have questions of more pressing moment than those asked so far. Please, we are busy people and need to get back to our duties, so ask what you will of us.*"

"*Well, you are perceptive.*" responded Lestrade, indicating to Fleming that Scotland Yard had taken the reins, "*My good colleague here, Inspector Fleming, has a case of some complexity and more than a good deal of worry on his hands. The Press has somewhat over-enthusiastically come up with the label of the Ley Line Murders and, as competent and dutiful as our Salisbury man is, the sheer number of necessary interviews has overwhelmed his resources. The fact that we come as a trio should indicate to you that we consider yourself, and your brothers, as prime sources of useful information, such is your standing in the region. Have you, yourself, or either of your brothers here, any information which may shed light on the victims' identities or reason they were killed and why their bodies would be dismembered and spread along the ancient ley lines? Have there been strangers roaming about and possibly upsetting local arrangements?*"

"*We do, as I have said,*" replied Richard, briskly cutting off his youngest brother's attempt to comment, "*have the occasional Druid entering our lands but we tolerate them only so far. The ley lines are real but not always distinct and, should any group, Druid or otherwise, approach and request access so that they may walk along them, we generally agree but stipulate what can and cannot be done. It is a matter of maintaining control for, if we didn't give in just a little, they would walk just where ever they wished and disturb our agricultural arrangements.*"

"Why they were murdered in the manner they were," Richard continued, *"I cannot say, nor could I hazard a guess as to any motive, nothing beyond the conjecture the Press has been making. Perhaps they were just that, ritual killings by some mysterious cult."*

"Perhaps they were," agreed Lestrade with more than a suggestion of impatience apparent in his tone, *"but perhaps they were made to look that way. But, strangers, beyond the usual assortment of Druids; have any left a lasting impression, something which may have left you less than comfortable with their presence?"*

"Any strangers?" Richard asked of himself, somewhat over-dramatically and dwelling on the final syllable far too long, *"Well, we have had the occasional knock on the door from the odd land speculator but, as I said previously, we refer them to our solicitors, give them a friendly glass of whiskey or a cool beverage, depending on the season, and see them on their ways."*

"Anyone you recall being over-zealous or of foreign origin?" Lestrade asked.

Richard leaned back and gave a ponderous *"Hmmm."* before answering with, *"No, not that I can recall. Perhaps you should speak with our solicitors in Salisbury, Freeman and Todd, in the High Street."*

"We certainly shall." declared Lestrade, less than satisfied with the answer given, *"Anyone who has had recent contact with strangers to the district will need to be interviewed."*

"So you really don't have any leads at this point." said James Fernmont, half in question, half by way of declaration.

"Actually," replied Lestrade, extra-serious in both manner and voice, *"we have several lines of enquiry currently running; some will prove fruitless while others, a much smaller number as time goes on, will bear the proverbial fruit and that fruit will lead someone straight to the gallows, mark my word. This Salisbury murderer has a debt to pay and, should you care to glance over my record, you will find that I am the most proficient and successful debt collector that Scotland Yard has. My patience is great and my hand, stuck on the end of the long arm of the Law as it is, is always eager to come to grips with the guilty party."*

"On a different tack, though." said Lestrade, now animated having just given James Fernmont the sternest of looks and the benefit of his most severe vocal tones and leaving the man a little unnerved, *"You have a neighbour, a man called Barraclough; could he have anything of interest to add to what you three Gentlemen have told us? He has the reputation of being somewhat of a recluse, we are informed, and his house is only three or four miles from where we sit, as I understand it."*

"Correct on both counts, Inspector." volunteered Richard, taking the pressure off his youngest brother, one prone to saying too much in his eldest brother's opinion, *"But it's more like four and a half miles by road. The man is a bit of an eccentric, I'm afraid, and given to all manner of wild stories concerning the spirit world hereabouts, that connected with Stonehenge and the other structures. He may have information useful to you but, then, he may lead you a merry chase along one of his flights of fancy on the ley lines. We don't see much of him, if the truth were to be told, he's just too engrossed in fairies and ghosts and such which he claims to have seen and which he talks constantly if given the chance. We find it's best to avoid him."*

Sherlock Holmes said nothing but noted the dynamic between the two brothers, Richard and James, and how the former had jumped in to stop the latter from adding more to his statement. There was obviously more to be asked but he could tell that Lestrade was getting ready to bring things to a close. Holmes had seen Lestrade at work before and, though he considered the man to have a less than adequate imagination, he knew that the Scotland Yard man's nose for deception and lies was second only to his own. He also knew that Lestrade, when on the scent, was relentless and would pursue his prey all the way to the kill, literally.

"Well, thank you, Gentlemen." said Lestrade rising slowly from his chair and indicating to his colleagues that it was time to go, *"Now, unless any one of you has anything more to add, anything which he thinks may have pertinence to the case or strikes him as being something or someone out of place, we must bid you goodbye but may have cause to call on you for future assistance with local matters."*

Holmes and Fleming rose in unison but not nearly as rapidly as Richard Fernmont who seemed to have been pushed from his chair by some hidden spring. The eldest brother hurried to grip the hand of Lestrade while manoeuvring the Scotland Yard man in the direction of the front door while the two younger brothers half rose from their seated positions only to retake them seconds later. The two remaining detectives made feeble and fruitless attempts at saying *"Thank you"* and *"Goodbye"* and quickly turned to follow Fernmont as he virtually marched Lestrade outside. A whistle from Fernmont caught the ear of Jenkins who stood upright on his driver's post and waved his hand to indicate he had gotten the message.

"*Now, Gentlemen,*" said an impatient Fernmont, "*you'll forgive me, I'll leave you now as I have pressing business to attend to. Your driver is on his way and I trust that Barraclough won't prove too difficult a prospect.*"

Having escorted his uninvited and less than welcome guests to the front porch and summoned their carriage for them, the senior Fernmont turned and disappeared indoors with such rapidity that the three detectives were left a little stunned.

"*I'd like to hang him right now,*" declared Lestrade, "*just for being obnoxious and rude. And what a strange household; I half expected to see the Fernmonts sprout horns and pointy tails. Richard was right to get rid of us as soon as he could; I wanted to use my boot on the fellow. And that John is a bit creepy in my book. How did they strike you, Holmes?*"

"*James Fernmont,*" Holmes declared to his colleagues, leaning in close lest he be overheard by the approaching Jenkins, "*seems a little simple but is at least honest and forthright with his feelings; but that Richard is hiding something, something nasty I'd wager. John, well I'd say he'd do whatever his big brother told him to. As for that James suffering from a youthful lack of restraint, the man is thirty five if he's a day. Also, and I don't know if either of you noticed it, there were no tell-tale signs of the feminine hand about the house, nothing to soften that atmosphere of male starkness and insensitivity, no signs of wives or even of a matronly cook or serving maid, just a couple of ancient male crones attending to the Fernmonts' needs.*"

"*But before anything can be decided, Gentlemen,*" the sleuth added, "*we must visit this Barraclough and hear what he has to say ... about the murders, and about his neighbours ... let us hope that his reputed eccentricity is based only on rumour greatly embellished by nosey and jealous types prone to*" *creating gossip where none of any substance actually exists. Parker said the man was not welcoming toward visitors but he cannot refuse to speak to two Police Inspectors on official business. That's enough for now; Jenkins is almost upon us."*

The Neighbour

The drive from the Fernmonts' estate to that of Barraclough was, as had been the drive outward from Salisbury, uneventful and silent but did give each detective the opportunity to go over the gathered facts still turning about in each man's mind. Discussion between them at this point would have been useful for reinforcing points of common interest and for removing or modifying points of misunderstanding; the mind of Holmes was capable of attending to such matters on its own but the official detectives had found that a meeting to discuss and argue points of view was the best way to test and mutually validate any evidence collected to date.

The trio had only a few short minutes to recover from the shock of what was effectively an ejection from the Fernmont house to discuss matters before Jenkins appeared, though that ejection had admittedly begun only after Lestrade had shown his readiness to leave. Each came away, though, with a keen distrust of Richard Fernmont and a bad feeling about John, the middle brother. James seemed almost likeable but definitely under the control of his eldest brother. The house they had just departed had left each man with a feeling of unease, as though the building and the land it stood upon was somehow sterile, not so much devoid of life but of that liveliness which one would expect from people who worked hard by day and then returned to a home full of welcoming laughter in the evening. There was not the least hint of human happiness in the place, that was it, and the notion suddenly and simultaneously occurred to all three detectives as they trundled down Fernmont's drive and out onto the public road.

Field workers were seen heads-down as Jenkins' carriage went by; there were no waves, no stopping to touch the forelock, no salutes, no polite calls of greeting to strangers passing by. The workers just worked and none could be seen to even look in the direction of the carriage and some were seen to turn away on its approach. It had been the same upon entry but the detectives had been too focussed on questions for the Fernmonts to notice.

"Friendly lot." commented Lestrade sarcastically, *"On the way here from Salisbury my arm darn near fell off from waving back to the field hands we passed, friendly sorts who were glad of an interruption to the grind they were involved in. Those Fernmonts had no machinery to speak of, no steam engines for threshing or dragging heavy loads about. Everything was done by hand or horse. It's hard to reconcile with their apparent prosperity; seems almost feudal."*

"Indeed." agreed Holmes, secretly pointing to Jenkins sitting high in the driver's seat to indicate the need for silence, unless the talking involve matters unrelated to the case. A quick nod from Lestrade signalled his compliance and the group travelled on speaking only of trivial matters, of past cases and of the growing hunger in each man's belly.

Barraclough's domain soon appeared and entry through two large and ancient gate posts told the travellers that they were on a quite old estate, one perhaps hiding a long history of prosperity and some degree of dominance over the greater region, also perhaps of conflict as the ebb and flow of the Civil War of two centuries past cut its destructive path across the long occupied plain to add even more layers of mystique to the ancient landscape.

The chimney stacks of Barraclough House could be seen from the roadway before they entered the property, though the house proper would not be encountered until a drive of ten minutes had taken the group through an ancient forest from which smoke rose and drifted toward them. The sight and smell of the smoke wafting from piles of smouldering wood made it seem as though they were being visited by the ghosts of the ancient inhabitants, though it was more likely that a few charcoal producers were refusing to yield to the benefits and convenience of coke and had customers of like mind. Salisbury Plain was a mixture of the old and the new, the ancient and the modern, and the detectives were slowly realising that they had entered a different world, one well apart from the modernity of the metropolis and the industrial cities, one where fairies might indeed be found fluttering about at the bottom of the garden and a ghost might creep up from behind and tap you on the shoulder on a dark night, or so it felt.

Field hands on the Barraclough estate were far more typical of the region than were those which had just been encountered, and waves and vocal salutes greeted the visitors as they passed by. A collection of dogs emerged as the carriage entered the house courtyard and noisily escorted the travellers to the impressive porch only to abruptly stop the commotion at the sound of their master's compelling voice.

Barraclough stepped over, saying to Jenkins, someone he recognised as a transporter of busybody tourists, *"I see three gentlemen in your carriage, Sir. I presume they have business and are not here to sightsee."*

Jenkins replied, taking some satisfaction in being able to claim official status whereas he had previously been given short shrift by Barraclough, *"I have been engaged to carry Inspector Fleming of the Salisbury Police and Inspector Lestrade of Scotland Yard to numerous locations on Salisbury Plain. They would appreciate a little of your valuable time and considerable local knowledge to clarify a few points about recent unpleasant events. Oh, and with them is Mr Sherlock*

Holmes, a consulting detective here to discover what others may miss."

"*Police, eh. Inspectors.*" grunted Barraclough, "*Well, have them come in. It's about time for a refreshment so your timing is good, almost planned I might say, were I a suspicious man. You can take yourself off around back, Jenkins, and see to your horses; they'll be in need of water and there's grass to be had beyond the trough.*"

Jenkins bowed silent compliance from his seat, quite impressed that Barraclough had remembered his name, though the man had on two occasions threatened him with a peppering of buckshot for appearing unannounced with touring groups desirous of visiting the old houses.

Barraclough stepped toward the detective trio as they stepped down and greeted each man cordially with a firm grip of his hand and words of apparent genuine welcome. "*Don't like tourists much.*" he added, "*They come around here disturbing the stock and interfering with the men's work and then want to be given private tours of the house and lands. They are at their leisure but we here are not. There's work to be done and that doesn't happen if we're off entertaining folks with too much spare time to waste. Idle hands will soon be about the Devil's work, you know.*"

"*Indeed they will.*" agreed Lestrade, "*And I can assure you that chasing up the after-effects and agents of that same Devil's work is our stock-in-trade and the reason we have need to disturb your arrangements this day. As Jenkins said, somewhat presumptively I may add, we have questions which you may be able to help us answer.*"

"*Questions about these Ley Line Murders, no doubt.*" prompted Barraclough.

"Exactly," responded Lestrade, *"and some other matters which may or may not have a bearing on the same."*

"Well, you'd better come inside and we'll sit and discuss what must be discussed." insisted a surprisingly compliant Barraclough, *"No true visitor to my home stands out in the elements while I have shelter and sustenance to offer, and certainly not men of official standing such as yourselves, and your consulting colleague."*

"Tell me, if you would be so disposed" he added, addressing himself to the unofficial accompanying detective, *"I had presumed that the famous Sherlock Holmes always travelled with his chronicler, Dr Watson. I do read of your exploits and find them intriguing and I trust that the good Doctor does not exaggerate your powers of observation, otherwise you would not be here boosting the Police numbers."*

"Dr Watson is attending to other matters at this time," replied Holmes, *"but it is true that I am able to claim an enhanced ability to see what others overlook, often features of seemingly trivial natures which can help me see through the murky mists of deception to the truth beyond."*

"I shall take your word for it, Mr Holmes." responded Barraclough with a hearty laugh, *"You do have a solid reputation. But you gentlemen are not here to talk about stories in the Strand but, rather, about those dire events upon Salisbury Plain. Firstly, though, our refreshments have come; so please let me offer you this little hospitality. My man will see to your driver's needs."*

Being somewhat famished after their travels, the visitors eagerly took to the cakes and buns proffered and sipped refreshing draughts of tea before settling back into their chairs to begin the interview. Fleming decided he should speak first as he was the Salisbury man and as he was, at least nominally, the detective in charge of the case. Before Fleming could open his mouth, though, Barraclough got in first with, *"Gentlemen, you must know, I'm sure, that the Army is after my land."*

Fleming looked at Holmes to see if he ought to make some sort of comment but Holmes took the initiative, saying, *"We are aware of talk of such things but have you been officially approached in any way? I would expect that such matters would be a closely guarded Government secret until the situation had been discussed with the land-holders and agreements were reached."*

"Nothing official," replied the host to his unofficial guest, *"but a man with your reputation for picking up on the minutiae of conversation and subtleties of people's behaviour would undoubtedly have noticed something brewing hereabouts. I, myself, have been subjected to the unwelcome attention of land speculators and local wisdom has this linked to rumours of military interest. Mind you, the suggestion of an application of non-military buckshot saw the blighters off smartly enough."*

"What you say is of some interest." admitted Holmes, *"But were these speculators local or otherwise? Could they have been foreigners seeking out secret and sensitive information about military affairs? We have had unsubstantiated suggestions of such intrigues occurring but we need solid information, not bar-room boasting or tea house gossip such as has been reported. We are here to investigate murders, certainly, but these other matters keep cropping up."*

"Well, I'm astute enough to see that you can only say so much on the matter I brought up," declared Barraclough, *"but I did wonder why a Frenchman would be after English land, even*

one accompanied by an Englishman, though I suppose a speculator is a speculator no matter where he's from."

"This Frenchman," insisted Holmes, "did he have a name? And what about his companion, the Englishman?"

"I truly cannot recall either one offering his name, even though they were here only a week since. I did think the English one said something about barrels to the other when they were approaching and in hushed discussions." was the reply, "But, there were other Frenchmen nosing about a few months back, though I can't be sure exactly when, certainly before these murders took place. They didn't ask anything of me but did ask questions of two of my day workers, and offered them money."

"And what did the Frenchmen get for their money?" broke in Lestrade, "It wouldn't have anything to do with covering up four murders, would it?"

"No. Seemingly not." came Barraclough's reply, "My men reported the matter to me and said they'd been asked to keep their eyes and ears open as to military types roaming about and visiting. They were given a pound each in consideration and promised more later if they had anything to tell. I told each to keep his pound and say nothing in future but report any more visits to me without delay. Oh, yes; only one of them seemed to speak much English which he apparently did quite well, as did the more recent one who had spoken to me, and his was as good or better than mine; well-dressed too, a dapper sort."

Holmes sat back in his chair, supporting his chin with the thumbs of his now joined hands and mentally noted the mention of barrels, something close enough to Barrallier if inadvertently overheard. "*Interesting.*" he said after a few moments thought, "*Very interesting, indeed.*"

"*But getting back to these murders.*" insisted Lestrade, "*Would you have any idea why four men might be killed and their bodies treated as they were. Now, before you answer, I can tell you that at least one of the victims could possibly have been French, and in the military at some time.*"

"*Ah, yes, That tattoo the newspaper reported; very suggestive.*" replied Barraclough, "*Too many Frenchmen out and about lately for there not to be some connection, I'm sure. But the act is far too barbaric a crime for these parts in this day and age.*"

"*And what of the strange religious practices we hear of up around Stonehenge?*" asked Fleming, having received numerous reports of unusual gatherings of people in robes, "*Could any of these deluded people be involved, in your opinion, you being so close to the area of their devotions, or whatever they might call them?*"

"*Ah, yes. The Druids.*" was the response, "*Mad as March hares, if you ask me. But I think they're harmless enough; just overgrown children playing at dress-up and having foolish fun, though they might be the sort to be open to suggestions from The Beast. You know, Satan.*"

"*So, not Devil-worshipers but foolish Christians playing a risky game.*" suggested Fleming, "*We get warnings about them from the pulpit every Sunday.*"

"*I don't really know how serious they all take it,*" replied Barraclough, "*but some about these parts do make money from it all and let them perform their ceremonies on their land. They get buckshot from me.*"

"*And your neighbours, the Fernmonts,*" queried Lestrade, "*would they ever get involved in such activities or let the Druids on their lands for such purposes?*"

"*The Fernmonts?*" shouted Barraclough, "*Would they have anything to do with the Druids? Good God, man; they are the Druids.*"

The Shock

"The Fernmonts are the Druids!" repeated Holmes, for once taken completely off-guard and realising that he had missed a vital clue which ought to have been obvious to someone with his powers of perception. It wasn't only Holmes who felt that way, the revelation had come as a complete shock to all three detectives and left each one dumbstruck for a few seconds while he took in the message and let its reality sink deep.

"You mean," asked Lestrade, finding his voice, *"that the three Fernmonts get dressed up and go about chanting with all of those others up at Stonehenge?"*

"Well, yes." was Barraclough's reply, *"Not only that, but that Richard leads them and presides over their rituals. He's the high priest or whatever they call the one calling everyone together and starting off all their heathen mumbo-jumbo."*

"But, do they take it seriously?" asked Fleming, himself a devout and enthusiastic church-goer and finding it extremely difficult to accept that such prominent though admittedly strange people as the Fernmonts could hold such radically different beliefs, *"Do they really believe in tree spirits and all that winter solstice stuff? No, this has got to be wrong; it can't be."*

"Richard Fernmont does have some power over people; he can be very persuasive, though I don't take much to him myself." replied Barraclough, *"His control of his brothers is virtually absolute, especially that John. And as for James, well I think there's more to him than first impressions would suggest, though he'd dare not oppose his eldest brother. I've had little enough to do with them over the past few years, just for matters of our properties' common fences and occasional*

straying stock and such. They don't welcome casual visitors and I don't move far from my own lands."

"I've two sons down in London, you know," he continued, *"but they have no interest in farming. I suppose that was my fault, sending them off to University as I did. When I go, the Army might as well have the land and my lads can have the money; all things must come to an end but at least I have no Druids in the family."*

Holmes felt the man starting to drift from the matters they had come to discuss and broke in, saying, *"We noticed that the field hands on Fernmont's lands are less than friendly, whereas yours and others we had seen had all been cheerful and courteous to strangers passing by. Does Richard Fernmont's influence extend to his workers' dispositions?"*

"The Fernmont's are hard taskmasters." was the reply, one bordering on anger, *"Richard can be a very stern man and woe betide any of his workers not giving his full measure of effort. But they all follow him and wear robes and chant and do all the other things, all for the high priest of Fernmont House. Every full moon they'll get up to their antics around the stones on Fernmont's land, they leave mine alone since I warned them off, and then they march off to Stonehenge to play at being good Druids."*

"But Stonehenge was around well before the Druids came into being," demanded Holmes, *"I mean the original Druids."*

"Just try telling these modern ones that." responded Barraclough, getting a little annoyed at the thought of grown men playing at things about which they knew nothing, *"They don't want to know. It gets them in, all the robes and the sense of secret knowledge; and, once in, that Richard keeps them there, though every so often one of them escapes and leaves*

the district, for fear of his life I expect ... well, I suspect ... some just disappear."

"When you say 'disappear', do you mean from around here or from the face of the Earth?" asked Lestrade, sensing a series of undetected crimes, *"I'm sure that Inspector Fleming here could do with a list, if such a thing might be put together. Perhaps these four Ley Line victims are only the ones which have come to light."*

"Or perhaps dragged into the light to be clearly visible to others." posed Fleming, *"A warning of what to expect if one strayed from the flock."*

"That would make sense were it not for the severity of the warning, the dismemberment and public display of the body parts." added Holmes, *"This smacks of something more, something involving retribution and punishment for some gross and unforgiveable indiscretion, not just for having a shaky commitment to Druid practices and beliefs."*

"Perhaps these four Frenchmen blundered into a secret rite of some sort." offered Barraclough, *"Though killing them for that would have been a risky venture. I agree with Mr Holmes, though Inspector Fleming's proposal does have considerable merit; some combination of the two proposals, I would suspect might explain it."*

"Well," said Holmes with a definite note of determination in his voice, *"I need facts, we all do, and I propose to witness these Druids in action. I can do it on my own or with others but, though my action might be beset by a modicum of danger, I would not expect Police Inspectors to be in on something which might turn out to be somewhat illegal. How far would it be to walk from here to Stonehenge, Mr Barraclough? Not too far I would expect."*

"*Less than two miles, Mr Holmes,*" replied Barraclough, "*but the ritual would no doubt start before moonrise on Fernmont land. up near the row of stones which run toward the great monument. They will do a bit of chanting there, dozens of them. I've seen them on numerous occasions, and then move off to Stonehenge, in a sort-of procession with Richard Fernmont dressed in his robes and holding up a stick of some sort, a staff sacred to the Druids I would think. I believe that others join them up there from other locations, all traipsing in along the ley lines, or so I presume. If you wish to start your venture from Barraclough House, you are more that welcome to do so. Just turn up early and don't let the Fernmonts see you. Oh, and I would suggest that, if you do come, you come armed.*"

"*I will take the matter under advisement.*" commented Holmes, "*But there is another factor of unknown sympathies who keeps cropping up and who we dare not get offside. We keep him as close as we might but say little in his presence.*"

"*I presume this person could be close by,*" responded Barraclough, "*perhaps out the back and attending to his horses as we speak.*"

"*Yes,*" Holmes conceded, "*our own inimitable cabbie. He's a type, a force of nature which resists all attempts to tame him. And he's a bit of a showman; he has a way of putting something which makes you think he wrote the book on the matter and could answer any question put to him. It's just that we've been told to keep him at arm's length and to remain tight-lipped about anything we don't want spread around Salisbury and beyond.*"

"*Nor do we know with any certainty that he's not involved in these matters,*" added Lestrade, "*He gets out and about and carting people and all sorts of material around, and it was he who discovered the body parts along the ley lines. We have nothing on him but his presence, I admit, can be a little disquieting."*

"Jenkins?" Barraclough barked, then tempered his response, *"Well I don't take to him much myself, he's a bit too pushy with those tourists of his, always looking to extend the range of his tours and he doesn't always understand the meaning of 'No'. Still, he's no idler, he does give his all when he's at his work, I'll give him that. As for his being in league with the Druids, I can't see it; he'd be too independent for them. In my book, the man is simply a big mouth in need of some gossip to pass on and an empty pocket in search of a shilling."*

"That is much the same as our general though tentative assessment." declared Holmes, *"But, if we can impose on your hospitality for just a little longer, we would ask you your opinion two other local landholders, by name of Franklin and Billings, and also of the Fernmonts' distant cousin, Captain Fernmount."*

Their surprisingly genial and forthcoming host looked around at his three visitors, took a deep breath and began a new discourse about these neighbours, though two were at some little distance as compared with the Fernmonts and the third was considerably farther away.

He then began, *"Franklin and Billings do not own the lands they work; they are not quite the tenant farmers of old but the do lease their lands from some of the older families hereabouts. Franklin has been in these parts since he was born and leases out part of Lord Balesworth's land starting about two miles north from here and extending until it comes up against that of Billings, though that land spreads more easterly. Billings leases his land from Lord Achill who also has holdings in Ireland. I believe that a purchase by the Army could leave both leasehold men somewhat out in the cold, though I do believe that there has been mention of positive arrangements for such good managers of land, crop, men and stock."*

"I have met the lessees," he continued, *"and have little but good to say of both. Poor managers tend not to last long on the land and these two men have lasted through times good and bad and should continue to do so, unless something happens to change the land arrangements, such as has been suggested. They seem amiable types, not fools, and certainly not given to running around in robes under a full moon, though I am not on intimate terms with either of them."*

Lestrade came in on this point with, *"But you would not expect either man to have some sort of grudge against the Army or any Government agent or representative?"*

"Not at all." replied the host, *"In fact, it is likely that such men could do quite well out of the new arrangement. The lands hereabout are screaming out for good managers, and good managers demand high payment. A move may be inconvenient but may also be unavoidable."*

"But Fernmount, our illustrious Captain." he continued, *"is neither a good manager of land nor of men and he holds his rank only by the efforts of others. He is not the most amiable of men nor the wisest and he has continued with the family tradition of squandering away his assets on hare-brained schemes and maintaining false appearances. I'm afraid that he may soon lose all but holds onto some ridiculous notion that he has some claim on the Fernmont estate. His two saving graces, in my book, are that he thinks the Druids are crazed lunatics and that his relations are mad, though there could be some little truth in these latter assertions. He makes his way here from time to time and can be quite a reasonable visitor;*

but at other times he is full of venom and can be quite unpleasant and unreasoning, though this, I believe, is out of frustration bordering on desperation."

Sherlock Holmes, having sat back and listened to all that had been discussed and revealed, thought about his previous night's walk to Wylye Station from Netherfield. He had seen the way clearly as the moon was nearly full. Perhaps it would reach its maximum this night? He asked his host, *"Tonight is the night of the full moon, is it not? I would expect it to rise about midnight."*

"No." replied Barraclough, knowing full well what the Great Sleuth was thinking, *"That apparition will occur on tomorrow's night, around twenty minutes past the hour you mentioned, so you will have time to prepare whatever it is that you have in mind to do. But, I warn you, take extreme care for a fanatic of any calling is a dangerous animal and anyone entering its lair will be attacked without mercy or restraint."*

"Like the four Frenchmen, perhaps?" posed Lestrade.

"More like four dead, dismembered and dispersed Frenchmen." was the emphatic reply.

The Surprise

Scenarios and working hypotheses fell away as Sherlock Holmes had listened to Barraclough and the sleuth felt that here was someone who spoke plainly but generally respectfully of his neighbours, though he obviously did not suffer fools gladly. The man had given him and his colleagues the name of the region's chief Druid and food for thought about the possible fate of four missing Frenchmen, though nothing of the Englishmen and two Frenchmen seen at Cooper's Inn, one of whom went by the name of Barrallier. He felt that he had come to an impasse which could only be overcome by taking a risky action involving spying on Druidic ceremonies, some of which may have involved ritual murder. At least he felt that he had an extra ally in Barraclough and that the possibility of a threat posed by Jenkins had evaporated, though he could still not be fully trusted to keep what he saw and heard to himself.

Holmes was keen, as were his two colleagues, to get back to Salisbury. Mycroft could well have responded by telegram though it was more likely that a letter would find him at Cooper's Inn the next day. Lestrade wanted to discuss matters with both Holmes and Fleming in private while Fleming was keen for news of his family. Matters, though, in these cases, would seem to have a way of sorting themselves out.

Before any of these desirable outcomes could be achieved, however, the three detectives would need to return to Salisbury and this would require the services of the ever-ready Fred Jenkins who had been snoozing the afternoon away in the back of his carriage, patiently waiting for his fares to return. The colourful cabbie was being paid whether he was actually working or not and this trip had turned out to be the most profitable and restful he had ever take on. Still, at the first call of his name, the man jumped into action, retaking the driver's seat in seconds and taking the reins to urge and steer the carriage toward Barraclough House's main porch.

"Back to Salisbury, Jenkins." came instructions from Holmes, the man actually paying for the cabbie's services, *"We could take the faster route back."*

Barraclough had walked out with his three visitors, more than pleased to have seen some action on the murders at last. The arrival of Inspector Lestrade from Scotland Yard and the famous Sherlock Holmes who had come with the stalwart John Watson, described as off attending to 'other matters', would put Salisbury's Inspector Fleming's investigations onto a far more professional footing. The host thanked each visitor effusively but gave Sherlock Holmes a special nod, saying, *"I shall see you very soon, Mr Holmes. Wear something dark and don't forget to bring a loaded gun and a friend with you; you may well have need of both."*

Holmes gave Barraclough a knowing smile and proceeded to join his colleagues in Jenkins' carriage. A crack of the whip and a sharp call from the driver and the team started off, leaving Barraclough House behind as the once-reluctant host turned and re-entered its hallway rather intrigued with his new acquaintances. The long days of Britain's summers gave the group ample opportunity to return to Salisbury in full daylight and attend to whatever crises, large or small, might have arisen in their absence.

The trip back would take something over an hour at a brisk trot, the first call being the Police Station where Fleming would take his leave for a few minutes and check his messages. It had been intended that the group would then proceed directly to Cooper's Inn for supper followed by discussions on the day's business but Fleming had received surprising and somewhat worrying news. Mrs Fleming, having fled Salisbury with her daughter for the safety and security of Netherfields, seemed to have had second thoughts and had sent a message saying she wanted to return to her home, being forced from which by a mere threat was not the way in which the wife of a Police Inspector should behave. This decision by Mrs Fleming, despite the level of planning and amount of effort expended in arranging the ruse to protect the mother and daughter, put the Salisbury Inspector in a dilemma.

"*She wants to come back.*" he said to the others, "*Just when we've got her and Nancy to safety and we're making some headway with this case. No, it can't happen; she must stay where she is so we can keep on with our investigations.*"

There was no indication as to whether Mrs Fleming had actually departed Netherfields but Holmes knew that Watson would have done everything in his power to persuade her otherwise or, that being unsuccessful, would have sent off an urgent message telling him that the 'special package' was on its way back to Salisbury. Holmes also knew that Watson would not leave her side and would guard the 'special package' all the way. Regardless of Mrs Fleming's decision, however, the action did have some positive results in that Fernmount had been confronted and this had led onto preparing the meetings with the Fernmonts and Barraclough, both of which yielded far more useful information than had been collected to date.

It was decided that, as nothing could be done about this new situation at that time and as Watson had not sent a warning message, the group ought to continue on with its plan. Jenkins was told to take the trio to Cooper's Inn but that Inspector Fleming would require transport back to his home at nine o'clock that evening. The cabbie complied and deposited his charges as requested and then made off to pick up a few extra fares on top of his retainer from Holmes. The trio was feeling a little famished and looked forward to pre-supper drinks and a generous repast courtesy of Cooper, the innkeeper.

Lestrade and Fleming adjourned to the bar while Holmes went in search of the all-important reply from his brother in Whitehall, someone whose work he often described as moving pawns around an Empire-wide chess board. No letter had been received, however, but Holmes did have a visitor.

"There's a gentleman by name of Croft waiting for you, Mr Holmes." said Cooper, keeping his voice low lest the visit be a confidential one, *"You'll find him in the saloon room. He came with two other men but they're in the front bar refreshing themselves."*

Holmes pondered on this unexpected visitor. *"A confidant of Barraclough's? No, too soon! A contact of Parker's? Possibly! Someone from Netherfields? Unlikely!"*

The Great Sleuth really had no idea who this person could be so he decided to confront the man directly. To his surprise, the saloon room was empty but, before he could retreat, he felt the shaft of a heavy walking stick tapping on his shoulder.

"Little Brother," said the large figure looming behind him, *"this place is appalling. I mean, it's unfit for horses let alone for human habitation. "It's dark and it's dingy, its clientele is malodorous and boorish and the food is atrocious, though I must admit that the beverage which I sampled was quite good. I'm staying at The Grand."*

Sherlock turned and looked at the figure, now so much larger than life seen away from its usual habitat, and, once he was able to move his lower jaw which had dropped in abject amazement, said, "*Mr Croft. Is it really you so far away from the hallowed corridors of Whitehall? The Empire must surely fall now that you have vacated its central hub for the delights of rural Wiltshire.*"

"*But what … why are you here?*" the younger Holmes asked worryingly, "*The situation must be dire indeed for you to leave Whitehall, let alone London.*"

"*Dire? No, but precarious, yes.*" was the simple reply, a reply which needed no further qualification for Sherlock Holmes to understand that his brother had come to ensure the continuation of the nation's wellbeing. "*I must find out first-hand what the situation is with these French types wandering around Salisbury Plain and who's possibly been killing them. The French Embassy staff is one thing but there is now a special French mission arrived in Britain to prepare the way for more intense negotiations on matters which cannot be discussed or even hinted at.*"

"*Then it seems you have arrived at a very opportune moment,*" was the sleuth's frank reply, pulling his brother into the room lest others hear what they had to say to each other, "*though the number of Frenchmen roaming Salisbury Plain may well have been significantly reduced and the remaining ones might turn out to be French land speculators in league with English partners or agents. Apart from everyone on Salisbury Plain, from the guttersnipe all the way up to the lord of the manor, openly discussing the fact that the Army is secretly about to invade the region, your greater secret would appear to be safe. The murders, as diabolical as they are, have provided a very convenient and fortuitous smokescreen for your special negotiations. If I didn't know better, I could imagine someone*" *at Whitehall arranging the whole thing, though I would be loath to put forward any names."*

"Then who's been upsetting the arrangements of both Britain and France?" asked the Whitehall man, now quite bewildered.

"Druids!" was his brother's reply, simple and succinct.

"Druids?" yelled Mycroft, forgetting his normal Whitehall reserve, *"What in blazes have Druids got to do with it?"*

Sherlock Holmes, always eager to have one up on his elder brother, replied, *"Well, nothing and everything, possibly. The real Druids fell by the wayside two thousand years ago but today's Druids seem to feel that they've have picked up where the dead ones left off or some may even claim that they've always been here in a long surviving line. If you would care to wait, though, we were all about to dine and then sit around and discuss the day's revelations and plan our next moves. You ought to dine with us; I don't know what you'd been gnawing on to describe Cooper's food as appalling. Though it might not quite come up to the standards of your favourite restaurant, we find it good, wholesome, filling and delicious. Or you can sit back and watch us eat; it's your choice."*

Sherlock had his brother wait in the saloon room while he collected both Lestrade and Fleming, telling Mycroft's men, who were both aware of parts of the situation and of Sherlock's involvement, they should take their meals in the main dining room. He then advised Cooper of the dining arrangements and returned to the saloon room. Cooper arrived to take the men's orders and Mycroft was introduced to Fleming, not as Croft but as the senior Holmes of Whitehall fame. Neither Police Inspector knew anything of the budding potential for some 'special arrangement' between Britain and

France and Sherlock knew a good deal less than did his elder brother. Drinks arrived and, after them, the meals, the standard of which, though falling short of Mr Croft's normal expectations, at least generated no adverse comment from him.

Before Sherlock or either of the two Inspectors could say anything, Mycroft addressed the assembly, as he liked to describe any gathering over which he might preside. "*Gentlemen, at present there are matters of supreme importance coming to a head, matters of which I can tell you absolutely nothing and of which you, being my ever-obedient brother and two loyal and sworn Queen's men, may not even ask. Four men of foreign origin seem to have lost their lives in a disturbing manner and, of those four men, one may well have been an official of a foreign embassy. That embassy has expressed its concern, not so much for the loss of the man who has actually been a source of some consternation to his countrymen, but for the difficulty, even danger, in which that country might be placed should word get out of those matters about which I may not speak.*"

"*Well,*" commented a confused and confounded Lestrade, "*I'm certain that all of us here are glad you've clarified that, whatever it is that you can't tell us.*"

Sherlock Holmes was now in possession of sufficient facts to begin laying down the foundations of the story he was intent on building, a story which was still, however, short a few load-bearing bricks in its fabric, bricks which he intended collecting on the following night. Mycroft listened as the three men took turns describing the events of the past few days and how every new fact seemed to contradict the previous one until their last visit, that to Barraclough, had allowed many such facts to fall into place.

The following night would be one of a full moon, a moon which did not rise, though, until after midnight. The Fernmonts, if the pattern of Druidic observances held true, would conduct preliminary services on their land, starting about eleven o'clock, before moving procession-style to Stonehenge, there to wait within the darkened circles of stone for the arrival of the lesser celestial light, the full moon.

Did the Fernmonts actually believe that Stonehenge was theirs, they who claimed to be the rightful heirs to the Druidic religion? It did seem so to the pilgrims who flocked to the ancient monument, there to discover and witness an ancient order performing its sacred rites. It seemed, also, that those same pilgrims had been looking for connection with the spirits of old and on Salisbury Plain had found someone telling them that what they had sought they had now found. The detectives found it hard not to be sceptical but had to admit that at least some of the adherents to the re-invented ancient rites were, in fact, true believers. Sherlock Holmes then declared that he would be going to Barraclough House late in the morning, there to prepare himself for his foray amid the Druids, or at least as close as he dare get.

"I do not expect anyone to come with me," he stated, *"but should anyone wish to join me, I would welcome the reinforcements who might back me up should things go awry. Mycroft, you're not coming, and that is final. You're not fit enough and it would be the height of stupidity for a man of your official standing to risk falling into the hands of these hooded fiends, if that is truly what they are. You must return to the Grand Hotel and wait out the night's events. I would like to recall Watson, and Mycroft's coming here has given me the way to do it without placing Mrs Fleming at risk."*

The two official detectives agreed to back up the Great Sleuth and Mycroft knew that the action described could not involve him. Being at least as astute as his younger brother, the Whitehall man could see that Sherlock intended that one of his men would stand in for Watson. Each man in the 'assembly' also understood that they were looking for murderers, but murderers of people who sought to discover military secrets and that those military secrets were somehow linked with something so incredibly sensitive that Mycroft Holmes had taken unprecedented action to leave his office in Whitehall and see for himself how things stood with matters about which he may not speak nor, it seemed in the most infuriatingly confounding way, was prepared to be asked.

That settled, Sherlock Holmes then declared, "*We've no other choice than to send Jenkins off in the morning with one of Mycroft's men, deposit him at Netherfields, and have our cabbie return with Watson. We must keep Mrs Fleming where she is – Mycroft's man will not be persuaded by tears and heartfelt sobbing but Watson would yield to her pleas sooner or later and then we'd have more problems than we have now.*"

"*But can we truly trust Jenkins?*" asked a worried Lestrade.

"*We must; we have no option.*" explained Holmes, "*Locals describe him as an over-talkative busybody but the general view seems to be that he is otherwise trustworthy and not likely to be tolerated by the Fernmonts playing at their Druidic games. It would be prudent, however, to ask him to call tomorrow morning and then tell him where he's going. He'll be calling tonight at nine to take Fleming home and he can do likewise for Mycroft who's staying at The Grand where the beds are softer; one of Mycroft's men can go to The*

Grand, one can stay here and leave for Netherfields in the morning."

There being no further point in extending or adding to the discussions, the four men retreated to the inviting charms of tobacco and whiskey and into their minds to ponder the day ahead.

The Advance

The clip-clop of Jenkins' horse once again announced his arrival right on time and the four men rose, Mycroft making his way to his two operatives. One, Wallis, he told to stay at Cooper's Inn and be prepared to travel to another location in the morning and be ready for a stay of several days. The other, Carruthers, he told to accompany him to The Grand Hotel, there to attend to matters of security. Jenkins' Hansom could not take all three men and so set off with Fleming to deliver him to his home; on his return he was directed to take Mr Croft and Mr Wallis to The Grand. Holmes also suggested that something more rugged might be needed in the morning at seven o'clock to take one man into the countryside and to bring another back. Jenkins agreed and promised to be there at the appointed hour. Lestrade then made off to retire to his room while Sherlock, Mycroft and Wallis remained in the main bar room, talking little while awaiting the return of Jenkins, after which Sherlock would follow Lestrade's lead and retire.

Morning found Holmes up and eager to get things started but knowing that he had to be patient as it would be some hours before Watson would return and their travel to Barraclough House could be arranged. This was another part of the plan to be kept from Jenkins until he needed to know the actual destination; the man did not seem to support any one particular faction in the region beyond being a private and independent cabbie, wagon master and tour guide, depending on the vagaries of demand. His relapses into a more refined speaking voice could be put down to showmanship for the benefit of his tourist clients but, beyond the man's incredible gossip collecting ability, there was nothing of any substance against him.

Seven o'clock sounded just as Jenkins pulled up in a light wagon; Holmes handed the cabbie a sealed letter for Watson containing the message that he should return while his place would be taken by a trusted man called Wallis. The message also contained a number of prearranged code words which Watson would recognise and know that the message was genuine and it was safe to trade places and return with Jenkins. Wallis climbed on board, throwing a small pack into the back, and the two men set off for Netherfields after Holmes had advised the cabbie that his services would be required on his return with Watson and that an overnight stay on the Plain would be required.

The departure of Jenkins left only Sherlock Holmes and Inspector Lestrade at Cooper's Inn, each with little to do for some hours. Nothing had been arranged with Mycroft or with Fleming for the morning so Holmes thought he might seek out Parker, if the man was still somewhere in town. Lestrade said he would prefer to go off to confer with his colleague Inspector Fleming while Holmes made off to visit Parker's hotel and, if the journalist could not be found, continue on to The Grand Hotel to continue discussions with his elder brother and hopefully find out more details about the antics of Baudin, details considered inappropriate for the ears of the two policemen.

Half an hour's walk saw Sherlock enter Parker's hotel and ask if the man was in. On being told "*No*", Holmes scribbled a quick note, sealed it within an envelope and left it at the front counter; hopefully the journalist would return in time to read it and hurry to catch him at The Grand Hotel or, if too late for that, before the party left for Barraclough House. Fifteen minutes' walk would find the sleuth watching his elder brother consume, in one sitting, enough food to keep the younger brother going for several days.

"Sherlock." called out the elder Holmes, *"I wasn't sure to expect you or not so I started without you. Come over and join me; The Grand's fare is delicious and the tea is brewed to perfection."*

Sherlock walked over and sat across from his brother at a table scattered with pastries and buns of a richness unexpected by a man used to eating at the best London restaurants. Tea was accepted but the rest was declined by the Great Sleuth who wanted only to concentrate on the upcoming foray into the midst of the Druids and matters which may pertain to the murders.

"I'll start off first." Sherlock announced to his brother, *"The overwhelming weight of probability has Baudin and his three ex-military cohorts dead at the hands of the Druids, or people posing as the Druids. I think this would come as no surprise to anyone though the motives behind the killings are still not clear. Tonight's little incursion should shed considerable light onto matter, provided that we, that is Watson and I, do not end up as sacrificial victims on the Slaughter Stone."*

"Slaughter Stone?" queried Mycroft, *"And what, pray tell, is that, though I can probably guess?"*

"It's what the locals call a stone situated just outside the stone circles of Stonehenge." explained his brother, *"A stone which look for all the world like it has blood dripping from it, though the red colour comes from a red algae growing in depressions in the rock and in which rainwater collects. For all we know, the name could be quite appropriate but some argue that it's some sort of altar stone positioned to catch the light of the dawn sun on the solstice. I actually tested some of the dried red matter, though, and my test indicated the presence of blood, though the quantity did not seem great."*

Sherlock had intended to elaborate further but the arrival of a note from the front desk saying that Parker had arrived and was asking for Mr Croft had put an end to the discussions. Sherlock explained that he had invited Parker to join them as it was his information which had set them on their current course, and as Mycroft had expressed some interest in the man's considerable abilities.

Mycroft watched his brother escort the journalist to his table and pull out a chair, indicating that he should sit. Before doing so, though, Parker looked at the elder Holmes, extended his hand and said, *"Mr Croft, is it? I'm Robert Parker, journalist reporting for The Times, primarily."*

If Parker could discern any fraternal similarities between the two Holmes brothers, he did not show it; he simply shook Mycroft's hand and took the seat offered by Sherlock, wondering what was actually afoot. Mycroft offered the journalist fresh tea and as much as he might care to eat. Being on a meagre sustenance allowance, Parker accepted the offer with enthusiasm and proceeded to make significant inroads on the remaining pastries before Sherlock spoke.

"Mr Croft,' he started, *"is not with the Police but is in the service of the Crown, in a roundabout way, and can often help facilitate cooperation between various official persons who might otherwise fail to find each other."*

"May I stop you there?" interrupted Parker, *"I do know who this gentleman is, though I will continue to address him as Croft until told otherwise. He is your elder brother Mycroft, a man living in Pall Mall and working in Whitehall and keeping the machinery of government ticking over, as it were. He arrived in Salisbury yesterday while you, Lestrade and Fleming were off to places we shall refrain from mentioning."*

"*Well,*" broke in Mycroft, "*now it's my turn to stop you. There are matters afoot which could get you placed behind bars indefinitely just in case you might know more that you ought. I do respect the Law but sometimes it gets a little inconvenient, if you take my meaning.*"

"*I do take your meaning, and have no argument to offer.*" replied Parker, "*My business is collecting information and reporting it to the Public with a commentary interesting enough to keep the readers intrigued right down to the last word so that those same readers will go out and buy the newspaper's next edition. Having said that, I do not report everything; there are some facts worthy of being withheld, facts which might help an offender evade capture and facts which might, dare I say it, start a war.*"

"*Your restraint is admirable,*" commented Mycroft, "*as is your ability to seek out facts which others have gone to some effort to conceal. Tell me, was my identity known to you before I came to Salisbury?*"

"*I did have an inkling,*" conceded Parker, "*but your actual identity was confirmed only minutes ago when you acted to stop me from speaking further and did not deny the assertion.*"

Mycroft looked straight at Parker for a few silent seconds before saying, "*Well done, young man. It is quite some time since I have so cleverly outfoxed. I must say that I am very impressed with the way you got me to tell you what I didn't want you to know, not yet anyway. We must talk further.*"

"*Sherlock.*" he continued, now addressing his brother, "*Mr Parker and I have important business to discuss. I would be obliged if you could leave us to ourselves for the day. Oh, and try not to get yourself sacrificed tonight, it would be a great inconvenience to me.*"

Having overdone his plan and outfoxed himself, Sherlock grinned, stood up from the table, gave an understanding nod to both men and walked from The Grand Hotel into the main street, there to hail a cab to take him back to Cooper's inn. Lestrade and Fleming had also returned after the Salisbury man had attended to a number of trivial matters and, on the way, the two official detectives had taken the opportunity of Holmes' absence to discuss the level of illegality they might have to overlook in the upcoming action.

Almost an hour went by before Jenkins would return, bringing with him John Watson who, as interesting as he found Professor Tilbury's studies, was keen to get off guard duty and into some action. Upon that return, Jenkins said he would come back in a short while with more-suitable transportation and the necessities for camping out. Basic supplies were had from the inn's considerable pantry and four armed men set off with Jenkins for a location beyond Stonehenge where Jenkins, Lestrade and Fleming would camp and from where Holmes and Watson would proceed to Barraclough House on foot. All four, however, were surprised to see Mycroft's man Caruthers waiting for them just outside the inn. He looked ready for action, dressed for the hunt and carrying a long object wrapped in light canvas, a rifle.

"Mr Croft said to go with you, Mr Holmes." said the man, *"He reckoned that you'd need me more than he would. I've seen action before, Royal Marines you know, well ex. I could do with some excitement."*

"Climb aboard." replied Holmes, quite overlooking the fact that Jenkins might be able to hear all, *"I think we may place you with Lestrade and Fleming, here. Watson and I will present a large enough profile to the gathering so you might*

act as a supernumerary to the official detectives with that artillery piece you're lugging about."

Sight-seeing and idle chit-chat was definitely not on anyone's agenda for the outward trip but it was hard to take in the vista of Salisbury Plain and not think back to the ancient times and to how many had made exhaustive excursions over its rolling profile, pushing and dragging large and incredibly heavy stones for weeks, perhaps months, out of religious devotion or perhaps out of fear of those who knew the secrets of the sun and the stars and who communed with the spirits of the Earth. Was this the sort of fearsome faith that Sherlock Holmes and John Watson could be facing in just a few hours, two determined men backed up at a distance by two Police detectives working at or beyond the limits of their authority? The facts had pointed to such a level of control over believers that a few simple and subservient people had become capable of acts of abject barbarity just to please one man in flowing robes and avoid his uncompromising wrath. Proof, however, was wanting and it was obvious to Holmes that he would have to catch the man in the act, perhaps even with his priestly hands dripping red with blood.

Time passed and the entrance to Barraclough's estate came into view; Holmes and Watson decided that they had ample time to walk the remaining distance and so hopped off to allow Lestrade, Fleming and Carruthers to proceed with Jenkins in the wagon. A ride which would have taken ten minutes along Barraclough's for a wagon turned out to take not much longer on foot and the two men soon found themselves outside Barraclough's porch and watching as the man himself came out of the darkness of the long hallway.

"Ah, Mr Holmes." came eagerly from Barraclough who then turned to face the second man with a welcoming, *"And this*

has to be Dr John Watson, the man who has kept the name of Sherlock Holmes in the public eye and ear."

"*At your service.*" came from Watson just as Holmes managed an embarrassed "*Indeed*".

Greetings were completed, and Barraclough continued, "*So, the game is truly afoot. Or does everyone say that to you whenever you turn up somewhere? Anyway, I've been dying to say it ever since you graced my doorstep yesterday and expressed an interest in ridding the Plain of these butchers.*"

"*Dr Watson has put many an extra word into my mouth, I fear, in those lurid accounts of our many adventures,*" replied Holmes, "*but in this case the phrase you used could not have been truer. There are butchers on the Plain and this night we may be well rid of them.*"

"*We have come to gather facts so that we may proceed in that general direction, Mr Barraclough.*" continued Holmes with a tone of conditional determination, "*But I do have a strong feeling that we may well fulfil both aims this night. Three men have gone ahead to camp beyond Stonehenge; Jenkins is with them despite our misgivings about the man, misgivings which have reduced significantly over the last day or so.*"

"*Two policemen, I would wager, and perhaps another.*" prompted Barraclough, "*One from London and another from Salisbury. They and that third man, whoever he is, would be well-placed beyond those stones and Jenkins can be watched, not because he may deliberately betray them but because he is so nosey that he can't help but give the game away with his snooping.*"

"Yes, indeed." was Holmes' simple reply, ignoring any reference to Carruthers, *"But Watson and I should get some rest before tonight's action."*

"Of course." responded an insistent Barraclough, *"Come in and we'll have a light refreshment, a little discussion on the lay of the land, and then as much rest as can be had until you must be off. You can have a light late supper at that time to carry you over till morning when we'll all be out counting the enemy's dead, so to speak."*

That said, the two London men entered the dark hallway to do as Barraclough suggested. They had advanced to a location just short of the battleground and were now readying themselves to face a mysterious enemy of unknown resolve.

ANGRY SPIRITS

The Ritual

Fernmont House was busy with selected Druidic adherents being allowed to enter while the Grand Master prepared himself both mentally and spiritually. It was not a simple matter of throwing some robes over his day to day clothes, a strict sequence of procedures had to be followed in a long-perfected ceremony involving ritual washing of this supreme earthly priest and a great many incantations to the spirits of the Earth, Moon and Sun which had to be flawlessly recited by lesser priests in the correct order and at the correct time.

The language used was derived from an archaic Gaelic dialect only just recognisable by those speaking the modern Welsh tongue and totally incomprehensible to speakers of English. None the less, the words spoken conformed to a set of oral chants set down as a scripture centuries before by an underground priesthood operating covertly throughout Britain, France and parts of Spain generally but having its greatest following in Wales and Brittany. Richard Fernmont could complete each section of the incantation without a single error but whether he actually understood what he was saying or was so practiced that no one could tell otherwise was unknown and nobody would dare pose such a disrespectful and dangerous question.

Outside, people had gathered for the forthcoming lunar ceremony. Numbers were not great, not such as would be attracted for the solstice observations when hundreds perhaps thousands might converge, all looking much like tourists but actually constituting pilgrims who would don their various robes only at the commencement of the ritual under the standing stones near Fernmont House, just prior to the Grand Master's appearance.

While Holmes and Watson were engaged in making their arrangements with Barraclough, and Lestrade and Fleming were preparing to camp beyond Stonehenge, Richard Fernmont was giving directions to his two brothers who were to emerge robed and on either side of their elder brother from Fernmont House to the waiting crowd of devotees. The night was not a night of celebration but of duty, a duty to perform a ceremony which many would find distasteful and even repulsive, particularly for those new to this aspect of their adopted religion. The gathered Druids would don their robes at a given signal and stand watchful and in silence as the High Priest and two lesser priests emerged, the latter with brown shoulder capes draped over their robes while the appearance of the former, the High Priest, would draw involuntary gasps from all around.

At the dawning ceremony of the winter solstice, his brilliant white robes would reflect the promise of renewal of life as the length of the new day ceased to diminish and began its first faltering steps back to supremacy, thus marking the annual victory of the spirit of the sun over the demons of the eternal black void which would claim the Earth should the Druids fail to honour the ways of the ancient ones. The robes of the ceremony of the full moon, however, could vary depending on the time of year and the mood of the Earth; gold celebrated the gathered harvest, green looked forward to the new shoots of Spring. This night's ceremony, however, like that two months previously, called for the High Priest to be robed in stark crimson, the ominous colour of freshly spilled blood and a sign that ritual human sacrifice was to be made.

Nobody knew who would be sacrificed; the victim or victims were provided by the lesser priests on behalf of the High Priest, sometimes selected at random, sometimes for infraction of the rules, sometimes for being perceived as enemies of the new Druids. The spirits of the wilful Earth had to be honoured and placated in the light of the full moon and before the stronger light of the sun could drive those same spirits below ground. While a ritual fiery death in the wicker man had been the ancient Celtic manner of immolation of the victims, beheading was now the manner of despatch as it attracted less attention from those who would consider either course of action abominable; the deaths would go ahead and, for the Earth, blood would slake its thirst and flesh would sate its hunger and its spirits would be content, for a time at least.

Two months before, a group of four men had been brought to the slaughter stone bound and gagged, there to be beheaded in full view of the gathered pilgrims who gathered to witness the blood gush forth and soak into the ground. The headless victims were then to be placed on the stone to have their hearts removed and their limbs lopped off; some blood would necessarily remain on the stone but the Earth would drink its fill of most. The heads, limbs and torsos would, under normal circumstances, be removed to be buried in one of the ancient burrows, tombs of old which provided access to the underworld, there to be deposited as food for the Earth, while the hearts would remain with the High Priest, preserved as gory trophies of the savage rite.

Unlike previous sacrifices, this one had been attended by many who objected and some discontent was expressed. The dissenters, however, were few and could be warned off with threats of being the next sacrificial victims and the lesser priests, John and James Fernmont, were instructed to distribute the remains as dire warnings along the ley lines stretching out from Stonehenge.

"This is madness." James had objected, *"Our secrets will be placed before the world and our people will be persecuted and killed as they had been through the centuries and calamity will befall the entire Earth."*

"Obey." was Richard's dire reply, *"Obey or die as they have just died, as will all who dissent and disobey."*

James was never strong enough to go far against any of his brother's orders and John would always obey as a matter of course. Instead of being buried in the ravenous Earth, the grizzly remnants were distributed as directed and found two days later by the ever-inquisitive, ever-intrusive Fred Jenkins. The Fernmonts and their ever-obedient farm hands retreated to their everyday activities and the rest of the Druids dispersed to all points of the compass. The Earth had slaked its thirst but would now demand its quota of human flesh; the spirits would seek out those who would deny them their rightful measure. Inspector Fleming of the Wiltshire Constabulary based in Salisbury found he had four murders, four unidentified victims, four sets of limbs and torsos, no heads or hearts, no one who knew anything, no one who saw anything, no one who heard anything and no earthly clue on why such a thing had happened on the normally quiet Salisbury Plain.

This night, however, those gathered were in no doubt as to what was to happen. Three victims had been chosen, though taken forcefully would be a more accurate way of describing their apprehension, and retained for ritual sacrifice. The three had the misfortune to enter onto Fernmont lands asking questions which the Fernmonts did not want raised, let alone answered, questions which others had asked before and had lived, for just a short while, to regret it.

Holmes and Watson were roused from a drowsy half-slumber by Barraclough, eager to have the two men sent on their ways to observe the first part of the ceremony at a distance. They would arrive some forty minutes before Richard Fernmont would emerge draped in deadly crimson to address the gathered faithful and commence the preliminary rite of the full moon. The two men waited and watched from their higher vantage point just inside Barraclough's land then saw some one or two hundred ordinary looking people, men and women, don their robes and face the main entrance of Fernmont House as their High Priest walked slowly outward, his two robed brothers at each side and a dozen officiating helper Druids walking along, six ahead and six behind.

Only the stars could be seen in the blackened sky overhead but blazing torches lit the amazing scene and Holmes and Watson were able to see most of the procedures. Sound did carry well on the still night but what was said was incomprehensible to the sleuths, the words being archaic terms known only to a few. The High Priest may have recounted the liturgy in an ancient form of Gaelic but he addressed those gathered in clear English, informing all that they would soon move onto Stonehenge, there to watch the full moon rise over the horizon and then to witness three sacrifices to the living Earth in the sacred light of the moon, the measurer of earthly time.

On hearing the word 'sacrifice', the two men looked at each other and knew that the night would bring danger; they could not ignore the fact that three people would die if they failed to act and that action would possibly generate violent retaliation. The three victims, they thought, could well be the three unaccounted-for commercial travellers, if that was what they truly had been, three men who had possibly pushed too hard in the wrong place at the wrong time. Hopefully, when the time came to act both Lestrade and Fleming would be in position and able to support them in whatever action had to be taken; there was no way that a message could be sent to them and the two men knew it would be certain suicide to send one of them off and leave the other to act alone.

Presumably at a signal unseen by any but the lesser priests and their helpers, Holmes and Watson saw the two younger Fernmont brothers head toward a rally point where they stopped while Richard, the crimson-clad High Priest, walked up and stood between them. The helpers then summoned the gathered followers to line up in pairs behind the leaders for the procession to Stonehenge. All seemed orderly to the two sleuths and they could not make out any sign of the intended victims. This was to change as the line of chanting Druids, at a given signal, paused outside a small hut, far too small to be workers' quarters, from which six of the helpers dragged three bound, gagged and struggling forms, obviously the sacrificial victims, all definitely unwilling.

As the London pair lost sight of the leading Druids, it was decided the time had come to make haste overland to their vantage point near the slaughter stone, hoping that Lestrade and Fleming might already be in place. There would be no time to warn the two official detectives of the circumstances but both had been prepared for some such eventuality; all four men were armed and their presence, as far as could be ascertained, was unsuspected.

The way to Stonehenge was along a slight two mile rise across Barraclough's lands, though the Druids had been barred from entering by an owner incensed by their constant taking of liberties and knocking over stone walls which impeded their progress. They now knew to avoid doing so as Barraclough's bark, as bad as it might be, was far inferior to the bite of the buckshot he loaded into his shotgun. Holmes and Watson would be able to proceed along a direct line toward their objective while the Fernmont procession had to stick to a more tortuous route until much closer. This would work well for the two sleuths as, though they would have to clamber over a few fences, they would arrive at Stonehenge well before the lumbering lines of Druids.

Going on what Barraclough had told them, given the man's close observation of some of the rituals, the pair could find cover within the main circle of stones behind a fallen lintel, one of the incredibly heavy horizontal stones once raised high atop two vertical pillars but now long fallen to ground, perhaps for thousands of years. The main body of Druids would form up beyond the Friar's Heel while the priests and helpers, and the sacrificial victims, would take their places close to the Slaughter Stone; Holmes and Watson would be able to see most of what was to happen but remain concealed, though they would have to take care for their faces not to shine out in the moonlight.

Scrambling over the boundary wall to Barraclough's land, the pair quickly advanced the remaining distance to the stone monument then, taking in what could be discerned by starlight, found and took up position behind the stone which had long awaited their arrival, or so it seemed to them at this time.

In the distance, they could hear the chanting of the approaching procession. There would be some time to wait before all the stragglers could catch up with the main body but, after a seemingly interminable wait, the two sleuths could make out the forms of Druids taking up their assigned positions around the stones to continue the ceremony and bring the ritual to its gory conclusion after the rising of the full moon. Holmes and Watson both looked at each other, each man hoping that their three armed colleagues had likewise taken up their positions only one hundred and fifty yards distant but out of their line of sight.

The Sword

On separating from the party in Jenkins' wagon and proceeding on foot to Barraclough House, Homes and Watson would have no practical way of keeping contact with the two policemen and their extra companion, the man provided by Mycroft at the last minute. They had no doubt that Jenkins would carry on at a steady pace to a point beyond and slightly below a line of sight to Stonehenge, a point out of sight and earshot of any who intended to gather, first at Fernmont House, and then at the monument. To any onlooker, the travellers would seem just that, travellers, not three men preparing to strike at a group of people most considered to be eccentric but harmless, and who could be particularly good for business.

Few would have thought that any of the robed visitors could be capable of the extreme violence exercised two months previously and it remained to be seen how many would rush to defend their priestly masters when finally confronted. Holmes had tried to get a feel for the mind of the modern Druid, what each actually believed and how far each might go when put under duress but, beyond discovering a Britain he barely knew had existed, he had to admit that the ancient mysteries would have little bearing on the way the case would be solved. Without hard evidence of particular people's involvement, there would be no way to proceed to a successful prosecution. The guilty parties just had to be caught in the act of committing a crime and this would entail standing back until such parties made the first move.

While Holmes and Watson had been conferring with Barraclough on the best way to approach the Druids, Jenkins had been unloading his wagon after Lestrade, Fleming and Carruthers had alighted and spread out to get their bearings in the dim pre-moonrise light. No fires were to be made and, so, no hot food. But the night was far from freezing, just a little chilled out on the Plain, and bread rolls and cold meat, washed down with water and whiskey, would keep the hunger pangs away, not that any one of them would admit to being more hungry than excited at the prospect of coming to grips with mass murderers.

Jenkins unfolded three camp beds for his passengers, just in case any cared to take advantage of the long wait before they could advance to their post just one hundred and fifty yards from Stonehenge but somewhat opposed to where they expected Holmes and Watson to take up their positions. Each group would have a good view of the Druids' expected ceremonial area but would not be able to see each other; each group would have to trust that the other had not met with some misadventure which would prevent them from proceeding.

Lestrade's group was some two and a half miles from Stonehenge and would need to take up its forward position by midnight, preferably well before. They could approach the monument with some ease and with little chance of being detected but a simple noisy fall by one of the party could give everything away. All three men were accustomed to long periods of waiting in the course of their duties, Lestrade and Fleming on police stake-outs and Carruthers on guard duty with the Royal Marines and more recently when on surveillance for Mycroft Holmes.

The three venturers thought it best to stretch out for one hour on Jenkins' camp beds and conserve their energy before setting off. They had eaten but refrained from swallowing whiskey lest they become too drowsy to perform at their peaks, though not one of the three could sleep thinking about the coming action. Jenkins said nothing after observing the men's disposition and, after eating a small meal, climbed into the back of his wagon to do a bit of light snoozing, something at which he was well practiced.

Lestrade was the first to rise, quickly followed by Carruthers and then by Fleming, all three being fed, rested and raring to go. Jenkins had parcels of bread and meat prepared for each man plus flat whiskey bottles filled with water, all easy to slip into each man's jacket pocket. Revolvers were checked and reholstered and Carruthers slung his rifle over one shoulder, recalling his days of action as a much younger man. Mycroft's man checked that his bullet pouch was in place and wondered just how much shooting he'd have to do and if those he would face would put up a fight and shoot back.

"Fleming should lead the way." declared Lestrade peering deeply into the dark of the night, *"It's his case and he is a local and should know his way about."*

"Carruthers eyes are younger than mine." countered Fleming, *"I can't see a thing and I don't know where I am anyway."*

Carruthers looked toward Jenkins and simply said, *"Point"*, carefully observing the direction the cabbie indicated against the position of two bright stars.

"Follow me," said Carruthers with a smile, *"and keep up. I might be tempted to shoot stragglers lest they be captured by the enemy. No noise, no talking, don't drop anything and don't cough. Small steps, steady and deliberate; no jumping, no tripping, no slipping, no falling over. Keep your eye on the back of the man in front. Understand?"*

"Understood." said both detectives in unison and with some amusement as they took positions in line behind the ex-Royal Marine.

Moving across strange ground in the dark and in silence made for a long and monotonous trek for the two detectives; Carruthers was in his element, though, and had much to keep his mind occupied as he kept the two bright stars to his right at his 'one o'clock' while watching ahead for the rocks and depressions which loomed menacingly as he led his blind charges across the open plain and into battle, he hoped. The Ex-Royal Marine had seen service in various parts of the world but, when his special gifts and his general usefulness had been mentioned by a mutual acquaintance, he was taken by Mycroft Holmes as a special operative, one of Mycroft's many descriptions for those he engaged for activities which did not appear in any book of official procedures. The 'special operative' did seem to do a lot of watching and waiting but, then, this had been his life since the age of sixteen when he found that the life of a sailor was far less exciting and far more strenuous than he anticipated and signed up. He found that life still involved quite a bit of heavy lifting and digging at times but there were moments of great excitement to be had. Mycroft Holmes offered him important and dangerous work and a far better rate of pay; he could think of no reason to say 'No'.

Faint sounds of chanting people shuffling their way across the ground began wafting toward the trio and Carruthers slackened his forward movement to a slow walk while he took stock of his position. He fancied that he could see the faint outline of Stonehenge ahead against a background of stars hanging low against the horizon. Lestrade could see little, though his eyes had adjusted to the low levels of light enabling what sight he had to stay focussed on the bolt of the rifle slung across the leader's back; Fleming could see only the vague outline of Lestrade and mostly followed the sound of the footfalls of the men in front. For either man to lose his way at this point would be both embarrassing and potentially deadly.

A few more minutes confirmed Carruthers' imaginings as the unmistakable monumental form of Stonehenge defined itself against a very slight glow on the horizon and the pace was picked up. The three men could not be certain of how high the ridge of land they were to locate would be; it seemed well defined on the field map which Holmes and Watson had prepared but might only be a slight rise worn down by centuries of trampling and grazing. In the covert raids in which Carruthers had been engaged, he had seen worse; maps had been provided by people who knew nothing of the general terrain to be covered and features both vague and distinct had been rendered in the same thick lines of black ink – he harboured no illusions about the difficulty he might face. The expanse of land, however, was not great and their target feature could likely be found from memory alone if such became necessary. As fortune would have it, though, the slight ridge was reasonably well defined across the landscape and the trio took a right turn along its reverse face and located their target, a depression sufficiently wide and deep to hold their three forms and offer cover from prying eyes. They could hear the procession approaching but it and the rising of the full moon were still some time off. All they could do now was check their weapons, lie back and look up at the stars in silence.

On and on came the sounds of chanting voices and shuffling feet and both groups of concealed men, heads draped with dark field blankets, cautiously peered out at the mass of caped figures beginning to spread out behind Friar's Heel as the priests and their helpers moved on toward the Slaughter Stone. A fire had been started at the Friar's Heel and, between the two groups of Druids, three more forms could be made out on the ground, two kneeling and one crouched, all bound and gagged and each one guarded by a helper who seemed oblivious to the looks of terror on his victim's face. Their time was approaching.

High Priest Richard Fernmount stood and faced the mass of followers, his two brothers on one side and three helpers on the other. The three victims, though firmly bound, twisted themselves around to see their executioner and hear his words as he spoke of blood and flesh which would be bathed in the sacred light of the full moon and then given to the living Earth to appease its restless spirits. The words of the High Priest seemed to mesmerise the mass of followers but, at a given signal, a particular phrase spoken loud and strong, two followers came slowly forth with a slow solemn exaggerated marching gait carrying an object, long and held horizontally to present to the High Priest. It was a sacred object, a broadsword of the type wielded by the wild Celts of old, once a weapon to cleave an enemy clean in two and now a sacrificial instrument wielded to sanctify an offering and give its life force back to the waiting Earth.

Out from the mass of followers, past the sacrificial victims and their helper guards, then onto the High Priest, the sword bearers continued, stopping and kneeling just yards from his crimson form. One of the lesser priests reached out to take the ceremonial staff, allowing the High Priest to accept the sword on the flattened palms of his extended hands; the High Priest said a brief incantation and gripped the instrument by its hilt. The other of the lesser priests stepped forward to remove the gilded scabbard to reveal the highly polished blade within. It had been honed to an extremely sharp edge, an edge which would soon cut into the necks of the victims now struggling impotently on the ground below it.

Now a further ceremony saw the sword carried around for the massed followers to witness and venerate; the High Priest held it out in front, holding its hilt so that its vertical blade caught the flickering light of the Friar's Heel fire and dazzled all who gazed upon it. Holmes and Watson could see much of the proceedings, as could their compatriots positioned on the other side of the monument, though each often lost sight of the High Priest and the victims as the milling of the lesser priests and helpers blocked their views.

On the horizon, the unmistakable glow of the approaching full moon signalled that it was time for the next part of the ritual to commence. The High Priest turned to face the point of the moon's anticipated appearance, the lesser priests and helpers following suit and the mass of followers falling silent and watching in their turns. Then came the time – a glint of light shot out above the horizon followed by a burst of reddish rays which stretched out and through the sacred stones and touched the gathered Druids, the light getting stronger as the curved outline of the moon began to show. Second by second, the form grew until the full lunar orb broke free of the horizon to the cheers of the Druids, all transfixed by the apparition and the sacred light which shone upon them. All under the full moon were being purified, the priests, the helpers, the followers and, most especially, the sacrificial victims. The High Priest turned and held up the brightly gleaming sword for all to see; it was time for the Earth to receive its due.

The Offerings

From their vantage point behind the fallen stone lintel, the sleuths were able to just make out the faces of the three sacrificial victims by the light of full moon and the Friar's Heel beacon fire; they could clearly see the man called Barrallier and also his two companions, all bound and gagged, all struggling, and all about to die and be dismembered. Worrying about the state of mind of the victims would not benefit any one of the captive three and Sherlock Holmes steeled himself to focus on what needed to be done. He knew, however, that he could not just walk over and shoot some Druid on the basis of what he thought would happen, he had to wait for the Druids to make the first move and then take action only when a victim's life was actually threatened. They had not expected quite so many to attend the ceremony and had only two revolvers between them, though their colleagues had at least two more and Carruthers had brought along a rifle; if the robed mob became enraged, however, they might not be able to effective intervene and could quickly be overwhelmed to suffer the same gory fate as the three sacrificial victims. Perhaps, Holmes thought, the action might have been better thought out.

As the sleuth looked on, waiting for some sign to commence action in defence of the three victims, he pondered on just who and what they actually were. *"In all probability,"* he silently mused, *"Barrallier is the actual name of one of their number, one of the two French members of the trio. We had first thought them to be commercial travellers and then we, that is I, took them to be operatives working for Mycroft but now we find they seem to be land speculators, or agents acting on behalf of distant principals. But what do the Fernmonts take them for?"*

Holmes could tell that he very little time to think about the 'whys' of the matter when Fernmont's sword had been unsheathed ready to go about its gory business. Both he and Watson, revolvers cocked and ready, were both poised to leap out from behind their cover and fire at the executioner should he make a move to carry out his deluded deadly duty. It was likely, he surmised, that Lestrade, Fleming and Carruthers had taken up their positions and had similarly readied themselves for rapid action. Neither of the parties, official or unofficial, could know of the mission upon which the three victims had embarked just two weeks previously upon their well-placed principals in London and Paris hearing rumours of bulk purchases of land near Salisbury for the Army, land which had some bearing, it was thought, on some significant understanding between Britain and France being imminent.

The three men had inadvertently blundered into an arena of death, probably thinking that the Ley Line Murders were the work of some madman and assuming that he had likely fled the region right after disposing of the body parts in a way which would confuse everyone; after all, there had been no further murders. It was to be their bad fortune that two of their number were French and that, being so, were assumed to be connected with four other Frenchmen who had been secretly assessing the expanses of land which formed Salisbury Plain, not for its real estate value but for its potential for holding war games which, to them, particularly to the paranoid arch-patriot Baudin, placed France between a burgeoning German Nation with an unstoppable war machine and a resurgent British Army supported by a world-wide empire and the world's most powerful navy.

Such considerations surged through the mind of Sherlock Holmes, not from a conscious determination to get at the truth but from that mind's automatic predilection for rapid, complex analytical thought. The Great Sleuth was starting to see the broader picture in more detail as possibilities transformed into probabilities and then gelled into hard notions fitting many of the available facts. There was no time, however, not now, for pondering on the implications; three men's lives were in dire peril and neither he nor Watson could act until the High Priest took action to kill the prisoners, the three sacrificial victims who had only been seeking the opportunity to make sizeable commissions from sales they might effect.

Lestrade and Fleming, crouching in what they considered an oversized ditch, had no such thoughts going through their minds. Like Holmes and Watson, they were ready to leap from cover and attack what they saw as merciless killers of innocent men and degenerate defilers of human remains. They did, however, have something their two unofficial colleagues did not, they had Carruthers and Carruthers had his rifle, the sights of which marked the centre of Richard Fernmont's forehead. Mycroft's man had no qualms about pulling the trigger; it was something he had done before and would no doubt be called on to do again. If the High Priest even so much as looked like he was about to use that sword, a bullet would shatter the brain of a man who had, as Carruthers saw it, no place in the ordered society he served. Unlike the Druids, though, he would not taunt his victim, he would despatch it quickly like the vermin he felt it was.

Both groups of interveners looked on as the light of the full moon spread and overwhelmed that of the Friar's Heel beacon fire. They would have to keep their heads covered with their dark blankets to avoid being seen; a small opening in the covering would permit an ample view of the proceedings to be made and they could not risk taking their eyes off the sword and the man who held it. Watson's heart was pounding, almost audibly to the man crouched beside him. Holmes, though, despite his heart rate having increased a little, was calm and composed with all extraneous emotions locked behind the door of his brain-attic and his emotions firmly chained to the walls of his mind's deepest dungeon. Both Lestrade and Fleming had seen action before, against criminal gangs whose vile crimes almost took on a note of respectability next to what they might witness this night. Carruthers, though, was as calm as the proverbial cucumber and saw the whole thing as a diversion; had he the intellect and imagination of Holmes, he might have challenged the Great Sleuth for predominance in practicing his craft with the least involvement of emotion, positive or negative.

Carruthers had his thoughts but they were not concerned with murders or justice or law, just carrying out a job he was assigned, a job he was very good at and which he liked enormously, though getting an evildoer of the ilk of Fernmont was a positive bonus. The other four men, their thoughts running wild, all except for those of Sherlock Holmes who held them under a strict discipline, could not help but think about four earlier victims whose dismembered remains had been discovered nearby. This must have been the way they met their fates, each man being bound and gagged and then beheaded before being ritually butchered, the last to die having seen the grizzly fates of his three compatriots before he, too, faced the sword of Richard Fernmont, High Priest of the British Druids.

What had been their crime, a crime which rated such a death and subsequent dismemberment? But what, then, had been the crime of these men now facing death at the hands of a madman in front of so many chanting fanatics? Had they committed the same offence or were they just unlucky innocent victims to fanaticism and bloodlust? This was not the time to ponder such matters; yet such questions, once loosed, would never find peace until they found answers.

That so many thoughts could rush through a mind at such a moment and in so short a time was as remarkable as it was confounding. The crime which needed their attention, despite the three men being bound up and held against their wills, crime enough in itself, was one which had not yet been committed. Lestrade knew well that there would be at least one death this night and he hoped to Providence that not one would be that of any of the three captives. He could have made arrests then and there on the basis of what he had seen but he might not have been able to prove murder in regards to the four earlier victims. Fleming may have been willing to accept the lesser victory but Lestrade was intent on the greater one, and the destruction of a dangerous cult which had grown out of an innocent though dedicated re-creation of an ancient religion passed into myth but recalling an intriguing mystical past.

The full moon had risen higher still, illuminating the drama being played out on an ancient stage to sate primeval desires. At yet another subtle signal, one helper guarding the victims raised a hand and two others came to help drag the unfortunate struggling captive toward the Slaughter Stone and the crimson-clad High Priest wielding the sacrificial sword. Knives were produced and the jacket and shirt of the selected victim were cut and ripped from his body, a living body which was cast to the ground to allow the High Priest to place his foot on the victim's neck, symbolising the power of life and death over anyone considered a threat to the Druids. Carruthers was itching to pull the trigger and all the others had to force themselves to remain still until death was on the point of being delivered. The victim would have been frantic at this point but acting prematurely might only result in the death of the rescuers as well.

Any compassion or leaning toward restraint which Richard Fernmont possessed was lost inside the fanatical Druid he had become. He chanted in the ancient dialect, the meaning of the words lost to all but the most dedicated and experienced of the helpers, helpers who joined in the abominable dedication to the spirits of the Earth and praising of those of the heavens. John Watson felt the hackles rise on the back of his neck as his revulsion gave way to anger and it was only the presence of the steadying hand of Sherlock Holmes on his arm which prevented him from charging in and emptying the contents of his revolver into the heart of this hooded abomination which called itself a priest.

"Not yet." Holmes mouthed silently to his friend and both men maintained their positions until the moment when the Druids could be brought down and the evil which had infiltrated their ranks could be expunged.

A second victim then found himself being dragged forward to suffer the same indignity as the first. The same guttural chant came forth from what was once Richard Fernmont, a chant which was then answered by moans and swaying from the followers, now transfixed by a mixture of awe and terror but unable to keep from watching the moment, some experiencing utter revulsion, some experiencing great elation and intense satisfaction. Then came the time of the third man and a repeat of the taunting preparation of the first two. Three men were now ready for their final ordeal and the first to be chosen, still bound and gagged, was dragged upward onto his knees before the High Priest who took a stance at one side so that all present could witness the strike which would severe the man's head and send blood gushing outward onto the sacred ground of

Stonehenge. The followers were all called to gather in closer so that none could miss the spectacle of sacrifice. The two lesser priests, John and James Fernmont, held the man's arms and pressed down on his shoulder blades so that his head push forward and out. Richard Fernmont then gently lowered the blade onto the victim's neck in calculated preparation for the kill.

The Intervention

High Priest of the British Druids, Richard Fernmont, raised the gleaming sword high above his head and held it there as his two brothers held the struggling victim still, forcing him to present his neck to the deadly blade. As the angle of the sword was seen to drop backward to increase the sweep and power of the delivery, a sharp crack rang out through the still night air. Holmes and Watson had risen as one at the sight of the readied sword, each having raised a revolver to fire at the sword-wielder but ducking and freezing on the spot at the sound of a rifle's ear-splitting discharge; they then saw delivery for the terrified would-be victim.

Before any descent could be effected, the sword dropped from the High Priest's hands as the back of his head exploded and splatters of bloodied brain and splinters of fractured skull peppered the lesser Druids standing behind to observe the gory proceedings. The intended victim, still very much alive, dropped senseless to the ground as the younger Fernmount brothers saw their elder sibling's head fly violently backward and his form collapse where it had stood seconds before, intent on delivering death which had, somewhat appropriately, found its way to him.

"*Got him!*" said Caruthers as though he had just won a prize at a carnival's shooting gallery, "*He won't be cutting off any more heads.*"

Holmes and Watson stood dumbfounded for a few seconds as Lestrade, Fleming and Caruthers came on at the run, the two detectives each firing a round into the air while the ex-Royal Marine dropped his rifle and extracted a revolver from his belt. Recovering their senses, the pair copied the action of their official colleagues and fired over the heads of the shocked and panicky Druids.

"Stop, Police!" was heard from Lestrade and Fleming as the ungainly robe-clad crowd turned yelling and screaming and started to run. More pistol shots into the air only seemed to make them run even faster but the group then heard the unmistakable double retort of a shotgun from the direction of Barraclough's boundary.

"That'll keep them going," yelled a greatly amused Barraclough as he broke the shotgun's breach to reload, *"and a backside full of buckshot will be a reminder for two of them not to return. Wonderful stuff, that buckshot; best argument ever invented."*

A few Druids stopped but most kept on as the bright moonlight lit the way before them. Robes were discarded en-masse as the mob found the Fernmonts' boundary and scrambled over sections of stonework and wooden rail then continued downward toward Fernmont House, beyond which were the carriages which had borne them from Salisbury and the townships scattered about.

Watson rushed to the unintelligible victim to render what medical assistance he could; he knew that the senior Fernmont was well beyond any help he could provide. Two other intended victims, both bound and gagged, looked on expectantly as Holmes rushed forward, knife in hand, to release them both and render assistance. Fleming grabbed James, the younger Fernmont, while he put his revolver barrel against John's forehead, seemingly itching to pull the trigger.

"Should I pop a few of them that's running?" asked a nearby and hopeful Carruthers, now disappointed that he had discarded his rifle, ideal for the long distance targets the retreating Druids were now presenting.

"*No.*" replied Lestrade, "*More killing won't help much. We'll round up who we can over the next few days. Some will get away but there are too many of them for us few to handle. Their victims are safe and that is a good result.*"

"*We have one dead Druid,*" he continued, staring at the two lesser priests, "*and two live Fernmonts; well, alive for now though I think they'll both be getting fitted for a special necktie before long, and not one from Savile Row. These two are for the drop, I'd say, unless they turn out to be mad. If I was in their shoes, though, I'd choose the rope over the madhouse; it'd get the misery over with quick smart.*"

"*Someone should go for Jenkins.*" suggested Fleming, "*We'll have to chain these two blighters inside his wagon, though I'd like to drag them back to Salisbury behind it. Beheading people; I mean, that's for barbarians, and for the French.*"

"*Two of these fellows are French, if they are who we think they are.*" said Holmes.

"*Well, they'd be used to it, then; them with their guillotines.*" commented Carruthers through a cheeky grin, "*I don't know why we even bothered.*"

"*Put handcuffs on those Fernmonts and keep those other three in sight.*" demanded Lestrade, "*There'll be some questions they'll need to answer, all of them. Perhaps you could go off for Jenkins, Carruthers, and bring him and his wagon here.*"

"*Right you are.*" replied Carruthers, "*I'll pick up my rifle on the way and be back in no time. He's not so far away.*"

Carruthers went off at a brisk trot retrieving his discarded rifle and continuing on to find Jenkins but discovered that the man had started getting prepared the moment the two detectives and their supernumerary had left to do battle. His horses had been harnessed and hitched in readiness and, on hearing the shooting, he had started off steadily in the direction of Stonehenge and was only half a mile distant when Carruthers found him.

"You're a good cabbie, Jenkins." declared Carruthers, *"You could sniff out a fare in a crowd of confirmed pedestrians. Got room for me up front?"*

"Hop aboard, whoever you are." replied the chuckling cabbie, *"It sound as though someone's declared war over there. Anybody hurt?"*

"Nobody I didn't shoot." laughingly admitted Carruthers as though the event had made his year, let alone his day, *"But, then, I did need the practice; my aim's been getting a bit off in my dotage. Not much of a challenge, though, the fellow was just standing there and about to cut someone's head off."*

"Well," commented Jenkins to his smiling passenger, *"I'm glad it was all in a good cause."*

Onward the two lumbered in the wagon till the illuminated form of Stonehenge and a vastly reduced number of people about it could be seen. Carruthers could make out the forms of Lestrade and Fleming speaking to two figures seated on one of the fallen stones, the gesturing of the London man indicating that the discussion was not at all friendly and was likely putting the fear of hemp ropes and hellfire into them if they didn't cooperate fully. Faint sounds of yelling were coming from the direction of Fernmont House as the fleeing mob of Druids argued over carriage ownership and complained of being held up by slow horses on the public road. They were too far away for him to waste any concern –

he had been sent to bring Jenkins' wagon to Stonehenge and that is what he would do.

A little further on and he could see what he presumed to be Holmes and Watson tending to the needs of the three intended victims, each of whom would be, after having been bound and gagged for some considerable time and brought to the brink of a grizzly end, in a weakened condition and a state of shock, especially the first one chosen. Each of the victims was wearing one of the blankets the interveners had used for cover, these having been retrieved as the victims' jackets and shirts had been cut and ripped from their bodies and as the night had taken on a definite chill. Several others figures were seen to be sitting on the ground still wearing robes and appearing to have their hands bound behind their backs. Whether these were fanatical Druids or just ordinary people caught up in something they thought to be innocent fun but which turned unbelievably horrific, Carruthers could not say, but he kept his rifle ready in case its persuasive capabilities should be further required. Somewhere on Salisbury Plain was the figure of Barraclough armed with his shotgun, each barrel loaded with a charge of argument-stopping buckshot, though the sound of its distinctive discharge had not been heard again since he first appeared – two shots into the backsides of two of the retreating mass of Druids seemed to have satisfied his eccentric urge to perforate but not permanently damage. Getting closer still, both Jenkins and Carruthers could see another form, a form clad in crimson though not standing but, rather, laying crumpled on the ground.

"That's Richard Fernmont," declared Carruthers with a note of some satisfaction, *"minus part of his head, that is. What's missing is scattered about the ground and over the robes of a few of those mad Druids. Hell, did they run when they saw his brains get splattered all over the place."*

Jenkins was having a hard time taking it all in. Had this respectable, though sometimes unpleasant and often aloof, gentleman been about to murder three innocent men just to satisfy the requirements of some ancient ritual he was performing? And all of those people were just looking on? As the reality sunk in, he looked at Carruthers and said with some measure of disbelief, "*You mean, you shot Richard Fernmont?*"

"*I did; and with this trusty rifle I'm holding.*" replied the ever-pragmatic Carruthers, "*It came down to his head or that other poor sod's. It's a pity he couldn't have seen the bullet coming, though, the way he taunted those fellows all bound up. Anyway, he won't be so heavy to carry back now. Will he?*"

"*I suppose not.*" agreed a somewhat rattled Jenkins, though the black humour of Carruthers was lost on him for a few moments, "*Yes, well ... no, indeed. I see what you mean.*"

Jenkins saw that each of the three now-released captives had something to eat and drink and he and Carruthers helped them into the back of the wagon. A sip of whiskey would settle their nerves somewhat though it would take some considerable time before anyone could recover from such an ordeal. Though two were French, all spoke English and Fleming could question them on the trip back to Salisbury where they would be admitted to Salisbury Hospital for any necessary treatment and observation. Delayed shock could fall upon them at any time in the next few days and it would be as well for them to be under close medical supervision. Watson had checked each man and was satisfied that all three were in a fit state to travel and had written notes to pass on to the hospital's medical staff. Fleming did get one of his wishes as the two younger Fernmonts and several de-robed Druids were tethered to the back of the wagon to walk behind it back to Salisbury. Space was at a premium in the wagon with the three rescued men reclining in the back while Fleming and Jenkins sat perched on the driver's seat; one Fernmont, however, did get to ride though his comfort was not of a high consideration. The body of Richard Fernmont was bundled up and also placed in the back of the wagon and covered; the three other passengers in the back were not aware of his presence but there was little choice but to take the body back and deposit in Salisbury Hospital's morgue after the three patients had been admitted to the wards.

Fleming was, with some little difficulty, able to ascertain the names of the three rescued men and assure them that they faced no charge that he could imagine and that they would have protection until they were fit to return to their normal lives, if such a thing could now be found for either of them, They were warned, however, that there were matters of a serious nature surrounding the events of the past two months and that they would be required to meet with the security forces of both Britain and France and agree to certain undertakings. Under no circumstances were they to speak to anyone about what happened, most especially the Press. Whether any of the three took in what he said, Fleming could not tell, but he would repeat the message more than once over the coming days, as would Lestrade waving the authority of Scotland Yard and the prospect of hefty prison terms in solitary confinement before them.

Holmes, Watson and Lestrade waited until the wagon had departed, took a last look around and then started off on foot toward Barraclough House, an easy task now that the full moon had risen. They would be picked up by Jenkins some time after daybreak, horses being willing. Lestrade had picked up the ceremonial sword and reunited it with its scabbard and Watson had located the Druidic High Priest's staff; all robes which could be found had been placed in the back of Jenkins' wagon on top of the dead Richard Fernmont. Holmes had nothing to carry and neither he nor any of the others wanted to pick up the scattered pieces of Fernmont's skull – that would be left to other policemen who would be out at first light with Fleming to gather evidence and begin their search for Druids who, no doubt, would have long-departed the scene.

Subsequent intense interrogation of the two younger Fernmonts was to reveal how the eldest brother Richard had become captivated by the ancient myths and monuments from an early age and had visited Professor Tilbury on numerous occasions to learn what he could about the ancient peoples and especially the Druids. That such an intriguing feature as Stonehenge and a great many stone and earthen structures could be found in abundance around Salisbury and across Britain convinced him that his immediate region was the centre of the spiritual Earth. He was also convinced, because of his great innate interest in the subject and his family's ancient affiliations with the land, that he was descended from those who survived the destruction of the Druids by the Romans so many centuries ago on the sacred island of Mona.

In recent years, however, the innocent ceremonies and entrancing rituals which had entertained so many and enthralled more than a few had come under the scrutiny of a more internationally focussed group of Druids from the European continent, particularly France, a group with a certifiable history of observance over many centuries, unlike that of Richard Fernmont. Considering himself to be the High Priest of the British Druids, Richard had studied and mimicked the many ceremonies of his European counterparts but refused to relinquish his claims to supremacy, swearing that blood would flow should any from the Continent come to enforce the same over him and his followers.

From what was revealed next, Lestrade and Fleming learned and communicated to other parties that it was a case of very bad timing which had placed the missing Baudin and his men on Salisbury Plain in search of military secrets, specifically the extent of intended land purchases for the Army's expanded requirements. Four Frenchmen poking their noses around Fernmont's land and taking map bearings and measurements from Stonehenge and other easily identifiable and accessible monuments had convinced Richard Fernmont that the French Druids had arrived and were preparing to absorb or destroy British Druidism. The fates of the four men were sealed and they were taken and retained for ritual execution, their dismembered bodies left as a warning to all who might follow.

Unfortunately, some did follow, two Frenchmen and one Englishmen appearing on Fernmont's doorstep asking questions about purchasing land. In Fernmont's eyes, this was proof that the French Druids were in league with British traitors and these three men would have to suffer the same fate as their predecessors. Fortunately for these latter three, Inspector Fleming had been joined by parties from London sceptical of the facts as presented in the newspaper headlines. Had that not occurred, three more dismembered victims would have been discovered on Salisbury Plain and the existence of any Frenchman visiting the district would have been precarious in the extreme.

No one, however, could explain the threat made to Mrs Fleming. It was surmised but never confirmed that someone from the French Embassy or other body had been investigating Baudin's disappearance and had made subtle but awkward approaches in technically good but colloquially clumsy English to Mrs Fleming in order to make unofficial contact with her husband. It was never to be established with great certainty that this was the case but, if it had been, Mrs Fleming had completely misunderstood the man's motives and message and may never have been in any danger.

The Legends

Mycroft Holmes had spent too long away from Whitehall enjoying what he described as the dubious comforts of a rural existence, despite being treated to the best the city of Salisbury was able to provide. It was with some urgency, and after having spent two nights in the Grand Hotel, that he summoned all parties to a closed meeting to render his verdict and deliver a warning.

Holmes and Watson had visited Professor Tilbury at Netherfields to advise the great lady and her guests that all had been resolved and that any danger for Mrs Fleming and her daughter had disappeared. Jenkins had been advised of the need for this visit and that he would be needed for a further trip to collect the Flemings and their bodyguard Willis and return them to Salisbury, the Flemings to return to their home and Wallis to report to Mr Croft.

Professor Tilbury was delighted to hear the news but somewhat disappointed at the fate of Richard Fernmont, though she knew that once he had chosen violence as a means to solve his problems, there would be no way to control how matters would end. She was also saddened to hear that the two younger Fernmonts had been arraigned on capital charges.

"A whole family gone, wasted, all for some stupid obsession." she ranted, *"Could they not have revelled in the region's long and spectacular history without believing in fairy tales and acting out their fantasies?"*

Another thought went through her mind, one more immediately disconcerting than any other.

"*Do you realise the implications of the Fernmonts' involvement and ultimate demise?*" she continued, well knowing that no one did, "*That self-styled Captain Fernmount will now have a considerably strong claim on the Fernmont lands and that could make him a very rich man and a positive pest. He has enough gall and a sufficient number of well-placed contacts to mount a strong claim to the old estate, and those lawyers of his will do all they can to see that he is successful; it would be their only chance of ever being paid what the man owes them, and then get a bit more in those exorbitant fees they charge for land title transfers. They're the sort that'd pull down Stonehenge and sell off the stones as building blocks – no feeling for history or heritage, just law books and money.*"

After taking the usual refreshments provided at Netherfields, Holmes and Watson were both struck by the attention given by Julia, the maid, to Mycroft's man Wallis. "*It would seem,*" whispered Watson to Holmes, "*that Parker has a rival and may well have his work cut out for him at Netherfields.*"

"*You would think so,*" replied Holmes, "*but if my brother gets wind of either man's interest, which he most assuredly will, given his penchant for finding things out, both men may find out just how far the empire does stretch.*"

"*Parker?*" Watson started.

"*Don't ask.*" broke in Holmes, "*My brother's tentacles are many and long.*"

"*You mean,*" Watson continued, probing for more, "*he's been Mycroft's man all along?*"

"*Perhaps not before,*" was the reply, "*but Mycroft can be very persuasive and Parker is the right type to keep on side and well rewarded. I would not be surprised to find that the out-of-character headlines in The Times were set as bait on which my brother knew I would bite. The mysterious ways of Providence are as nothing to the wiles of my illustrious and manipulative brother. It is also noteworthy that Parker pointed us in the right direction without actually telling us anything and quite possible that my meeting with Parker and Mycroft was all an act staged to keep me distracted."*

"He has a way about him, that Parker, and I see great things for him in the years to come." Holmes continued, "I expect that his journalistic style with alter considerably and perhaps he'll find certain attractions of Wiltshire too strong to resist. But no more of this, there are some things which are better left alone."

Train timetables dictated the timing of next meeting as Mycroft was keen to get back to the metropolis – too many things may have happened on which he had not been able to make comment. Much that happened in government depended on his ability to put information into the right hands at the right moment, and to stave off looming disasters, and only the most urgent of situations could get him away from his desk in Whitehall, hence his appearance at Salisbury.

With one hour until the London train's departure, Mycroft had all parties gather in a private room in the Grand Hotel for one of his 'assemblies'. Tea and cakes were served at Mycroft's insistence and chairs were distributed around a circular table, the Whitehall man sitting high before everyone. Holmes and Lestrade sat to the left, Fleming at centre, while Parker and Wallis were seated on the extreme right next to Barraclough. Jenkins came in last and room was made next to Watson. All present, except for Mycroft and Wallis, had been present and witnessed the events at Stonehenge and were about to hear an edict which all would abide by or face quite dire circumstances. One man, Carruthers, was very obvious by his absence.

"*Gentlemen,*" Mycroft started, "*as you all may or may not know, there are matters about this Ley Line Murder case which go beyond the ritual killing of four men and the intended demise of three more. Those killings are a Police matter and will be treated as such but other matters concerning the case are so sensitive that it is desirable for things to be finalised without fanfare.*"

Mycroft sat back, took a deep breath, and continued, "*As the instigator and main perpetrator of the crimes is now deceased, and as it seems that the man's two brothers will be found unfit to plead due to their degenerate mental states and are to be confined in an asylum at Her Majesty's pleasure, a public trial will thankfully be unnecessary. It will be necessary, however, for the Public to see Justice done and the fact that a man of some high standing has been killed by a government operative who had acted to save the lives of three innocent men will, after some suitable embellishment by Mr Parker here, go a long way to settling the Public's irratiblity on the matter. Mr Wallis has a document for each person present, a document which, when signed, will bind its signatory to silence on certain matters. I am certain that Mr Jenkins will like to tell his stories to tourists and that is not discouraged but he is warned not to go beyond the basic facts. Momentous things, things of great international importance, are at a formative stage and real dangers remain until such matters are settled. I tell you all, Gentlemen, than no one will leave this room before swearing an oath and putting his signature to that document.*"

When Mycroft spoke in earnest nobody could take his words lightly, such was the presence of the Whitehall man acting with full executive authority. All present did come forward to swear the oath and sign the document and each was thanked personally by Mycroft Holmes for his cooperation and patriotism. Professor Tilbury would receive a special letter of appreciation from the Wiltshire Constabulary for her intellectual and practical assistance in bring the case to a successful conclusion. Numerous local adherents to Druidism would be contacted and questioned as to their degrees of involvement in the murders but, as further publicity on the case was undesirable, those people were sternly warned about the inadvisability of such associations and told that a watch list had been prepared and that they had been placed on it. The only wild card to be considered was Fernmount but his involvement had been due to his envious desires to regain his distant cousins' lands, an unlikely situation which was now thrown wide open by his distant cousins' death or being declared insane; he would have to be watched but certainly not trusted with any further information.

At the conclusion of the assembly, the two Holmes brothers, accompanied by Watson, Lestrade and Fleming, made their ways to Salisbury Station where Mycroft boarded for London. The others went about their business but Jenkins had been engaged to take Watson and Sherlock Holmes to Netherfields, there to personally thank the Professor for all she had done. As the London train moved out of Salisbury, Lestrade and Fleming made their ways back to the Police Station while Holmes and Watson went off in search of Jenkins.

Fred Jenkins had been dozing, not atop his cab but in the seat of his carriage. On seeing the two men approach, he jumped up and grabbed the reins saying, *"I thought something a little special was in order, Gents, so I dusted off the carriage."*

"Netherfields is it?" he continued as the two men hopped in and took their comfortable seats, *"And then maybe a spin around the countryside; just to say goodbye, you know."*

"That sounds delightful," said Watson, *"We leave for London in the morning but will be sad to say goodbye to Salisbury and its Plain despite all which has occurred."*

Goodbyes at Netherfields turned into a late lunch and the men finally stepped back into the carriage for a final tour of the immediate region. Jenkins took his clients, as he called people who hired his carriage, along back roads and tracks unknown to all but one long accustomed to finding his way to and from every point of interest upon Salisbury Plain. Two hours saw them jumping to the ground before Stonehenge; no trace of any assembly of Druids or of any intervention in their deadly ritual could be found, no skull fragments, traces of blood no cartridge shells. It looked as if no one had been there in a month.

Jenkins took out a flask of whiskey, something he always seemed to have on hand, and poured a draught into each of three mugs. *"Gentlemen,"* he began, *"here's to Stonehenge and all the stories she has generated."* The toast was made and three more draughts were poured 'just for the constitution'.

"She?" commented Watson, a quizzical look on his face.

"Yes. She!" replied Jenkins, *"You know ... Mother Earth and Father Sky and all that. It's like coming home every time I see the place. She's gentle, always there with a welcome, though she has been ill-used at times by certain types. They'll come and go but the welcoming stones will remain always. Don't you feel her? She's real and she'll never leave you as long as you live."*

Watson knew that Jenkins was right; even Sherlock Holmes had to admit that there was a definite presence about the place and knew that the Druids and others would return, all trying to absorb the atmosphere generated by a monument set in place so long ago by people whose spirits still seemed to pervade its form.

It was time to return to Salisbury, to Cooper's Inn, and rest. The case was solved but not explained, nor could it ever be, not in its entirety. Still, people were saved and Mycroft's secrets were safe, safe enough, though Sherlock Holmes had been asked to embark on a delicate mission on behalf of the French nation in a semi-official capacity by his brother. Watson knew better than to ask. Thoughts wandered about as the carriage wound its way back Salisbury till finally coming to a halt at the entrance to Cooper's Inn. Goodbyes were exchanged with the cabbie and Sherlock handed the man a generous wad of banknotes which were accepted graciously, though the cabbie neglected to advise his clients that similar generosity had been extended by Mycroft Holmes.

Tired and eager for a good long sleep, the pair stepped down from the carriage and made way to the inn's main counter and greeted the innkeeper. *"Hello there, Mr Cooper."* said Holmes, *"Would you have two rooms for a pair of weary investigators?"*

"Indeed I would." came the reply, *"I have your original rooms all ready for you – I have anticipated your return and reserved them exclusively. Your belongings are within, all waiting for you."*

Billy, the innkeeper's lad, always prepared to accept an extra thruppence, was called and carried what luggage the pair did have to the two reserved rooms upstairs and deposited his loads on the two central tables. Holmes and Watson ordered a couple of whiskeys to bolster themselves after an arduous week and to settle their thoughts which might otherwise run amok and keep them awake.

After ten minutes or so of general banter with the innkeeper, Holmes and Watson wearily made their ways up the stairs and along the corridor but stopped dead in their tracks upon reaching their rooms. On both doors they saw that the innkeeper had removed the simple room number signs and they gazed on two carved wooden plaques telling the guests that they were about to take their rests in the 'Sherlock Holmes Room' and the 'John Watson Room', their silhouettes adorning the plaques above the names.

"*Well, Watson,*" declared Holmes with a rare and rather wry smile, "*It would appear that you and I now have our own local monuments - we are now legends of Salisbury and can join those ancients in a well-earned sleep, though preferably not of such duration as theirs.*"

"*Indeed.*" replied Watson, "*And I do fear that our good innkeeper, and our intrepid cabbie, will prove to be imaginative and inventive sources of a new series of highly embellished and well lubricated tales about our mysterious past. Perhaps I ought to write as much of the story as I dare before they stretch the truth too far and Mycroft takes my pen away.*"

The Great Sleuth, eyes rolling, yawned and pushed opened his door; he then started inward while saying with a note of some exasperation, "*If you must, Watson. If you must.*"

....

An Addendum
to the Case of The Ley Line Murders

(from materials graciously provided by the heirs to the estate, and the administrators of the collected literary works, of the late John Watson M.D. known in late Victorian London's literary circles as Dr Watson, colleague and chronicler of the famous consulting detective of Baker Street, Sherlock Holmes, of unknown fate though presumed deceased)

Sherlock Holmes and myself rarely had entered into a case of such complexity, a case of such diabolical involvement and potential for serious international complications as when we, some few years ago out of frustration bred of sensational newspaper reporting, stepped into a quagmire of intrigue upon the Salisbury Plain and back into the mists of antiquity at Stonehenge to assist the local authorities investigating what people were calling The Ley Line Murders.

These were matters of grave concern to all those in the district, particularly to those whose habitations were distant from neighbours who might render assistance in the case of an attack. Local Police resources were stretched at the time Sherlock Holmes made his offer of help, an offer readily taken up by the beleaguered officers responsible for such a vast area. Several matters combined and compounded upon each other to render the whole affair so complex that even his great intellect was at times strained. The situation was eventually brought under control but some matters were deemed to be of too sensitive a nature to permit their disclosure.

I find myself in the dilemma of knowing so much more but being permitted to say little further beyond the fact that the matters we encountered and prevailed over had been matters of such sensitivity that the accounts which would ordinarily have been placed before the Public have been withheld lest certain powerful parties misunderstand the situation and other powerful parties take advantage of any confusion produced. A full century and more may have to pass before the stresses building up in late eighteenth century Europe may have abated sufficiently to permit all details to be divulged.

It was with this in mind, and after consultation with the highest approachable civil authority in the land that a voluntary stay of publication has been agreed to for a requested period of twenty five years plus a mandatory one century, by which time, it is to be presumed, the countries of the world will have abandoned the use of violence in settling their differences.

That said, I commend to my heirs my unfinished manuscript and its accompanying notes in trust for future times, and should the same materials survive until the year of Our Lord two thousand and seventeen, I leave their disposal to my heirs' considerable discretion. They may decide to destroy them, publish them as they stand or empower some other agent to finish the work I had started or to reconstitute them in his own words. The only stipulation that I would make in doing so is that my good friend, Mr Sherlock Holmes, be given full credit for cutting through the shifting mists of superstition to discover those hard facts which lay strewn upon solid ground.

Since our Ley Line Murders Case, a sad occurrence had made me hesitant to further recount our many adventures but, should this manuscript, in whatever form it takes, see the light of day in years long into the future, let its dedication read 'to the memory of a great and dear friend'.

John Watson M.D. London 1892

Also from Allan Mitchell

Sherlock Holmes novellas in verse

All four novellas have been released also in audio format with narration by Steve White

Sherlock Holmes and The Menacing Moors
Sherlock Holmes and The Menacing Metropolis
Sherlock Holmes and The Menacing Melbournian
Sherlock Holmes and The Menacing Monk

"The story is really good and the Herculean effort it must have been to write it all in verse—well, my hat is off to you, Mr. Allan Mitchell! I wouldn't dream of seeing such work get less than five plus stars from me…" **The Raven**

Also from MX Publishing

MX Publishing is the world's largest specialist Sherlock Holmes publisher, with over a hundred titles and fifty authors creating the latest in Sherlock Holmes fiction and non-fiction.

From traditional short stories and novels to travel guides and quiz books, MX Publishing cater for all Holmes fans.

The collection includes leading titles such as *Benedict Cumberbatch In Transition* and *The Norwood Author* which won the 2011 Howlett Award (Sherlock Holmes Book of the Year).

MX Publishing also has one of the largest communities of Holmes fans on Facebook with regular contributions from dozens of authors.

www.facebook.com/BooksSherlockHolmes

www.mxpublishing.com

Also from MX Publishing

  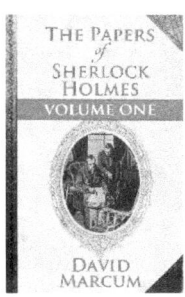

Our bestselling books are our short story collections;

'Lost Stories of Sherlock Holmes' , 'The Outstanding Mysteries of Sherlock Holmes', The Papers of Sherlock Holmes Volume 1 and 2, 'Untold Adventures of Sherlock Holmes' (and the sequel 'Studies in Legacy) and 'Sherlock Holmes in Pursuit', 'The Cotswold Werewolf and Other Stories of Sherlock Holmes' – and many more......

Also from MX Publishing

"Phil Growick's, 'The Secret Journal of Dr Watson', is an adventure which takes place in the latter part of Holmes and Watson's lives. They are entrusted by HM Government (although not officially) and the King no less to undertake a rescue mission to save the Romanovs, Russia's Royal family from a grisly end at the hand of the Bolsheviks. There is a wealth of detail in the story but not so much as would detract us from the enjoyment of the story. Espionage, counter-espionage, the ace of spies himself, double-agents, double-crossers...all these flit across the pages in a realistic and exciting way. All the characters are extremely well-drawn and Mr Growick, most importantly, does not falter with a very good ear for Holmesian dialogue indeed. Highly recommended. A five-star effort."
The Baker Street Society

www.mxpublishing.com

Also from MX Publishing

The Missing Authors Series

 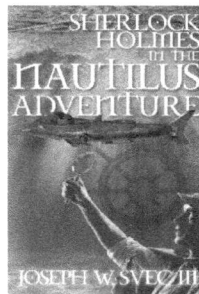 

Sherlock Holmes and The Adventure of The Grinning Cat
Sherlock Holmes and The Nautilus Adventure
Sherlock Holmes and The Round Table Adventure

"Joseph Svec, III is brilliant in entwining two endearing and enduring classics of literature, blending the factual with the fantastical; the playful with the pensive; and the mischievous with the mysterious. We shall, all of us young and old, benefit with a cup of tea, a tranquil afternoon, and a copy of Sherlock Holmes, The Adventure of the Grinning Cat."
Amador County Holmes Hounds Sherlockian Society

www.mxpublishing.com